When Lucy Watson left her hometown in the desert, she planned to escape the stigma of being a saloonkeeper's daughter by becoming a backwoods welfare worker. Her sister Clara had already eloped with a cowboy she hardly knew, and Lucy was free to start a new life.

But Lucy wasn't really free of Clara's romantic mistake. For the errant Clara had left a living legacy—one that threatened to keep Lucy from the love that was offered by Edd, the love she desperately wanted!

It was only when gunfire erupted that Lucy's fate—and Clara's—was finally decided.

Zane Grey

UNDER THE TONTO RIM

PUBLISHED BY POCKET BOOKS NEW YORK

**POCKET BOOKS, a Simon & Schuster division of
GULF & WESTERN CORPORATION
1230 Avenue of the Americas, New York, N.Y. 10020**

Published by arrangement with Harper & Row, Publishers, Inc.

ISBN: 0-671-82879-7

First Pocket Books printing May, 1976

10   9   8   7   6   5   4

Trademarks registered in the United States and other countries.

Printed in the U.S.A.

UNDER THE
TONTO RIM

CHAPTER I

Lucy Watson did not leave home without regrets. For a long time she gazed at the desert scenery through tear-blurred eyes. But this sadness seemed rather for the past—the home that had been, before the death of her mother and the elopement of her younger sister with a cowboy. This escapade of Clara's had been the last straw. Lucy had clung to the home in the hope she might save her sister from following in the footsteps of others of the family. Always she had felt keenly the stigma of being the daughter of a saloon-keeper. In her school days she had suffered under this opprobrium, and had conceived an ideal to help her rise above the circumstances of her position. Clara's defection had left her free. And now she was speeding away from the town where she had been born, with an ache in her heart, and yet a slowly dawning consciousness of relief, of hope, of thrill. By the time she reached Oglethorpe, where she was to take a branch-line train, she was able to address all her faculties to a realization of her adventures.

Lucy had graduated from high school and normal school with honors. Of the several opportunities open to her she had chosen one of welfare work among backwoods people. It was not exactly missionary work, as her employers belonged to a department of the state government. Her duty was to go among the poor families of the wilderness and help them to make better homes. The significance of these words had prompted Lucy to make her choice. Better homes! It had been her ideal to help make her own home better, and so long as her mother lived she had succeeded. The salary offered was small, but that did not cause her concern. The fact that she had the welfare department of the state behind her, and could use to reasonable extent

1

funds for the betterment of these primitive people, was
something of far greater importance. When she had accepted this position two remarks had been made to her,
both of which had been thought-provoking. Mr. Sands,
the head of the department, had said: "We would not
trust every young woman with this work. It is a sort of
state experiment. But we believe in the right hands it will
be a great benefit to these uncultivated people of the
backwoods. Tact, cleverness, and kindliness of heart will
be factors in your success."

Lucy had derived gratification from this indirect compliment. The other remark had aroused only amusement.
Mrs. Larabee, also connected with the welfare work, had
remarked: "You are a good-looking young woman, Miss
Watson. You will cause something of a stir among the
young men at Cedar Ridge. I was there last summer. Such
strapping young giants I never saw! I liked them, wild
and uncouth as they were. I wouldn't be surprised if one
of them married you."

Oglethorpe was a little way station in the desert. The
branch-line train, consisting of two cars and the engine,
stood waiting on a side track. Mexicans in huge sombreros
and Indians with colored blankets stolidly watched Lucy
carry her heavy bags from one train to the other. A young
brakeman espied her and helped her aboard, not forgetting
some bold and admiring glances. The coach was only
partly filled with passengers, and those whom Lucy noticed
bore the stamp of the range.

Soon the train started over an uneven and uphill road-
bed. Lucy began to find pleasure in gazing out of the
window. The flat bare desert had given place to hills, fresh
with spring greens. The air had lost the tang of the cattle
range. Occasionally Lucy espied a black tableland rising
in the distance, and this she guessed was timbered mountain country, whither she was bound.

At noon the train arrived at its terminal stop, San
Dimas, a hamlet of flat-roofed houses. Lucy was interested
only in the stagecoach that left here for her destination,
Cedar Ridge. The young brakeman again came to her

assistance and carried her baggage. "Goin' up in the woods, hey?" he queried, curiously.

"Yes, I think they did say woods, backwoods," laughed Lucy. "I go to Cedar Ridge, and farther still."

"All alone—a pretty girl!" he exclaimed, gallantly. "For two cents I'd throw up my job an' go with you."

"Thank you. Do you think I need a—a protector?" replied Lucy.

"Among those bee hunters an' white-mule drinkers! I reckon you do, miss."

"I imagine they will not be any more dangerous than cowboys on the range—or brakemen on trains," replied Lucy, with a smile. "Anyway, I can take care of myself."

"I'll bet you can," he said, admiringly. "Good luck."

Lucy found herself the sole passenger in the stagecoach and soon bowling along a good road. The driver, a weather-beaten old man, appeared to have a grudge against his horses. Lucy wanted to climb out in front and sit beside him, so that she could see better and have opportunity to ask questions about the country and the people. The driver's language, however, was hardly conducive to nearer acquaintance; therefore Lucy restrained her inquisitive desires and interested herself in the changing nature of the foliage and the occasional vista that opened up between the hills.

It seemed impossible not to wonder about what was going to happen to her; and the clinking of the harness on the horses, the rhythmic beat of their hoofs, and the roll of wheels all augmented her sense of the departure from an old and unsatisfying life toward a new one fraught with endless hopes, dreams, possibilities. Whatever was in store for her, the worthy motive of this work she had accepted would uphold her and keep her true to the ideal she had set for herself.

The only instructions given Lucy were that she was to go among the families living in the backwoods between Cedar Ridge and what was called the Rim Rock and to use her abilities to the best advantage in teaching them to have better homes. She had not been limited to any method or restricted in any sense or hampered by any

church or society. She was to use her own judgment and
report her progress. Something about this work appealed
tremendously to Lucy. The responsibility weighed upon
her, yet stimulated her instinct for conflict. She had been
given a hint of what might be expected in the way of diffi-
culties. Her success or failure would have much to do
with future development of this state welfare work. Lucy
appreciated just how much these isolated and poor families might gain or lose through her. Indeed, though beset
by humility and doubt, she felt that a glorious opportunity
had been presented to her, and she called upon all the
courage and intelligence she could summon. There was
little or nothing she could plan until she got among these
people. But during that long ride through the lonely hills,
up and ever upward into higher country, she labored at
what she conceived to be the initial step toward success—
to put into this work all her sympathy and heart.

Presently she plucked up spirit enough to address the
stage driver.

"How far is it to Cedar Ridge?"

"Well, some folks calkilate it's round twenty-five miles,
then there's tothers say it's more," he drawled. "But I
don't agree with nary of them."

"You would know, of course," said Lucy, appreciat-
ingly. "How far do you call it?"

"Reckon aboot twenty miles as a crow flies an' shinnyin'
round forty on this uphill road."

Lucy felt rather bewildered at this reply and did not
risk incurring more confusion. She was sure of one thing,
however, and it was that the road assuredly wound uphill.
About the middle of the afternoon the stage reached the
summit of what appeared rolling upland country, grassy
in patches and brushy in others, and stretching away toward a bold black mountain level with a band of red rock
shining in the sun. Lucy gazed westward across a wide
depression, gray and green, to a range of ragged peaks,
notched and sharp, with shaggy slopes. How wild and
different they seemed to her! Farther south the desert
mountains were stark and ghastly, denuded rock surfaces
that glared inhospitably down upon an observer. But these

mountains seemed to call in wild abandon. They stirred something buoyant and thrilling in Lucy. Gradually she lost sight of both ranges as the road began to wind down somewhat, obstructing her view. Next to interest her were clearings in the brush, fields and fences and cabins, with a few cattle and horses. Hard as she peered, however, Lucy did not see any people.

The stage driver made fast time over this rolling country, and his horses trotted swingingly along, as if home and feed were not far off. For Lucy the day had been tiring; she had exhausted herself with unusual sensation. She closed her eyes to rest then and fell into a doze. Sooner or later the stage driver awoke her.

"Say, miss, there's Cedar Ridge, an' thet green hill above is what gives the town its name," he said. "It's a good ways off yit, but I reckon we'll pull in aboot dark."

Lucy's eyes opened upon a wonderful valley, just now colored by sunset haze. A cluster of cottages and houses nestled under a magnificent sloping ridge, billowy and soft with green foilage. The valley was pastoral and beautiful. This could not be the backwoods country into which she was going. Lucy gazed long with the most pleasing of impressions. Then her gaze shifted to the ridge from which the town derived its name. Far as she could see to east and west it extended, a wild black barrier to what hid beyond. It appeared to slope higher toward the east, where on the horizon it assumed the proportions of a mountain.

To Lucy's regret, the winding and ascending nature of the road again obscured distant views. Then the sun set; twilight appeared short; and soon darkness settled down. Lucy had never before felt mountain air, but she recognized it now. How cold and pure! Would the ride never end? She peered through the darkness, hoping to see lights of the village. At last they appeared, dim pin-points through the blackness. She heard the barking of dogs. The stage wheeled round a corner of trees, to enter a wide street, and at last to slow down before looming flat-topped houses, from which the yellow lights shone.

"Miss, anybody goin' to meet you?" queried the driver.

"No," replied Lucy.

"Wal, whar shall I set you down? Post office, store, or hotel?"

Lucy was about to answer his question when he enlightened her by drawling that she did not need to make any choice, because all three places mentioned were in the same house.

When the stage came to a halt Lucy saw a high porch upon which lounged the dark forms of men silhouetted against the yellow light of lamps. Despite the lights, she could scarcely see to gather up her belongings. To her relief, the stage driver reached in for her grips.

"Hyar we air—Cedar Ridge—last stop—all out," he drawled.

Lucy stepped down hurriedly so that she could stay close to him. The darkness, and the strangeness of the place, with those silent men so close, made her heart beat a little quicker. She followed her escort up wide rickety steps, between two lines of men, some of whom leaned closer to peer at her, and into a large room, dimly lighted by a hanging lamp.

"Bill, hyar's a party fer you," announced the driver, setting down the baggage. "An', miss, I'll thank you fer ten dollars—stage fare."

Lucy stepped under the lamp so that she could see to find the money in her purse, and when she turned to pay the driver she espied a tall man standing with him.

"Madam, do you want supper an' bed?" he asked.

"Yes. I am Lucy Watson of Felix, and I shall want room and board, perhaps for a day or two, until I find out where I'm to go," replied Lucy.

He lighted a lamp and held it up so that he could see her face.

"Glad to help you any way I can," he said. "I'm acquainted in these parts. Come this way."

He led her into a hallway, and up a stairway, into a small room, where he placed the lamp upon a washstand. "I'll fetch your baggage up. Supper will be ready in a few minutes."

When he went out Lucy looked first to see if there was a key in the lock on the door. There was not, but she found a bolt, and laughed ruefully at the instant relief it afforded.

"I'm a brave welfare worker," she whispered to herself, scornfully. Then she gazed about the room. Besides the washstand before noted it contained a chair and a bed. The latter looked clean and inviting to Lucy. There would be need of the heavy roll of blankets at the foot. The cold air appeared to go right through Lucy. And the water in the pitcher was like ice. Before she had quite made herself ready to go downstairs she heard a bell ring, and then a great trampling of boots and a scraping of chairs on a bare floor.

"Those men coming in to supper!" she exclaimed. "Bee hunters and white-mule drinkers, that brakeman said! . . . Well, if I *have* to meet them I—I can stand it now, I guess."

The hall and stairway were so dark Lucy had to feel her way down to the door. She was guided by the loud voices and laughter in the dining room. Lucy could not help hesitating at the door. Neither her courage nor her pride could prevent the rise of unfamiliar emotions. She was a girl, alone, at the threshold of new life. Catching her breath, she opened the door.

The dining room was now brightly lighted and full of men sitting at the tables. As Lucy entered, the hubbub of voices quieted and a sea of faces seemed to confront her. There was a small table vacant. Lucy seated herself in one of the two chairs. Her feeling of strangeness was not alleviated by the attention directed toward her. Fortunately, the proprietor approached at once, asking what she would have to eat. When she had given her order Lucy casually looked up and around the room. To her surprise and relief, none of the young men now appeared to be interested in her. They had lean hard faces and wore dark rough clothes. Lucy rather liked their appearance, and she found herself listening to the snatches of conversation.

"Jeff's rarin' to plow right off," said one. "Reckon it'll be plumb boggy," was the reply. And then others of them spoke. "My hoss piled me up this mawnin'," and, "Who air you goin' to take to the dance?" and, "Lefty March paid what he owed me an' I near dropped daid," and, "Did you-all hear about Edd Denmeade makin' up to Sadie again, after she dished him once?" and, "Edd's shore crazy fer a wife. Wants a home, I reckon."

The talk of these young men was homely and crude. It held a dominant note of humor. Probably they were as fun-loving as the riders of the low country. Lucy had expected to be approached by some of them or at least to hear witticisms at her expense. But nothing of the kind happened. She was the only woman in the room, and she might not have been there at all, for any attention she received. Something of respect was forced from Lucy, yet, woman-like, she suffered a slight pique. Soon her supper came, and being hungry she attended to that.

After supper there was nothing for her to do but go to her room. It was cold and she quickly went to bed. For a while she lay there shivering between the cold sheets, but presently she grew warm and comfortable. The darkness appeared pitch-black. Distant voices penetrated from the lower part of the house, and through the open window came the sound of slow footsteps accompanied by clink of spurs. Then from somewhere far off sounded the bay of a hound and it was followed by the wild bark of a coyote. Both bay and bark struck lonesomely upon her spirit.

Lucy realized that actually to experience loneliness, to be really cut off from family and friends, was vastly different from the thought of it. She had deliberately severed all ties. She was alone in the world, with her way to make. A terrible blank sense of uncertainty assailed her. Independence was wholly desirable, but in its first stage it seemed hard. Lucy was not above tears, and she indulged in a luxury long unfamiliar to her. Then she cried herself to sleep.

When she awoke the sun was shining in upon her. The air was crisp and cold and bore a fragrance wild and sweet, new to Lucy. With the bright daylight all her courage returned, even to the point of exhilaration. She put on a woolen dress and heavier shoes. The cold air and water had greatly accelerated her toilet. When had her cheeks glowed as rosily as now? And for that matter, when had her hair been as rebellious? But she had no time now to brush it properly, even if her hands had not been numb. She hurried down to the dining room. A wood fire blazed and cracked in the stove, to Lucy's great satisfaction. The dining room was empty. Presently the kitchen door opened and a stout woman entered with pleasant greeting.

"Miss Watson, my husband said we might find somethin' we could do for you," she said, kindly.

"Yes indeed, you may be able to give me information I need," replied Lucy.

"I'll fetch your breakfast an' then you can tell me what you want to know."

The proprietor's wife introduced herself as Mrs. Lynn, and appeared to be a motherly person, kindly and full of curiosity. Lucy frankly explained the nature of the work she was about to undertake.

"I think it's a fine idea," responded Mrs. Lynn, emphatically. "If only the Denmeades an' the rest of them will have it."

"Will they be too proud or—or anything to give me a chance?" asked Lucy, anxiously.

"We're all plain folks up here, an' the backwoods families keep to themselves," she replied. "I don't know as I'd call them proud. They're ignorant enough, Lord knows. But they're just backwoods. Like ground-hogs, they stay in their holes."

On the moment the woman's husband came in from the street. He appeared to be a gaunt man, pallid, and evidently suffered from a lung complaint, for he had a hoarse cough.

"Bill, come here," called his wife. "Miss Watson has what I think a wonderful mission. If it will only work! . . . She's been hired by the state government to go among our people up here in the backwoods an' teach them things. She has explained to me a lot of things she will do. But in few words it means better homes for those poor people. What do you think about it?"

"Wal, first off I'd say she is a plucky an' fine little girl to take such a job," replied Mr. Lynn. "Then I'd say it's

good of the state. But when it comes to what the Denmeades an' the Claypools will think about it I'm up a
stump."

"Bill, it's such a splendid idea," said his wife, earnestly.
"She can do much for the mothers an' children up there.
We must help her to get a start."

"I reckon. Now let's see," returned her husband, ponderingly. "If our backwoods neighbors are only approached right they're fine an' hospitable. The women
would welcome anyone who could help them. But the men
ain't so easy. Miss Watson, though, bein' young an' nice-
lookin', may be able to make a go of it. . . . If she can
keep Edd Denmeade or one of them bee hunters from
marryin' her!"

Here Lynn laughed good-humoredly and smiled know-
ingly at Lucy. Mrs. Lynn took the question more seriously.

"I was goin' to tell her that myself," she said. "But we
mustn't give her the wrong impression about our neighbors. These backwoodsmen are not Bluebeards or Mor-
mons, though they are strong on gettin' wives. They are
a clean, hardy, pioneer people. Edd Denmeade, for instance now—he's a young man the like of which you
won't see often. He's a queer fellow—a bee hunter, wonderful good to look at, wild like them woods he lives in,
but a cleaner, finer boy I never knew. He loves his sisters.
He gives his mother every dollar he earns, which, Lord
knows, isn't many. . . . Now, Miss Lucy, Edd like as not
will grab you right up an' pack you off an' marry you.
That would settle your welfare work."

"But, Mrs. Lynn," protested Lucy, laughing, "it takes
two to make a bargain. I did not come up here to marry
anyone. With all due respect to Mister Edd's manner of
courting, I feel perfectly capable of taking care of myself.
We can dismiss that."

"Don't you be too sure!" ejaculated Mrs. Lynn, bluntly.
"It's better to be safe than sorry! . . . I ain't above tellin'
you, though—if Edd Denmeade really fell in love with
you—that'd be different. Edd has been tryin' to marry
every single girl in the country. An' I don't believe he's

been in love with any one of them. He's just woman hungry, as sometimes these backwoodsmen get. That speaks well for him bein' too clean an' fine to be like many others. An' as to that, Edd is only one of a lot of good boys."

"Thanks for telling me," replied Lucy, simply. "Of course I want to know all I can find out about these people. But just now what I need to know is how to get among them."

"Mary, I've been thinkin'," spoke up Mr. Lynn, "an' I've an idea. Suppose I call in the Rim Cabin schoolteacher. He's in the post office now—just rode in. I reckon he's the one to help Miss Watson."

"Fetch him in pronto," replied Mrs. Lynn, with alacrity; and as her husband went out she continued: "It's Mr. Jenks, the school-teacher. First man teacher ever here. You see, the youngsters at Rim Cabin school never got much teachin', because whenever a schoolmarm did come one of the boys would up an' marry her. So they're tryin' a man. It's workin' out fine, I hear. Mr. Jenks is in this high, dry country for his health, same as my husband. I reckon he wasn't always a school-teacher. Anyway, he's a good Christian man, not young enough to have the girls makin' sheep eyes at him."

At this juncture Mr. Lynn returned with a slight, stoop-shouldered man whose thin serious face showed both suffering and benevolence. He was introduced to Lucy, who again, somewhat more elaborately, explained the reason for her presence in Cedar Ridge.

He made her a very gallant bow, and seated himself at the table, to bend keen kind blue eyes upon her.

"You are a courageous young woman," he said, "and if you are sincere these people will take you into their homes."

"No one could be more sincere," replied Lucy, with spirit. "I have absolutely no motive but to do good. I chose this out of a number of positions offered me. I wanted something different—and not easy."

"You have found it," he said. "The opportunity is here and it is big. There are a score or more of children who might as well belong to savages for all the civilization they get. No doctor when they are sick, no church, no amusement, no pretty things common to children, no books or toys—nothing except what little schooling I can give them. They have no school in winter, on account of weather. I've been here a month. There are twenty-seven pupils in my school, the eldest a boy of nineteen—a man, really—and the youngest a girl of four. They are like a lot of wild Hottentots. But I really think more of them than any children I ever taught. The problem is to win them."

"It must be a problem for an outsider," replied Lucy, seriously.

"I believe they will take more quickly to a girl," he went on. "At least the children and boys will. Your problem will be a different one from mine. I'll not dwell on it, lest I discourage you. What's more to the point, I can say as their teacher I've learned a good deal about their lives. At first this seemed a tragedy to me, but I am learning that a good many of our necessities are not really necessary, after all. These children and young people are really happy. They have few wants because they do not know what more civilized people have in their lives. It is not through sophistication that you will benefit them. To brighten their surroundings, change the primitive squalor, teach the children useful things—therein lies your opportunity."

"Can you advise me how to start—whom to approach first?" asked Lucy.

"Come with me," replied Mr. Jenks, earnestly. "I'm driving back to-day. I live at Johnson's—five miles down from the Rim Cabin, which, by the way, is the name of my school. I'll take you up to see Lee Denmeade. He lives some miles farther on, up in the woods under the Rim Rock. He's probably the most influential man among these backwoodsmen. I rather incline to the opinion that he will like your proposition."

"It's very good of you. Thank you," replied Lucy, gratefully. "I am ready now to go with you."

"I'll call for you in an hour," said Mr. Jenks, rising.

After he had gone out Lucy turned to Mrs. Lynn to ask: "I wonder—when he hinted about my problem and said he didn't want to discourage me—did he mean this—this marrying propensity you spoke of?"

"I reckon you hit it plumb," replied Mrs. Lynn, gravely, yet with a smile. "It's the only problem you have. You will be a blessin' to them overworked mothers an' a godsend to the children."

"Then—I can stand anything," rejoined Lucy, happily, and she ran upstairs to repack the grip she had opened. While her hands were busy her mind was preoccupied, now humorously and then thoughtfully, and again dreamily. She was indeed curious about these backwoods people —earnestly and sympathetically curious. It was impossible not to conjecture about this Edd Denmeade. She made a mental picture of him, not particularly flattering. Poor fellow! So all he wanted was a wife, any girl he could get. The thought afforded Lucy amusement, yet she felt pity for the lonesome fellow. "I hope to goodness he doesn't run after *me!*" soliloquized Lucy, suddenly aghast. "I certainly wouldn't marry a backwoodsman—or a cowboy. . . . Poor little foolish sister! I wonder how soon she'll find out her mistake. That Jim Middleton was no good. . . . I wish everybody wouldn't make me think of marriage. It'll be a long time until I want to—if ever."

Lucy sighed, dispelled her dreams, and finished her packing, after which she gazed out of the window.

It was considerably longer than an hour before Lucy found herself seated in an old buckboard beside Mr. Jenks, rattling along a dusty road behind the heels of two big shaggy horses.

But the brisk trot soon ended at the base of the steep ridge, up which the road zigzagged through a low-branched thick-foliaged forest, remarkable for its fragrance.

"What smells so sweet?" was one of Lucy's many questions.

"Cedar. Those gnarled trees with the gray sheafs of bark, hanging like ribbons, and the dense fine light-green foliage, are the cedars that give name to the ridge and village," replied Mr. Jenks. "They are an upland tree, an evergreen. I like them, but not so well as this more graceful tree with the checkered bark. That's a juniper. See the lilac-colored berries. They grow ripe about every two years. And this huge round green bush with the smooth red-barked branches is manzanita. And that pale green plant with the spear-pointed leaves like a century plant— that's mescal. . . . But perhaps you would be more interested to hear about the people."

"Yes. But I love the outdoors and all that grows," replied Lucy, enthusiastically. "I've never had a chance to live in the country, let alone in the wilds."

"You may find it too wild, as I did at first," replied the teacher, in grim amusement. "I walk from Johnson's to the school—five miles. I used to see fresh bear tracks in mud or dust. I seldom see them now, as the bears have moved up higher. Almost every day I see deer and wild turkey. One night I was late leaving the cabin. It was moonlight. A big gray animal followed me halfway down to Johnson's. I didn't know what it was until next day, but anyhow my hair stood on end."

"And what was it?" queried Lucy.

"A mountain lion," replied Mr. Jenks, impressively.

"A lion?" echoed Lucy, incredulously. "I didn't know there were lions in this country."

"It was a panther, or cougar. But mountain lion is the proper name. I'll show you his skin. Lee Denmeade put his hounds on the track of the beast and killed it. He gave me the skin. . . . Oh, it'll be wild enough for you. After we get on top of the ridge you won't wonder that bears and lions live there."

Lucy, being an artful questioner and inspiring listener, led Mr. Jenks to talk about the people among whom she expected to dwell.

He told how some of his child pupils rode their little burros six and eight miles to school; how a slip of a boy came on horseback from his home twelve miles away; how sometimes they were frightened by wild animals and cattle. He told of the dance that was held at the schoolhouse once every week—how everyone for miles around attended—babies, children, young people, and grown-ups —and stayed from sundown to sunrise. All of which time the boys and girls danced! It was their one and only time to be together. Distance and hard work precluded the pleasure of company. Sometimes on a Sunday or a birthday one family would visit another. The girls spent what little leisure they had in sewing. The boys passed their spare time in hunting and fighting. Mr. Jenks said he had at first been dreadfully concerned at the frequent fights. But as these young backwoodsmen appeared to thrive on it, and seldom were any less friendly for all their bloody battles, he had begun to get used to it.

So interesting was the talk of the school-teacher that Lucy scarcely noted the tedious miles up the long ascent of the ridge, and was only reminded of distance when he informed her they were almost on top and would soon have a magnificent view. Despite his statement, however, Lucy was wholly unprepared for what suddenly burst upon her gaze from the summit.

"Oh—how glorious!" she cried.

It seemed she gazed down on an endless green slope of massed tree-tops, across a rolling basin black with forest, to a colossal wall of red rock, level and black fringed on top, but wildly broken along its face into gigantic cliffs, escarpments, points, and ledges, far as eye could see to east or west. How different from any other country Lucy had ever viewed! A strong sweet breath of pine assailed her nostrils. Almost she tasted it. In all the miles of green and black there was not a break. If homes of people existed there, they were lost in the immensity of the forest. An eagle soared far beneath her, with the sun shining on his wide-spread wings. A faint roar of running water floated up from the depths, and that was the only sound to disturb the great stillness. To one who had long been used to flat desert, the drab and yellow barrenness, how fertile and beautiful these miles and miles of rolling green! That wild grand wall of rock seemed to shut in the basin, to bar it from what lay beyond. Lastly the loneliness, the solitude, gripped Lucy's heart.

"We're on top of Cedar Ridge," the school-teacher was

saying. "That mountain wall is called the Red Rim Rock.
It's about thirty miles in a straight line. . . . We're looking
down upon the homes of the backwoodsmen you've come
to live among."

CHAPTER II

The road down into this forest-land contrasted markedly
with the ascent on the other side of the ridge; it was no
longer steep and dusty; the soil was a sandy loam; the
trees that shaded it were larger and more spreading. Birds,
rabbits, and squirrels made their presence known.

Some ferns and mosses appeared on the edge of the
woods, and pine trees were interspersed among the cedars.
Mr. Jenks was nothing if not loquacious, and he varied
his talk with snatches of natural history, bits of botany,
and considerable of forestry. It appeared he had once
been a forest ranger in one of the Northern states. Lucy
had a natural thirst for knowledge, something that her
situation in life had tended to develop.

They descended to a level and followed the road
through pine thickets above which an occasional monarch
of the forest reared itself commandingly. At length they
abruptly drove out of the woods into the first clearing.
Lucy's thought was—how hideous! It was a slash in the
forest, a denuded square, with dead trees standing in the
brown fields, a rickety fence of crooked poles surrounding a squat log cabin, with open door and dark window
suggestive of vacancy.

"Family named Sprall once lived here," said Mr. Jenks.
"Improvident sort of man. He has a large family, more
or less addicted to white mule. They moved back in some
canyon under the Rim."

"I've heard of this white mule," replied Lucy. "Of

course it's a drink, and I gather that it kicks like a mule. But just what is it?"

"Just plain moonshine whisky without color. It looks like alcohol. It *is* alcohol. I once took a taste. Fire and brimstone! I nearly choked to death. . . . The people of this district make it to some extent. They raise a kind of cane from which they distill the liquor. But I'm bound to say that seldom indeed do I see a drunken man."

Beyond this deserted clearing the road tunneled into a denser forest where the pungent odor of pine thickly pervaded the atmosphere. The ground was a smooth mat of pine needles, only sparsely grown over with under-brush. Live-oak trees appeared, at first stunted, but grad-ually developing into rugged members of the forest. Noon found the travelers halted beside the first brook, a tiny trickling rill of clear water. Lucy was grateful for a cool drink. Mr. Jenks had been thoughtful to provide a lunch, of which they partook while sitting in the shade of an oak.

Here Lucy had opportunity to observe a small reddish-brown squirrel that was the sauciest little animal she had ever beheld. It occupied a branch above her and barked in no uncertain notes its displeasure and curiosity. Pres-ently its chatter attracted a beautiful crested blue jay that flew close and uttered high-pitched notes, wild and fierce in their intensity.

"I hope the people here are not as antagonistic as this squirrel and bird," observed Lucy.

"A few of them are—like the Spralls, for instance," re-plied Mr. Jenks. "Well, we still have far to go. I call it five miles from here to Johnson's. You'll say it's five leagues."

If Lucy had not been eager and anxious to establish her position securely here in the region she would have reveled in the winding shady road through the green-canopied, sun-flecked forest. Along here it had a consider-able sameness, that added to the distance. About two o'clock Mr. Jenks drove into another clearing, somewhat less hideous than the first one, but still a crude, ragged, unpastoral kind of farm. A wide green field dotted by cows and horses was the only redeeming feature. Log corrals and pole fences led the eye to a large log cabin surrounded by shacks old and moldy-roofed, manifestly the first buildings erected.

"This is the Johnson place, where I live," said Mr. Jenks, with a smile. "That framework of boards, covered by a tent, is my humble domicile. Do you know, Miss Watson, I have actually grown to love sleeping out there? . . . This is Sunday, which means the Johnsons will all be home or all away visiting."

The school-teacher drove through an open gate in the log fence, and past a huge flat barn, dark and odorous of horses, to draw rein at the back of the cabin.

"I was wrong. Sam Johnson is home, at least. I don't know the boy with him," said Mr. Jenks, as he threw the reins and got down.

"I'd like to walk a little," rejoined Lucy.

"You'll probably walk, and climb, and besides ride horse-back, before you're through to-day," replied Mr. Jenks, laughing, as he reached for his parcels on the seat.

"Oh, that'll be fine!" exclaimed Lucy, delighted. And naturally she gazed over at the young men sitting on the rude porch. They might have been two of the boys she had seen in the dining room at Cedar Ridge.

"Sam, she's a looker," drawled one of them, in a perfectly audible voice.

The other stood up, disclosing a tall, lithe form clad in blue jeans. He had a shock of tousled chestnut hair and a freckled face that on the moment bore a broad grin.

"Dog-gone me!" he ejaculated. "Teacher has fetched back a wife."

Lucy met the teacher's eyes. They were twinkling. She could not restrain a laugh, yet she felt a blush rise to her face.

"Sam flatters me, Miss Watson," said Mr. Jenks, in a low voice. "But that illustrates."

"They must have this wife business on the brain," retorted Lucy, half nettled.

The teacher called to the young man, Sam, who approached leisurely, a young giant somewhere over twenty years of age, clean-eyed and smooth-faced.

"Howdy, teacher!" he drawled, but his light hazel eyes were fixed on Lucy.

"This is Sam Johnson," spoke up Mr. Jenks, turning to Lucy. "Sam, meet Miss Lucy Watson of Felix. She has come to sojourn awhile with us."

"Right glad to meet you," said Sam, somewhat shyly.

"Thank you, Mr. Johnson," replied Lucy.

"Sam, will you saddle two horses for us? I'm taking Miss Watson up to Denmeade's," interposed Mr. Jenks.

"Shore will, teacher," rejoined Sam, and moved away with sidelong glance at Lucy.

"Have you any riding clothes?" inquired Mr. Jenks, as if suddenly reminded of something important.

"Yes. I was careful not to forget outdoor things," replied Lucy.

"Good! I'll carry your grips to my tent, where you can change. Of course we'll have to leave your baggage here until we interview Denmeade. If all goes well it can be packed up to-night."

The interior of Mr. Jenks's abode was vastly more prepossessing than the exterior. It was such an attractive little place that Lucy decided she wanted one similar to it, for the summer at least. The furnishings included a comfortable-looking cot, a washstand with mirror above, a table, books, lamp, and pictures. Several skins, notably a long gray furry one she took to have belonged to the lion Mr. Jenks had mentioned, served as rugs for the rude board floor. A picture of a sweet, sad-looking woman occupied a prominent place. Lucy wondered if she was his wife.

It did not take her many minutes to get into her riding clothes. Fortunately they had seen a service which now appeared likely to serve her in good stead. At normal school Lucy had ridden horseback once a week, and felt that she was not altogether a tenderfoot. Finding her gauntlets, she had the forethought to pack her traveling suit, so that in case she remained at Denmeade's her baggage could be sent for. Then, with a last and not unsatisfied glance at herself in the mirror, she sallied forth from the tent, keen for this next stage of her adventure.

A glossy, spirited little bay pony stood there saddled and bridled, champing his bit. Another horse, dusty and shaggy, large in build and very bony, was haltered to the hitching rail near by. Mr. Jenks was lacing something on the saddle of the smaller horse. Sam Johnson lounged beside him and the other fellow had approached. He did not appear so tall or so lean as young Johnson.

Lucy felt uncertain how these backwoodsmen would take her rather trim and natty riding suit, but as she knew she looked well it gave her no great concern. She had made up her mind to win the liking of all these people, if possible.

"What a pretty pony!" she exclaimed. "Am I to ride him, Mr. Jenks?"

"Yes—if you can," returned the teacher, dubiously, as he looked up from his task. "I assure you he is no pony, but a very mettlesome mustang."

"Aw, teacher, Buster's as gentle as a lamb," protested Sam. Then, indicating his companion by a sweep of his long arm, he said, "Miss Lucy, this here is my cousin, Gerd Claypool."

Lucy had to give her hand to the brown-faced young man, for he had extended a great paw. She liked his face. It was rich and warm with healthy blood, and expressive of both eagerness and bashfulness. Lucy was not going to forget his remark, "Sam, she's a looker!" and she gazed as demurely as possible into his blue eyes. It took only one glance to convince her that he was of the type Mrs. Lynn had praised so heartily. Lucy also saw that he was quite overcome.

"Mettlesome mustang?" echoed Lucy, gazing from Mr. Jenks to Sam. "Does that mean anything terrible? I assure you I'm no cowgirl."

Sam's shrewd eyes sought her boots and then her gauntlets. "Wal, you're shore no stranger to a hoss. Buster isn't a bronc. He's never pitched with a girl yet. Talk to him some an' pat him as if you'd no idea a hoss could be mean."

Lucy did as she was bidden, successfully hiding her nervousness; and it appeared that Buster did not show any viciousness or fear. He had a keen, dark eye, somewhat fiery, but not at all fierce. As he was a small horse, Lucy mounted him easily, to her satisfaction.

"How's the length of your stirrups?" asked Mr. Jenks.

"Just right, I think," replied Lucy, standing up in them.

"Wal, I reckon they're a little long—I mean short," drawled Sam, approaching.

Lucy was quick to grasp the guile in this young gentleman of the woods. He was as clear as an inch of crystal water. She grasped just as quickly the fact that she was going to have a good deal of fun with these boys. Sam knew her stirrups were all right; what he wanted was a chance to come close to her while she was in the saddle. It was an old cowboy trick.

"Thanks, I'm very comfortable," she said, smiling at him.

Meanwhile Mr. Jenks had mounted and turned his horse toward the road.

"I never rode this nag," he said. "Come now, Miss Watson."

"Teacher, look out she doesn't run off from you," called Sam, as they started. His voice was full of mirth. "An', Miss Lucy, that's shore a regular hoss you're ridin'."

Lucy turned in the saddle. "I nearly forgot to thank you, Mr. Johnson. It is good of you to let me ride him."

She found Buster rather hard to hold in. Before she had followed Mr. Jenks many paces she heard Sam blurt out to his cousin, "Gerd, by golly! it's shore worth a lot to have Edd Denmeade see *that* girl ridin' my best hoss."

"Haw! Haw!" roared Gerd, and then made reply Lucy could not distinguish.

Presently she caught up with her guide and together they rode out through the corral.

"Mr. Jenks, did you hear what they said?" inquired Lucy.

"Indeed I did. They're full of the old Nick, those boys. I'd like to be in your boots, yet again I wouldn't."

"What did he mean by saying it was worth a lot to have Edd Denmeade see me riding his horse?"

"It was a compliment to you, especially his emphasis on the qualifying adjective before girl," replied the teacher, with a chuckle. "You see, Edd Denmeade seems a superior sort of person to most of the boys. Really he is only forceful—a strong, simple, natural character. But the boys don't understand him. And the girls do still less. That is why I suspect some have refused to marry him. Sam now is tickled to have Edd see the very prettiest girl who ever came to Cedar Ridge ride up on his horse. Edd will be wild with jealousy."

"Goodness! I'm afraid most girl visitors here have been homely," replied Lucy.

"No, they haven't been, either," declared the teacher. "Now, Miss Watson, we have a mile or so of good sandy road before we cut off on the trails. Let's have a gallop. But be sure you don't do what Sam hinted—run off from me. You might get lost."

With that he urged his mount from walk to trot and from trot to gallop. Lucy's horse did not need urging; he bolted and shot down the road ahead of Mr. Jenks. Lucy was alarmed at first and found it hard to keep her feet in the stirrups. But soon she caught the swing of the mustang and then a wild impulse prompted her to let him run. How fast he sped on under the pines! His gait made the saddle seem like a rocking-chair. But she hauled hard on Buster, obedient to the resolve she had made—that she would restrain herself in all ways. Pulling him to a swinging canter, Lucy took stock of pleasant sensations. The rush through the pine-scented air was exhilarating; soon the exercise had her blood dancing all over her; low branches of pine tore at her hair; the turns of the winding road through the woods allured with their call of strange new scenes. Rabbits darted ahead of her, across the open, into the pine thickets. At length, some distance ahead she saw where the road forked, and here she brought Buster to a stand. She was tingling, pulsing with heated blood, and felt that she could have cried out with the joy of the moment.

Mr. Jenks came galloping up to halt beside her. "That was bully," he said. "Miss Watson, you need not be ashamed of your riding. . . . We take the left-hand road. That to the right goes on to my log-cabin school. I wish we had time to see it. A little way farther we strike a trail."

Soon after that Lucy was riding behind the teacher along a narrow trail that almost at once began to lead downhill. The forest grew denser and the shade became dark and cool. Rocks and ledges cropped out of the ground, and all about her appeared to tend toward a wilder and more rugged nature. The dreamy, drowsy hum which filled Lucy's ears swelled to a roar. It came from far down through the forest. It was running water and it thrilled Lucy. How sweet and welcome this verdant forest to eyes long used to desert glare!

The trail took a decided pitch, so that Lucy had to cling to the pommel of her saddle. It led down and down, into a ravine full of mellow roar, deep, murmuring, mystical, where the great trees shut out the sky. Only faint gleams of sunlight filtered down. They came to a rushing brook of amber water, brawling and foaming over rocks, tearing around huge mossy bowlders, and gleaming on down a wild defile, gloomy with its shadows.

The horses stopped to drink and then forded the brook, crashing on the rocks, plunging on to splash the water ahead. Lucy had a touch of that sweet cold water on her face. On the other side the trail turned up this beautiful glen, and followed the brook, winding in and out among bowlders that loomed high overhead. Ferns and flowers bordered the trail. Maples and birches grew thickly under the stately pines. Lucy became aware of another kind of tree, the most wonderful she had ever seen, huge-trunked, thick with drooping foliage, and lifting its proud height spear-shaped to the sky. Her guide informed her that this tree was a silver spruce, which name seemed singularly felicitous.

Again they forded the brook, to Lucy's mingled dismay and delight, and after that so many times that she forgot them and also her fears. The forest became a grand temple. Higher towered the forest patriarchs, two hundred feet and more above her head, mingling their foliage in a lacy canopy, like a green veil against the blue. She caught a glimpse of wild sleek gray creatures bounding as on rubber legs into the brush. Deer!

At last the trail led out of the fragrant glen and zigzagged up a slope, to the dry forest of pines, and on and upward, farther and higher until Lucy felt she had ascended to the top of a mountain. She lost the mellow roar of the brook. The woodland changed its aspect, grew hot with dusty trail and thick with manzanita, above which the yellow-barked pines reached with great gnarled arms. Open places were now frequent. Once Lucy saw a red wall of rock so high above her that she gasped in astonishment. That was the Red Rim Rock, seemingly so close, though yet far away. Lucy became conscious of aches and pains. She shifted from side to side in the saddle, and favored this foot, then the other. Often she had to urge Buster on to catch up with her guide.

Suddenly she turned a corner of the brushy trail to ride out into a clearing. Bare brown earth, ghastly dead pines, like specters, seemed to lift her gaze, to where, sky-high, the red wall heaved, bold, strange, terrific, yet glorious with its zigzag face blazing in the hues of sunset, and its black-fringed crown wandering away as if to the ends of the earth.

Strangely then into her mind flashed a thought of this backwoods boy whose name had been on the lips of everyone she had met. Born under that colossal wall! All his life in this forest and rock solitude! Lucy could not help but wonder what manner of man he was. She resented an involuntary interest. The force of a personality had been thrust upon her. It was feminine intuition that caused her, unconsciously, to fortify herself by roused antagonism.

Mr. Jenks pointed to a little rough gray house, half log, half stones, that dominated the clearing. "Denmeade built it twenty-three years ago," said the teacher. "He and his wife walked up here, from no one knows where. They had a burro, a cow, a gun, and an ax, and some dogs.

They homesteaded this section. He has five girls and four boys, all born in that little one-room hut. Edd is the oldest—he's twenty-two. Last year they built quite a fine log cabin, up in the woods beyond the fields. You can't see it from here."

The surroundings seemed fitting for such heroic people as these Denmeades.

"They may be backwoodsmen," declared Lucy, voicing her thought, "but I'd call them pioneers. Which is to say real Americans!"

"Miss Watson, I like that," replied the teacher warmly. "You have gotten the significance. These people are great."

Over against that impulsive impression Lucy had the crudeness of the scene to oppose it. She was intelligent enough to accept crudeness as a part of pioneer life. It could not be otherwise. But she gazed over the slash cut in the forest, and found it lacking in anything she could admire. The Red Rim Rock and the encircling belt of mighty green were facts of nature. The space of bare ground with its ghastly dead trees, its ruined old hut, its uncouth shacks of board and poles, its pigs rooting around, its utter lack of what constituted her idea of a farm, somehow did not seem to harmonize with the noble pioneer spirit. Lucy hesitated to make this impression permanent. She did not like the look of this place, but she was broad-minded enough to wait. She hoped she would not find these people lazy, shiftless, dirty, existing in squalid surroundings. Yet she feared that would be exactly what she would find.

The trail led along a patchwork fence of poles and sticks, here rotting away and there carelessly mended by the throwing of an untrimmed branch of tree. At the corner of the huge field snuggled the rude shacks she had seen from afar, all the worse for nearer view. They rode between these and a round log corral, full of pigs of all sizes, and from which came an unbearable stench. Some of the hogs were stuck in the mud. Lucy saw some tiny baby pigs, almost pink, with funny little curly tails, and sight of these gave her unexpected pleasure. So she experienced two extremes of feeling in passing that point.

From there the trail led through an uncared-for orchard of peach trees, into a narrow lane cut in the woods. The pines had been left where they had fallen, and lay brown and seared in the tangle of green. This lane was full of stumps.

"You appreciate why we needed horses to get here, don't you?" inquired Mr. Jenks.

"Indeed I do!" replied Lucy.

"Denmeade said he'd never live in a place where wheels could go. I rather sympathize with that spirit, but it is not one of a progressive farmer. I dare say you will have it to combat."

Th lane descended into a ravine, where clear water ran over stones that rang hollow under the hoofs of the horses. Lucy saw cows and calves, a very old sheep, woolly and dirty, and a wicked-looking steer with wide sharp horns. Lucy was glad to get safely past him. They rode up again, into a wider lane, at the end of which showed a long cabin, somewhat obscured by more peach trees. A column of blue smoke curled up against the background of red wall. A fence of split boards surrounded the cabin. A strip of woods on the right separated this lane from the bare field. Lucy could see light through the pine foliage. The brook meandered down a shallow ravine on this side; and on the other a deep gully yawned, so choked with dead trees and green foliage and red rocks that Lucy could not see the bottom. She heard, however, the fall of water.

A dog barked. Then rose a chorus of barks and bays, not in the least a friendly welcome. It increased to an uproar. Lucy began to be conscious of qualms when a loud sharp voice rang out. The uproar ceased.

"Hyar, you ornery dawgs, shet up!" the voice continued.

Then Lucy saw a tall man emerge from the peach trees and come to the gate. His garb was dark, his face also at that distance, and they gave a sinister effect.

"That's Denmeade," whispered Mr. Jenks. "We're lucky. Now, young lady, use your wits."

They rode on the few remaining rods, and reaching the rude hitching rail in front of the fence, they halted the horses. Mr. Jenks dismounted and greeted the big man at the gate.

"Howdy, teacher!" he replied, in a deep, pleasant drawl.

"Fine, thank you, Denmeade," returned Mr. Jenks, as he extended his hand over the fence. "I've brought a visitor to see you. This is Miss Lucy Watson of Felix."

Lucy essayed her most winning smile as she acknowledged the introduction.

"Glad to meet you, miss," responded Denmeade. "Get down an' come in."

Dismounting, Lucy approached the gate, to look up into a visage as rugged as the rock wall above. Denmeade was not old or gray, though his features showed the ravages of years. Lucy had no time to mark details. The man's eyes, gray and piercing as those of an eagle, caught and held her gaze.

"If you please, I'd like to talk to you alone before I go in," she said, appealingly.

Denmeade removed the huge battered black sombrero, and ran a brawny hand through his thick dark hair. The gray eyes twinkled and a smile changed the craggy nature of his face.

"Wal, seein' as Edd ain't hyar, I reckon I can risk it," he drawled.

Mr. Jenks suggested that they sit in the shade; and presently Lucy found herself seated on a stump, facing this curious backwoodsman. He seemed a more approachable person than she had pictured, yet there was something about him, strong, raw, fierce, like the wilds in which he lived. Lucy had worried about this coming interview; had schooled herself to a deliberate diplomacy. But she forgot worry and plan. The man's simplicity made her sincere.

"Mr. Denmeade, I want a job," she announced, bluntly.

It was good to see his astonishment and utter incredulity. Such a situation had never before happened in his life. He stared. His seamed visage worked into a wonderful grin.

"Wal, reckon yore foolin'," he said, and he turned to Jenks. "Teacher, shore you've hatched some kind of a joke."

"No, Denmeade. Miss Watson is in earnest," replied the school-teacher.

"Indeed I am," added Lucy, trying to restrain her impulsiveness.

But Denmeade still could not take her seriously. "Wal, can you chop wood, carry water, pick beans, an' hop around lively—say fer a fellar like my Edd?"

"Yes, I could, but that is not the kind of a job I want," returned Lucy.

"Wal, there ain't no other kind of work up hyar fer a woman," he said, seriously.

"Yes, there is. . . . It's to make better homes for the children."

"Better homes! What you mean?" ejaculated Denmeade.

Briefly Lucy explained some of the ways the homes in the wilderness could be made happier for women and children. Denmeade was profoundly impressed.

"Wal now, young woman, I reckon it's good of you to think of them nice an' pretty ways fer our kids an' their mothers. But we're poor. We couldn't pay you, let alone fer them things they need so bad."

Lucy's heart throbbed with joy. She knew intuitively that she had struck the right core in this old backwoodsman. Whereupon she produced her papers.

"It's a new thing, Mr. Denmeade," she said, earnestly. "State welfare work. My salary and the expenses I incur are paid by the state. It's all here for you to read, and my references."

Denmeade took her papers in his horny hands, and began to read with the laborious and intense application of one to whom reading was unfamiliar and difficult. He took long to go over the brief typed words, and longer over the personal letter from the superintendent of the state department that had engaged Lucy. Finally he absorbed the import.

"Welfare! State government! Dog-gone me!" he ejaculated, almost bewildered. "Say, Jenks, what ails them fellars down thar?"

"Perhaps they have just waked up to the needs of this north country," replied the teacher.

"Shore them papers don't read like they had an ax to grind. Reckon it ain't no politics or some trick to make us pay taxes?"

"Denmeade, they read honest to me, and my advice, if you ask it, is to accept their help."

"Humph! It shore took them a long time to build us a schoolhouse an' send us a teacher. Whar did they ever get this hyar welfare idee?"

"Mr. Denmeade," spoke up Lucy, "I had something to do with this idea. It really developed out of my offer to go into welfare work in a civilized district."

"Wal, comin' from a girl like you, it ain't hard to accept," he declared, and he extended his great brown hand. His gray eyes flashed with a softened light.

Lucy placed her hand in his, and as he almost crushed it she was at considerable pains to keep from crying out. When he released it she felt that it was limp and numb.

"You—you mean it—it's all right?" she stammered. "You'll let me stay—help me get started?"

"I shore will," he replied, forcefully. "You stay hyar with us as long as you want. I reckon, though, the other four families close by in this high country need you more'n us. Seth Miller's, Hank Claypool's, Ora Johnson's, an' Tom Sprall's."

"Miss Watson, the Ora Johnson he means is a brother of the Sam Johnson you met," interposed Mr. Jenks.

Lucy was too happy to express her gratitude, and for a moment lost her dignity. Her incoherent thanks brought again the broad grin to Denmeade's face.

"Jenks, come to think about it, thar's angles to this hyar job Miss Lucy is aimin' at," he remarked, thoughtfully. "She can't do a lot for one family an' slight another. If she stays hyar with us she'll have to stay with the others."

"Of course. That's what I expect to do," said Lucy.

"Wal, miss, I ain't given to brag, but I reckon you'll find it different after staying with us," rejoined Denmeade, shaking his shaggy head.

Plain it was for Lucy to see that Mr. Jenks agreed with him.

"In just what way?" queried Lucy.

"Lots of way, but particular, say—Ora Johnson has an old cabin with one room. Countin' his wife, thar's eight in the family. All live in that one room! With one door an' no winder!"

Lucy had no ready reply for such an unexpected circumstance as this, and she gazed at Mr. Jenks in mute dismay.

"I have a tent I'll lend her," he said. "It can be erected on a frame with board floor. Very comfortable."

"Wal, I reckon that would do fer Johnson's. But how about Tom Sprall's? Thar's more in his outfit, an' only two cabins. But shore no room for her. An' the tent idee won't do—sartin not whar Bud Sprall goes rarin' around full of white mule. It wouldn't be safe."

"Denmeade, I had that very fear in mind," said Mr. Jenks, earnestly. "Miss Watson will have to avoid Sprall's."

"Shore, it'd ought to be done. But I'm reckonin' that'll raise hell. Tom is a mean cuss, an' his outfit of wimmen are jealous as coyote poison. They'll all have to know Miss Lucy is hyar helpin' everybody equal. They'll all want equal favors from the state. I ain't sayin' a word ag'in' Tom, but he's a rustler. An' thar's turrible bad blood between Bud Sprall an' my boy Edd."

"You see, Miss Watson, it's not going to be as rosy as we hoped," said Mr. Jenks, regretfully.

"I'm not afraid," replied Lucy, resolutely. "It never looked easy. I accept it, come what may. The Spralls shall not be slighted."

"Wal, you've settled it, an' thar ain't nothin' wrong

with your nerve," replied Denmeade. "Come in now an' meet my folks. Teacher, you'll eat supper with us?"

"I'm sorry, Denmeade. I must hurry back and send Sam up with her baggage," returned Jenks, rising. "Goodby, Miss Watson. I wish you luck. Come down to school with the children. I'll see you surely at the dance Friday night."

"I'm very grateful to you, Mr. Jenks," replied Lucy. "You've helped me. I will want to see you soon. But I can't say that it will be at the dance."

"Shore she'll be thar, teacher," said Denmeade. "She can't stay hyar alone, an' if she wanted to, Edd wouldn't let her."

"Oh—indeed!" murmured Lucy, constrainedly, as Denmeade and the school-teacher exchanged laughs. How irrepressibly this Edd bobbed up at every turn of conversation! Right then Lucy resolved that she would certainly not go to the dance. And she realized an undue curiosity in regard to this backwoods boy.

CHAPTER III

Lucy followed her escort into the yard and between the blossoming peach trees to the cabin. She saw now that it was a new structure built of flat-hewn logs, long and low, with a peaked roof of split shingles covering two separate square cabins and the wide space between them. This roof also extended far out to cover a porch the whole length of the building. Each cabin had a glass window, and the door, which Lucy could not see, must have faced the middle porch. The rude solid structure made a rather good impression.

A long-eared hound stood wagging his tail at the head of the porch steps. Lucy's roving eye took in other dogs asleep in sunny spots; several little puppies with ears so long they stumbled over them as they ran pell-mell to meet Denmeade; heavy rolls of canvas, no doubt blankets or bedding, were piled along the wall; saddles and saddle blankets were ranged in similar order on the opposite side; the cabin wall on the right was studded with pegs upon which hung kitchen utensils and tools; that on the left held deer and elk antlers used as racks for hats, guns, ropes. The wide space of porch between the two cabins evidently served as an outdoor dining room, for a rude home-carpentered table and benches occupied the center.

At Denmeade's call a flock of children came trooping out of the door of the left cabin. They were big-eyed, dirty and ragged, and sturdy of build. A sallow, thin-faced little woman, in coarse dress and heavy shoes, followed them.

"Ma, this hyar is Miss Lucy Watson from Felix," announced Denmeade.

Mrs. Denmeade greeted Lucy cordially and simply, without show of curiosity or astonishment. Then Denmeade told her in his blunt speech what Lucy had come for. This information brought decided surprise and welcome to the woman's face. Lucy was quick to see what perhaps Denmeade had never known in his life. She added a few earnest words in her own behalf, calculated to strengthen Mrs. Denmeade's impression, and to say that when convenient they would talk over the work Lucy was to undertake.

"Reckon you're a new kind of teacher?" queried Mrs. Denmeade. "Sort of home-teacher?"

"Why yes, you could call me that," replied Lucy, smiling.

"Shore that'll please the kids," said Denmeade. "They sort of look up to a teacher. You see we've only had school-teachers a few years. Edd went four years, Allie three, Dick an' Joe three, Mertie two, Mary an' Dan one. Liz an' Lize, the twins hyar, five years old—they haven't started yet."

Whereupon the children were presented to Lucy, a situation rich in pleasure and interest for her. The twins

were as like as two peas in a pod, chubby, rosy-cheeked
little girls, fair-haired, with big eyes of gray like their
father's. To Lucy's overtures they were shy, silent, yet
fascinated. Dan was a dark-headed youngster, with eyes
to match, dirty, mischievous, bold, and exceedingly responsive to Lucy. Mary, too, was dark, though lighter
than Dan, older by a year or two, a thin overworked girl
who under favorable conditions would be pretty. The
several other children present were Claypools, visiting
the Denmeades. When Lucy had greeted them all she was
to meet Denmeade's older daughters Allie, a young
woman, huge of build, with merry face, and Mertie, a
girl of sixteen, quite beautiful in a wild-rose kind of way.
She was the only one of the family who showed anything
of color or neatness in her attire. Manifestly she wore
her Sunday dress, a coarse print affair. Her sharp dark
eyes seemed more concerned with Lucy's riding habit, the
way she had arranged her hair and tied her scarf, than
with Lucy's presence there.

Lucy was taken into the left-hand cabin, to meet the
mother and sister of the Claypool children. They, too,
were hard-featured, unprepossessing, and bore the unmistakable marks of hard labor in a hard country. All
these impressions of Lucy's were hasty ones that she
knew might pass entirely or change. Intense as was her
interest, she could not stare at or study these people. She
had to confess that they put her at her ease. There was
not a suspicion of inhospitality, or, for that matter, except
on the part of the children, the betrayal of anything
unusual about this newcomer. Lucy was given one of the
few home-made chairs, a rude triangular board affair
that could be set two ways. And then the conversation
which no doubt her advent had interrupted was resumed
by the older women.

The twins began to manifest signs of being irresistibly
drawn to Lucy. They were in the toils of a new experience. Lucy had been used to children, and had taken
several months of kindergarten work, which was going
to be of infinite value to her here. She listened to the
conversation, which turned out to be homely gossip,

differing only in content from gossip anywhere. And while doing so she had a chance to gaze casually round the room.

The walls were bare, of rough-hewn logs, with the chinks between plastered with clay. There was a window on each side. A huge rough stone fireplace occupied nearly all the west end of the cabin. In a left-hand corner, next to the fireplace, was a closet of boards reaching from floor to ceiling. This ceiling appeared to be of the same kind of shingling Lucy had observed on the roof. The floor was rough clapboard, like that of the porch outside. The two corners opposite the fireplace contained built-in beds, bulky with a quilted covering. There were no other articles of furniture, not even a table or lamp.

Lucy appreciated that this living room, despite its lack of comforts, might be far superior to the dark, clay-floored cabin rooms she had heard about. It was at least dry and light. But its bareness jarred on her. What did these people do with their leisure time, if they had any? The younger women talked of nothing save dances and boys; their elders interpolated their gossip with bits of news about the homely labors that spring had brought. Mary was the only one of the children whom Lucy could induce to talk; and she had, apparently, a limited range of subjects. School, the burro she rode, the puppies she played with, appeared to be in possession of her mind.

At length the Claypools announced that if they were to reach home by dark they must hurry.

"Come an' see us," invited the mother, addressing Lucy, and the grown daughter added: " 'By. Reckon Edd'll be fetchin' you an' Mertie to the dance."

Lucy murmured something noncommittal in reply, and accompanied the women and children outside. They left the porch at the far end of the cabin, and went through a side gate out into the woods, where two horses and a burro were haltered to trees. Dogs, sheep, and chickens tagged at their heels. There was a rather open clearing under the pines, trodden bare, and covered with red and white chips of wood. Women and children talked all together, so that it was impossible for Lucy to distinguish

much of what was said. She gathered, however, that
Mrs. Denmeade told Mrs. Claypool something about
Lucy's welfare work. Then mother and daughter, unmind-
ful of their skirts, mounted the two horses.

The burro raised one long ear and cocked the other at
the three Claypool youngsters. Mrs. Denmeade and Allie
lifted them up on the back of the burro. It had a halter
tied round its nose. The little boy, who could not have
been more than four years old, had the foremost position astride the burro. He took up the halter. His sisters,
aged, respectively, about three and two, rode behind him.
The older girl got her arms round the boy, and the
younger did likewise by her sister. Lucy was not only
amazed and frightened for the youngsters, but also so
amused she could scarcely contain herself.

"Aren't you afraid you'll fall off?" she asked, standing
abreast of them.

"Naw!" said the boy. And the elder girl, with a sober
smile at Lucy, added: " 'Tain't nuthin' to fall off. But it's
hard gettin' back on."

It required considerable beating and kicking on the
part of the three to start the burro after the horses, but
at last he decided to move, and trotted off.

"How far have they to go?" inquired Lucy, as she
watched them disappear in the woods.

"Reckon five miles or so. They'll get home about
dark," replied Mrs. Denmeade. "Now, girls, there's supper
to get. An', Miss Watson, you're goin' to be more one
of the family than company. Make yourself to home."

Mary attached herself to Lucy and led her around the
corner of the cabin to see the puppies, while the twins
toddled behind. Lucy wanted to know the names of the
puppies and all about them. When Mary had exhausted
this subject she led Lucy to see her especial playground,
which was across the ravine in a sheltered spot redolent
of pine needles. She showed Lucy a nook under a large
manzanita where she played with pine cones and bits of
Indian pottery, which she said she had found right there.
Lucy had to see the spring, and the stone steps across the
brook, and the big iron kettle and tub which were used in

washing. Lucy looked in vain for an outhouse of any description. There was none, not even a chicken-coop. Mary said the chickens roosted in trees, like the wild turkeys, to keep from being eaten by beasts. Lucy inquired about these beasts, and further if there were snakes and bugs.

"Rattlers, trantulars, an' scorpions in summer. That's all that's bad," said Mary.

"Goodness! That's enough!" exclaimed Lucy.

"They won't hurt nobody," added the child, simply. Then she led Lucy across the clearing, where the twins tarried on an enterprise of their own, and down a trail into the deep gully. Here among the rocks and ferns, overshadowed by the pines and sycamores, they got away from the despoiled forest above. Lucy was glad to rest a little and listen to Mary's prattle. How wild and rugged this gully! Yet it was scarcely a stone's-throw from the cabin. The clear water babbled over smooth red stone and little falls and gravelly bars.

"It dries up in summer," said Mary, indicating the brook. "Sometimes the spring does, too. Then we all have to pack water from way down."

They came at length to a green bench that had been cleared of brush and small trees, yet, owing to the giant spreading pines above, did not long get direct rays of the sun. Rude boxes, some of them painted, were scattered around on little platforms of stones.

"Edd's beehives," said Mary, with grave importance. "We must be awful good. Edd doesn't mind if we behave."

"I'll be very careful, Mary. I don't want to get stung. Are they real wild bees?"

"Shore. But Edd tames them. Oh, Edd loves bees somethin' turrible," answered the child, solemnly. "Bees never sting him, even when he's choppin' a new bee tree."

"Why does Edd do that?" inquired Lucy.

"Didn't you ever, ever hear of Edd Denmeade's honey?" returned Mary, in great surprise. "Pa says it's the best in the world. Oh-umum! He'll shore give *you* some. Edd likes girls next to his bees. . . . He's a bee hunter. Pa says Edd's the best bee liner he ever seen."

"Bee liner! What's that, Mary?"

"Why, he watches for bees, an' when they come he lines them. Bees fly straight off, you know. He lines them to their hive in a tree. Then he chops it down. Always he saves the honey, an' sometimes he saves the bees."

The child added to the interest accumulating round the name of Edd Denmeade.

"Where is Edd now?" asked Lucy.

"He went to Winbrook with the pack burros," replied Mary. "That's up over the Rim an' far off, to the railroad. Edd's promised to take me there some day. Shore he ought to be back soon. I want him awful bad. Candy! Edd always fetches us candy. He'll come by Mertie's birthday. That's next Wednesday. He's fetchin' Mertie's new dress. Her first boughten one! She's sixteen. An' Edd's givin' it to her. Oh, he'll come shore, 'cause he loves Mertie."

"Of course he loves you, too?" queried Lucy, winningly.

"Ma says so. But Mertie's his favorite. She's so pretty. I wish I was," replied Mary, with childish pathos.

"You will be, Mary, when you are sixteen, if you are good and learn how to take care of yourself, and have beautiful thoughts," said Lucy.

"Ma told Mrs. Claypool you was a home-teacher. Are you goin' to teach me all that?"

"Yes, and more. Won't you like to learn how to make nice dresses?"

"Oh!" cried Mary, beamingly, and she burst into a babble of questions. Lucy answered. How simple! She had anticipated cudgeling her brains to satisfy these backwoods children. But Mary was already won. They remained in the gully until the sun sank, and then climbed out. Mary ran to confide her bursting news to the little twin sisters, and Lucy was left to herself for the time being. She walked down the lane, and across the strip of woodland to the open fields, and out where she could see.

Westward along the Rim vast capes jutted out, differing in shape and length, all ragged, sharp, fringed, reaching darkly for the gold and purple glory of the sunset.

Shafts and rays of light streamed from the rifts in the clouds, blazing upon the bold rock faces of the wall. Eastward the Rim zigzagged endlessly into pale cold purple. Southward a vast green hollow ran like a river of the sea, to empty, it seemed, into space. Beyond that rose dim spectral shapes of mountains, remote and detached. To the north the great wall shut out what might lie beyond.

How unscalable it looked to Lucy! Points of rim ran out, narrow, broken, sloping, apparently to sheer off into the void. But the distance was far and the light deceiving. Lucy knew a trail came down the ragged cape that loomed out over Denmeade's ranch. She had heard some one say Edd would come back that way with the pack-train. It seemed incredible for a man, let alone a burro. Just to gaze up at that steep of a thousand deceptive ridges, cracks, slants, and ascents was enough to rouse respect for these people who were conquering the rock-confined wilderness.

This lifting of Lucy's spirit gave pause to the growth of something akin to contempt that had unconsciously formed in her mind. After hearing and reading about these primitive inhabitants of the wild she had developed abstract conceptions of kindliness, sympathy, and close contact with them. They had been very noble sentiments. But she was going to find them hard to live up to. By analyzing her feelings she realized that she did not like the personal intimations. Her one motive was to help these people and in so doing help herself. She had come, however, with an unconscious sense of her personal aloofness, the height to which, of course, these common people could not aspire. Yet their very first and most natural reaction, no doubt, was to imagine a sentimental attachment between her and one of these backwoods boys.

From amusement Lucy passed to annoyance, and thence to concern. She had experienced her troubles with cowboys even in town, where there were ample avenues of escape. What would she encounter here? Would she find at the very outset a ridiculous obstacle to her success, to the fine record of welfare work she longed to establish?

The matter became a problem, no less because a faint accusing voice had begun to reach her conscience. She listened to it and strained at it until she heard something like doubt of her being big enough for this job. She humiliated herself. It had never occurred to her that she might be found wanting. A wonderfully stabilizing though painful idea this was. After all, what excuse had she for superiority?

Standing there in the open fields, Lucy forgot the magnificent red wall and the gorgeous sunset-flushed panorama. She realized her vanity, that she had wounded it, that in all probability it would have to be killed before she could be wholly worthy of this work. Her humility, however, did not withstand the rush of resentment, eagerness, and confidence of her youth. Lucy stifled in its incipiency a thought vaguely hinting that she would have to suffer and grow before she really was what she dreamed she was.

Presently she heard the crack of hoofs on rock, and, turning, she espied two riders entering the corral at the end of the field. She decided they must be two more of the Denmeades, Dick and Joe, if she remembered rightly. They dismounted, threw their saddles, turned the horses loose. They appeared to be long, lean, rangy young men, wearing huge sombreros that made them look top-heavy. They whistled and whooped, creating sounds which clapped back in strange echo from the wall. It emphasized the stillness to Lucy. Such hilarity seemed out of place there. Lucy watched the tall figures stride out of sight up the lane toward the cabin.

"One thing sure," soliloquized Lucy, gravely, "I've got to realize I have myself to contend with up here. Myself! . . . It seems I don't know much about *me*."

She returned to the cabin, entering the yard by the side gate. Some of the hounds followed her, sniffing at her, not yet over their hostility. The Denmeades were collecting round the table on the porch. The mother espied Lucy and greeted her with a smile.

"Reckon we was about ready to put the hounds on your trail," she called, and when Lucy reached the table she added: "You set in this place. . . . Here's Dick an' Joe. You've only one more to see, an' that's Edd. Boys, meet Miss Lucy Watson of Felix."

Lucy smiled at the young men, waiting to sit down opposite her. Which was Dick and which Joe she could not tell yet. The younger was exceedingly tall and thin. The older, though tall and angular, too, appeared short by comparison. Both had smooth, still, shining faces, lean and brown, with intent clear eyes.

"Hod-do!" said the older boy to Lucy, as he took his seat across the table. He was nothing if not admiring.

"Joe, did you meet teacher Jenks?" asked Denmeade, from the head of the table.

"Yep. Saw him at Johnson's. He told us aboot Miss Watson. An' we passed Sam on the trail. He was packin' her baggage."

Before Allie and Mertie, who were carrying steaming dishes from the kitchen, had brought in all the supper, the Denmeades set about the business of eating.

"Help yourself, miss," said the father.

The table was too small for so many. They crowded close together. Lucy's seat was at one end of a bench, giving her the free use of her right hand. Mary sat on her left, happily conscious of the close proximity. The heads of the little girls and Dan just topped the level of the table. In fact, their mouths were about on a level with their tin plates. At first glance Lucy saw that the table was laden with food, with more still coming. Pans of smoking biscuits, pans of beans, pans of meat and gravy, and steaming tin cups of black coffee! Lucy noted the absence of milk, butter, sugar, green or canned vegetables. She was hungry and she filled her plate. And despite the coarseness of the food she ate heartily. Before she had finished, dusk had settled down around the cabin, and when the meal ended it was quite dark.

"I hear Sam's hoss," said Dick, as he rose, clinking his spurs. "Reckon I'll help him unpack."

Lucy sat down on the edge of the porch, peering out into the woods. The children clustered round her. Mrs. Denmeade and her older daughters were clearing off the

supper table. A dim lamplight glimmered in the kitchen.
Lucy was aware of the tall form of Dick Denmeade
standing to one side. He had not yet spoken a word.
Lucy addressed him once, but for all the answer she got
he might as well have been deaf. He shifted one of his
enormous boots across the other. In the dim light Lucy
made out long spurs attached to them. Then Mrs. Denmeade ordered the children off to bed. One by one they
vanished. Mary's pale face gleamed wistfully and was
gone.

It dawned on Lucy, presently, that the air was cold. It
had changed markedly in an hour. Big white stars had
appeared over the tips of the pines; the sky was dark
blue. The blackness of the night shadows had lightened
somewhat or else her eyes had become accustomed to it.
Quiet settled over the cabin, broken only by low voices
and sounds from the kitchen. It struck Lucy as sad and
somber, this mantle of night descending upon the lonely
cabin, yet never before had she felt such peace, such
sweet solitude. By straining her ears she caught a dreamy
murmur of the stream down in the gorge, and a low
mourn of wind in the pines. Where were the coyotes,
night hawks, whippoorwills, all the noisy creatures she
had imagined lived in the wilderness?

Pound of hoofs and clink of spurs became audible
in the lane, approaching the cabin. Lucy heard a laugh
she recognized, and low voices, merry, subtle, almost
hoarse whisperings. Then the gate creaked, and the musical clink of spurs advanced toward the porch. At last
Lucy made out two dark forms. They approached, and
one mounted the steps, while the other stopped before
Lucy. She conceived an idea that this fellow could see
in the dark.

"Wal, Miss Lucy, here's your bags without a scratch,"
said Sam Johnson's drawling voice. "Shore I bet you was
worried. How'd you find my hoss Buster?"

"Just fine, thank you," replied Lucy. "Full of spirit and
go. Yet he obeyed promptly. I never had a slip. Now
were you not trying to frighten me a little—or was it
Mr. Jenks?—telling me he was some kind of a mustang?"

"Honest, Buster's gentle with girls," protested Sam. "Shore he pitches when one of these long-legged Denmeades rake him. But don't you believe what anyone tells you."

"Very well, I won't. Buster is a dandy little horse."

"Wal, then, you're invited to ride him again," said Sam, with subtle inflection.

"Oh, thank you," replied Lucy. "I—I'll be pleased— if my work allows me any spare time."

"Howdy, Sam!" interposed Allie, from the kitchen door. "Who're you goin' to take to the dance?"

"Wal, I ain't shore, jest yet," he returned. "Reckon I know who I'd like to take."

"Sadie told me you asked her."

"Did she? . . . Sent her word. But she didn't send none back," protested Sam, lamely.

"Sam, take a hunch from me. Don't try to shenanegin out of it now," retorted Allie, and retreated into the kitchen.

Lucy was both relieved and amused at Allie's grasp of the situation. No doubt Sam had been approaching another invitation.

Denmeade's heavy footfall sounded on the porch, accompanied by the soft pad of a dog trotting. "That you, Sam? How's yore folks?"

"Tip top," replied Sam, shortly.

"Get down an' come in," drawled Denmeade as the other shuffled restlessly.

"Reckon I'll be goin'," said Sam. "I've a pack-hoss waitin'. . . . Evenin', Miss Lucy. Shore I hope to see you at the dance."

"I hardly think you will," replied Lucy. "Thank you for fetching my baggage."

Sam's tall form disappeared in the gloom. The gate creaked as if opened and shut with forceful haste. Almost directly followed the sound of hoofs going off into the darkness.

"Hey, Sam!" called Joe, coming out of the cabin, where he had carried Lucy's grips.

"He's gone," said his father, laconically.

"Gone! Why, the dinged galoot had somethin' of mine! Funny, him runnin' off. He shore was rarin' to get here. Never saw him make such good time on a trail. What riled him?"

"Wal, I have an idee," drawled Denmeade. "Allie give him a dig."

"I shore did," spoke up Allie, from the kitchen, where evidently she heard what was going on outside. "It's a shame the way he treats Sadie."

Lucy began to gather snatches of the complexity of life up here. After all, how like things at home! This girl Sadie had refused to marry Edd Denmeade. There was an intimation that she was attached to Sam Johnson. On his part, Sam had manifested a slight interest in a newcomer to the country.

Mrs. Denmeade came out of the kitchen carrying a lighted lamp, and she called Lucy to accompany her into the other cabin. She set the lamp on the high jutting shelf of the fireplace.

"You sleep in here with the children," she said simply.

"Yes—that will be nice," rejoined Lucy, peering around. Dan was asleep on the floor in a corner, his bed a woolly sheep skin, his covering a rag quilt. Mary and the twins were fast asleep in one of the beds. Lucy stepped close to peer down at them. Liz and Lize lay at the foot, curly fair heads close together. Their faces had been washed and now shone sweet and wan in the lamplight. Their chubby hands were locked. Mary lay at the head of the bed, and her thin face bore a smile as if she were having pleasant dreams.

"Where—shall I wash?" asked Lucy, with diffidence.

"You'll find water, basin, towel out on the porch. . . . Good night. I reckon you're tired. Hope you sleep good."

Lucy bade her hostess good night and turned musingly to the opening of one of her grips. She could hear the low breathing of the sleepers. Somehow, to be there with them, under such circumstances, touched her deeply. It was for the sake of such as they that she had forsaken personal comfort and better opportunities. Despite a somewhat depressed spirit, Lucy could not regret her action. If only she won their love and taught them fine, clean, wholesome ways with which to meet their hard and unlovely futures! That would transform her sacrifice into a blessing. •

The room was cold. A fire in the big stone fireplace would have been much to her liking. By the time she got ready for bed she was chilled through. Before blowing out the lamp she took a last look at the slumbering children. They seemed so still, so calm, so white and sweet. Lucy trembled for them, in a vague realization of life. Then, with some difficulty she opened one of the windows. Once in bed, she stretched out in aching relief. That long ride, especially on the horse, had cramped and chafed her. The bed was as cold and hard as ice. There were no sheets. The blankets under her did not do much to soften the feel of what she concluded was a mattress filled with corn husks. It rustled like corn husks, though it might have been coarse straw. The coverings were heavy rag quilts.

Nevertheless, Lucy had never before been so grateful for a bed. If this bed was good enough for those innocent and happy and unfortunate children, it was good enough for her. Unfortunate! She pondered. She would have to learn as much as she taught.

She heard heavy boots and the jangle of spurs on the porch, the unrolling of one of the canvas packs, faint voices from the kitchen, and then footsteps over her head in the attic. One of the boys spoke up there. Probably that was where they slept. Lucy now remembered seeing the ladder that led from the middle porch to a wide hole in the ceiling. She wondered where the rest of the Denmeades slept. No doubt she was robbing father and mother of their room and bed.

Gradually all sounds ceased, except the faint murmur of water and wind, out in the woods. Lucy grew warm and sleepy. Yet so novel and strange were her sensations that she fought off the drowsy spell. She was really there up in the backwoods. She could scarcely credit it. The blackness of the room, the silence, the unfamiliar fragrance of pine and wood smoke, were like unrealities of a dream. She lived over the whole journey and would not have changed any of it. Suddenly the stillness broke to a deep-ringing, long-drawn bay of a hound. It made her flesh creep. How it rang out the truth of her presence in the wild forest, in the hard bed of these lowly pioneers! The home that had failed her was gone forever. The one person she had loved most—her sister Clara—had failed her. And in the lonely darkness she wept, not as on the night before, childishly and unrestrainedly, but with sorrow for loss and gratefulness for the future that promised so much.

She would be happy to face the morrow, come what might. It could only bring another kind of strife, that in itself might be good for her soul. With such hope and a prayer that it would be so she fell asleep.

CHAPTER IV

Lucy awakened in a half-conscious dream that she was in a place unfamiliar to her. Before she opened her eyes she smelled wood smoke. Then she saw that daylight had come and she was looking at her open window through which blue smoke and sunlight were pouring in. Bewildered, she gazed around this strange room—bare wood and clay walls—big stone fireplace—rude ceiling of poles and shingles. Where was she?

With a start she raised on her elbow. Then the effort that cost her, the sense of sore muscles, and the rustling of the corn-husk mattress brought flashing to memory her long ride of yesterday and the backwoods home of the Denmeades.

She was surprised, and somewhat mortified, to see that the children were up and gone. On the moment Lucy heard the patter of their feet outside on the porch and the ringing strokes of an ax on hard wood. Whereupon she essayed to hop out of bed. She managed it all right, but not without awkwardness and pain.

"Oh, I'm all crippled!" she cried, ruefully. "That ride! . . . And say, it's Greenland's icy mountains here."

The plain, substantial woolen garments that she had brought for cold weather were going to be welcome now. Lucy dressed in less time than ever before in her life. Then with soap, towel, comb, and brush she sallied out on the porch and round to the side of the cabin. The children were in the kitchen. An old man sat on a bench. He was thin, gray, with cadaverous cheeks, a pointed chin bristling with stubby beard.

"Good mawnin'," he said.

Lucy greeted him and asked where the water was.

"I jest fetched some," he said, pointing to a stand at the end of the porch. "Right pert this mawnin'. I reckon the frost won't do them peach blossoms no good."

Lucy indeed found the water pert. Her ablutions, owing to her impetuosity, turned out to be an ordeal. Evidently the old fellow had watched her with interest, for as she finished her hair and turned back he said with a huge grin, "Rosy cheeks!"

"Thanks," replied Lucy, brightly. "I'm Lucy Watson. I didn't meet you last night."

"Nope. But I seen you. I'm Lee's oldest brother. Thar's four of us brothers hyar in the woods. Uncle Bill the kids call me."

Upon her way back to the room she encountered the extremely tall young Denmeade who appeared too bashfull to return her greeting. Lucy hurriedly put her things away and made her bed, then presented herself at the kitchen door, to apologize for being late.

"Reckoned you'd be tired, so I wouldn't let the children call you," replied Mrs. Denmeade. "Come an' eat."

They were having breakfast in the kitchen. Mary was the only one of the children to answer Lucy's greeting. Dan did not appear bashful, but his mouth was so full he could not speak. Mrs. Denmeade and Mertie were sitting at the table, while Allie stood beside the big stove. They did not seem stolid or matter-of-fact; they lacked expression of whatever they did feel. Lucy sat down to ham, eggs, biscuits, coffee. "Some of Edd's honey," indicated Mrs. Denmeade, with pride, as she placed a pan before her. Lucy was hungry. She enjoyed her breakfast, and as for the honey, she had never tasted anything so delicious, so wild and sweet of flavor.

After breakfast, Lucy was greatly interested in the brief preparations for school. Dan had to be forced away from the table. He was bareheaded and barefooted. Lucy went out to the gate with him and Mary. Dick was coming up the lane, leading two little gray lop-eared burros and a pony, all saddled. Dan climbed on one burro and Mary the other. Mertie came out carrying small tin buckets, one of which she handed to each of the children. Mary seemed reluctant to leave Lucy, but Dan rode off down the lane, mightly unconcerned. Mertie mounted the pony, and then had her brother hand up books and bucket. She smiled at Lucy. "You must get the boys to lend you a horse, so you can ride down to school with us," she said.

"That'll be fine," replied Lucy. "But the ride I had yesterday was enough for a while. I'm afraid I'm a tenderfoot."

Dick picked up a bucket and a rifle, and made ready to start.

"Do you walk to school?" queried Lucy, smiling.

"Yes'm. I like walkin'," he replied.

"Look at his legs," said Mertie. "Pa says Dick can outwalk any of them, even Edd."

"He does look as if he could take long steps," returned Lucy, laughing.

"Reckon it'd be nice if you could teach us at home," said Dick, shyly.

"Yes, it would, and I shall teach you a good deal," replied Lucy. "But I'm not a regular school-teacher."

Lucy watched them go down the lane after Dan and was unexpectedly stirred at sight of the little procession. When she turned back up the path, Mrs. Denmeade met her.

"They're gone. It was fun to see the little burros,"

said Lucy. "How far do they have to ride and why does Dick carry the gun?"

"It's five miles. Woods all the way. An' Dick doesn't pack that gun for fun. There's bears an' cats. An' hydrophobia skunks. I'm afraid of them. But when Dick's with the children I don't worry."

"What in the world are hydrophobia skunks?" queried Lucy.

"Nothin' but polecats with hydrophobia," replied the other. "Lee reckons the skunks get bitten by coyotes that have hydrophobia. It makes the skunks crazy. They come right for you. If you ever run across a pretty white-an'-black cat with a bushy tail—you run!"

"I will indeed," declared Lucy. "An ordinary skunk is bad enough. But this kind you tell of must be dreadful."

"Wal, Miss Lucy, this is wash-day for us," said Mrs. Denmeade. "An' we never seem to have time enough to do all the work. But I want to help you get started. Now if you'll tell me——"

"Mrs. Denmeade, don't you worry one minute," interrupted Lucy. "I'm here to help you. And I shall lend a hand whenever I can. As for my work, all I want is your permission to plan for what I think necessary—to buy things and make things for the house."

"Reckon I'm glad to agree on anythin' you want," replied Mrs. Denmeade. "Just call on me, an' Lee or the boys."

As they walked up the path to the cabin Lucy was telling Mrs. Denmeade how it had been the decision of the welfare board to endeavor to teach the people living in remote districts to make things that would further easier and better living.

Denmeade, coming from the fields, apparently, met them and could not help but hear something of what Lucy said. It brought the broad grin to his weatherbeaten face.

"Wife," he said, as he surveyed Lucy from head to foot, "this hyar city girl has got sense. An' she looks like she might grow into a strappin' fine young woman. 'To

work with their hands,' she says. She's hit it plumb.
That's all we ever done in our lives. That's why we
never learned new tricks. . . . All the same, if Miss Lucy
teaches us somethin', we can do the same for her."

"I certainly expect you to," said Lucy, gladly. "I'd
like to learn to take care of a horse, chop wood, and line
bees."

Denmeade let out a hearty laugh.

"Wal, now, listen to her," he ejaculated. "Take care,
young woman, an' don't let my boy Edd hear you say
you want to line bees. 'Cause if you do he'll shore take
you. An' say, mebbe hangin' to that long-legged boy
when he's on a bee line, mebbe it ain't work!"

"All the same, I shall ask him to take Mertie and me
sometime," declared Lucy.

"You couldn't hire Mertie to tramp up an' down these
woods all day for anythin', let alone bees," replied Mrs.
Denmeade, with scorn. "Mertie sews clothes for herself
or me all day, an' shore she dances all night. But she's
not like the rest of the Denmeades. I reckon Dick would
be the best one to go with you an' Edd."

"Wal, how'd you like to help me an' Uncle Bill plow
today?" asked Denmeade quizzingly.

"Plow! Oh, that would be a little too much for me just
yet!" laughed Lucy. "Why, that ride yesterday knocked
me out! I'm stiff and sore this morning."

"Shore. That's no easy trail to anyone new to hosses,"
said Denmeade.

"Mr. Denmeade, I'd like to accept the loan of that
tent the school-teacher offered," rejoined Lucy. "I think
I could make myself very comfortable and I would not
be depriving you and your wife of your room."

"Shore. Anythin' you like. Reckon the boys could
make a tent tight enough to keep out bugs, snakes, dogs,
wild cats, lions an' bears—an' mebbe hydrophobia
skunks."

"Goodness! . . . Mr. Denmeade, you're teasing me,"
exclaimed Lucy.

"Wal, reckon I was," he replied. "Fact is, though, it
ain't a bad idee. Summer is comin' an' the weather will

soon get fine fer sleepin' outdoors. I seen the way Jenks had his tent fixed. Reckon me an' the boys can do it. But to-day we want to get through plowin' before the rain. . . . See them clouds comin' up out of the southwest? That means storm. Mebbe to-night or to-morrow or next day—but storm shore an' sartin."

"I hope Edd gets in before the rain," said Mrs. Denmeade. "Mertie would be sick if her new dress got spoiled."

"Ahuh! I reckon," returned Denmeade, gruffly. Then as Lucy mounted the steps to the porch he said to her, "You have the run of the place now, Miss Lucy, an' you can call on me or the boys any time."

"Who's the best carpenter?" queried Lucy.

"Wal, I reckon Dick is shore handy with tools," replied Denmeade. "An' he has time before an' after school. But tools is all-fired scare about hyar."

"Can we buy them at Cedar Ridge?"

"Shore. An' I reckon some one will be ridin' down after the dance."

Lucy did not need to spend much more time looking around the cabins, inside or outside. The possessions of the Denmeades were so few that a glance had sufficed to enumerate them. Manifestly also their wants were few. But the comfort and health of a home did not depend upon how little was necessary. The children of pioneers should have some of the conveniences of civilization. Lucy did not underestimate the problem on her hands.

She found that Mrs. Denmeade had removed from the closet whatever had been there, leaving it for Lucy's use. This enabled Lucy to unpack most of her belongings. When that was done she took pencil and pad and went outdoors to find a place to sit down and think and plan.

One of the old black hounds, a dignified and solemn dog, looked at Lucy as if he realized she should have company, and he went with her. How amused Lucy was to see the hound walk along with her, manifesting no evidence of friendliness other than his accompanying her.

Lucy crossed the strip of woods to the edge of the field, and then walked along under the pines toward the slope.

Through the green and black of the forest she could see the looming red wall. At the end of the field she halted. Deep dark woodland merged upon the edge of the clearing. She sat down under a huge pine, from which position she could see out across the open.

"Oh, I'll never be able to concentrate on anything here!" murmured Lucy, thrilled with the wildness and splendor of the forest. Birds and squirrels were boisterous, as if rejoicing at the spring. The wind moaned through the tree-tops, a new sound to Lucy, stirring her blood. Most striking of all was the fragrance of pine. Lucy reveled a few moments in this sweet wild solitude, then made a valiant effort to put her mind on her work. At the very outset she made notes on her pad. The fact that expenditure of funds for the betterment of living conditions up here had been trusted to her common sense and discretion made Lucy extremely conscientious. She would purchase only what was absolutely necessary, and superintend the making of many useful things for the Denmeades. To this end she applied herself to the task of choosing the articles she must buy and those she must make.

It turned out to be a fascinating task, made easy by the course of manual training she had taken at normal school. Prominent among the articles selected to buy were tools and a sewing-machine. Tools meant the constructing of chairs, tables, closets, shelves, and many other household articles; a sewing-machine meant the making of sheets, pillows, towels, curtains, table-covers, and wearing apparel.

Lucy pictured in her mind what the inside of that cabin would look like in a couple of months. It filled her with joy for them and pride for herself. The expense would be little; the labor great. She had already convinced Denmeade that this welfare work was not charity; in the long run it must be for the good of the state.

Between such dreams and calculations Lucy mapped out the letters and orders she would write that afternoon. Then she would have to wait so long until the things arrived. Still, she reflected, a number of necessities could be obtained at the store in Cedar Ridge. She would persuade Denmeade to go or send some one at once.

At length Lucy discovered that without thinking about if she had changed her position several times to get out of the shade into the sun. The air had grown chill. Then she became aware of the moan of wind in the pines. How loud, mournful, strange! Clouds were scudding up from the southwest. They were still broken, but much heavier and darker than they had been in the early morning. They made great dark shadows sail along the rolling green crest of the forest. Gazing upward, Lucy was amazed to see that the clouds obscured the Rim at the high points. From up there drifted down a low, steady roar. Wind in the pines! It was a different sound from the sough in the nearby tree-tops. Birds and squirrels had ceased song and chatter.

Once more Lucy applied herself diligently to her task, and for a while forgot herself. The wind increased to a gale, intermittent, but steadily growing less broken. She heard it and thrilled, yet went on with her figuring. Suddenly a heavy crash somewhere in the woods close at hand thoroughly frightened her. No doubt a dead tree had blown over. Nervously Lucy gazed about her to see if there were other dead trees. She espied several and many bleached gnarled branches shaking in the wind. A great primeval forest like this seemed to be a dangerous place.

"I always imagined it would be wonderful to live like an Indian—wild in the woods," soliloquized Lucy. "But I guess it might be fearful on occasions."

She became prey then to conflicting impulses—one to run back to the cabin, the other to stay in this roaring forest. For a moment the latter dominated her. She stepped out from under the pine into a glade and threw back her head. How the wind whipped her hair! The odor of pine was now so strong that it was not far from suffocating. Yet its sweetness seemed intoxicating. The cold air was exhilarating, in spite of its increasing chill. Against the background of blue sky and gray cloud the pine crests waved wildly and thin streams of brown pine needles flew before the gale.

Lucy's daring did not extend beyond a moment or so. Then the old black dog appeared, to eye her solemnly and trot off. She followed as fast as she could walk, sometimes breaking into a little run. Soon she was breathless and light-headed. Such little exertion to tire her! Lucy recollected that high altitudes affected some persons thus. Her heart pounded in her breast. It became absolutely imperative that she go slower, or give out completely. Even then, when she reached the cabin porch she was glad to sink upon it with a gasp.

The golden sunshine was gone. A gray mantle appeared to be creeping over the forest world. The roar of the wind now seemed behind and above the cabin. Presently Mrs. Denmeade, coming out for a pail of water, espied Lucy sitting there.

"Storm comin'," she said. "It'll blow for a while, then rain."

"Oh—I'm—so—out of—breath!" panted Lucy. "It was —wonderful, but—scared me. . . . The children! Will they stay at school?"

"Not much. They'll come home, rain or shine. Edd is goin' to catch it good. Dave Claypool just rode by an' stopped to tell me he met Edd up on the mountain."

"Met E—your son! When?"

"This mornin'. Dave was ridin' through. He lets his hosses range up there. Said he'd run across Edd about fifteen miles back down the Winbrook trail. Shore now Edd can drive a pack-train of burros. But they're loaded heavy, an' Edd will spare the burros before himself. I reckon he'll hit the Rim just about dark. An' if the storm breaks before then he'll have somethin' tough. Rain down here will be snow up there. But he'll come in to-night shore."

Her matter-of-factness over what seemed exceedingly serious and her confidence in the return of her son through gale and darkness awakened in Lucy a first appreciation of the elemental strength of these backwoods people. Lucy respected strength to endure above all virtues. How infinitely she herself had been found wanting! She hurried to her room, conscious that again this Edd Denmeade had been forced upon her attention.

Lucy got out her writing materials and set herself to the important task of the letters she had planned. At intervals she found her mind wandering, a thing not habitual with her. Yet the circumstances here were extenuating. And all the time she was aware of the gale. It swooped down the chimney with hollow roar. She was able to think and write consistently through the hours. The Denmeades ate whenever some of them came in hungry, a bad and labor-consuming habit, Lucy thought, which she would endeavor to break. She was glad, however, that there was no midday meal except Sundays. She grew cramped and cold from sitting so long on the uncomfortable chair, writing on her lap. But she accomplished the task of a dozen letters, and an enlarging and copying of her notes.

This accomplishment afforded her great satisfaction. Putting on a heavy coat, she went outside to walk off the chill in her blood. She found Mrs. Denmeade and Allie carrying the day's wash up from the brook down in the gully. Lucy promptly lent her assistance, and when she had made four trips, carrying a heavy burden, she was both out of breath and hot from the effort.

The gray mantle overhead had darkened. Only occasional rifts showed a glimpse of blue sky. The air was perceptibly damper. And the roar of wind now had no break.

Lucy rested a little, trying the while to win Liz and Lize to talk to her. They did not sidle away from her any longer, but had not yet reached the communicative stage.

Lucy was conscious of worry, of dread, and not until she saw Mary and Dan, with Mertie behind them, coming up the lane, did she realize the significance of her feelings. They were safe. And by the time they reached the gate the tall form of Dick came stalking into sight.

Manifestly for them the journey home through the forest, under the threshing boughs of the trees, was merely an incident of school days. However, when Mertie heard from her mother that Edd had been seen back up on the Rim and would surely be caught in the storm, she gave

vent to an excited concern. Not for her brother's safety
and comfort, but for her birthday present of the new dress!
Mrs. Denmeade petted and soothed her. "Don't worry,
Mertie," she concluded. "Reckon you ought to know Edd.
There's sacks of flour on them pack-burros. It ain't likely
he'll see that flour spoiled, let alone your new dress."

"But, ma!" protested Mertie, miserably, "Edd's only
human! An' you know how terrible storms are up there."

"Wal, it was your fault Edd packed to Winbrook," retorted her mother. "He could of got the flour at Cedar
Ridge, only one day's pack. But you had to have a city
dress."

Mertie subsided into sullen restless silence and took no
part in the preparations for supper. The children gravitated to Lucy, who essayed to play with them on the
windy porch. The afternoon darkened. Presently the men
returned from their labors, loud-voiced and cheery, smell-
ing of horses and newly plowed earth. At the wash-bench
they made much splashing.

"Wal, ma, we got the field plowed, an' now let her
rain," announced Denmeade.

"Let her rain!" cried Mertie, shrilly, as if driven.
"That's all anybody cares. Storm—rain—snow! For Edd
to be caught out!"

"Aw, so thet's what ails you," returned her father.
"Wal, don't you worry none about him."

During supper Denmeade again silenced his unhappy
daughter, and though he drawled the reprimand in cool,
easy words, there was a note in them that gave Lucy an
idea of the iron nature of these backwoodsmen. This was
the only instance so far in which the slightest discord or
evidence of authority had appeared in the Denmeade
family. To Lucy they seemed so tranquil, so set in their
rugged simplicity.

After supper the gray twilight deepened and a misty
rain blew in Lucy's face as she stood on the porch. Above
the sound of the wind she heard a patter of rain on the
roof.

"Reckon she'll bust directly," said Denmeade, as he

passed Lucy, his arms full of wood. "I'm buildin' a fire fer you. It's shore goin' to storm."

By turning her ear to the north and attending keenly Lucy was able to distinguish between the two main sounds of the storm—the rush and gusty violence of the wind around the cabin, and the deep mighty roar of the gale up on the Rim. She shivered with more than cold. At dark the fury of the storm burst. Torrents of rain fell, drowning all other sounds. Lucy was forced back against the wall, but the rain, driving under the porch roof in sheets, sent her indoors.

A bright log fire blazed and cracked in the open fire-place of the room she occupied. The children were sitting on the floor, talking, and such was the roar on the roof and the bellow down the chimney that Lucy could not hear a word they said. Evidently, however, something in the fire attracted them. Mary was looking at it, too, thoughtfully, even dreamily, her thin face and large eyes expressive of a childish hunger for something.

The hour seemed a restless, uncertain one for Lucy. How the storm raged and lashed! She had an almost irre-sistible desire to run out into it, a sensation at once over-come by abject fear. Even the porch, with its two open doors of lighted rooms, was as black as pitch. Lucy knew she could not have gone a rod from the cabin without being lost. The gale outside would howl and shriek ac-companiments to the roar on the roof; now and then a gust of wind sent a volley of raindrops, thick as a stream, against the windowpanes. The red fire hissed with the water that dripped down the chimney. Lucy walked from window to window, from the fireplace to the door; she sat down to gaze with the children at the opalescent embers settling on the hearth; and she rose to pace the floor. Her thoughts were wholly dominated by the sensations of the storm. At last Lucy put on her long heavy coat and braved the porch. But this time she went to the back, where in the lee of the cabin she was out of the fury of wind and rain. There she stood against the wall, peering out into the blackness, feeling the whip of wind, the cold wet sting of flying hail.

It had grown colder. The rain was lessening in volume and some of it was freezing to sleet. While she cowered there the roar on the roof subsided, and gradually the strife of the elements around the cabin slowed and softened. Presently Lucy became aware of the terrific roar of the storm up on the Rim. It shook her heart. It seemed a continuous thunder; and it roused in her unaccustomed feelings. How strange to realize that she both feared and loved the black wild roaring void out there!

She seemed thousands of miles from her home, from the desert where she had lived always, the hot glaring little city, with its sun-baked streets winter and summer, its throng of people, intent upon money-making, marrying, living. What a contrast they presented to these few hardy families of the mountains! Lucy wondered if a race of people, in their gregarious instincts, their despoliation and destruction of the wilderness, could not lose something great and beautiful. She felt it vaguely. How had men lived in the long ages before there were cities or settlements?

How was it possible for this Edd Denmeade to find his way home, in this ebony blackness, under the roaring and cracking pines, down over a two-thousand-foot-mountain wall? The thing was incredible. Yet his father and his mother expected him as a matter of course. He had done it before. They trusted him. Even the vain Mertie, despite her fears and doubts, knew he would come. Then considering all this, what manner of man was Edd Denmeade? Lucy no longer repudiated her interest. In her heart there was a vague longing for she knew not what, but in this case she imagined it due to her disappointment at home, with Clara and her suitors, with the type of young men that had the good will of her father. They had received scant courtesy from Lucy. No understanding of sentiment stirred in Lucy. What could a boy of the backwoods be to her? But this wild-bee hunter was surely pretty much of a man, and Lucy was curious to see him.

She remained out on the porch until she was thoroughly cold and wet, and still longer, until she had convinced herself that she had a faint realization of what a storm was in this high timbered country. Then she went in.

All the family, including Uncle Bill, had assembled in her room. Denmeade, his brother, and Dick and Joe, were grouped near the fireplace. Denmeade knelt on one knee, in what Lucy later discovered was his characteristic resting position, his dark face in the light, his big black hat pushed back on his head. The others were sitting on the floor, backs to the wall, listening to what he was saying. The mother and Allie were seated, silent, on the children's bed. Mertie, crouched on one of the chairs, stared somberly into the fire. Mary was bent over, so she could catch the light on a book. The children played as before.

As Lucy went in, it was Mary who got up to offer her chair. Lucy, as she advanced to the blazing logs, was astonished to see how wet her coat had become. She held it to the fire, most gratefully conscious of the warmth. Then at the moment Joe interrupted his father's talk.

"I hear bells. Reckon some of the burros got in. Edd won't be far."

"Wal, he'll be with the pack outfit. Rustle out thar," replied his father.

While Denmeade replenished the fire the others stamped out, their spurs clanking. Mrs. Denmeade and Allie went into the kitchen. Mertie's apathy vanished and she rushed out into the darkness of the porch. Her voice pealed out, calling to Edd. Likewise the children responded to the home-coming of their brother.

Lucy felt happy for all of them. Hanging up her coat, she wiped the raindrops from her face and gave a touch here and there to her disheveled hair. Then she stood, back to the fire, palms turned to the genial heat, and, watching the door, she waited with sustained interest, with something of amusement, yet conscious of a vague unformed emotion.

Presently clamor of childish voices, pitched high above the deeper ones of men, and the thump of heavy boots, and jingle of spurs, moved across the porch to the door of the cabin. Lucy stepped aside into the shadow. Then the light of the fire streamed out of the door.

"In thar, all of you," boomed Denmeade. "Let Edd get to the fire."

It seemed to Lucy that a tall dark form emerged from the gloom into the light, and entered the door with the children and girls. For a moment there was a hubbub. The older members of the household came in, somewhat quieting the mêlée.

"Mertie, here's your present," said the newcomer. His voice seemed rather drawling and deep. Disengaging himself from clinging hands, he laid a large parcel, wrapped in a wet slicker, upon a vacant chair. Mertie let out a squeal, and pouncing upon the package, dropped to her knees and began to tear it open.

"Oh, Edd! . . . If you got it—wet!" she panted.

"No fear. It's wrapped in paper an' oilskin, under the slicker," he said. Then he drew another package from the inside of his huge fur-collared coat. "Liz! Lize! Danny!"

"Candy!" screamed the children in unison. And straightway pandemonium broke loose.

When the young man threw his wet sombrero on the floor near the hearth, and removed his rain-soaked coat, Lucy had a better chance to see what he looked like. Certainly his face was not handsome, but she could not say how much of its dark, haggard rawness was due to exposure. He did not change expression as he gazed down upon those whom he had made happy. But Lucy's keen sight and power to read divined the fact that he worshiped Mertie and loved the children. He untied a wet scarf from his neck and threw that beside his sombrero. All the older members of the family were silently gazing down upon the fortunate one. Mary seemed to be reveling in Mertie's excitement, yet as she gazed up at Edd her large eyes questioned him.

"Mary, reckon I have somethin' for you in my pack," he said. "Wait till I warm my hands. I'm near froze."

With that he strode to the fire and knelt before it, one knee on the floor, in a posture Lucy had descried as characteristic of his father. Edd extended big, strong, capable-looking hands to the blaze. They were actually stiff and blue. Seen nearer, his face, with the firelight shining directly upon it, was an open one, lean, smooth, with prominent nose and large firm-lipped mouth and square chin. His eyes were larger than any of the other Denmeades', light in color, intent in gaze. Still, Lucy could not be certain she liked his face. It looked bruised, pinched, blackened. His hands, too, were grimy. Water dripped from him and ran in little streams over the hearth to sizzle on the hot ashes. He seemed to bring with him the breath of the open, cold and damp, the smell of the pines and burros, odorous, rank.

Gasps of delight emanated from those surrounding Mertie as she held up a white beribboned dress, and many were the mingled exclamations that followed. It was the mother who first recovered from the spell. Peering into the shadow, she at last espied Lucy.

"There you are," she said. "I was wonderin' if you was seein' the circus. . . . This is my oldest boy. Edd, meet Miss Lucy Watson from Felix. She's our home-teacher, come to live with us for a spell." \

Lucy spoke from the shadow. Edd peered out of the firelight, as if locating her with difficulty. She did not see the slightest indication that he was surprised or interested. What had she expected from this much-talked-of wild-bee hunter?

"Can't see you, but hod-do just the same," he drawled.

Then Denmeade advanced to lean his tall form against the mantel.

"Dave rode down early—said he'd seen you, an' figgered you'd hit the Rim trail before the storm busted."

"Wind held us back all afternoon," replied the son. "An' some of the packs slipped. Reckon I'd made it shore but for that. The storm hit us just back from the Rim. I'll be doggoned if I didn't think we'd never get to where the trail starts down. Hard wind an' snow right in our faces. Shore was lucky to hit the trail down before it got plumb dark. I led my hoss an' held on to Jennie's tail. Honest I couldn't see an inch in front of my nose. I couldn't hear the bells. For a while I wasn't shore of anythin'. But when we got down out of the snow I reckoned we might get home. All the burros but Baldy made it. I didn't miss him till we got here. He might have slipped over the cliff on that narrow place. It shore was wet. Reckon, though, he'll come in. He was packin' my camp outfit."

"Edd, come an' eat, if you're hungry," called his mother from the kitchen.

"Nary a bite since sun-up. An' I'm a-rarin' to feed," he replied, and gathering up his smoking coat, scarf, and sombrero, he rose.

"Boy, did Blake buy your honey?" queried his father, accompanying him toward the door.

"I reckon. Every bucket, an' I whooped it up to a dollar a gallon."

"Whew! Dog-gone me! Why, Edd, you'll make a bizness of your bee huntin'!" ejaculated Denmeade.

"Shore I will. I always meant to," asserted the son. "Pa, if I can find an' raise as much as five hundred gallons this summer I'll sell every pint of it."

"No!" Denmeade's exclamation was one of mingled doubt, amaze, and wondering appreciation of a fortune. They crossed the porch into the kitchen, from which Lucy heard them but indistinctly. Then Mrs. Denmeade appeared at the farther door.

"Lucy, take the candy away from the children an' put it where they can't reach it," she called. "Else they'll gorge themselves an' be sick."

Lucy approached this dubious task with infinite tact, kindliness, and persuasion. Liz and Lize were presently prevailed upon, but Dan was a different proposition. He would not listen to reason. When he found Lucy was firm he attempted to compromise, and, failing of that, he gave in ungraciously. Flouncing down on his sheepskin rug, he pulled the rag coverlet over him. Lucy could see his eyes glaring in the firelight.

"Danny, don't you undress when you go to bed?" asked Lucy, gently.

"Naw!" he growled.

"Don't you ever?" she went on.

"Not any more. The kids do, but not me."

"Why not you?" demanded Lucy. "It's not healthy to

sleep in your clothes. Tell me, Danny. I'm your home-teacher, you know."

"Nobody ever said nuthin' to me," retorted the lad. "Pa an' Joe an' Dick sleep in their clothes. An' Edd——why, I've slept with him up in the loft when he never took off nuthin'. Went to bed right in his boots an' spurs."

"Oh, indeed!" murmured Lucy, constrainedly, some-what taken aback. "Well, Danny, all the same it's not a healthy thing to do, and I shall teach you not to."

"Teacher, you'd make me sleep naked?" he protested. "Aw, it'd be cold in winter, an' I never have enough covers nohow."

"Danny, I shall make you nightclothes to sleep in. Nice soft warm woolly stuff."

"No long white thing like Mertie sleeps in," he as-serted, belligerently.

"Any way you want. Shirt and pants, if you like," said Lucy.

"Then I can wear them all day, too," he rejoined with interest, and lay down.

Lucy turned her attention to the twins, very pleased to find them growing less shy with her.

"Tan we have some, too?" asked Lize, timidly.

"Have what, my dear?" queried Lucy, as she drew the children to her.

"Them Danny'll have to sleep in."

"Indeed you shall! Long white nightgowns, like the little princess in the fairy story."

The twins had never heard of princesses or fairies, but they manifested the most human trait of children——love of stories. Lucy held them entranced while she undressed them and put them to bed. She was quick to realize her power over them. Her victory was assured.

Then Denmeade entered, carrying some sticks of wood.

"Reckon you can put them on, if you want to keep up the fire," he said. "Wal, you've put the kids to bed. Now, Miss Lucy, shore that will please ma."

When Mrs. Denmeade came in with towel and basin she appeared astounded to find the children undressed and in bed.

"You rascals never did it all by your lonesome," she averred. "Teacher has been takin' you in hand. But she forgot your dirty faces an' hands."

"Teacher told us stories," whispered Liz, rapturously.

"Candy an' stories all at once!" exclaimed the mother as she wielded the towel. "Reckon that'll make bad dreams. . . . Stop wigglin'. Don't you ever want a clean face? . . . An' your teacher is tired an' needs sleep, too."

After Mrs. Denmeade had gone Lucy closed the door, catching as she did so a glimpse into the dimly lighted kitchen with its dark faces, and she dropped the bar in place, quite instinctively. The action made her wonder why she did it, for last night she had left the door unbarred. But tonight she had found the Denmeades walking in and out, as if she were not domiciled there. She did not put it beyond any one of them to burst unbidden in upon her at any hour. And she wished for the tent Mr. Jenks had offered. Yet, suppose she had been in a tent to-night, out there alone in the blackness, with a flimsy shelter overhead and a scant flooring under her feet! It actually gave her a tremor.

Lucy made no effort to hurry to bed. Drawing the chair closer to the dying fire, she toasted her hands and feet and legs that had felt like ice all evening. Outside, the wind moaned under the eaves, and from high on the Rim came that thrilling roar. Rain was pattering steadily on the roof, a most pleasant sound to desert ears. Heat Lucy knew in all its prolonged variations; but cold and rain and snow were strangers. She imagined she was going to love them.

Gradually as the fire died down to a pale red glow the room darkened. It seemed full of deep warm shadows, comforting Lucy, easing the strain under which she had unconsciously labored.

The event that had hung over the Denmeade home ever since she reached it had been consummated—the bee hunter had returned. Lucy had no idea what she had expected, but whatever it had been, it had not been realized. An agreeable disappointment dawned upon her. Edd Denmeade had not struck her as bold, or as a bully or a backwoods lout, foolish over girls. His indifference to her presence or appearance had struck her singularly. Her relief held a hint of pique.

"I think I had a poor opinion of him because everybody talked of him," she mused. "He fooled me."

But that could not account for her sensations now. Never before in her life had Lucy welcomed the firelit shadows, the seclusion of her room, to think about any young man. During school, too, she had imagined she had been falling in love. This feeling which grew strangely upon her now was vastly dissimilar from that mawkish sentiment. She could analyze nothing clearly. Edd Denmeade had impressed her profoundly, how or why or just what moment she could not tell. Had she been repelled or attracted? She fancied it was the former. She could be repelled by his raw, uncouth, barbarian presence, yet be fascinated by the man of him. That hurried return through the storm, down over the fearful trail, in a Stygian blackness—a feat none the less heroic because it had been performed to please a shallow little peacock of a sister—that called to something deep in Lucy. She thought of her sister Clara, selfish, unloving, thoughtless of others. Lucy felt that she and Edd Denmeade had something in common—a sister going the wrong way!

She recalled his look as Mertie had frantically torn at the package. Serene, strong, somehow understanding! It flashed over Lucy, intuitively as much as from deduction, that Edd Denmeade knew his sister's weakness and loved her perhaps all the more because of it. That thrilled her, warmed her heart, as did her memory of his smile at the twins, Liz and Lize.

But all the rest was incomprehensible. Her pride, not of family, but of personal attainments and consciousness of her power to rise above her station, precluded any romantic thought of Edd Denmeade. He was a backwoodsman. She had come there to teach his people and their relatives and neighbors how to alleviate the squalor of their homes. The distance between her and them could not be bridged. So her interest and admiration must have been impersonal: it was the strange resentment which grew on her, the sense of being repelled by a hunter of the woods, that was personal and intimate.

Lucy crouched there before the fire till the red embers faded. The rain pattered steadily, the wind mourned, the wild night wore on. Forced thoughts, trying to solve riddles of her mind and heart, did not bring her tranquillity. At night her imagination and emotion were always active. Lucy did not trust them. She fought the insidious drifting toward dreams, repelled it, and went to bed sure of herself.

CHAPTER V

On Mertie Denmeade's birthday several of her girl schoolmates rode up from the school with her. They were to stay overnight and go back to school next morning. Lucy could not help wondering where they were going to sleep.

Among these girls was Sadie Purdue, whom Lucy observed with attention. Sadie possessed but little charm, so far as Lucy could see. Her face and figure were commonplace, not to be compared with Mertie's and her complexion was pitted and coarse-fibered, well suited to her bold eyes and smug expression. Her shoulders were plump, her hands large, her feet clumsy. Lucy could not but wonder what Edd Denmeade saw in this girl. She reflected then that it was absurd for her to have assumptions or opinions, until she knew more of these people. Every one of these Jacks had their Jills. It seemed inconceivable for Lucy to pass critical judgment on this Sadie Purdue and not include her companions. Lucy found them colorless, civil, hardy girls, somewhat like Allie Denmeade. She was gravely astonished to find that she had an inexplicable antagonism toward Sadie. For that reason she went out of her way to engage Sadie in conversation.

The girl, as well as her companions, was exceedingly

curious about Lucy's work. She asked numerous questions, the gist of which appeared to be a greedy interest in what they all were going to gain through Lucy's presence.

"We live 'way down near Cedar Ridge," she informed Lucy. "I stay with my cousin, Amy Claypool, while I'm goin' to school. This's my last term, thank goodness."

"What will you do then?" inquired Lucy. "Teach school?"

"Me teach? Laws no! I couldn't teach. Reckon a girl in this country has nothin' to do but marry when she leaves school. I've had offers, but I'm in no hurry."

"Do girls up here marry so young?" asked Lucy.

"From fifteen up. I'm sixteen, same as Mertie."

Lucy encouraged the girl to talk, which seemed to be very easy to do. Sadie was impressed by Lucy's interest, and besides that manifestly had motives of her own for establishing a repute. Lucy gathered that neither Sadie nor Mertie wanted to marry one of these bee-hunting, corn-raising, wood-chopping "jacks." They aspired to homes in Winbrook, or at least Cedar Ridge. But they were not averse to being courted and taken to dances.

"Trouble is, when a fellow keeps company with you, he ain't long satisfied with just courtin'," confided Sadie, giggling. "He wants to marry—wants a woman. Here's Edd, Mertie's brother. He took me to one dance an' spent a Sunday callin' on me. Asked me to marry him! . . . When he'd never even kissed me or put his arm round me!—The big boob! I told him he hadn't learned much from his honey-bee huntin'."

Lucy found that remark a difficult one to answer, and she was at some pains to conceal her own reaction. Fortunately Sadie was rushed off by her several friends for the purpose of a joint attack upon Mertie, to make her display the birthday dress. It amused Lucy to see how Mertie refused and affected modesty, when underneath she was burning to reveal herself in the new dress. At last she allowed herself to be persuaded. "All right, but only you girls can see me."

They were in the room Lucy occupied. Mertie barred

the door, saying: "I don't mind you, teacher. But you mustn't tell."

Whereupon, with utter lack of modesty, and obsessed by a strange frenzy, Mertie donned the dress, to create consternation and rapture among her friends. By a lucky chance, which Lucy appreciated more than the others, the dress actually fitted the girl, and changed her wondrously. Many were the exclamations uttered, and one found lodgment in Lucy's memory. "Mertie," said Amy Claypool, soberly, "you an' Sadie call Edd a big boob. But I think he's grand."

Late in the afternoon Mrs. Denmeade and Allie began to spread the porch table with a birthday dinner for Mertie and her visitors. Several young men had ridden in, foremost of whom Lucy recognized as Sam Johnson. These young people arranged themselves around the porch and began what seemed to Lucy a remarkable exhibition of banter and absurdity.

The children dragged Lucy out on the porch, where Sam Johnson performed the office of introduction that Mertie neglected or omitted by choice. Gerd Claypool was a blue-eyed young giant with tawny hair, and Hal Miller was a lean, rangy cowboy type, solemn of face, droll of speech. These new visitors manifested enough interest in Lucy to convince her that it was not pleasing to Mertie and Sadie, so Lucy made excuses and left them to their peculiar fun. She played with the children, helped Mrs. Denmeade, and then sat in her room, the door and window of which were open. Part of the time Lucy was aware of the banter going on, but she did not become acutely interested until the Denmeade boys came on the scene.

"Wal, if here ain't the ole bee hunter, home early an' all shaved nice an' clean," drawled Sam Johnson.

"Mertie's birthday, Sam," replied Edd. "How are you all?"

"Jest a-rarin' to go," said Gerd Claypool.

"Edd, I reckon we'd like a lick of that honey pot of yours," added Hal Miller.

"I gave ma the last half-gallon for Mertie's party," replied Edd. "You might get some, if you don't hold back on your halter too long."

"What's become of all your honey?" queried Sam, with interest. "I remember you had a lot."

"Sold. An' I'm offered a dollar a gallon for all I can fetch to Winbrook."

Sam whistled. "Say, you ain't such a dog-gone fool as we thought, chasin' bees all the time."

"I'll make it a business," said Edd.

"Edd, it wouldn't be a bad idea for you to save some of your honey," interposed Sadie Purdue, slyly.

"What you mean?" asked Edd, bluntly.

"Girls like honey," she answered, in a tormenting tone no one could mistake.

"Reckon I savvy," returned Edd, with good humor. "But honey words an' honey ways with girls don't come natural to me, like with Sam."

His reply raised a howl of laughter at Sam's expense.

"Wal, I ain't noticin' that I ever go to any dances alone," rejoined Sam, sarcastically.

Lucy could see from the shadow of her room through the door most of the group of young people on the porch. Sam leaned behind Sadie, who sat by the porch rail. Gerd and Hal occupied seats on the canvas packs. The other girls sat on a bench. Dick was the only one of the Denmeade boys in sight. He appeared rather out of it, and stood in the background, silent, listening, with a rather pleasant smile on his keen face.

It was most interesting and instructive for Lucy to observe and hear these young people. What struck her most was the simple, unrestrained expression of what she divined as a primitive pleasure in tormenting. At the bottom of it was the unconscious satisfaction at another's pain. Sadie's expression was a teasing, joyful malignance. Manifestly she was reveling in the fun at the boys' expense. Mertie wore a bored look of superiority, as if she were tolerating the attentions of these young men for the moment. Amy Claypool's face, honest and comely, was wreathed in smiles. The boys near them wore lazy, bantering expressions, without selfish or unfriendly hint. But to the sensitive Lucy, used to the better educated, their talk seemed crude, almost brutal.

For a while the sole topic of conversation was the dance on Friday night. It expressed the wholesome and happy regard these youths and maidens held in the only recreation and social function that fell to their lot. Personalities and banterings were forgotten for the moment; other wonderful dances were remembered; conjectures as to attendance, music, ice cream, were indulged in. Presently, however, when they had exhausted the more wholesome reactions to this dance subject they reverted to the inevitable banter.

"Say, Dick, have you found a girl tall enough to take to the dance—one you wouldn't have to stoop 'way over to reach?" drawled Sam Johnson.

Dick's youthful face turned ruddy. The attention suddenly and unexpectedly thrown upon him caused him intense embarrassment. The prominent bone in his throat worked up and down.

"Boy, yore handy with tools," interposed Hal. "Make a pair of stilts for that fat little sister of mine yore sweet on. She's four feet eight an' weighs one fifty. Reckon you'd make Sam 'an' Sadie look sick."

Other sallies, just as swift and laugh-provoking, gave the poor boy no time to recover, even if he had been able to retaliate. It was his sister Allie who came to the rescue from the door of the kitchen.

"Sadie, who're you goin' with?" she inquired, sweetly.

"Sam. He's the best dancer in this country," she announced.

"So it's settled then," rejoined Allie, casually. "When I asked him the other day who he was goin' with I kind of got a hunch it might not be you."

Sadie flashed a surprised and resentful look up at Sam. He took it, as well as the mirth roused by Allie's covert remark, with an equanimity that showed him rather diplomatic.

"Sadie, I told Allie you hadn't accepted my invite, which you hadn't," he said.

"Reckon it wasn't necessary," she retorted, in a tone that conveyed the impression of an understanding between them.

"Wal, Sadie," drawled Edd's slow, cool voice, "I reckon you'll find it necessary to hawg-tie Sam for dances —or *any other* kind of shindig."

This sly speech from Edd Denmeade gave Lucy an unexpected and delightful thrill. Almost she joined in the hilarity it stirred. Even the self-conscious Mertie burst into laughter. For a moment the tables had been turned; Sam was at a loss for a retort; and Sadie gave a fleeting glimpse of her cat-like nature under her smugness and pleasant assurance.

"Edd, have you asked any girl yet?" she inquired, sweetly.

"Nope. Not yet. I've been away, you know," he replied.

" 'Course you're goin'?"

"Never missed a dance yet, Sadie."

"It's gettin' late in the day, Edd," she went on, seriously. "You oughtn't go alone to dances, as you do sometimes. It's not fair to break in on boys who have partners. They just have to set out those dances. . . . Edd, you ought to be findin' you a regular girl."

Sadie's voice and face were as a transparent mask for the maliciousness of her soul.

"Shore, Edd," put in Sam, "an' you ought to hawg-tie her, too."

"Funny about Edd, ain't it?" interposed Gerd. "The way he can see in the woods. Say, he's got eyes! He can line a bee fer half a mile. But he can't line a girl."

"Nope, you're wrong, boy," replied Edd, with evident restraint. "Never had no trouble linin' a girl. But I haven't got the soft soap stuff you fellows use."

"Who are you goin' to ask to the dance?" insisted Sadie.

They nagged him, then, with this query, and with advice and suggestions, and with information that no matter what girl he asked he would find she had already accepted an invitation. It must have been their way of having fun. But to Lucy it seemed brutal. Almost she felt sorry for Edd Denmeade. It struck her that his friends and relatives must have some good reason for so unmercifully flaying him. For, despite the general bantering, they had made him the center and the butt of their peculiar way of enjoying themselves. The girl Sadie seemed the instigator of this emphasis thrown upon Edd, and Sam ably seconded her.

Amy Claypool, however, manifested a kindlier spirit, though apparently she did not realize the tirade was little short of a jealous brutality.

"Edd, I'd ask the new schoolmarm," she said, lowering her voice. "She's awful pretty an' nice. Not a bit stuck-up!"

Lucy heard this suggestion, and at once became a prey to amusement and dismay. Why could not the young people, and their elders, too, leave her out of all reckoning? Her pulse quickened with an excitation that displeased her. How her very ears seemed to burn!

Sadie Purdue burst into a peal of laughter. "Amy, you're crazy!" she exclaimed. "That city girl wouldn't go dancin' with a wild-bee hunter!"

This positive assertion did not produce any mirth. No doubt Sadie had no intention now of being funny. A red spot showed in her cheek. The sudden scrape of boots and clank of spurs attested to the fact that Edd Denmeade had leaped to his feet.

"Sadie Purdue, I reckon it's no disgrace to hunt bees," he said, sharply.

"Who said it was?" she retorted. "But I've been among town folks. You take my hunch an' don't ask her."

Edd stalked off the porch, coming into range of Lucy's sight when he got down into the yard. His stride seemed to be that of a man who was hurrying to get away from something unpleasant.

"Sadie, you shore don't know it all," said Amy, mildly. "If this home-schoolmarm wasn't a nice an' kind sort she'd not be up heah. Fun is fun, but you had no call to insult Edd."

"Insult nothin'," snapped Sadie. "I was only tryin' to save his feelin's."

"You never liked Edd an' you don't want anyone else to," returned Amy. "I know two girls who might have liked Edd but for you."

Lucy's heart warmed to this mild-voiced Amy Claypool. She did not make the least show of spirit. Sadie turned petulantly to Sam, and there was a moment of rather strained silence.

"Come an' get it, you birthday party," called Allie from the door.

That call relieved the situation, and merriment at once reclaimed the young people. Lucy was glad to see them dive for seats at the table. She was conscious of a strength and depth of interest quite out of proportion to what should have been natural to her. Still, she had elected to undertake a serious work among these mountaineers. How could she help but be interested in anything that pertained to them? But the wild-bee hunter! Quick as a flash then Lucy had an impulse she determined to satisfy. Would Edd Denmeade give these guests of his sister's the last bit of the honey upon which he set such store? Lucy felt that he ought not do so and would not, yet she contrarily hoped that he might. There appeared to her only one way to ascertain, and that was to walk by the table and see. Despite her determination, she hesitated. Then fortunately the problem was solved for her.

Allie, sailing out of the kitchen door, set a pan rather noisily upon the table. "There's the last of Edd's honey. Fight over it!"

The next few moments' observation afforded Lucy the satisfaction of seeing the birthday guests actually engaged according to Allie's suggestion. From that scene Lucy formed her impression of the deliciousness of wild-bee honey.

Lucy did not lay eyes upon Edd Denmeade until late the following morning, when, after the visitors and school children had ridden away, he presented himself before her where she played with the twins on the porch.

"Mornin'. Reckon I'd like a few words with you," he said.

"Why, gladly!" replied Lucy, as she sat up to gaze at him.

Edd was standing down in the yard, holding his sombrero in his hands and turning it edgewise round and round. On the moment he did not look at her. Seen now at close range, with all the stains of that terrible ride home removed from garb and face, he appeared vastly different. He was laboring with thought.

"Ma an' pa have been tellin' me about you, but I reckon I'm not satisfied."

"Yes? Is there anything I can tell you?" said Lucy, relieved. She had actually been afraid he would ask her to go to the dance.

"Shore. I want to know about this here work you're goin' to do."

Then he looked up to meet her eyes. Lucy had never met just such a glance. His eyes were so clear and gray that they seemed expressionless. Yet Lucy conceived a vivid impression of the honesty and simplicity of the soul from which they looked. Whereupon Lucy took the pains to explain quite at length the nature of the work she had undertaken among his people. He listened intently, standing motionless, watching her with a steady gaze that was disconcerting.

"Pa an' ma talked more about things you were goin' to get the state to buy for us," he said, reflectively. "I'm wonderin' if they don't take more to that."

"It would be only natural," responded Lucy, earnestly. "I must have time to show actual good, rather than gain."

"I reckon. Pa's sendin' me to Cedar Ridge, where I'm to post your letters an' buy all that outfit you want. I'm takin' three burros to pack. Reckon I'll put the sewin' machine on Jennie."

"Oh—a little burro to carry it—all alone!" exclaimed Lucy.

"Shore. Jennie packed the kitchen stove up that trail you come on. An' she packed a hundred an' fifty pounds of honey to Winbrook."

"Well, I'll say that Jennie is a wonderful little beast of burden," replied Lucy.

"Now—you aim to stay with us awhile, an' then go to Claypool's an' Johnson's an' Miller's an' Sprall's?"

"Yes, that is my plan, but no definite time is set. I have all the time there is, as I heard your Uncle Bill say."

"Wal, it's a bad idea. It won't do," he declared.

"How? Why?" queried Lucy, anxiously.

"First off, you're too young an' pretty," he said, wholly unconscious of the language of compliment.

"Oh!" returned Lucy, almost confused. "But, surely, Mr. Denmeade——"

"Nobody ever called me mister," he interrupted.

"Indeed! . . . I—well—surely my youth—and my good looks, as you are kind to call them, need not stand in my way?"

"Shore they will. If you were an old woman, or even middle-aged, it might do. But you're a girl."

"Yes, I am," rejoined Lucy, puzzled and amused. "I can't deny that."

Manifestly he regarded his bare statement as sufficient evidence on the point, whatever this was; for he went on to say that the several families would quarrel over her and it would all end in a row.

"Reckon no matter what pa said I'd never let you go to Sprall's," he concluded, simply.

"You! . . . May I ask what business it would be of yours?"

"Wal, somebody has to take these here things on his shoulders, an' I reckon most of them fall on me," he replied.

"I don't understand you," said Lucy, forcibly.

"Wal, somethin' wrong is always happenin' up here among us people. An' I reckon I'm the only one who see it."

"Wrong! How could it be wrong for me to go to Sprall's?" protested Lucy. "From what I hear, they need me a great deal more than any family up here."

"Miss, I reckon you'd better not believe all you hear," he returned. "If you was to ride over to Sprall's you'd say they'd ought to be washed an' dressed, an' their cabin burned. But that's all you'd see unless you stayed a day or so."

"Oh! . . . Suppose I'd stay?" queried Lucy.

"You'd see that was long enough."

"But don't you understand I'm here to help poor families, no matter how dirty or ignorant or—or even wicked?" cried Lucy, poignantly.

"Shore I understand. An' I reckon it's your goodness of heart, an' of these people who sent you. But it won't do, maybe not for us, an' shore an' certain never for such as the Spralls."

"You must tell me why, if you expect me to pay the least attention to what you say," retorted Lucy, stubbornly.

"Shore I can't talk about the Sprall women to a girl like you," he protested. "If ma won't tell you, it's no job for me. But I reckon there's no need. You're not goin' to Sprall's."

Lucy was at a loss for words. His bare assertion did not seem to stir her anger so much as a conviction that for some reason or other she would not go to Sprall's.

"I've heard, since I've been here, that there was bad blood between you and Bud Sprall. It must have been your mother who said it," replied Lucy, slowly, trying to keep her temper.

"Nope. The bad blood is on Bud's side. Reckon if there'd been any on mine I'd have killed him long ago. . . . Now, miss, you're a city girl, but you ought to have a little sense. If I told you I couldn't let Mertie stay where Bud Sprall was—you'd understand that, I reckon."

"Yes. I am not quite so stupid as you seem to think," retorted Lucy.

"Wal, for the same reason I'd not let you go, either. . . . Now we're wastin' time talkin' about Sprall's. To come back to this here work of yours, I'm sorry I can't see it favorable like pa an' ma. But I just can't."

"I'm sorry, too," replied Lucy, soberly. "It'll be discouraging to have even one person against me. But why —why?"

"I reckon I can't figure that out so quick," he replied. "It's the way I feel. If you was goin' to live among us always I might feel different. But you won't last up here very long. An' suppose you do teach Liz an' Lize an' Danny a lot of things. They've got to grow up an' *live* here. They might be happier knowin' less. It's what they don't know that don't make any difference."

"You're terribly wrong, Edd Denmeade," replied Lucy with spirit.

"Ahuh! Wal, that's for you to prove," he returned, imperturbably. "I'll be goin' now. An' I reckon I'll fetch your outfit in about midday to-morrow."

Lucy stared after the tall figure as it stalked with a flapping of chaps keeping time with a clinking of spurs. Edd Denmeade was six feet tall, slender, yet not lean like his brothers. He was built like a narrow wedge, only his body and limbs were rounded, with small waist, small hips, all giving an impression of extraordinary suppleness and strength. Lucy had seen riders of the range whose form resembled this young bee hunter's. They had been, however, awkward on their feet, showing to best advantage when mounted on horseback. This Denmeade had a long, quick, springy stride.

When he had passed out of sight down the lane Lucy let the children play alone while she pondered over his thought-provoking words. She realized that he was right in a way, and that it might be possible to do these children more harm than good. But never if she could only impress them lastingly. The facts of the case were as plain as printed words to her. These backwoods people were many generations behind city people in their development.

In a fairly intelligent and broad way Lucy had grasped at the fundamentals of the question of the evolution of the human race. Not so many thousands years back all the human family, scattered widely over the globe, had lived nomad lives in the forests, governed by conditions of food and water. Farther back, their progenitors had been barbarians, and still more remotely they had been cave men, fighting the cave bear and the saber-toothed tiger. Lucy had seen pictures in a scientific book of the bones of these men and beasts. In ages back all the wandering tribes of men had to hunt to live, and their problems were few. Meat to eat, skins to wear, protection from beasts and ravaging bands of their own species! Yet, even so, through the long ages, these savages had progressed mentally and spiritually. Lucy saw that as a law of life.

These backwoods people were simply a little closer to the old order of primitive things than their more fortunate brethren of civilization. Even if they so willed with implacable tenacity they could not forever hold on to their crude and elemental lives. They could never evade the line of progress. Edd Denmeade's father was a backwoodsman; Edd himself was a bee hunter; his son would most likely be a forest ranger or lumberman, and his grandson perhaps become a farmer or a worker in the city.

Naturally this giant boy of the woods understood nothing of all this. Yet he had a quaint philosophy which Lucy felt she understood. In a sense the unthinking savage and the primitive white child were happier than any children of civilized peoples. In a way it might be a pity to rob them of their instincts, educate them out of a purely natural existence. But from the very dawn of life on the planet the advance of mind had been inevitable. Lucy was familiar with many writers who ascribed this fact to nature. Her personal conviction was that beyond and above nature was God.

If Edd Denmeade was not stupid and stubborn she believed that she could enlighten him. It might be interesting to teach him; yet, on the other hand, it might require more patience and kindliness than she possessed. Evidently he was the strongest factor among the young Denmeades, and perhaps among all these young people. Despite the unflattering hints which had fostered her first impression, she found that, after talking seriously with him, she had a better opinion of him than of any of the other young men she had met. In all fairness she was bound to admit this.

All the rest of the day and evening Lucy found the thoughts Edd had roused running in her mind, not wholly unsatisfying. Somehow he roused her combativeness, yet, viewed just as one of the Denmeades, she warmed to the problem of helping him. Moreover, the success of her venture with this family no doubt hinged mostly upon converting the elder son to her support. Perhaps she could find an avenue open to her through his love of Mertie and devotion to the children.

Next morning found Lucy more energetic and active mentally than she had been so far. She had rested; the problem she confronted had shifted to a matter of her own powers. Nevertheless, neither the children, nor helping Mrs. Denmeade, nor reading over some half-forgotten treatises relative to her work, interested her to the point of dismissing Edd Denmeade from mind. Lucy realized this, but refused to bother with any reflection upon it.

She was in her room just before the noon hour when she heard Uncle Bill stamp up on the porch and drawl out: "Say, Lee, hyar comes Edd drivin' the pack-burros."

Denmeade strode out to exclaim. "So soon! Wal, it do beat hell how that boy can rustle along with a pack-outfit."

"Heavy load, too. Jennie looks like a camel," replied Uncle Bill. "Reckon I'll lend a hand onpackin'."

Lucy quite unnecessarily wanted to run out to see the burros, a desire that she stifled. She heard the tinkle of their bells and the patter of their little hoofs as they came up to the porch.

"Wal, son, you must been a-rarin' to git home," drawled Denmeade.

"Nope. I just eased them along," replied Edd. "But I packed before sunup."

"Fetch all Miss Lucy's outfit?"

"Some of it had to be ordered. Sewin' machine an' a lot of dry goods. It'll be on the stage next week, an' I'll pack it then. Reckon I had about all I could pack to-day, anyhow."

"Say, Edd," called Allie's lusty voice from the kitchen, "who'd you go an' storm for the dance?"

"Reckon I haven't asked nobody yet," replied Edd, laconically.

"You goin' to stay home?" rejoined Allie, her large frame appearing in the kitchen doorway. Her round face expressed surprise and regret.

"Never stayed home yet, Allie, did I?"

"No. But, Edd, you musn't go to any more dances alone," said his sister, solicitously. "It makes the boys mad, an' you've had fights enough."

"Wal, you didn't notice I got licked bad, did you?" he drawled.

Allie went back into the kitchen, where she talked volubly in the same strain to her mother.

"Edd, reckon we'd better carry this stuff in where Miss Lucy can keep the kids out of it, huh?" queried Denmeade.

"I shore say so. It cost a lot of money. I hope to goodness she makes out with it."

Lucy heard his quick step on the porch, then saw him, burdened with bundles and boxes, approaching her door. She rose to meet him.

"Howdy! I got back pronto," he said. "Pa thinks you'd better have this stuff under your eye. Where'll we stack it? Reckon it'll all make a pile."

"Just set light things on the beds, heavy ones on the floor. I'll look after them," replied Lucy. "Indeed you made spendid time. I'm very grateful. Now I shall be busy."

Sometime during the afternoon, when the curious members of the household had satisfied themselves with an exhaustive scrutiny of the many articles Lucy had in her room, and had gone about their work and play, Edd Denmeade presented himself at the door.

"Reckon I'd like to ask you somethin'," he said, rather breathlessly and low.

"Come in," replied Lucy, looking up from where she knelt among a disarray of articles she had bought.

"Will you go to the dance with me?" he asked.

Lucy hesitated. His shyness and anxiety manifestly

clashed. But tremendous as must have been this issue for him, he had come out frankly with it.

"Oh, I'm sorry! Thank you, Edd, but I must decline," she replied. "You see what a mess I'm in here with all this stuff. I must straighten it out. To-morrow work begins."

He eyed her with something of a change in his expression or feeling, she could not tell what. "Reckon I savvied you'd say no. But I'm askin' if you mean that no for good. There's a dance every week, an' you can't help bein' asked. I'm givin' you a hunch. If any schoolmarm stayed away from dances, folks up here would believe she thought she was too good for us."

"Thank you. I understand," replied Lucy, impressed by his sincerity. "Most assuredly I don't think I'm too good to go to a dance here, and enjoy myself, too."

"Maybe, then—it's just me you reckon you'd not like to go with," he returned, with just a tinge of bitterness.

"Not at all," Lucy hastened to reply. "I'd go with you the same as with anyone. Why not?"

"Reckon I don't know any reason. But Sadie Purdue was pretty shore she did. . . . You wouldn't really be ashamed of me, then?"

"Of course not," replied Lucy, at her wits' end to meet this situation. "I heard you spoken of very highly by Mrs. Lynn at Cedar Ridge. And I can see how your parents regard you. At my home in Felix it was not the custom for a girl to go to a dance upon such slight acquaintance as ours. But I do not expect city customs up here in the woods."

"Reckon I like the way you talk," he said, his face lighting. "Shore it doesn't rile me all up. But that's no matter now. . . . Won't you please go with me?"

"No," answered Lucy, decidedly, a little nettled at his persistence, when she had been kind enough to explain.

"Shore I didn't ask any girl before you," he appealed, plaintively.

"That doesn't make any difference."

"But it means an awful lot to me," he went on, doggedly.

It would never do to change her mind after refusing him, so there seemed nothing left but to shake her head smilingly and say she was sorry. Then without a word he strode out and clanked off the porch. Lucy went on with the work at hand, becoming so interested that she forgot about him. Sometime later he again presented himself at her door. He was clean shaven; he had brushed his hair while wet, plastering it smooth and glossy to his fine-shaped head; he wore a light colored flannel shirt and a red tie; and new blue-jeans trousers. Lucy could not help seeing what a great improvement this made in his appearance.

"Reckon you haven't thought it over?" he queried, hopefully.

"What?" returned Lucy.

"About goin' to the dance?"

"I've been very busy with all this stuff, and haven't had time to think of anything else."

"Shore I never wanted any girl to go with me like I do you," he said. "Most because Sadie made fun of the idea."

This did not appear particularly flattering to Lucy. She wondered if the young man had really been in love with that smug-faced girl.

"Edd, it's not very nice of you to want me just to revenge yourself on Sadie," rejoined Lucy, severely.

"Reckon it's not all that," he replied, hurriedly. "Sadie an' Sam an' most of them rake me over. It's got to be a sore point with me. An' here you bob up, the prettiest an' stylishest girl who ever came to Cedar Ridge. Think what a beat I'd have on them if I could take you. An' shore that's not sayin' a word about my own feelin's."

"Well, Edd, I must say you've made amends for your other speech," said Lucy, graciously. "All the same, I said no and I meant no."

"Miss Lucy, I swear I'd never asked you again if you'd said that for good. But you said as much as you'd go sometime. Shore if you're ever goin' to our dances why not this one, an' let me be the first to take you?"

He was earnest; he was pathetic; he was somehow

most difficult to resist. Lucy felt that she had not been
desired in this way before. To take her would be the
great event in his life. For a moment she labored with
vacillation. Then she reflected that if she yielded here it
would surely lead to other obligations and very likely to
sentiment. Thereupon she hardened her heart, and this
time gave him a less kindly refusal. Edd dropped his
head and went away.

Lucy spent another hour unpacking and arranging the
numerous working materials that had been brought from
Cedar Ridge. She heard Mrs. Denmeade and Allie pre-
paring an early supper, so they could ride off to the
dance before sunset. Lucy had finished her task for the
afternoon and was waiting to be called to supper when
again Edd appeared at the door.

"Will you go to the dance with me?" he asked, precisely as he had the first time. Yet there seemed some
subtle change in both tone and look.

"Well, indeed you are persevering, if not some other
things," she replied, really annoyed. "Can't you understand plain English? . . . I said no!"

"Shore I heard you the first time," he retorted. "But
I reckoned, seein' it's so little for you to do, an' means
so much to me, maybe you'd——"

"Why does it mean so much to you?" she interrupted.

" 'Cause if I can take _you_ I'll show them this once,
an' then I'll never go again," he replied.

It cost Lucy effort to turn away from his appealing
face and again deny him, which she did curtly. He disappeared. Then Mrs. Denmeade called her to supper.
Edd did not show himself during the meal.

"Edd's all het up over this dance," observed Mrs.
Denmeade. "It's on account of Sadie's sharp tongue. Edd
doesn't care a rap for her now an' never did care much,
if my reckonin' is right. But she's mean."

"Laws! I hope Edd doesn't fetch that Sally Sprall,"
interposed Allie. "He said he was dog-goned minded to
do it."

"That hussy!" ejaculated Mrs. Denmeade. "Edd
wouldn't take her."

"Ma, he's awful set on havin' a girl this dance," responded Allie.

"I'll bet some day Edd gets a better girl than Sadie Purdue or any of her clan," declared the mother.

A little while later Lucy watched Mrs. Denmeade and Allie, with the children and Uncle Bill, ride off down the lane to disappear in the woods. Edd had not returned. Lucy concluded he had ridden off as had his brothers and their father. She really regretted that she had been obdurate. Coming to think about it, she did not like the idea of being alone in the cabin all night. Still, she could bar herself in and feel perfectly safe.

She walked on the porch, listening to the murmur of the stream and the barking of the squirrels. Then she watched the sun set in golden glory over the yellow-and-black cape of wall that jutted out toward the west. The day had been pleasantly warm and was now growing cool. She drew a deep breath of the pine-laden air. This wild country was drawing her. A sense of gladness filled her at the thought that she could stay here indefinitely.

Her reflections were interrupted by the crack of iron-shod hoof on rock. Lucy gave a start. She did not want to be caught there alone. Peering through the foliage, she espied Edd striding up the lane, leading two saddled horses. She was immensely relieved, almost glad at sight of him, and then began to wonder what this meant.

"If he's not going to ask me again!" she soliloquized, and the paradox of her feeling on the moment was that she was both pleased and irritated at his persistence. "The nerve of him!"

Edd led the two horses into the yard and up to the porch. His stride was that of a man who would not easily be turned back. In spite of her control, Lucy felt a thrill.

"Reckon you thought I'd gone?" he queried as he faced her.

"No; I didn't think about you at all," returned Lucy, which speech was not literally true.

"Wal, you're goin' to the dance," he drawled, cool and easy, with a note in his voice she had never heard.

"Oh—indeed! I am?" she exclaimed tartly.

"You shore are."

"I am not," flashed Lucy.

With a lunge he reached out his long arms and, wrapping them round her, he lifted her off the porch as easily as if she had been an empty sack. Lucy was so astounded that for an instant she could not move hand or foot. A knot seemed to form in her breast. She began to shake. Then awakening to this outrage, she began to struggle.

"How-dare you? Let me down! Release me!" she cried.

"Nope. You're goin' to the dance," he said, in the same drawling tone with its peculiar inflection.

"You—you ruffian!" burst out Lucy, suddenly beside herself with rage. Frantically she struggled to free herself. This fierce energy only augmented her emotions. She tore at him, wrestled and writhed, and then in desperation fraught with sudden fear she began to beat him with her fists. At that he changed his hold on her until she seemed strung in iron bands. She could not move. It was a terrible moment, in which her head reeled. What did he mean to do with her?

"Reckon I'll have to hold you till you quit fightin'," he said. "Shore it'd never do to put you up on Baldy now. He's a gentle hoss, but if you kicked around on him I reckon he might hurt you."

"Let—me—go!" gasped Lucy, hoarsely. "Are—you crazy?"

"Nope. Not even riled. But shore my patience is wearin' out."

"Patience! Why, you lout—you brute—you wild-bee hunter!" raved Lucy, and again she attempted to break his hold. How utterly powerless she was! He had the strength of a giant. A sudden panic assailed her fury.

"My God! You don't mean—to hurt me—harm me?" she panted.

"You dog-gone fool!" he ejaculated, as if utterly astounded.

"Oh! . . . Then what—do you mean?"

"I mean nothin' 'cept you're goin' to that dance," he

declared, ruthlessly. "An' you're goin' if I have to hawg-
tie you. Savvy?"

Whereupon he lifted her and set her in the saddle of
one of the horses, and threw her left foot over so that
she was astride.

"No kickin' now! Baldy is watchin' out of the corner
of his eye," said this wild-bee hunter.

The indignity of her position, astride a horse with her
dress caught above her knees, was the last Lucy could
endure.

"Please let—me down," she whispered. "I'll—go—
with you."

"Wal, I'm shore glad you're goin' to show sense,"
he drawled, and with action markedly in contrast to his
former ones he helped her dismount.

Lucy staggered back against the porch, so weak she
could hardly stand. She stared at this young backwoodsman, whose bronze face had paled slightly. He had
bruised her arms and terrified her. Overcome by her
sensations, she burst into tears.

"Aw, don't cry!" Edd expostulated. "I'm sorry I had
to force you. . . . An' you don't want to go to a dance
with red eyes an' nose."

If Lucy had not been so utterly shocked she could have
laughed at his solicitude. Hopeless indeed was this backwoodsman. She strove to regain control over her feelings,
and presently moved her hands from her face.

"Is there any place down there—to change—where
a girl can dress?" she asked, huskily. "I can't ride horseback in this."

"Shore is," he said, gayly.

"Very well," returned Lucy. "I'll get a dress—and go
with you."

She went to her room and, opening the closet, she
selected the prettiest of the several dresses she had
brought. This, with slippers, comb, and brush and mirror,
she packed in a small grip. She seemed stunned, locked
in a kind of maze. Kidnapped! Forced by a wild-bee
hunter to go to a backwoods dance! Of all adventures
possible to her, this one seemed the most incredible! Yet

had she not been selfish, heartless? What right had she to come among such crude people and attempt to help them? This outrage would end her ambition.

Then hurriedly slipping into her riding clothes, Lucy took the bag and returned to the porch.

"Wal, now that's fine," said Edd, as he reached for the grip. He helped her mount and shortened the stirrups without speaking. Then he put a big hand on the pommel of her saddle and looked up at her.

"Shore now, if it'd been Sadie or any girl I know she'd have gone in an' barred the door," he said. "I just been thinkin' that over. Shore I didn't think you'd lie."

Lucy endeavored to avert her gaze. Her horror had not faded. But again the simplicity of this young man struck her.

"Do you want to back out now an' stay home?" he went on.

"You are making me go by force," she returned. "You said you'd 'hawg-tie' me, didn't you?"

"Wal, reckon I did," he replied. "But I was riled an' turrible set on takin' you. . . . Your havin' a chance to lock yourself in! Now you didn't do it an' I savvied you wouldn't."

Lucy made no reply. What was going on in the mind of this half-savage being? He fascinated while he repelled her. It would have been false to herself had she denied the fact that she felt him struggling with his instincts, unconsciously fighting himself, reaching out blindly. He was a living proof of the evolution of man toward higher things.

"Wal, reckon I'll let you off," he declared at length.

"Are you afraid I'll tell what a brute you were?" she flashed, sarcastically.

His lean face turned a dark red and his eyes grew piercing.

"Hell, no!" he ejaculated. "Shore I don't care what you tell. But I'd hate to have you think same as Sadie an' those girls."

"It doesn't matter what I think," she replied. "You'd never understand."

"Wal, I would, if you thought like them."

"Is it possible you could expect me to think anything but hard of you—after the way you treated me?" she demanded, with returning spirit.

"Hard? Reckon I don't mind that," he returned, ponderingly. "Anyway, I'll let you off, just because you wasn't tricky."

"No, you won't let me off," asserted Lucy. "I'm going to this dance . . . and you'll take the consequences!"

CHAPTER VI

At the corral gate Edd Denmeade swung his long length off his horse and held the gate open for Lucy to ride through.

"Wal, want to go fast or slow?" he asked, as he mounted again.

"Prisoners have no choice," retorted Lucy.

Evidently that remark effectually nipped in the bud any further desire for conversation. His gray eyes seemed to be piercing her, untroubled yet questioning. He put his horse to a trot. Lucy's mount, without urging, fell in behind. His easy gait proved to be most agreeable to her. He was a pacer, and Lucy recognized at once that he was the kind of a horse it was a great pleasure to ride. He appeared to be eager, spirited, yet required no constant watching and holding.

The trail led into the forest, a wide, dusty, winding path full of all kinds of tracks, one of which Lucy thought she recognized as Dick's. She had noticed his enormous feet. Patches of manzanita, clumps of live-oak, thickets of pine, bordered the trail. Above these towered the stately rugged-barked monarchs of the forest. The last of the afterglow of sunset flowed rosily on the clouds; through the green lacework of the trees gleamed the gold of the wandering wall far above her. Shadows were lying low in the ravines that headed away from the trail. Presently this level bench of woodland ended and there was a sharp descent, down which the trail zig-zagged by easy stages. Then again the forest appeared level. Lucy heard the dreamy hum of a waterfall. Here Edd took to a swinging lope, and Lucy's horse, as before, fell into the faster stride.

The forest grew darker and cooler. The trail wound in and out, always hiding what was beyond. Sometimes Edd's horse was out of sight. Lucy found herself in a strange contention of mind. Despite her anger and the absurdity of her being dragged virtually a prisoner to this dance, the novelty of the situation and the growing sensations of the ride seemed to be combining to make her enjoy them, whether she wanted to or not. That would be a humiliation she must not suffer. Yet no doubt the horse Baldy was the finest she had ever ridden. She had to fight herself to keep from loving him. Nor could she help but revel in this lonely, fragrant trail through the wild dales and glades. They rode out levels and down steps, and crossed rushing brooks; and it appeared that Edd kept going a little faster all the time. Yet he never looked back to see how she fared. No doubt he heard her horse.

Twilight turned the greens and browns to gray. In the denser parts of the forest Lucy could scarcely see the dim pale trail ahead. Suddenly she caught a glimpse of a fire. It disappeared as she loped along, and then reappeared. Then, all too soon, she thought, they rode into a clearing dominated by a large low building, half logs and half rough boards. A fire burned brightly under a huge pine near the edge of the clearing, and it was surrounded by noisy boys and girls. Horses were haltered to saplings all around. Wagons and queer-looking vehicles attested to the fact that a road led to this forest schoolhouse.

Edd halted at the rear of the building, and, dismounting, he set Lucy's grip on the ground and turned to help her off. But Lucy ignored him and slipped quickly down.

She was warm, throbbing from the brisk exertion of riding, and in spite of herself not wholly unresponsive to the adventure.

"Wal, we're shore here," drawled Edd, happily, no doubt keenly alive to the shouts of the young people round the fire. "You can dress in there."

He led her to a door at the back of the schoolhouse. Lucy mounted the high log steps to enter. The room was bare, a small addition built against the building. There was no one in it, a fact that relieved Lucy. A lighted lamp stood on a table. On one side was a built-in couch covered with dried pine boughs. Besides these articles of furniture there was a box to serve as a chair.

Lucy closed the door and hurriedly set about the business of dressing. She was not in any hurry to go out to meet Edd and the people at this dance; but she found it expedient to do so, owing to the cold. The bare room was like a barn. Once dressed, Lucy rather regretted bringing her best and most attractive gown. She had selected it hastily and in a moment of stress. Excitement and exertion had left her pale, with eyes darker than usual. She could not spare time on her hair, but it looked the better for that.

"If this mirror doesn't lie I never looked half so well," she murmured. "Now, Mr. Edd Denmeade, wild-bee hunter and wild kidnapper, we'll see!"

Lucy's mood did not tolerate the maxims and restraints she had set for herself. On the moment she was ready to abandon her cherished ambition to succeed in welfare work. Gorillas and outlaws and bee hunters were a little beyond her ken. Edd Denmeade had laid hold of her in a savage manner, to which the dark-blue marks on her white arms could attest. Lucy did not stop to analyze her anger and the limits to which it might drive her. One thing at least was clear to her, and it was that she would use all a woman's guile and charm to make Edd Denmeade rue this night. At first she had intended to go straight to his father and mother and tell of the indignity that had been done her. But she had changed her mind during the ride, and now that she was dressed in her

best her mood underwent further change. She had brought
a light-blue silk scarf to go with her white gown, and
throwing this round her bare shoulders she sallied forth.
As she stepped down to the ground the bright blaze
from the fire blinded her, yet she saw a tall dark form
detach itself from the circle there and approach her.

"You shore dressed pronto," drawled Edd.

Lucy put her hand on his arm and walked beside him,
perfectly aware of his long stare. He led her round the
schoolhouse to a front entrance, where another crowd of
boys and girls whispered and gaped.

"Our old fiddler's late," said her escort, "an' I reckon
the gang is rarin' to dance."

Edd had to push himself through a crowd just inside
the door, and he did it in a rather imperative way. Once
through this line, Lucy saw a large bare board floor,
then a large room lighted by many lamps, and many
people sitting and standing around the walls. Edd was
leading her across the room toward a corner where there
were a stove and a table. Here was congregated another
group, including women and children. Mrs. Denmeade
and Allie came to meet them; and if Lucy had wanted
any evidence of creating a sensation, she had it now.

"Wal, ma, here we are," drawled Edd, as coolly as
if there were no strained situation. Perhaps for him there
was none.

"For goodness' sake!" exclaimed his mother, in delight.
"Lucy, I'm shore awful glad to see you here. You fooled
us bad. That boy of mine is a fox."

Lucy's murmured reply did not include any of the
epithets she might have laid upon Edd Denmeade. Allie
appeared even more delighted to see her.

"Oh, it was good of you to come!" she whispered,
taking Lucy's arm and squeezing it. "You look perfectly
lovely. An' all the boys will die."

"I hope it'll not be so bad as that," laughed Lucy,
softening unexpectedly. The warmth of her welcome and
the extravagant praise of her appearance were too much
for her. Whatever she felt toward Edd Denmeade, she
could not extend to these simple, impulsive people. This

was their social life, the one place they gathered to have pleasure, and here they seemed very different. Lucy was at once the cynosure of all eyes, and was surrounded by old and young alike. The twins, Liz and Lize, after their first blank bewilderment as at an apparition in white, clung to her with the might of conscious pride of possession. Denmeade and Uncle Bill greeted her with wrinkled faces wreathed in smiles. Lucy met Claypools, Millers, Johnsons, and numberless others whose names she could not remember. Edd brought young men, all lean, rangy giants, whom she could not have distinguished one from another. It dawned on Lucy that he wanted most of the boys there to meet her and dance with her. Indeed, he showed no selfish interest. But Lucy did not really look at Edd until Mrs. Denmeade, during an opportune moment, whispered to her:

"Lucy, I reckon Edd's the proudest boy in the whole world. Pa said the same. We never seen him this way before. He was never happy at our dances. But you've done him good by comin', an' I'm thankin' you."

Whereupon Lucy forced herself to gaze upon the escort who had gone to such an extreme to bring her to this dance. And she was to discern that, whatever his misconduct toward her, he was now wearing his laurels with becoming modesty. For Lucy could not blind herself to the fact that she was the star attraction of this dance and that Edd had brought his rivals to a state of envy. Both circumstances pleased her. Seldom had she ever been the belle of a dance. Every young man who met her begged the privilege of dancing with her. And as introductions were quick and many she could not remember names. How she enjoyed seeing Sam Johnson beg Edd for a dance with her! And Edd showed no rancor, no remembrance of insults, but with a courtesy that would not have ill become one in higher walks of life he gratified Sam. Lucy found the situation different from what she had anticipated. To revenge herself upon Edd Denmeade she had determined to be frigid to him and as sweet as she could make herself to every other boy there, particularly Sam Johnson. Not yet did

she repudiate that unworthy resolve, though something
was working on her—the warmth of her welcome—the
pleasure she was giving—the honor she had unwittingly
conferred upon this crude woodsman, the simplicity with
which he took his triumph.

It dawned upon Lucy that there was only one reason
why she could not thoroughly enjoy this dance, and it
was because of what she called the brutal circumstances
of her coming. Why had she not been willing and glad
to come? Too late! The indignity had been perpetrated
and she could not forget it. Nevertheless, she felt stir
in her something besides the desire to shine and attract
for the sole purpose of making Edd Denmeade miserably
jealous. It was an honest realization that she could like
these people and enjoy herself.

Commotion and stamping of feet and merry voices
rose from the front of the schoolhouse. Lucy was informed that the music had arrived. She saw an old man
proudly waving a violin and forging his way to the tiny
platform. The children screeched and ran for him. Edd
joined the group with whom Lucy was standing. Then
a loud twang from the fiddler set everyone to expectancy.
When he began to play the couples moved out upon
the floor. Edd said no word, but he reached for Lucy.

"Wait. Let me watch a moment," she said. "I want
to see how you dance."

"Wal, shore we're no great shucks at it, but we have
fun."

Soon the floor was half full of wheeling, gliding
couples, with more falling in line every moment. Their
dancing had only one feature in common with what she
understood about dancing, and that was they caught
the rhythm of the old fiddler's several chords.

"Very well, Mr. Denmeade, I think I can catch the
step," said Lucy.

As he took hold of her it was not possible to keep
from stiffening somewhat and to hold back. Still, she was
to ascertain that Edd showed no thought of holding
her closely. How serious he was about this dancing! He
was surprisingly easy on his feet. At first Lucy could

not fall in with his way of dancing; gradually, however, she caught it, and after several rounds of the room she was keeping time with him. It required a great deal of effort and concentration for Lucy to live up to her repute as a dancer. Manifestly Edd Denmeade did not talk while he danced. In fact, none of the dancers talked. They were deadly serious about it, and the expressions on different faces highly amused Lucy. She could not see that dancing held any sentimental opportunities for these young people. It seemed to Lucy a bobbing, gyrating performance, solemnly enjoyed by boy and girl in markedly loose contact. Really they danced wholly with their own intent and energy. Lucy found Edd's arm as rugged and unyielding as the branch of an oak. At last the dance ended, to Lucy's relief.

"Shore you can dance!" exclaimed Edd, heartily. "Like a feather! If you hadn't leaned on my arm I'd not have known you was there. New kind of dancin' for me!"

Lucy did not deign to reply. He led her back to the corner, where he found her a seat beside his mother. "Shore I hope you dance them all down," he whispered. "Reckon I wouldn't be in Sam Johnson's boots for a lot."

"What did he mean?" inquired Lucy of his mother, after he had left them.

"Dancin' anyone down is to make him give up—tire him out," she replied. "An' that about Sam Johnson is funny. Sam is reckoned to be the best dancer in these parts. An' so is Sadie. Wal, as everybody seen right off, Sadie can't hold a candle to you. An' Sam is goin' to find it out."

"Some one will surely dance *me* down," replied Lucy, with a laugh. "I am out of practice."

It developed that the time between dances was long, and given over to much hilarity and promenading around. The children took advantage of this opportunity to romp over the floor. Lucy soon was surrounded again, so that she could not see very much of what was going on. Sam Johnson claimed her for the next dance. He struck Lucy as being something of a rural beau, quite taken with himself, and not above intimating that she would surely

like dancing with him better than with a big-footed bee
hunter.

As a matter of fact, when the fiddler started up again
Lucy found Sam's boast to be true. He was a surprisingly
good dancer and she enjoyed dancing with him. But it
was not this that prompted her to be prodigal of her
smiles, and to approach audacity, if not actual flirtation,
to captivate Sam. She did not stop to question her
motive. He and his girl Sadie had been largely responsible for Edd Denmeade's affront to her. Yet Lucy did
not dream that she was championing Edd. She had been
deeply roused. The primitive instincts of these young
people were calling to the unknown in her.

Once in the whirling maze of flushed faces Lucy found
herself looking right into Sadie Purdue's eyes. Lucy
nodded smilingly. Her greeting was returned, but Sadie
failed to hide her jealousy and resentment.

When that dance ended Lucy was beseiged by the
young men, and gradually she gave herself up to the
novelty of the occasion. Now and then she saw Edd
dancing or attending some one, but he did not approach
her. Mrs. Denmeade apparently took great pride in Lucy's
popularity. The children gradually drooped and were
put to sleep in the corner back of the stove. Lucy had
to take a peep at them, some dozen or more of curly-
headed little boys and girls, and several babies, all worn
out with excitement and now fast asleep.

Dance after dance followed, stealing the hours away.
By midnight, when the intermission and supper were
announced by Mr. Denmeade, it seemed to Lucy that
she had allowed her impulsiveness and resentment to
carry her away. Sam Johnson had more than lived up to
the reputation Edd had given him. Only Lucy's tact saved
him from utterly neglecting Sadie; and as it was he made
a fool of himself. Mr. Jenks, the teacher, did not dance,
and devoted himself to the older people. He had not
found opportunity for more than a few words with Lucy,
but several times she had caught him intently watching
her, especially while she was with Sam. This, more than
any other thing, made her reflect that perhaps she had

already forgotten the ideal she had propounded to him. She suffered a moment of regret; then, when at the intermission Edd presented himself before her, cool and nonchalant, she could not help being rebellious.

"Wal, reckon I'll have to lick somebody before this night's over," he drawled as he led her across the room.

"Indeed! How interesting!" replied Lucy, icily.

"Shore will, unless somebody backs down on what he said. . . . Ma wants you to set with her at supper. Teacher Jenks has somethin' to say to you. Shore tickles me. . . . Why, Lucy Watson, you've made this night the wonderfulest of my life! I've had enough dancin' an' gettin' even an' crawlin' of these here corn-huskers to last forever."

Lucy was afraid that for her, too, something wonderful lurked under the commonplaces of this experience, but she could not confess that Edd Denmeade had created it. She felt how little she was to regret that he had surprised her by not living up to the status of boor and ruffian. Instead of this he had turned out to be something approaching a gentleman. He became an enigma to her. It must be that he had no conception of his rude seizure of her person, his utter disregard of her feelings. Yet here at the dance he had eliminated himself, content to see her whirled about by his cousins and friends, simply radiating with the pride of being her cavalier.

"Reckon I'll help feed this outfit," he said, leaving her in a seat between his mother and Mr. Jenks.

"Well, I'd hardly have known you," said the schoolteacher, with a smile and cordial greeting.

"Wal, I said the same," averred Mrs. Denmeade. "Shore she just looks lovely."

Lucy had the grace to blush her pleasure. "I declare this night will ruin my promise as a welfare worker. Too many compliments!"

"Not your promise, but your possibility," whispered Mr. Jenks, significantly. "Young lady, I intend to talk to you like a Dutch uncle."

"Indeed, I hope you do," replied Lucy, soberly. "Then I'll have something to tell you."

A corps of young men, among whom was Edd, passed round the room, distributing sandwiches and coffee, cake and ice cream. Soon the large hall-like place hummed with voices. Every seat along the walls was occupied. Around the entrance clustered a group of youths who had come without partners, and it was plain they felt their misfortune. Nevertheless, they had established some kind of rapport between themselves and other boys' partners. Lucy's keen susceptibilities grasped the fact that many of the girls welcomed this state of affairs.

Presently Mr. Jenks found opportunity to say, "You have created a havoc, Miss Lucy."

"Have I? Well, Mr. Jenks, I'm surely afraid that I wanted to," she confessed.

"I am not joking," he continued, more earnestly. "Indeed, I make all allowance for a girl's natural vanity and pleasure in being admired. You are 'shore good fer sore eyes,' as I heard one old codger say. You have stormed this schoolhouse crowd. If looks could kill, Sadie Purdue would have had you dead hours ago. They all say, 'Sam is gone!' . . . It would be funny—if it were anywhere else but up in this backwoods."

"Oh, have I forgotten myself?" exclaimed Lucy, aghast.

"Pray don't misunderstand," said Mr. Jenks, hastily. "I think you very modest and nice, considering the unusual situation. But you *have* forgotten your welfare work. Of course I don't see how you can avoid these dances. And that's the rub. Your popularity will make enemies among the girls and fights among the boys."

In self-defense Lucy related briefly and vividly how Edd Denmeade had seized her and held her powerless, threatening to tie her, until in her shame and fear she had consented to come to the dance.

"I'm not surprised," said Mr. Jenks, gravely. "These fellows are built that way, and Edd is really what they call him, a wild-bee hunter. I believe that implies almost an Indian's relationship to the woods. But you must not mistake Edd and do him injustice. It never dawned on him that violence would be a profanation to a girl such as you. . . . Could you honestly accuse him of the least boldness—you know what I mean?"

"No, I'm bound to confess that he handled me as if I were a boy or an old sack," replied Lucy, honestly.

"Well, then, try to understand him. It will not be easy. He's a savage. But savages are closer to nature than other men, and somehow the better for it. . . . What surprises me is that Edd has not made any fuss yet over Bud Sprall's attention to you."

"Bud Sprall!" exclaimed Lucy, with a start of amaze. "Have I met him?"

"Wal, I reckon, as Edd would say," rejoined the teacher, amused at Lucy's consternation. "You have danced twice with Bud, and showed that you liked it."

"Oh, but I didn't know," wailed Lucy. "I didn't catch half the names. . . . Show him to me."

The school-teacher managed presently, in an unobtrusive manner, to indicate which one of Lucy's partners had been the disreputable Bud Sprall.

"That handsome young fellow!" she burst out, incredulously.

"Handsome, yes; Bud's good-looking enough and he can dance. But he is not just the fellow you can have dangling after you."

"I took him for one of the relations. There're so many. And I didn't see anything wrong with him except, come to think of it, he might have been drinking a little. But he was not the only one upon whom I detected drink."

"White mule! These boys will fetch a bottle to the dances. It's the one objectionable feature about their social family affairs. Naturally white mule kicks up fights."

"Oh, how unfortunate! How thoughtless of me not to *know* what I was doing!" cried Lucy.

"Don't be distressed," he returned, kindly. "No harm yet. But I advise you to avoid Bud hereafter."

"I'm sure I promised him another dance," said Lucy, in perplexity.

"Get out of it, then. And that's the worst of it. Bud will be sore and make trouble, unless you are very clever."

"Oh dear! How can I get out of a dance I've promised?

. . . And that Sam Johnson! I *was* nice to him, deliberately. He's such a conceited fellow. I'm afraid I let him think he'd made a wonderful impression on me."

"Miss Watson, I have an inspiration," rejoined Mr. Jenks, animatedly. "Confide in Edd. Get him to help you out of your dilemma."

"Edd! How could I? Impossible!" replied Lucy, heatedly.

"Of course that's for you to say. But if you don't, and cannot extricate yourself, I imagine you will only get in deeper."

Lucy, seeing Mrs. Denmeade approaching with friends, was unable to continue discussing the situation with Mr. Jenks. The parents of the children present were eager to talk to Lucy, and they asked innumerable questions. Before she realized the fleeting by of the supper hour the fiddler started one of his several tunes, and there followed a rush of dancers to the floor.

Edd did not exhibit any considerable alacrity in approaching her for this first number after the intermission.

"Want to dance this with me?" he queried, coolly.

"Isn't it customary?" replied Lucy as she glanced over the dancers to select some she knew.

"Shore. But if you don't *want* to dance with me I'd as lief not have you."

"Oh, really! . . . Would you expect me to be dying to dance with you?" retorted Lucy, with sarcasm.

"Nope. I'm not thinkin' about myself. But you think I am. My folks all reckon you're havin' the wonderfulest time. Wal, I hope so, but I've a hunch you're not. For I've been watchin' you. I saw you with Mr. Jenks."

"Really, it'd only be honest to confess that—that I'm enjoying myself—when I forgot how I happened to come," said Lucy.

"So I reckoned. An' you can have this dance with anyone you want."

"But—you brought me here. Won't it look strange if you don't dance with me?" she queried, with concern.

"Wal, the strangest thing that ever happened in this

schoolhouse was for a Denmeade's girl to dance with a Sprall," he returned, bitterly.

"Oh! I am not your girl. . . . And I had not the remotest idea I was dancing with Bud Sprall. I only just found out. Mr. Jenks told me."

"Say, you didn't know it was Bud Sprall you danced with twice?" he demanded, with piercing eyes of doubt.

"Absolutely no. I never caught his name," confessed Lucy.

"Wal, I'll be dog-goned! I wish everybody knew that. Shore I can tell my folks," he said, ponderingly.

"Edd, I'm afraid I promised him another dance—after supper," went on Lucy, nervously. She realized there was an undercurrent here, a force of antagonism quite beyond her. When his face turned white she was nearer the truth. Abruptly he wheeled to leave her, but Lucy was quick to catch his sleeve and draw him back. The dancers crowded them to the wall.

"Do not leave me alone," she said, swiftly. "Remember that I am a stranger here. You brought me against my will. I can hardly be blamed for dancing with Bud Sprall when I did not know who he was."

"Reckon that's all right," he replied, gazing down on her. "But you was sweet on Bud an' you've shore turned Sam Johnson's head."

Lucy strove valiantly to keep her temper and find her wits. She began to have an inkling why Mr. Jenks was so concerned over her predicament.

"Suppose I was? Didn't you deserve to be punished?" she queried.

"Reckon I don't savvy you," he rejoined, doubtfully. "Shore you strike me a little like Sadie Purdue."

"We are all women. Nevertheless, I don't consider that a compliment. But . . . you brought me here. I've made a mess of it. I was—well, never mind now. Only, it's your duty to help me not make it *worse*."

"Who's sayin' I wouldn't help you?" he queried.

"You started to leave me."

"Wal, you said you'd another dance with Bud."

"But I didn't know who he was. Now I do know. I

won't dance with him. I don't want to. I'm very sorry I
blundered. But he seemed nice and——and——"

"Bud has a way with girls," said Edd, simply. "Shore
he's slicker than Sam."

"Will you take me home?" she asked, urgently.

"Shore. But I reckon that'd make worse talk. You'd
better stay an' let me take care of you."

"I——I'll do what you want me to," replied Lucy, faintly.

"Wal, dance this with me. Then I'll hang around an'
keep an eye on you. Keep out of that ring-around dance
where they change partners all the time. When Bud or
Sam comes up, you give me a look, an' I'll be there
pronto. Shore all your dances are mine, an' I don't have
to give any more to Bud or Sam."

"Thank you. I——I hope it turns out all right," replied
Lucy.

While she danced her mind was active. She regretted
her rash determination to make this crude backwoods
youth jealous. He had certainly disappointed her in that
regard. After awakening to the situation, first through
her conversation with Mr. Jenks and later with Edd, she
realized she had jeopardized her welfare work. No matter
what affront she had suffered, she should not have been
so silly, so reckless, so undeserving of the trust placed
in her. Yet what provocation! Her nerves tingled at the
thought.

When the dance ended Edd relinquished her to one
of his cousins, and gradually Lucy lost her worry for the
time being. The next dance was the ring-around, which
Lucy refused to enter, remaining beside Mrs. Denmeade.
Here she had opportunity to watch, and enjoyed it immensely. The dancing grew fast and furious. When the
dancers formed in a ring and wheeled madly round the
room, shrieking and laughing, they shook the schoolhouse
till it rattled.

It developed that Edd Denmeade was more than a
match for Bud Sprall when he presented himself for the
dance Lucy had promised. But the interchange of cool
speech struck Lucy keenly with its note of menace. Sprall's

dark handsome face expressed a raw, sinister hate. Denmeade wore a laconic mask, transparent to any observer. The advantage was his. Finally Sprall turned to Lucy.

"I ain't blamin' you, for I know you want to dance with me," he said. "Reckon I'll not forget. Good night."

Sam Johnson was not so easy to dispose of. Manifestly he and Edd were friends, which fact made the clash devoid of rancor.

"Wal, Sam, see here," drawled Edd, finally. "You go an' fetch Sadie up. Reckon I'd like a dance with her. You've only had five dances with Miss Lucy. This here one will be six, if Sadie is willin' to trade off. So fetch her up."

"Edd, I haven't got Sadie for this dance," fumed Sam.

"Then you're out of luck. For I shore won't give up my partner."

Sam tramped away in high dudgeon. Lucy danced once round the room with Edd, and then joined the group outside eating ice cream beside the fire. Dawn was gray in the east. How dark the forest and mournful the wind! Lucy edged nearer the fire. She had become conscious of extreme fatigue, and longed for this unforgettable night to end.

Nevertheless, she danced until daylight. Her slippers were worn through. Her feet were dead. Never before in her life had Lucy expended such physical energy. She marveled at those girls who were reluctant to let the old fiddler off.

Lucy changed the white dress and slippers for her riding clothes. Though the morning was frosty, she did not feel the cold. How she could ever ride up to the Denmeade cabin she had no idea.

"Better get me on your horse before I drop," she told Edd.

He wanted her to remain there at the schoolhouse with the children and girls, who were not to go home until evening. Mrs. Denmeade and Mrs. Claypool were getting breakfast for those who stayed. Lucy, refusing, was persuaded to drink a cup of coffee. Then Edd put her up on Baldy. All around the clearing boys and girls were mounting horses, and some of the older folk were driving off in wagons. Gay good-bys were exchanged. Lucy rode into the woods with the Denmeades.

At first the saddle and motion seemed a relief after such incessant dancing. But Lucy soon discovered that her strength was almost spent. Only vaguely did she see the beauty of the forest in the clear, crisp, fragrant morning. She had no sense of the stirrups and she could not catch the swing of the horse. The Denmeades trotted and loped on the levels, and walked up the slopes. Lucy could not have endured any one kind of riding for very long. She barely managed to hang on until they reached home.

The sun was rising in rosy splendor over the eastern wall. Wild turkeys were gobbling from the ridge behind the cabin. The hounds rang out a chorus of bays and barks in welcome.

Lucy almost fell out of the saddle. Edd was there beside her, quick to lend a hand.

"Wal, I reckon it was a night for both of us," he said. "But shore I don't want another like it, unless what I pretended was really true."

Murmuring something in reply, Lucy limped to her room, and barring the door she struggled to remove her boots. They might as well have been full of thorns, considering the pangs they gave her.

"Oh—oh—what a—terrible night!" she gasped, falling on the bed, fully dressed. "Yet—I know I wouldn't have missed it—for worlds . . . Oh, I'm dead! I'll never wake up!"

CHAPTER VII

It was midsummer. The mornings were pleasant, the days hot and still, the evenings sultry and purple, with massed clouds in the west.

The July rains had left the ridges and open patches and the edges of the clearings colorful and fragrant with flowers. Corn and cane and beans were green and wavy in the fields. A steady line of bees flew by the cabin porch, to and fro from hives to woods. And a drowsy murmuring hum made music down by the shady stream.

At sunrise the home of the Denmeades seemed to be a rendezvous for the frisky chipmunk and chattering red squirrel, for squalling blue jay and whistling hawk and cawing crow, and for the few wild singing birds of the locality. At noon the woods were locked in hot, drowsy stillness; the pine needles did not quiver; heat veils rose smokily from the glades. At evening a melancholy pervaded the wildness.

One Saturday Lucy sat meditating in the tent that had long been her abode. It was situated out under the pines on the edge of the gully. The boys had built a platform of rough-hewn boards, and a framework of poles, over which the canvas had been stretched. The floor was high above the ground, so that Lucy had long lost the fear of snakes and tarantulas. Indeed this outdoor home had grown wonderfully dear to her. By day she heard the tiny patter of pine needles on the tent; at night the cool winds blew through, and in the moonlight shadows of swaying branches moved above her.

Lucy had problems on her mind. As far as the Denmeades were concerned, her walfare work had been successful beyond her dreams. The time was approaching when in all fairness she must go to another family. She would keenly regret leaving this place she had learned to love, yet she wanted to do as well by others as she had done by the Denmeades. When to go—that was part of the problem.

Another disturbing factor came in the shape of a letter from her sister Clara. It had shocked her and induced a regurgitation of almost forgotten emotions. The letter lay open in her lap. It must be reread and considered and decided upon—matters Lucy was deferring.

The last and perhaps most perplexing question concerned Edd Denmeade. Lucy had to go back in retrospect. The trouble between Edd and her dated back to the dance in May, the one which he had forced her to attend. Lucy had gone to other dances since then, but Edd had never attended another. She might in time have forgiven him for that exhibition of his primitiveness, but shortly afterward he had precipitated something which resulted in their utter estrangement. The bee hunter was the only one of the Denmeades who had not wondrously benefited by her work. He had lost by her presence. He had gone back farther. He exhibited signs of becoming a solitary wanderer in the woods most of the time, a violent and dangerous young man when he did mingle with people. Lucy had forced upon her the undoubted fact that she was the cause of this. No one else knew yet, not even Edd's mother. Lucy could not take unadulterated pride and joy in her success. She did not see how she could have avoided such a situation, yet regret haunted her. And now with decisions to make she vacillated over the important ones, and brought to mind the scene that had turned Edd Denmeade aside from the happier influences and tasks which she had imposed upon his family.

Shortly after that dance Edd had come up to her where she sat on the corral fence watching the boys roping and shoeing a horse.

"I reckon I'm goin' to ask you a question," he announced. Almost his tone was the cool drawling one habitual with him; here, however, there seemed something deep, inevitable behind his words.

"Goodness! Don't ask me to go to another dance," laughed Lucy.

"Reckon I'll never dance again, unless——" He broke off. "An' what I'm goin' to ask you I've asked other girls. Shore this is the last time."

"Well, what is it?" queried Lucy, suddenly perturbed.

"Will you marry me?"

Notwithstanding the fact that she was startled, Lucy burst into mirth. It must have been the opposite to what she felt, a nervousness expressing itself in laughter. But it appeared to be unfortunate.

"I—I beg pardon, Edd," she made haste to say. "Really I didn't mean to laugh at you. But you—you surprised me so. . . . You can't be serious."

"Reckon I don't know just what I am," he replied, grimly. "But I'm askin' you to marry me."

"Because you want a home and a woman? I heard your father say that."

"Shore. That's the way I've felt. Reckon this is more. I've told my folks an' relations I was askin' you. Wanted them to know."

"Edd, I cannot marry you," she replied, gravely.

"Why not?" he demanded. "You're here. You want to work for us. An' I reckon I could help you as much as you could me."

"That's true. You *could* help me a great deal. But I'm sorry I can't marry you."

"Reckon you're too good for a backwoodsman, a wild-bee hunter who's been jilted by other girls," he asserted, with a strange, deep utterance.

"No. You're wrong," declared Lucy, both touched and angered by his speech. "I don't think I'm too good. That dance you dragged me to cured me of my vanity."

"Wal, then, what's the reason?" he went on. "Ma says you're goin' to stay among us people for years. If that's so you'll *have* to marry one of us. I'm askin' you first."

"Edd, an honest girl could not marry a man she didn't love," replied Lucy. "Nor can a man be honest asking a girl whom *he* does not love."

"Shore I am honest. I'm no liar," he retorted. "I'm

just plain man. I don't know much of people or books. But I know the woods, an' reckon I can learn what you want me to."

"I don't mean honest in that sense," rejoined Lucy. "I meant you don't love me."

"Love you! Are you like Sadie, who told around that I'd never kissed her?"

"No, I'm not like Sadie," answered Lucy, with rising temper.

"Wal, I'm askin' your pardon," he said. "Shore you're different from Sadie. . . . As for this love you girls talk about I don't know——I always felt a man should keep his hands an' his lips to himself until he had a wife."

"Edd, I respect you for that," replied Lucy, earnestly. "And understand you better. . . . But love is not kisses and all that."

"Wal, what is it, then?"

"It is something beautiful, spiritual as well as physical. It is a longing for the welfare, the happiness, the good of some one as well as the sweetness of desire. For a woman love means what Ruth said in the Bible. 'Whither thou goest, I will go. Thy people shall be my people, thy God my God.' . . . A man who loves a woman will do anything for her——sacrifice himself. The greater his sacrifice the greater his love. And last he ought to feel that he could not live without the object of his affections."

"Wal, I reckon I don't love you," replied Edd, ponderingly.

"Of course you don't. You're only thinking of yourself," rejoined Lucy.

"Reckon I can't help what I think. Who put all this in my head?"

"Edd, you haven't got anything in your head," retorted Lucy, unable to restrain her pique and scorn. "That's the trouble. You need education. All your people need education more than anything else."

"Wal, why don't you teach me same as you do Liz an' Lize?" he complained.

"You're a grown man!" ejaculated Lucy. "You want to marry me! And you talk like a child."

"Shore I could make you marry me—same as I made you go to the dance," he said, ruthlessly.

For an instant Lucy stared at him, too stunned to reply. The simplicity of his words and conviction was as monstrous as the idea they conveyed. How strange that, though a fury suddenly flamed up in her breast, she had a doubt of herself, a fear that he could do what he wanted to do with her!

"Make me marry you! Never!" she burst out, thickly.

"Shore I'd not care what you said," he replied.

Lucy's amaze and wrath knew no bounds. "You—you——" She choked, almost unable to express herself. "You savage! You couldn't even love yourself. You're——" She was utterly at a loss to find words. "Why, you're a fool—that's what you are! . . . If you mention marriage again I'll give up my work here and leave."

Then and then only did it seem to dawn upon him that there was something wrong with his mind. He gave Lucy a blank, dead stare, as if he saw something through her. The vitality and intensity withered out of his face. He dropped his head and left her.

That scene had been long weeks past. For days Edd had remained out in the woods, and when he returned there was a difference in him. None of the family, however, apparently attributed it to Lucy. But she knew. At first, such was her antagonism, she did not care what he did or what became of him; but gradually, as the weeks wore on and she had such wonderful success with her work, while he grew wilder and stranger, she began to pity instead of despising him. Poor backwoods boy! How could he help himself? He had been really superior to most of his cousins and friends. Seldom did he do any work at home, except with his bees. Rumor credited him with fights and brawls, and visits to the old moonshiner who distilled the liquor called white mule. His mother worried incessantly. His father passed from concern to grief. "Doggone me!" he ejaculated. "Edd's headed like them Sprall boys. An' who'd ever think it!"

Likewise, Lucy passed from pity to worry, and from

that to a conscience-stricken accusation. If for no other reason she was to blame because she had come to Cedar Ridge. This fall of Edd's was taking the sweetness out of her success. Could the teaching of a few children balance the ruin of their brother? How impossible not to accuse herself of the change in him! She felt it every time she saw him.

At last Lucy saw clearly that her duty consisted in a choice between giving up her welfare work there and winning Edd Denmeade back to what he had been before she came. Thought of abandoning that work would scarcely stay before her consciousness, yet she forced herself to think of it. She had found a congenial, uplifting vocation for herself. But it was one that she could give up, if it were right to do so. There were other things she could find to do. Coming to think of the change in the Denmeade household, the cleanliness and brightness, the elimination of unsanitary habits, the saving of labor, the development of the children's minds, she could not persuade herself that it would be otherwise than cowardice for her to quit now.

"I must stay," soliloquized Lucy, at last seeing clearly. "If I quit now, all my life I'd be bitter because I failed of the opportunity I prayed for. . . . Then, if stay I must save Edd Denmeade. . . . It would be welfare work of the noblest kind. . . . What it costs me must not matter."

Lucy deliberately made the choice, for good or ill to herself, with her eyes wide open and all her faculties alive to the nature of her task and the limits it might demand. Her home life had inured her to sacrifice. That thought brought her back to Clara and the letter which lay open in her lap. With a wrench of her spirit she took it up and reread:

FELIX, *July 10.*

DEAREST LUCY:

I came back from Mendino to find you gone. I deserved my disappointment, because I've never written you. But, Lucy, it wasn't because I'd forgotten. I was ashamed. I eloped with Jim, as you know, because father had no use for him. Well, if I had listened to you I'd not be miserable and alone now. Jim turned out worse than anyone thought. He didn't even marry me. I'm as much to blame for the whole business as he. The most shameful thing for me, however, was to discover I didn't love him. I was just crazy.

Father shut the door in my face. I've been staying with an old schoolmate, Mamie Blaize, who has been kind. But, Lucy, I can't stay here. Felix will be no place for me, after they find out.

I went to the State Department who employ you. From them I got your address. The woman there was very nice. She spoke of your success, and that you had paved the way for extensive welfare work in other parts of the state. Lucy, I'm proud of you. It was always in you—to do good.

I'm not very well or very strong. Won't you please let me come out there and stay with you? I'll get well and I'll work my fingers to the bone for you. Let me show you I've had my bitter lesson. I need you, Lucy dear, for sometimes I grow reckless. I have horrible spells of blues. I'm afraid. And if you fail me I don't know what in the world I'll do. But you won't fail me. I seem to feel that deep inside me. It makes me realize what I lacked.

Send me money at once to come, and tell me what to do—how to get there. Please, Lucy, I beg you. I'm in the dust. To think after scorning your love and advice I'd come crawling on my knees to you! Judge what has happened to me by that. Hurry and write.

Love,
CLARA.

This letter saddened Lucy more because of its revival of memory of the beloved little sister than the news it contained. Lucy had never expected anything but catastrophe for Clara. It had come, and speedily. Clara had been away from Felix a year and a half. She was now nearly nineteen. This frank letter revealed a different girl.

Lucy reread it, pondered over what she confessed, wept over the ruin of her, yet rejoiced over the apparent birth of soul. Clara had never been one to beg. She had been a sentimental, headstrong girl and she could not be restrained. Lucy forgave her now, sorrowed for the pitiful end of her infatuation for the cowboy Jim Middleton, and with a rush of the old sisterly tenderness she turned to her table to answer that letter. Her response was impulsive, loving, complete, with never a word of reproach. She was accepting Clara's changed attitude toward life as an augury of hope for the future. She would help take the burden of responsibility for that future. It was never too late. Clara must reconstruct her life among new people, and if her disgrace became public she could never return to Felix. Better perhaps that Felix become only a memory!

Lucy concluded that letter with interesting bits of information about this wilderness country, the beauty of its forests, and the solitude of its backwoods homes. She did not include any remarks anent the stalwart young backwoodsmen or their susceptibilities to the charms of young girls. Even as she thought of this Lucy recalled Clara's piquant, pretty face, her graceful form, her saucy provocative ways. How would Edd Denmeade, and that fine quiet brother Joe, respond to the presence of the pretty sister? Lucy had to dispel misgivings. The die was cast. She would not fail the erring Clara. Inclosing a money order on her office, Lucy sealed the letter and stamped it with an air of finality and a feeling of relief and happiness. It had taken a calamity to drive Clara to her heart and protection.

"There!" she breathed low, almost with a sob. "That's done, and I'm glad. . . . Come to remember, that's the second decision in regard to my problem. There was a third—when should I leave the Denmeades? . . . I can't leave just yet. I will stay. They have begged me to stay. . . . It cannot matter, just so long as I do my duty by these other families."

Then Lucy assuaged her conscience and derived a

strange joy out of the decision she had made. Where might they lead her? The great forest arms of the wilderness seemed to be twining round her. She was responding to unknown influences. Her ideals were making pale and dim the dreams she had once cherished of her own personal future—a home—children—happiness. These were not for everyone. She sighed, and cast away such sentiment.

"Edd would say I'm bogged down in welfare work," she said. "Now to go out and begin all over again!"

It seemed significant that as she stepped out of her tent she espied Edd stalking the lane toward the cabin. He had not been home for days and his ragged apparel showed contact with the woods. As Lucy halted by the gate to wait for him she felt her heart beat faster. Whatever sensations this wild-bee hunter roused, not one of them was commonplace.

"Good morning, Edd," said Lucy, cheerfully, as if that greeting had always been her way with him. "You're just the person I want to see. Where have you been so long?"

"Howdy!" he replied as he stopped before her. He gave her one of his piercing looks, but showed no surprise. He appeared thin, hard, hungry, and strained. He had not shaved for days, and his dark downy beard enhanced the strange wild atmosphere that seemed to cling round him. "I've been linin' new bees. Reckon it was high time I set to work. It's shore a fine year for bees. You see, there wasn't much rain. A rainy spring makes lots of yellow-jackets, an' them darn insects kill the wild bees an' steal their honey. This dry season keeps down the yellow-jackets. Reckon I'll have my best year findin' honey. Lined two trees to-day."

"When will you get the honey?" inquired Lucy.

"Not till after frost comes. October is best."

"Will you take me some day when you line bees and also when you get the honey?" asked Lucy, plunging headlong into her chosen task. She wanted to burn her bridges behind her. If she listened to caution and selfish doubts she could never keep to her decision. She expected her deliberate request to amaze Edd and cause him to show resentment or bitterness. But he exhibited neither.

"Shore will. Any time you say," he drawled, as he dragged his trailing rope to him and coiled it.

"I've news for you. I'm having my sister Clara come out to live with me," she announced.

"Shore that'll be good," he replied, with interest. "How old is she an' what's she like?"

"Clara is nearly nineteen. She's blond, very different from me. And very pretty."

"Wal, you're light-headed yourself, an' I reckon not so different."

"Edd, are you paying me a compliment?" she asked, archly.

"Nope. I just mean what I say. When'll your sister come?"

"If all goes well she'll arrive in Cedar Ridge on the stage Wednesday week. But some one must ride in to-morrow so my letter can catch Monday's stage."

"Give it to me. I'm ridin' to Cedar Ridge this afternoon."

"Edd, did you intend to go anyway?"

"Wal, reckon I didn't," he declared, honestly. "I've had about enough of town."

"You've been drinking and fighting?"

"Shore," he answered, simply, as if there were no disgrace attached to that.

"I don't want you to go to town with my letter unless you promise me you'll neither drink nor fight," she said, earnestly.

Edd laughed. "Say, you're takin' interest in me mighty late. What for?"

"Better late than never. I refuse to discuss my reasons. But will you promise?"

"Wal, yes, about the white mule. Sorry I can't promise about fightin'. I've too many enemies I've licked, an' if I happened to run into one of them, drunk or no drunk, they'd be a-rarin' to get at me."

"Then I'd rather you stayed away from Cedar Ridge."

"Wal, so would I. Honest, Lucy, I'm sort of sick. Don't

know what it is. But to-day in the woods I began to feel a little like my old self. It's bee huntin' I need. To get away from people!"

"People will never hurt you, Edd. It's only that you will not like them. . . . Tell me, have you had trouble with Bud Sprall?"

"Nope. Funny, too. For Bud's been lookin' powerful hard for me. He never goes to town an' I never go to dances, so we haven't bucked into each other."

"What's this trouble between you and Bud? Doesn't it date back to that dance you took me to?"

"Wal, it's part because of somethin' he said about you at that dance. I'd have beat him half to death right there, only I didn't want to spoil your good time."

He seemed apologizing to her for a softness that he regretted.

"About me!" exclaimed Lucy, in surprise. "What was it?"

"Reckon I'm not hankerin' to tell," he replied, reluctantly. "Shore I always blamed myself for lettin' it happen. But that night I was plumb locoed."

"Edd, if it is something you *can* tell me, do so at once," demanded Lucy.

"Wal, I can tell it easy enough," returned Edd, with a smile breaking the hardness of his grimy face. "Bud just bragged about peepin' through the cracks of the shed back of the schoolhouse. Swore he watched you undress."

"Oh—the sneak!" burst out Lucy, suddenly flaming.

"Wal, don't let the idea upset you," drawled Edd. "For Bud was a liar. He never saw you. He just hatched that up after you wouldn't give him the other dance."

"How do you know?" queried Lucy, in swift relief.

"Reckon I didn't know that night. But shore I found out afterward. I rode down to the schoolhouse an' looked. There wasn't a crack in that shed anywheres. Not a darn one! You can bet I was careful to make shore. Bud just lied, that's all. He's always been a liar. But I reckon I hold it as much against him as if he had seen you. . . . An' now there's more I'm sore about."

Lucy did not delve into her mind to ascertain why she

had no impulse to nullify Edd's anger against Bud Sprall. The subject seemed natural to Edd, but it was embarrassing for her.

"How about my letter?" she asked, ignoring his last speech.

"Gerd's ridin' in to-day an' he'll go by here. Fetch me the letter an' I'll see he gets it."

Lucy ran back to her tent, and securing it she returned to hand it to Edd, with a word as to its importance.

"Shore. More trouble for us backwoods boys!" he ejaculated, amicably, as he grinned.

"Trouble! What do you mean?" she asked, though she knew perfectly well.

"Another pretty girl ridin' in," he rejoined, with a hint of pathos, "an' one that wouldn't an' couldn't care a darn for the likes of us."

"Edd, that is unkind," protested Lucy, uncertain how to meet such speeches of his. There seemed only one course to pursue and that called on all her courage.

"Reckon it is. I'm not as kind feelin' as I used to be."

"Indeed you're not," returned Lucy, hastily. "And I want to talk to you about that. Not now. Sometime when you're rested and cheerful. . . . Come here. I want to show you what I have done during this last absence of yours."

She led him across the open clearing and along a new-cut path into the woods. It ended abruptly on the edge of the gully. A board walk had been erected on poles, extending some yards out over the gully, to a point just above the spring. By means of a pulley and rope a bucket could be lowered into the spring and hauled up full of water, at very little expenditure of energy. Lucy demonstrated it with ease, showing the great saving of time and effort. Mrs. Denmeade and Allie had been compelled to make many trips a day to this spring, going down the steep trail and climbing back.

"Now what do you say to me? I thought that out and had your father and Uncle Bill put it up," declared Lucy, with pride.

Edd appeared to be either dumfounded or greatly im-

pressed. He sat down rather abruptly, as if this last mani-
festation of Lucy's practical sense had taken something
out of him.

"Simple as a b c," he ejaculated. "Why didn't pa or
me—or somebody think of that long ago? I reckon ma
an' Allie are ashamed of us."

His torn black sombrero fell to the ground, and as he
wiped his moist face with a soiled scarf his head drooped.
How tremendously he seemed to be struggling with a
stolid mind! He resembled a man learning to think. Finally
he looked up squarely at her.

"Reckon I'm about licked," he declared. "I've been
dyin' hard—Miss Lucy Watson from Felix. But thick as
I am I'm shore no darned fool. This here job to make
fetchin' water easy for ma an' Allie is shore enough to
make me kick myself. It makes me understand what you
mean. I was against you. Every time I came home ma
showed me somethin' new. Shore that livin' room, as they
call it now, seemed no place for my boots an' spurs an'
chaps—for *me*. But I couldn't help seein' a difference in
ma an' Allie an' the kids. They began to look like that
room, with its furniture an' curtains an' pictures an' rugs
an' bright both day an' night. Reckon I can't tell you just
how, but it felt so to me. Clean clothes, pretty things,
must mean a lot to women an' kids. . . . An' so I'm comin'
down off my hoss an' I'm thankin' you."

"Then you really believe I'm helping to make your
people live better and happier?" asked Lucy, earnestly.

"It's hard for me to knuckle, but I do. I'm not blind.
You've been a blessin' to us," he replied, with emotion.

"But—Edd," she began, hurriedly, "I—I haven't helped
you."

"Me! . . . Wal, some fellows are beyond helpin'. I'm
a savage. A big fool! . . . Only a wild-bee hunter!"

As his head drooped and his bitter reply ended Lucy
divined the havoc that had been wrought by those words
of hers, uttered long weeks before, in an anger she could
not brook. He had taken them to heart. Lucy yearned to
retract them, but that was impossible.

"Edd, judged by my standard for men, you were—

what I called you," she said. "But I was unjust. I should have made allowance for you. I was hot-tempered. You insulted me. I should have slapped you good and hard."

"Wal, reckon I could have stood that," he replied. "You must have heard what Sadie an' other girls called me. An' *you* said it, too. Shore that was too much for me."

"If you'll promise not to—to talk the way you did then—never again, I'll forgive you," said Lucy, hesitatingly.

"Wal, don't worry, I'll shore never do it again. But I'm not askin' you to forgive me," he returned, bluntly, and rising, he stalked away toward the cabin.

Lucy realized that somehow she had been too impulsive, too hasty in her approach toward friendliness. Perhaps the old lofty superiority had unwittingly cropped out again. Nevertheless, something had been gained, if only her deeper insight into this wild-bee hunter. He was vastly ignorant of an infinite number of things Lucy knew so well. Somehow she had not accorded him a depth of emotion, a strength of individuality, the same that abided in her. Because he was a backwoodsman she had denied him an intimate personal sense of himself. She had not tried to enter into his way of looking at life or people or things. As far as he was concerned she had been a poor judge of humanity, a poor teacher. No easy task would it be to change him. Her reflection brought out the fact that the brief conversation with him had only added to her concern. His confession gratified her exceedingly. She had wanted more than she knew to have him see that she was helping his people to a better and happier life. How powerfully this motive of hers had seized hold of her heart! It had become a passion. He had called her a blessing to his family. That was sweet, moving praise for Lucy. No matter how he had been hurt in his crude sensitiveness, he surely was grateful to her. He was not wholly unapproachable. Only she must be tactful, clever, sincere. The last seemed the most important. Perhaps Edd Denmeade would see through tact and cleverness. Lucy pondered and revolved in mind the complexity of the situation. It must be made so that it was no longer complex. The solution did not dawn on her then, but she divined that she could learn more about him through his love of bees and the forest where he roamed.

Mary Denmeade espied Lucy sitting by the path to the spring, and, as always, she ran to her. The children could not get enough of Lucy's companionship. Through her their little world had widened wonderfully. Games and books, work and play, had already made incalculable differences. These backwoods children were as keen mentally as any children Lucy had been associated with in the city, and vastly easier to interest.

"Here you are," cried Mary, excitedly, her eyes wide. "Edd is scolding Mertie. She's awful mad. So's ma. But ma is mad at Mertie and Mertie's mad at Edd."

"Oh, I'm sorry, Mary. Perhaps I had better not go in yet," returned Lucy. "What's the trouble? Isn't it very strange for Edd to scold anyone, much less Mertie?"

"Strange? I don't know. He never scolds any of us *but* Mertie. Ma says it's because he loves her best. . . . Miss Lucy, Edd's not like he used to be. He stays away more an' when he does come home he's no time for us. Mertie said he was moony about you."

"Was that what caused the trouble?" asked Lucy, quickly.

"Oh no. Mertie said that a long time ago. . . . I wasn't in the kitchen, but I peeped in and heard him say: 'Mert, you've been ridin' with Bud Sprall again.' An' Mertie said: 'I've no such thing. But it'd be no business of yours if I had.' An' Edd said: 'Don't lie to me. Some one saw you.' Then Mertie had one of her bad spells. She raved an' cried. Ma took her part. Edd got hold of Mertie an' said he'd choke the truth out of her. He looked awful. Ma made him let Mertie go. An' Edd said: 'Wal, you stayed last night at Claypool's. Now what time did you get there after school?' Mertie said she couldn't remember. She had the reddest spots in her cheeks an' she couldn't look at Edd."

"Mary, did you listen to all that?" asked Lucy, disapprovingly, as the child halted to catch her breath.

"I couldn't help hearing," went on Mary. "But I did peep in the door. But they didn't see me. Edd said: 'I had a hunch before, Mert Denmeade. An' yesterday when I was told by some one who seen you I just rode down to Claypool's, an' I found out you didn't get there till near dark. Took you three hours to ride from school to Amy's home! I asked Amy when she seen you last. She looked darn queer, but I made her tell. You went off down the road with Sadie Purdue.' Then ma pitched into Mertie so mad that I run."

Lucy soothed the excited child and importuned her not to tell anyone else about the family quarrel and that perhaps it was not so much against Mertie as it looked. Mary shook her head dubiously, and presently, finding Lucy preoccupied, she gravitated toward the other children playing in the yard.

This was not the first time Lucy had been cognizant of an upset among the Denmeades owing to Mertie's peculiar ways of being happy. She had been the idol of the family, solely, no doubt, because of her prettiness. Lucy considered Mertie a vain little ignoramus with not enough character to be actually bad. Nevertheless, Lucy reflected, she might be as mistaken in Mertie as she had been in Edd. Of all the Denmeades, this second daughter was the easiest to influence because of her vanity. Lucy had won the girl's regard with a few compliments, a few hours of instruction in dressmaking, and perhaps that was why Lucy did not value it very highly. Still, for Edd's sake, and, more seriously considered, for the girl's sake also, Lucy was now prepared to go to any pains to bring about a happier relation between brother and sister. Perhaps, however, before she could be accused of meddling in personal affairs she had better wait until her kind offices were invited.

On her way back to her tent she heard the gate chain clank violently, and upon turning she espied Edd stalking away, black as a thundercloud. Should she let him go or halt him? Inspirations were not altogether rare with Lucy, but she had one now that thrilled her. This was her opportunity. She called Edd. As he did not appear to hear, she raised her voice. Then he wheeled to approach her.

"My, but you were tramping away fast and furiously!" said Lucy, amiably.

"Reckon I was. What you want?"

"Are you in any great hurry?"

"No, I can't say I am. Fact is I don't know where I'm goin'. But I'm a-rarin' to go, just the same." His voice was strained with spent passion and his lean face seemed working back to its intent, still expression.

"Come over in the shade and talk with me," said Lucy, and led him into the pines to a nook overlooking the gully, where she often sat. Plain it was that Edd followed her under compulsion. But this rather stimulated than inhibited Lucy.

"Don't go away angry," she began, and seating herself on the clean brown pine mats, she clasped her knees and leaned back to look up at him.

"Reckon it's not with you," he rejoined, drawing his breath hard.

"Of course not. I know what's wrong. Mary heard you quarreling with Mertie. She told me. . . . Now, Edd, I wouldn't for worlds meddle in your affairs. But my job is as wide as your woods. It's hard for me to tell where to leave off. The question is, if I can be good for Mertie, you want me to, don't you?"

"Wal, I shore do," he declared, forcibly. "More'n once I had a hunch to ask you. But I—I just couldn't."

"You should have. I'm sorry I've been so—so offish. It's settled, then. Now tell me what you think is wrong with Mertie."

"Reckon I don't think. I know," he replied, heavily. "Mertie is just plain no good. All she thinks of is her face an' of somethin' to deck herself in so she'll attract the boys. Any boy will do, though she sticks up her nose at most of them, just the same. She's got one beau, Bert Hall, who lives in Cedar Ridge. Bert is sweet on Mertie an' I know she likes him best of all the fellows who run after her. Bert owns a ranch an' he's got a share in his father's sawmill. Course he wants to marry Mertie an' Mertie wants to run wild. Dance an' ride! I reckon Sadie Purdue hasn't helped her none. . . . Wal, this summer

Mertie has taken on airs. She says if she's old enough to be asked to dances an' to marry, she's her own boss. Pa an' ma can't do nothin' with Mertie. I used to hold her down. But shore—I've a hunch my time is past."

"Well?" queried Lucy, as he ended haltingly. "I understand. What about this Bud Sprall?"

"Mertie always liked that black-faced pup!" declared Edd, darkly. "She's been meetin' him on the sly. Not alone yet, but with Sadie, who's got the same kind of interest in Bud's pard, a hoss-wrangler who lives over Winbrook way. Mertie lied about it. . . . Wal, if I can't break it up one way I can another."

"You mean you'll go to Bud Sprall?" queried Lucy, instantly.

"I shore do," he said, tersely.

"You two will fight—perhaps spill blood," went on Lucy, intensely. "That might be worse than Mertie's affair with Bud, whatever it is. Edd, surely it is just a flirtation."

"Reckon I fooled myself with ideas like that," returned Edd, bluntly. "Boys an' girls up here do their flirtin' at dances. Straight out, Miss Lucy, this here sneakin' has a bad look. I know Sadie Purdue. She jilted me because I was too slow. Reckon she'd never have married me. Funny thing is she *never* would, even if she'd wanted to, because I found her out. Nobody but you knows that. Wal, Mertie is thick with Sadie. An' they're meetin' these boys. Reckon you know how it will end, unless we stop it. Bert's an easy-goin' boy. But Mertie could go too far. . . . You see, Miss Lucy, you haven't guessed yet just how —how thick many of us backwoods boys an' girls get. Not me! That's one reason why I'm a big boob. . . . An' I always hoped an' prayed I could keep Mertie different. Shore it goes kind of hard to see I'm failin'."

"Edd, you've failed yourself," asserted Lucy, ringingly. "You're on the down grade yourself. You've taken to the bottle and to fights. How can you expect to influence your sister to go straight if you're no good yourself?"

"By God! that shore's been—eatin' into me!" he ejaculated, huskily, and hid his somber face in his grimy hands.

"Oh, I'm glad you see it!" cried Lucy, putting a hand

on his shoulder. "Edd, you must come back to your old self."

"Yes, I reckon I have to," he agreed. "If only it's not too late—for Mertie!"

"Let us hope and pray it is not," rejoined Lucy, earnestly. "I'm shocked at what you say, but yet I feel absolutely sure Mertie is still good. She's vain, she's wild. I know her kind. And, Edd, I promise to devote myself to Mertie. I must go to Felix for a week this fall. I'll talk about that to Mertie, hold it out to her. I'll take her with me. Oh, I know how to manage her. We'll marry her to Bert before she knows it."

"Wal, what ma said about you is shore true," he said, lifting his dark face stained with tears. "An' I'll make you a promise."

"Yes?" queried Lucy, encouragingly.

"I'll go back to my wild-bee huntin'."

Lucy divined the import of that strange promise and she rejoiced over it, happily proud for him and the Denmeades.

CHAPTER VIII

The news that Lucy's sister was coming spread all over the immediate country. Lucy was hugely amused at the number of gallants who visited Denmeade's on Sunday and found transparent excuses to interview her. There was no use to try to avoid them on the issue that portended.

Lucy exhibited Clara's picture with conscious pride, and did not deem it necessary to explain that the likeness dated back several years. She was both delighted and concerned over the sensation it created. Of all the boys she had met there, Joe Denmeade appeared to be the quietest and nicest, the least given to dances, white mule, and girls. Lucy experienced one acute qualm of conscience before she approached Joe to ask him to meet her sister at Cedar Ridge. That qualm was born of a fear that Joe might meet his downfall in Clara. She silenced it with the resigned conviction that circumstances were beyond her. What a feeble little woman she was!

Sunday afternoon on the Denmeade porch found the usual visiting crowd largely augmented. Sam Johnson paid his first call for weeks, this time without Sadie. He seemed less debonair and obtrusive than had been his wont. Least of all did he question Lucy about the pretty sister, but he drank in all that was said. Lucy watched Sam closely as he looked at Clara's picture; and soberly she judged by his expression that, unless, as she devoutly hoped, Clara had changed, there would be some love-lorn gallants haunting the Denmeade homestead.

"When's she comin'?" queried Sam.

"I'll hear in to-morrow's mail. Wednesday or Saturday," replied Lucy.

"Reckon you're goin' in to meet her?"

"Indeed I am. Joe will drive me to town from the schoolhouse. Mr. Jenks has offered his buckboard."

"Joe! So he's the lucky cub?" snorted Sam. "Reckon you'd need a man."

Lucy's choice was news to all the listeners, including Joe himself, who, as usual, sat quietly in the background. She had shot him a quick glance, as if to convey they had an understanding. Whereupon Joe exhibited surprising qualifications for the trust she had imposed upon him.

"Sam, you don't get the hunch," he drawled. "Miss Lucy's sister isn't a well girl. She's goin' to need *rest!*"

The crowd was quick to grasp Joe's import, and they laughed their glee and joined in an unmerciful bantering of the great backwoods flirt.

After supper, as Lucy sat on the steps of her tent, Joe approached her.

"Now, teacher, how'd you come to pick on me?" he asked, plaintively.

"Pick on you! Joe, you don't mean——"

"Reckon I mean pick me *out,* as the lucky boy," he interrupted. "I'm just curious aboot it."

Lucy liked his face. It was so young and clean and brown, square-jawed, fine-lipped, with eyes of gray fire!

"Joe, I chose you because I think you will give my sister a better impression than any other boy here," replied Lucy, with deliberation.

"Aw, teacher!" he protested, as shyly as might have a girl. "Are you jokin' me? An' what you mean by this heah impression?"

"Joe, I ask you to keep what I tell you to yourself. Will you?"

"Why, shore!"

"My sister is not well and she's not happy. It would give her a bad impression to meet first thing a fellow like Sam or Gerd or Hal, who would get mushy on sight. Edd now would be too cold and strange. I ask you because I know you'll be just the same to Clara as you are to me. Won't you?"

"An' how's that, teacher?" he queried, with his frank smile.

"Why, Joe, you're just yourself!" answered Lucy, somewhat taken at a disadvantage.

"Never thought about bein' just like myself. But I'll try. I reckon you're not savvyin' what a big job you're givin' me. I mean pickin' me out to take you to town. If your sister comes on Saturday's stage every boy under the Rim will be there in Cedar Ridge. Reminds me of what I heard teacher Jenks say once. Some men are born great an' some have greatness thrust on them. Shore I'm goin' to be roped in that last outfit."

"I like you, Joe, and I want you to live up to what I think of you."

"Miss Lucy, are you shore aboot me bein' worth it?" he asked solemnly.

"Yes, I am. . . . To-morrow you stay till the mail comes for Mr. Jenks. He'll have mine. Then we'll know whether Clara is coming Wednesday or Saturday. I'd like you to borrow Edd's horse Baldy for Clara to ride up from the schoolhouse. Any horse will do for me. We'll have to leave early."

"It'd be better. I can drive in from the schoolhouse in

three hours. The stage arrives anywheres from eleven to four. I'm givin' you a hunch. We want to be *there* when it comes."

The following day when Joe rode home from school he brought Lucy's mail, among which was the important letter from Clara—only a note, a few lines hastily scrawled, full of a wild gratitude and relief, with the news that she would arrive at Cedar Ridge on Saturday.

"It's settled, then, she's coming," mused Lucy, dreamily. "I don't believe I was absolutely sure. Clara was never reliable. But now she'll come. There seems some kind of fate in this. I wonder will she like my wild, lonesome country."

Lucy had imagined the ensuing days might drag; she had reckoned falsely, for they were singularly full of interest and work and thought. Edd had taken to coming home early in the afternoons, serious and moody, yet intent on making up for his indifference toward Lucy's activities with his family. He veered to the opposite extreme. He would spend hours listening to Lucy with the children. He was not above learning to cut animals and birds and figures out of paper, and his clumsy attempts roused delight. Lucy had, in a way vastly puzzling to the Denmeades, succeeded in winning Mertie to a great interest in manual training, which she now shared with Mary. Edd wanted to know the why and wherefore of everything. He lent Dick a hand in the carpentry work, of which Lucy invented no end. And he showed a strange absorption at odd moments in the children's fairy-story books. He was a child himself.

Naturally, during the late afternoon and early evening hours of the long summer days he came much in contact with Lucy. She invited his co-operation in even the slightest tasks. She was always asking his help, always inventing some reason to include him in her little circle of work and play. She found time to ask him about his bee hunting, which was the one subject that he would talk of indefinitely. Likewise she excited and stimulated an interest in reading. As he read very slowly and laboriously, he liked best to listen to her, and profited most by that, but Lucy always saw he was left to finish the passage himself.

At night when all was dark and still, when she lay wide-eyed and thoughtful under the shadowy canvas, she would be confronted by an appalling realization. Her sympathy, her friendliness, her smiles and charms, of which she had been deliberately prodigal, her love for the children and her good influence on Mertie—all these had begun to win back Edd Denmeade from the sordid path that had threatened to lead to his ruin. He did not know how much of this was owing to personal contact with her, but she knew. Edd was unconsciously drawn toward a girl, in a way he had never before experienced. Lucy felt he had no thought of sentiment, of desire, of the old obsession that he "must find himself a woman." Edd had been stung to his soul by his realization of ignorance. She had pitied him. She had begun to like him. Something of pride, something elevating, attended her changing attitude toward him. What would it all lead to? But there could be no turning back. Strangest of all was for her to feel the dawn of a real happiness in this service.

Saturday morning arrived earlier for Lucy than any other she remembered. It came in the dark hour before dawn, when Joe called her to get up and make ready for the great ride to Cedar Ridge—to meet Clara. Lucy dressed by lamplight and had her breakfast in the dim, pale obscurity of daybreak. Mrs. Denmeade and Edd were the only others of the household who had arisen. Even the dogs and the chickens were asleep.

It was daylight when Lucy arrived at the corrals, where the boys had the horses saddled.

"I'd like to ride Baldy as far as we go horseback," said Lucy.

"Shore," replied Edd. "An' I reckon you'd better ride him back. For he knows you an' he might not like your sister. Horses have likes an' dislikes, same as people."

"Oh, I want Clara to have the pleasure of riding him."

"Shore she'll take a shine to him, an' then you'll be out of luck," drawled Edd as he held the corral gate open.

"Indeed, I hope she takes a shine to Baldy and everything here," declared Lucy, earnestly.

"Me an' Joe, too?" he grinned.

"Yes, both of you."

"Wal, I reckon it'll be Joe. . . . Good-by. We'll be lookin' for you all about sundown."

Joe rode into the trail, leading an extra horse, which would be needed upon the return; and he set off at a gait calculated to make time. Lucy followed, not forgetting to wave a gloved hand back at Edd; then she gave herself up to the compelling sensations of the hour and thoughts of the day.

There were scattered clouds in the sky, pale gray, pearly white where the light of dawn touched their eastern edges, and pink near the great bright flare above the Rim. The forest seemed asleep. The looming wall wandered away into the soft misty distance.

Joe did not take the schoolhouse trail, but the wilder and less traveled one toward Cedar Ridge. The woodland was dark, gray, cool. Birds and squirrels had awakened noisily to the business of the day. Deer and wild turkey ran across the trail ahead of the horses. The freshness and fragrance of the forest struck upon Lucy as something new and sweet. Yet the wildness of it seemed an old familiar delight. Green and brown and gray enveloped her. There were parts of the trail where she had to ride her best, for Joe was making fast time, and others where she could look about her, and breathe freely, and try to realize that she had grown to love this wilderness solitude. Her grandfather had been a pioneer, and her mother had often spoken of how she would have preferred life in the country. Lucy imagined she had inherited instincts only of late cropping out. How would her sister react to this lonely land of trees and rocks? Lucy hoped against hope. There was a healing strength in this country. If only Clara had developed mind and soul enough to appreciate it!

Lucy well remembered the dark ravine, murmurous with its swift stream, and the grand giant silver spruces, and the mossy rocks twice as high as her head, and the gnarled roots under banks suggestive of homes for wild cats, and the amber eddying pools, deep like wells, and the rushing rapids.

The climb out of this deep endlessly sloped canyon brought sight of sunrise, a rose and gold burst of glory over the black-fringed Rim. Then a brisk trot through a lighter and drier forest ended in the clearing of the Johnsons'.

Early as was the hour, the Johnsons were up, as was evidenced by curling blue smoke, ringing stroke of ax, and the clatter of hoofs. Mr. Jenks, too, was stirring, and soon espying Lucy, he hastened to come out to the fence.

"Mawnin', folks," he drawled, imitating the prevailing mode of speech. "Miss Lucy, I shore forgot this was your great day. Reckon I'm out of luck, for I'll not be here when you drive back. I'm going to visit Spralls', to see why their children are absent so much from school."

"Mr. Jenks, will you please take note of these Spralls, so you can tell me about them?" asked Lucy, eagerly. "I feel that I *must* go there, in spite of all I hear."

"Yes, I'll get a fresh line on them," he replied. "And if that isn't enough to keep you away I'll find other means."

"Oh, you are conspiring against me," cried Lucy, reproachfully.

"Yes, indeed. But listen, I've news for you," he went on as Joe led the unsaddled horses inside the fence. "Your sister's coming has given me a wonderful idea. When she gets well, which of course she will do here very quickly, why not let her take my school? Affairs at my home are such that I must return there, at least for a time, and this would provide me with a most welcome opportunity."

"I don't know," replied Lucy, doubtfully. "Clara had a good education. But whether or not she could or would undertake such a work, I can't say. Still, it's not a bad idea. I'll think it over, and wait awhile before I speak to her."

Mr. Jenks made light of Lucy's doubts, and argued so insistently that she began to wonder if there were not other reasons why he wanted a vacation. She had an intuitive feeling that he wanted to give up teaching, at least there, for good. They conversed a few moments longer, until Joe drove up in the buckboard. Then Mr. Jenks helped Lucy to mount the high seat beside Joe and bade them a merry good-by.

Whatever the trail had been, the road was jarringly new to Lucy. There developed ample reason for Joe's advice to "hang on to the pommel," by which he must have meant anything to hold on to, including himself. The big team of horses went like the wind, bowling over rocks, ruts, and roots as if they were not there at all. Lucy was hard put to it to remain in her seat; in fact, she succeeded only part of the time.

"Say—Joe," cried Lucy, after a particularly sharp turn, which the buckboard rounded on two wheels, and Lucy frantically clung to Joe, "are you—a regular—driver?"

"Me? Say, I'm reckoned the best driver in this heah country," he declared.

"Heaven preserve me—from the worst," murmured Lucy.

"You picked me out, Miss Lucy, an' I shore mean to beat that outfit of boys in to Cedar Ridge," said Joe. "The whole darned caboodle of them will be there. Gerd an' Hal slept heah all night with Sam. An' they're already gone. Suppose the stage beats us to Cedar Ridge! . . . Say, Sam is up to anythin'."

"Drive as fast as you want, only don't upset me—or something awful!" returned Lucy, desperately.

On the long descent of the cedared ridge Joe held the big team to a trot. Lucy regained her breath and her composure. When at last they turned out of the brush into the main road of the little town Lucy was both thrilled and relieved.

"Wal, heah we are, an' we beat the stage," drawled Joe.

"You must be a wonderful driver, Joe, since we actually got here," averred Lucy. "But there'll be no need to drive that way going back—will there?"

"Reckon we want Clara to know she's had a ride, don't we?" he queried, coolly.

"Joe!"

"What'd you pick me out for? Reckon I've got to be different from that outfit. Look at the hosses. Whole string of them!"

"You mean the boys will waylay us?" queried Lucy, anxiously.

"Like as not they'd bust this heah buckboard if I left it long enough. Shore they'll expect to meet Clara an' have a chance to show off. But we'll fool them. When the stage comes you grab her. Go in to Mrs. Lynn's an' get some grub to pack with us. Don't eat in there. Sam'll be layin' for that. Hurry out an' we'll leave pronto, before the gang get their breath."

"But, Joe, why all this—this fear of the boys, and the rush?" queried Lucy.

"Reckon you know the boys. They'll be up to tricks. An' on my side, since you picked *me,* I want to have Clara first."

"Oh, I—see!" ejaculated Lucy. "Very well, Joe. I trust you, and we'll do your way."

They reached the post office, where Joe reined in the team. Lucy espied a porch full of long-legged big-sombreroed clean-shaven young men, whose faces flashed in the sun.

"Miss Lucy, I'll feed an' water the hosses," said Joe. "Reckon you need a little stretch after that nice easy ride."

"It'll be welcome," declared Lucy, getting down. "You keep an eye open for the stage while I run in to see Mrs. Lynn."

By going into the hotel entrance Lucy avoided the boys slowly gravitating toward her. Mrs. Lynn greeted her most cordially, and was equally curious and informative. Lucy took advantage of the moment, while she was chatting, to peep out of the window. The cavaliers of Cedar Ridge lounged on the porch, and stalked to and fro. One group in particular roused Lucy's amused suspicions. Sam Johnson was conferring most earnestly with several of his cronies, two of whom were Hal Miller and Gerd Claypool. They were not particularly amiable, to judge from their faces. A gesture of Sam's attracted Lucy's gaze toward two picturesque riders, lean and dark and striking. She recognized the handsome face and figure of one of them. Bud Sprall! The other was a taller lither man, with flashing red face and flaming hair of gold. Young, bold, sinister, dissipated as he appeared, the virility and physical beauty of him charmed Lucy's eye.

"Who is that man—there, with Bud Sprall?" queried Lucy, trying to appear casual.

Mrs. Lynn peeped out. "I was askin' my husband that very question. He didn't know the fellow's name. Pard of Bud's he said. Two of a kind! Some of the boys told him Bud was thick with cowboys of the Rim outfit. This one is new in Cedar Ridge."

Presently as Joe appeared driving the buckboard to a shady place under a cottonwood, some rode from the front of the post office. Through the window, which was open, Lucy caught amusing and significant remarks.

"Howdy, boys!" drawled Joe, in answer to a unity of greetings.

"What you-all doin' here with them work clothes on?" queried one.

"Joe, yore shore kinda young to tackle this hyar city proposition," said another.

"Wal, Joe, I reckon you can't drive that big team with your left hand," asserted a third, banteringly.

"Hey, Joe, I see you're a Denmeade all over," said another. "But take a hunch from Edd's cold tricks."

These remarks and others in similar vein attested the dominant idea in the minds of these young countrymen— that a new girl was soon to appear upon the scene and that only one attitude was possible. She was to be seen, fought over humorously and otherwise, and to be won. It afforded Lucy much amusement, yet it was also thought-arresting.

She went out and climbed to a seat beside Joe, careful to appear very vivacious and smiling. The effect was to silence the bantering boys and to cause, on the part of Sam and several others, a gradual edging toward the buckboard. Lucy appeared not to notice the attention she was receiving and she quite bewildered Joe with a flood of rather irrelevant talk. Then one of the boys shouted that the stage was coming.

That checked all fun-loving impulses in Lucy. Her heart gave a lift and began to pound against her side. Glimpses she caught of the dusty well-remembered stage, while many thoughts flashed through her mind. Would Clara come, after all? How much had she changed? Would she be as sweet and repentant and appealing as her letters had implied? What a situation would arise if she did not like this wilderness country! Then a thrilling, palpitating joy that Clara had at last yearned for her!

The stage wheeled round the corner of cottonwoods, and the old driver, with great gusto and awareness of his importance, hauled the sweaty horses to a halt in front of the post office.

Lucy leaped down and ran. There was four or five passengers, and a great store of bags, boxes, and bundles, all of which she saw rather indistinctly. But as she reached the stage she cleared her eyes of tears and gazed up expectantly, with a numbness encroaching upon her tingling nerves. Clara might not have come.

There was a hubbub of voices. Manifestly others of these passengers had friends or relatives waiting.

"Hello—Lucy!" cried a girl's excited, rather broken voice.

Lucy almost screamed her reply. Behind a heavy old woman, laboriously descending the stage steps, Lucy espied a slim, tall, veiled girl clad in an ultra-fashionable gown and hat the like of which had not been seen at Cedar Ridge. Lucy knew this was her sister, but she did not recognize her. As the girl stepped down to the ground she threw back her veil, disclosing a pale face, with big haunting blue eyes that seemed to strain at Lucy with hunger and sadness. Indeed it was Clara—vastly changed!

"Sister!" cried Lucy, with a sudden rush of tenderness. Clara met her embrace, mute and shaking. How strange and full that moment! Lucy was the first to think of the onlookers, and gently disengaging herself from clinging hands she burst out: "Oh, I—I didn't know you. I was

afraid you'd not be in the stage. . . . I'm so glad I'm half
silly. . . . Come, we'll go in the hotel a moment. . . . Don't
mind all this crowd."

Thus Lucy, talking swiftly, with no idea of what she
was saying, led Clara away; but she was acutely aware of
the fierce clutch on her arm and the pearly whiteness of
her sister's cheek. Lucy did not dare look at her yet.

The sitting room inside the hotel happened to be
vacant. Clara did not seem to be able to do anything but
cling mutely to Lucy.

"You poor dear! Are you *that* glad to see me?" murmured Lucy, holding her close.

"Glad!—My God!" whispered Clara, huskily. "You'll
never—know how glad. For you've never—been without
—friends, love, home, strength."

"Oh, Clara, don't—don't talk so!" cried Lucy, in distress. "Don't break down here. Outside there are a lot of
young backwoods boys, curious to see you. We can't avoid
that. They are nice, clean, fine chaps, but crazy over
girls. . . . Don't cry. I'm so glad to see you I could cry
myself. Brace up. We'll hurry away from here. There's
a long ride in a buckboard and a short one on horseback.
You'll love the horse you're to ride. His name is Baldy.
You'll love the woods. I live in a tent, right in the pines."

This meeting had proved to be unexpectedly poignant.
Lucy had prepared herself for a few moments of stress,
but nothing like this. Clara seemed utterly changed, a
stranger, a beautiful, frail, haunted-eyed young woman.
Lucy was deeply shocked at the havoc in that face. It
told her story. But strange as Clara seemed, she yet radi-
ated something Lucy had never felt in the old days, and
it was love of a sister. That quite overpowered Lucy's
heart. It had come late, but not too late.

"Clara, I hope you're strong enough to go on to-day—
to my home," said Lucy, gently.

"I'm not so weak as that," replied Clara, lifting her
face from Lucy's shoulder. It was tear-stained and convulsive. "I was overcome. I—I never was sure—till I saw
you."

"Sure of what?" asked Lucy.

"That you'd take me back."

"You can be sure of me forever. I can't tell you how happy it makes me to know you want to come. . . . Let us sit here a few moments. As soon as you rest a little and compose yourself we'll start. I've ordered a lunch which we'll eat as we ride along."

"Ought I not tell you—about my trouble—my disgrace —before we go?" asked Clara, very low.

"Why should you—now?" rejoined Lucy, in surprise.

"It might—make a difference."

"Oh no! You poor unhappy girl. Do you imagine anything could change me? Forget your troubles," returned Lucy, tenderly.

"I wanted to—at least when I met you after so long a separation. But those tall queer men outside. Such eyes they had! They must know about me."

"Only that you're my sister and coming to stay with me," said Lucy, hurriedly. "They've ridden into town to see you—meet you. Don't worry. They won't meet you. I have told only that you were ill."

Clara seemed passionately grateful for Lucy's thoughtfulness. She had little to say, however, yet listened strainingly to Lucy.

A little later, when they left the hotel, Clara had dropped the veil over her white face, and she clung closely to Lucy. Meanwhile Joe had driven up to the high porch, from which Lucy helped her sister into the buckboard.

"Clara, this is Joe Denmeade," said Lucy as she stepped in beside Clara.

Joe quaintly doffed his huge sombrero and spoke rather bashfully. Lucy was pleased to see his fine brown, frank face smile in the sunlight.

"Wal, reckon we're all heah," he said, briskly. "The stage driver gave me five valises—four big an' one small. They were tagged Clara Watson. I packed them in. An' if that's all the baggage we can be movin' along."

"That is all, thank you," returned Clara.

"Miss Lucy, did you fetch the lunch?" asked Joe, with his eye on the boys, who had nonchalantly sauntered closer to the buckboard.

"I have it, Joe. Drive away before——" whispered Lucy.

Sam Johnson, the foremost of the group, stepped forward to put a foot on the wheel of the buckboard. His manner was supremely casual. No actor could have done it better.

"Howdy, Joe! Good afternoon, Miss Lucy," he drawled, blandly.

Lucy replied pleasantly, and introduced him to Clara, and after they had exchanged greetings she added: "Sorry we've no time to chat. We must hurry home."

Sam made rather obtrusive efforts to pierce Clara's veil. Then he addressed Joe: "My hoss went lame comin' in, an' I reckon I'll ride out with you."

"Awful sorry, Sam," drawled Joe, "but I've got a load. Heah's Miss Clara's five valises, an' a pack of truck for ma."

"I won't mind ridin' in the back seat with the girls," rejoined Sam, in the most accommodating voice.

"Shore reckon you wouldn't," returned Joe, drily. "But this heah's Mr. Jenks's buckboard an' he asked me particular not to load heavy. So long, Sam."

Joe whipped the reins smartly and the team started so suddenly that Sam, who had been leaning from the porch with one foot on the wheel, was upset in a most ridiculous manner. The boys on the porch let out a howl of mirth. Lucy could not repress a smile.

"Serves him right," said Joe. "Sam's shore got a nerve. All the time with Sadie in town!"

"Joe! Did you see her?" asked Lucy, quickly.

"I shore did. She was across the road, peepin' out of Bell's door when Sam got that spill."

Lucy, relieved as well as amused at the quick start, turned to find Clara removing the veil. Her face was lightened by a smile. Slight as it was, it thrilled Lucy.

"Young men are—funny," she said, with a tinge of bitterness.

"Indeed they are," vouchsafed Lucy, heartily. "Well, we're free of that crowd. Joe, are they apt to ride after us?"

"Like as not," drawled Joe. "But the road is narrow. They shore can't pass us, an' all they'll get will be our dust."

"Suppose we eat lunch while we don't have to hold on," suggested Lucy. "Presently the road will be rough, and—to say the least, Joe drives."

"Let him drive as fast as he can," replied Clara, tensely. "Oh—the breeze feels so good! The air seems different."

"Clara, you'll find everything different up here. But I'm not going to say a word till you ask me. . . . Now, let's eat. We'll not get supper till dark or later. . . . Biscuits with jam. Chicken—and pie. Joe, I overheard one of those boys speak of your driving with one hand. So, surely you can drive and eat at the same time?"

"I reckon," rejoined Joe. "But see heah, Miss Lucy. Gerd Claypool said that, an' he shore didn't mean I'd be usin' my free hand to eat."

"Joe, do you think me so dense? Don't those boys ever think sense about girls?"

"Never that I reckoned. Edd used to be worse than any of them. But he's over it. I guess, since you came, Miss Lucy!"

Whereupon Clara's quick glance caught Lucy blushing, though she laughed merrily.

"Joe Denmeade! That is a doubtful compliment. . . . Come, you'd better begin to eat—this and this and this. . . . Clara, I get ravenously hungry up here. It's the wonderful air. I hope it will affect you that way."

Whereupon they fell to eating the ample lunch, during which time Lucy made merry. Nevertheless she took occasion now to observe Clara, unobtrusively, at opportune moments. Out in the clear bright sunlight Clara seemed indeed a pale frail flower. Always as a girl she had been pretty, but it would have been trivial to call her so now. Her face had strangely altered, and the only features remaining to stir her memory were the violet eyes and golden hair. They were the same in color, though Clara's eyes, that had once been audacious, merry, almost bold in their bright beauty, were now shadowed deeply with pain. Clara had been an unconscionable flirt; to-day no trace of pert provocativeness was manifest. Indeed, suffering, shock, whatever had been the calamity which was recorded there, had removed the callow coarseness of thoughtless adolescence, and had left a haunting, tragic charm. Lucy thought the transformation almost incredible. It resembled that birth of soul she had divined in Clara's letters. What had happened to her? Lucy shrank from the truth. Yet her heart swelled with wonder and ache for this sister whom she had left a wild girl and had found a woman.

By the time the lunch had vanished Joe was driving up the narrow zigzag road leading to the height of the cedared ridge. Here he ceased to look back down the road, as if no longer expecting the boys to catch up with him. But he lived up to his reputation as a driver.

"Reckon you froze them off," he said, at length. "Sam, anyhow. He'll shore never get over bein' dumped on the porch."

Lucy, talking at random, discovered that Clara was intensely interested in her welfare work in this backwoods community. Thus encouraged, Lucy began at the beginning and told the story of her progress in every detail possible, considering that Joe was there to hear every word. In fact, she talked the hours away and was amazed when Joe drove into the Johnson clearing.

"What a hideous place!" murmured Clara as she gazed around. "You don't live here?"

"No, indeed!" replied Lucy. "This is where Sam Johnson lives. We have a few miles to go on horseback. Clara, have you anything to ride in?"

"Yes; I have an old riding suit that I hate," said her sister.

"It doesn't matter how you feel about it," laughed Lucy. "Where's it packed? We can go into Mr. Jenks's tent while Joe tends to the horses."

Lucy conducted Clara to the teacher's lodgings, and then made some pretext to go outside. She wanted to think. She had not been natural. Almost fearing to look at Clara, yearning to share her burdens, hiding curiosity

and sorrow in an uninterrupted flow of talk, Lucy had
sought to spare her sister. What a situation! Clara the
incorrigible, the merciless, the imperious, crawling on her
knees! Lucy divined it was love Clara needed beyond
all else. She had been horribly cheated. She had cheated
herself. She had flouted sister, mother, home. Lucy began
to grasp here the marvelous fact that what she had
prayed for had come. Years before she had tried in
girlish unformed strength to influence this wayward sister.
When she gave up city life to come to the wilderness it
had been with the settled high resolve to do for others
what she had been forced to do for herself. The failure of
her home life had been its sorrow, from which had
sprung this passion to teach. She had prayed, worked,
hoped, despaired, struggled. And lo! as if by some omni-
scient magic, Clara had been given back to her. Lucy
choked over the poignancy of her emotion. She was
humble. She marveled. She would never again be shaken
in her faith in her ideals. How terrible to contemplate
now her moments of weakness, when she might have
given up!

Her absorption in thought and emotion was broken
by Clara emerging from the tent.

"Lucy, here's all that's left of me," she said, whim-
sically.

It was not possible then for Lucy to say what she
thought. Clara's remark about an old riding suit had
been misleading. It was not new, but it was striking.
Clara's slenderness and fragility were not manifest in this
outdoor garb. If she was bewitching to Lucy, what would
she be to these simple girl-worshiping backwoodsmen?

When Joe came up with the horses, and saw Clara,
there was no need for Lucy to imagine she exaggerated.
The look in his eyes betrayed him. But if he had been
struck as by lightning it was only for a moment. "Reckon
I can pack one of the valises on my saddle, an' carry
another," he said, practically. "To-morrow I'll fetch a
burro to pack home the rest. I'll put them in Mr. Jenks's
tent."

"This is Baldy. Oh, he's a dear horse!" said Lucy. "Get up on him, Clara. . . . Have you ridden lately?"

"Not so—very," replied Clara, with voice and face sharply altering. Then she mounted with a grace and ease which brought keenly home to Lucy the fact that Clara had eloped with a cowboy and had gone to live on a ranch south of Mendino. Clara had always been an incomparable rider.

Soon they were traveling down the road, Joe in the lead, Lucy and Clara side by side. For Lucy there was an unreality about the situation, a something almost like a remembered dream. Clara's reticence seemed rather to augment this feeling. Gradually there welled into Lucy's mind a happy assurance, tinged perhaps with sadness.

Once Clara remarked that it was new to her to ride in the shade. She began to show interest in the trees, and when they turned off on the trail into the forest she exclaimed, "Oh, how beautiful!"

Lucy was quick to observe that Clara managed Baldy perfectly, but she was not steady in the saddle. She showed unmistakable weakness. They rode on, silent, on and on, and then down into the deep green forest, so solemn and stately, murmurous with the hum of the stream. Clara subtly changed.

"If anything could be good for me, it would be this wild forest," she said.

"Don't say if, dear. It *will* be," responded Lucy.

"It makes me feel like going out of the cruel hateful light—that I hate to face—down into cool sweet shadow. Where I can feel—and not be seen!"

At the fording of the rushing brook Clara halted her horse as if compelled to speak. "Lucy, to be with you here will be like heaven," she said, low and huskily. "I didn't think anything could make me really want to live. But *here!* . . . I'll never leave this beautiful, comforting woods. I could become a wild creature."

"I—I think I understand," replied Lucy, falteringly.

From the last crossing of the rocky brook Clara appeared perceptibly to tire. Lucy rode behind her. Halfway up the long benched slope Clara said, with a wan smile:

"I don't know—I'm pretty weak."

Lucy called a halt then, and Joe manifested a silent solicitude. He helped Clara dismount and led her off the trail to a little glade carpeted with pine needles. Lucy sat down and made Clara lay her head in her lap. There did not seem to be anything to say. Clara lay with closed eyes, her white face and golden hair gleaming in the subdued forest light. Her forehead was wet. She held very tightly to Lucy's hand. Lucy was not unaware of the strange, rapt gaze Joe cast upon the slender form lying so prone. Several times he went back to the horses, and returned, restlessly. On the last of these occasions, as he reached Lucy's side Clara opened her eyes to see him. It was just an accident of meeting glances, yet to Lucy, in her tense mood, it seemed an unconscious searching, wondering.

"You think me—a poor weak creature—don't you?" asked Clara, smiling.

"No. I'm shore sorry you're sick," he replied, simply, and turned away.

Presently they all mounted again and resumed the journey up the slope. When they reached the level forest land above, Clara had to have a longer rest.

"What's that awful wall of rock?" she asked, indicating the towering Rim.

"Reckon that's the fence in our back yard," replied Joe.

"I couldn't very well jump that, could I?" murmured Clara.

Meanwhile the sun sank behind scattered creamy clouds that soon turned to rose and gold, and beams of light stretched along the wandering wall. Lucy thrilled to see how responsive Clara was to the wildness and beauty of the scene. Yet all she said was, "Let me live here."

"It'll be dark soon, and we've still far to go," returned Lucy, with concern.

"Oh, I can make it," replied Clara, rising. "I meant I'd just like to lie here—forever."

They resumed the ride. Twilight fell and then the forest duskiness enveloped them. The last stretch out of the woods and across the Denmeade clearing, up the lane, was ridden in the dark. Lucy leaped off and caught Clara as she reeled out of the saddle, and half carried her into the tent to the bed. The hounds were barking and baying; the children's voices rang out; heavy boots thumped on the cabin porch.

Lucy hastened to light her lamp. Joe set the valises inside the tent.

"Is she all right?" he asked, almost in a whisper.

"I'm—here," panted Clara, answering for herself, and the purport of her words was significant.

"She's worn out," said Lucy. "Joe, you've been very good. I'm glad I 'picked you,' as you called it."

"What'll I tell ma?" he asked.

"Just say Clara can't come in to supper. I'll come and fetch her something."

Joe tramped away in the darkness, his spurs jingling. Lucy closed the door, brightened the lamp, threw off gloves, hat, coat, and bustled round purposely finding things to do, so that the inevitable disclosure from Clara could be postponed. Lucy did not want to know any more.

"Come here—sit by me," said Clara, weakly.

Lucy complied, and felt a constriction in her throat. Clara clung to her. In the lamplight the dark eyes looked unnaturally big in the white face.

"I'm here," whispered Clara.

"Yes, thank Heaven, you are," asserted Lucy, softly.

"I must tell you—about——"

"Clara, you needn't tell me any more. But if you must, make it short."

"Thank you. . . . Lucy, you never saw Jim Middleton but once. You didn't know him. But what you heard was true. He's no good—nothing but a wild rodeo cowboy— a handsome devil. . . . I ran away with him believing in him—thinking I loved him. I was crazy. I might have —surely would have loved him—if he had been what I thought he was. . . . We went to a ranch, an awful hole, in the desert out of Mendino. The people were low trash. He told them we *were* married. He swore to me we *would* be married next day. I refused to stay and started off. He caught me, threatened me, frightened me. I was only a kid. . . . Next day we went to Mendino. There was no preacher nearer than Sanchez. We went there, and found he was out of town. Jim dragged me back to the ranch. There I learned a sheriff was looking for him. We had a terrible quarrel. . . . He was rough. He was not at all—what I thought. He drank—gambled. . . . Of course he meant to marry me. He wanted to do so in Felix. But I was afraid. We hurried away from there. But after . . . he didn't care—and I found I didn't love him. . . . To cut it short I ran away from him. I—couldn't go home So I went to work at Kingston. I tried several jobs. They were all so hard—the last one too much for me. I went downhill. . . . Then——"

"Clara," interrupted Lucy, distraught by the husky voice, the torture of that face, the passion to confess what must have been almost impossible, "never mind any more. That's enough. . . . You poor girl! Indeed you were crazy! But, dear, I don't hold you guilty of anything but a terrible mistake. You thought you loved this Jim Middleton. You meant well. If he had been half a man you would have turned out all right. God knows, no one can judge you harshly for your error. It certainly does not matter to me, unless to make me love you more."

"But—sister—I must tell you," whispered Clara, faintly.

"You've told enough. Forget that story. You're here with me. You're going to stay. You'll get well. In time this trouble will be as if it had never been!"

"But Lucy—my heart is broken—my life ruined," whispered Clara. "I begged to come to you—only for fear of worse."

"It's bad now, I know," replied Lucy, stubbornly. "But it's not as bad as it looks. I've learned that about life. I can take care of you, get back your health and spirit, let you share my work. Sister, there's no worse, whatever you meant by that. This wilderness, these backwoods people, will change your whole outlook on life. I *know,* Clara. They have changed me."

Mutely, with quivering lips and streaming eyes, Clara drew Lucy down to a close embrace.

CHAPTER IX

"Wal, didn't you-all invite yourselves to pick beans?" drawled Edd, coming out at the head of a procession of big and little Denmeades.

"Wal, we shore did aboot that," drawled Lucy, mimicking him. "Don't you see I'm rigged out to chase beans, bears, or bees?"

"Which reminds me you haven't gone wild-bee huntin' yet," said he, reflectively.

"Humph! I'd have to invite myself again to that, also," declared Lucy.

"Honest, soon as the beans are picked I'll take you. An' I've lined a new tree. Must have a lot of honey."

Mrs. Denmeade called out: "Make him stick to that, Miss Lucy. He's shore awful stingy about takin' anyone bee huntin'."

"Come, Clara," called Lucy, into the tent. "We're farmers to-day. Fetch my gloves."

When Clara appeared the children, Liz and Lize, made a rush for her and went romping along, one on each side of her, down the trail ahead of the procession. Lucy fell in beside Edd, and she was thinking, as she watched Clara adapting herself to the light steps of the youngsters, that the improvement in her sister was almost too good to be true. Yet the time since Clara had arrived at the Denmeades', measured by the sweetness and strength of emotion it had engendered, seemed very much longer than its actual duration of a few weeks.

"Wal, teacher, summer's about over," Edd was saying. "An' soon the fall dances will begin."

"Indeed? What a pity you can't go!" exclaimed Lucy, tantalizingly.

"Why can't I?"

"Because you vowed you had enough after taking *me* that time."

"Wal, reckon I did. But shore I could change my mind —same as you."

"Am I changeable? . . . I was only teasing, Edd. I got a hunch that you're going to ask me again."

"Correct. You're a smart scholar. How do you feel about goin'?"

"Shall I refuse, so you can indulge your—your wild-bee-hunter proclivities and pack me down on your horse?" queried Lucy, demurely.

"Sometimes I don't savvy you," he said, dubiously. "Reckon all girls have a little Sadie Purdue in them."

"Yes, they have, Edd, I'm ashamed to confess," replied Lucy, frankly. "I'd like to go with you. But of course that'll depend on Clara. To be sure, she's getting well, wonderful! It makes me happy. Still, she's far from strong enough for one of your dances."

"Joe asked her, an' she said she'd go if you went, too. I reckon she meant with me."

"Edd, you're learning from Sam Johnson."

"Nope, not me. I'd choke before I'd copy that honey-bee."

"So Joe asked her? . . . Well!" murmured Lucy, thoughtfully.

"Reckon she likes him, Lucy."

"Oh, I hope—I know she does. But, Edd——"

"Wal, I get your hunch," he interrupted. "You think maybe she oughtn't go with Joe because it'll only make him worse."

"Worse?" queried Lucy, turning to eye Edd.

"Yes, worse. But, Lucy, I reckon it couldn't be worse.

Joe thinks of Clara by day an' dreams of her by night. He's been that way since the day she came to us."

"Edd, you're pretty sharp. I imagined no one but me had seen that. I'm sure Clara hasn't. . . . It's a problem, Edd. But I knew it'd come."

"Wal, you're shore good at problems. What're you goin' to do about this one?"

"What would *you* do?" Lucy countered.

"I'd let Joe take her to the dance. You can manage her. Why, your slightest wish is law to Clara. That shore makes me think heaps of her. Wal, she could dance a few, an' look on some. Then we'd come home early."

"Would you promise that?"

"I shore would."

"Well, Edd, I'll think it over. You know if we go to this dance we'll be inclined to go again—perhaps often."

"Not with Joe an' me. I reckon this one would do us for a spell."

"Oh, that is different! And why?"

"Wal, you forget how you drove them boys crazy. I reckon this time, with Clara, you'd break up the dance. I've a hunch once would be enough for a spell. But shore I'd like it. So would Joe."

"Edd, this little sister of mine has broken up more than one dance—and a cowboy dance at that. Why couldn't we go and have a nice time, dance a little, and leave early, without what you hinted?—Fights!"

"That'd be easy, if you an' Clara could behave," he drawled.

"Edd Denmeade!" cried Lucy.

"Wal, you know you played hob with the boys. Why can't you be honest? Shore, Lucy, I wouldn't want to go if you did that again."

"All right. I promise to behave if I go. I'll talk to Clara."

"Wal, suit yourself. But I reckon you know I'll never go to another dance unless I can take you."

"Never?" echoed Lucy.

"Yes, never," he retorted.

"Why, Edd? That's a strong statement."

"Reckon because every dance before that one I was made fun of, most when I took a girl. But when I had you they didn't dare. That shore was sweet."

"Thanks, Edd. Sometimes you say nice things."

So they talked as they walked along the cool, sandy, pine-mat bordered trail. It was quite a walk from the cabin to what the Denmeades called the High Field. This was a level piece of ground, perhaps fifty acres in area, irregular in shape, and surrounded by the green forest of cedar and pine.

Of all the slashes cut into the woodland, this appeared to Lucy the most hideous. It was not a well-cultivated piece of ground. These Denmeades were hunters, wood-hewers, anything but farmers. Yet they were compelled to farm to raise food for themselves and grain for horses and hogs. Nevertheless, the hogs ran wild, subsisting most of the year upon roots, nuts, acorns, and what the back-woodsmen called mast.

A hundred or more dead trees stood scattered round over this clearing, cedars and pines and oaks, all naked and bleached and rotting on their stumps. They had been girdled by an ax, to keep the sap from rising, which eventually killed them. This was done to keep the shade of foliaged trees from dwarfing the crops. Corn and beans and sorghum required the sun.

It was the most primitive kind of farming. In fact, not many years had passed since Denmeade had used a plow hewn from the fork of an oak. High Field was fenced by poles and brush, which did not look very sure of keeping out the hogs. Right on the moment Danny and Dick were chasing hogs out of the field. Corn and weeds and yellow daisies, almost as large as sunflowers, flourished together, with the corn perhaps having a little advantage. The dogs were barking at some beast they had treed. Hawks and crows perched upon the topmost branches of the dead pines; woodpeckers hammered on the smooth white trunks; and the omnipresent jays and squirrels vied with each other in a contest calculated to destroy the peace of the morning.

Beyond the large patch of ground that had been planted in potatoes lay the three acres of beans, thick and brown in the sunlight. Beans furnished the most important article of food for the backwoods people. Meat, potatoes, flour, honey mostly in place of sugar, were essential and appreciated, but it was as Denmeade said, "We shore live on beans."

This triangle of three acres, then, represented something vastly important in their simple lives. They made the picking of beans a holiday, almost a gala occasion. Every one of the Denmeades was on hand, and Uncle Bill packed two big bags of lunch and a bucket of water. The only company present, considering that Lucy and Clara were not classified under this head, was Mertie's beau, young Bert Hall, a quiet boy whom all liked. Lucy regarded his presence there as a small triumph of her own. The frivolous Mertie really liked him, as anyone could plainly see. She had only been under the influence of Sadie Purdue. By a very simple expedient Lucy had counteracted and so far overcome this influence. She had devoted herself to Mertie; roused her pride through her vanity, subtly showed Bert's superiority to the other boys who ran after her, and lastly had suggested it would be nice to have Bert go with them to Felix. How important little things could become in this world of the Denmeades! It caused Lucy many pangs to reflect upon how often their lives went wrong for lack of a little guidance.

Manifestly Edd was the captain of this bean-picking regiment. He was conceded to be a great picker, and had a pride in his prowess second only to that of his lining of bees. Denmeade, the father, had two great gifts, according to repute—he could wield an ax as no other man in the country, and he was wonderful with his hunting hounds. Joe was the best one with horses, Dick with tools. Uncle Bill would plow when, according to him, all his relatives had been laid away in the fence corners. Thus they all excelled in some particular thing peculiarly important to their primitive lives.

"Wal, all hands get ready," called out Edd, cheerily.

"Reckon we got to clean up this patch to-day. You girls an' the kids can pick here in the shade. We'll pack loads of beans to you. . . . Bert, seein' you're company, I'll let you off pickin' out there in the sun. You can set with the girls. But I'm recommendin' you set between Lucy an' Clara. Haw! Haw!"

So the work of picking beans began. The children made it a play, a game, a delight, over which they screamed and fought. Yet withal they showed proficiency and industry.

The men fetched huge bundles of beans on the vines, and deposited them on the ground under the shady oaks at the edge of the field. Mrs. Denmeade and Allie picked with nimble and skillful hands. The girls sat in a little circle, with Bert in attendance and the children monopolizing all the space and most of the beans. Bert, having deposited piles of beans in front of each member of the party, was careful to sit down between Lucy and Clara, an action that caused Mertie to pout and laugh.

The process of stripping beans appeared a simple one to Lucy, yet she saw at once where experience counted. She could not do so well even as Mary. It piqued her a little. After all, intelligence and reason were not factors that could at once bridge the gap between inexperience and dexterity.

As they sat there talking and laughing and working, Lucy's thought ran on in pleasant and acquiring trend. Above all, what brought her happiness in this hour was the presence of her sister. Clara had begun to mend physically, and that, with the lonely environment, the simplicity of the Denmeades, the strength of natural things, had unconsciously affected her spiritually. She loved the children. She was intensely interested in their little lives. She fell to this fun of bean picking with a pleasure that augured well for the blotting of trouble from her mind. Clara had begun to be conscious of the superficiality of many sides and points of life in civilized communities. Here in the backwoods life seemed an easier, happier, simpler thing.

From time to time Lucy stole a look out into the

field at Edd, as he worked. He moved forward on his
knees, keeping a sack pushed in front of him, and his
hands flew. He was an engine of devastation to the rows
of beans. She seldom heard his voice. When he finished
a row he would get up, and gathering a huge bundle
of vines he would carry them to where the women were
picking. Dust and sweat had begrimed his face; his
shirt was wet through. There seemed something tremendously rugged, vital, raw about his physical presence.
He took this task seriously. Lucy wondered what was
going on in his mind. Did things she had talked of or
read to him revolve as he worked? There was a suggestion
of the plodding nature of his thought, strangely in contrast with the wonderful physical energy of his work.
She mused over the fact that she liked him as he was,
yet was striving to teach him, change him, put him on the
road to being a civilized man. Yet——! Something
vaguely regretful stirred deeply within her consciousness.

These more serious thoughts, however, only recurred
at intervals; for the most part she was alive to the objective task of learning to pick beans, and to the conversation around her. Allie Denmeade was as incessant a
talker as Joe was a listener; she had a shrewd wit and
a sharp tongue. Mertie was charming under favorable
influence and when she was receiving her meed of attention. Mrs. Denmeade had a dry geniality and a store of
wilderness wisdom. Mary was the sweet dreaming one
of the family.

Lucy had no idea that the noon hour had arrived
until the dusty men stalked in from the field, hungry
and thirsty, bringing with them an earthy atmosphere.

"Nineteen rows for me," declared Edd, "an' I'm
spittin' cotton. . . . Where's the bucket? I'll fetch fresh
water from the spring."

"Wal, ma, how'd you-all git along?" queried Denmeade, wiping his sweaty face.

"I disremember any better mawnin' for pickin'," she
replied. "Bert has been fillin' the sacks. Reckon there's
quite a few."

"Even dozen," exulted Bert.

"Good! We'll finish early. Edd shore is a cyclone for pickin' beans. . . . An' now, ma, spread out the grub. I'm a hungry old Jasper."

Uncle Bill carried forth the packs of food, which he had hidden from the children.

"It was a tolerable pickin', though I've seen better," he said. "The season's been dry an' thet's good for beans an' pickin' . . . . Wal, Lee, I'm noticin' Miss Lucy an' her sister have shore done themselves proud, fer tenderfeet."

Denmeade surveyed the respective piles of beans, one before Lucy, and a smaller one in front of Clara.

"Not so bad," he said, genially. "An' it shore is good to see you both settin' thar."

"Lee, tell their fortune with beans," suggested Mrs. Denmeade.

"I reckon I wouldn't risk that," he replied.

"Ma, you tell them. An' Bert's, too. It'll be fun. He's never been here to a bean pickin'," said Mertie.

"All the same, I had mine told once, down at Sadie's. Her old aunt told it," said Bert. "An' once is enough for me."

"A Mexican woman once told my fortune," interposed Clara, with a smile that was not all mirth. "It came true. And I—I don't want to know any more what's going to happen to me."

"Oh, I'm not afraid," called out Lucy. "Come, Mrs. Denmeade. Tell mine."

Whereupon Mrs. Denmeade, to the infinite delight of the children, selected some differently colored beans and pressed these into Lucy's palm. Then she intently studied Lucy's face, after which she struck the out-stretched hand, causing some of the beans to roll off and others to change position and settle.

"Wal, you're goin' to find happiness takin' some one else's troubles on your shoulders," said Mrs. Denmeade, impressively. "Your past has been among many people who didn't care for you. Your future will be among a few who love you. . . . I see a journey—a secret—somethin' that'll never come out—two dark years with white ones followin'. A child! . . . A cabin! A happy wife!"

This conclusion was greeted with a merry shout from the children and girls. Lucy, in her amusement, wished to carry the thing as far as possible to please them all. It struck her that Clara's faint color had vanished. How a few words could pain her! Lucy had no faith in any kind of fortune telling; she hardly took Mrs. Denmeade seriously.

"Wonderful!" she ejaculated. "Do the beans tell what kind of a husband I get?"

"No," rejoined Mrs. Denmeade, "but I reckon he won't be a city man."

"How interesting! I think I'm rather glad. Clara, I'm to have a country man for a husband. These red and white beans have foretold my fate."

She became aware then that Edd had returned and, standing behind her, evidently had heard her concluding words. Quite absurdly the fact embarrassed Lucy. The gay remarks forthcoming from all around fell upon her somewhat unfelicitously.

"Wal, Lucy, I see ma an' Allie have worked an old trick on you," he drawled. "Shore I told you to look out for them."

"Oh—it was only fun!" exclaimed Lucy, relieved despite her common sense.

Mrs. Denmeade smiled enigmatically. She seemed to possess some slight touch of mysticism, crude and unconscious. Lucy dispelled any idea that there was connection between the red and white beans and Mrs. Denmeade's prophecies. For that reason she found herself fixing in mind the content of those statements regarding her past and future.

"Come set around, folks," called Uncle Bill, with gusto.

The lunch hour of the bean pickers was as merry as a picnic dinner. The Denmeades had rushed through the morning hours; now they had leisure to eat slowly and to talk and joke. Lucy enjoyed this pleasant interval. It had but one break, an instant toward the end, when she espied Joe Denmeade sitting as always quietly in the background, with eyes of worship fixed upon Clara's face. That troubled Lucy's conscience.

Lucy wore out her gloves and made blisters on her fingers, acquiring along with these accidents a proficiency in the art of picking beans. Clara wearied early in the afternoon, and went to sleep under a pine tree. Mertie and Bert finished their allotment of beans, and wandering along the edge of the forest, they seemed to become absorbed in each other. Mrs. Denmeade and Allie worked like beavers, and the children drifted to playing.

The men soon finished picking and sacking the beans. Then Edd and his brothers stalked off to fetch the pack-burros. Uncle Bill still found tasks to do, while Denmeade rested and talked to his wife. Lucy leaned comfortably against the oak, grateful for relief from work, and because of it, appreciating infinitely more the blessing of rest. She did not try very hard to resist a drowsy spell, out of which she was roused to attention by a remark of Denmeade to his wife.

"Wal, it'd shore make bad feelin' between the Denmeades an' Johnsons if Sam homesteaded on the mesa."

"Reckon it would, but he's goin' to do it," returned Mrs. Denmeade. "Mertie told me."

"Sadie Purdue's back of that," said Denmeade, meditatively.

"She's never forgive Edd. . . . It'd be too bad if Sam beat Edd out of that homestead."

"Don't worry, wife. Sam ain't agoin' to," returned her husband. "Edd located the mesa, found the only water. He's just been waitin' to get himself a woman."

"But Edd oughtn't to wait no longer," protested Mrs. Denmeade.

"Wal, I reckon," rejoined Denmeade, thoughtfully. "We'll begin cuttin' logs an' get ready to run up a cabin. It's bad enough for us to be on the outs with Spralls, let alone Johnsons. . . . I'm goin' to walk up to the mesa right now."

Suiting action to word, Denmeade started off. Lucy sat up and impulsively called. "Please take me with you, Mr. Denmeade. I—I'd like to walk a little."

"Come right along," he responded, heartily.

Lucy joined him and entered the woods, taking two steps to one of his long strides.

"I'm goin' up to a place we call the mesa," he was saying. "Edd has long set his heart on homesteadin' there. It ain't far, but uphill a little. Sam Johnson has been talkin' around. Shore there ain't no law hyar to prevent him stealin' Edd's homestead. An' I reckon there's bad blood enough. So I'm goin' to begin work right off. That'll throw Sam off the trail an' then we won't have no call to hurry."

Lucy was interested to ask questions until she became out of breath on a rather long and steep slope. Here she fell back and followed her guide, whose idea of distance, she averred, was vastly different from hers.

At last, however, they reached a level. Lucy looked up, to be stunned by the towering, overpowering bulk of the Rim, red and gold, with its black-fringed crown, bright and beautiful in the westering sun. She gazed backward, down over a grand sweep of forest, rolling and ridging away to the far-flung peaks. Her position here was much higher than on any point she had frequented, and closer to the magnificent Rim.

"There's two or three hundred acres of flat land hyar," said Denmeade, sweeping his hand back toward the dense forest. "Rich red soil. Enough water for two homesteads, even in dry spells. It's blue snow water, the best kind, comin' down from the Rim. Wal, I'm hopin' Dick or Joe will homestead hyar some day. It's the best farm land I know of."

"Why, Mr. Denmeade, it's all forest!" exclaimed Lucy.

"Shore. It'll have to cleared. An' that's a heap of work."

"Goodness! It looks like it. How do you go about making a farm out of a thick forest?"

"Wal, we'll cut logs first to run up a cabin," replied Denmeade. "Then we'll clear off timber an' brush, an' set fire to it, leavin' the stumps. They'll rot out in a few years. The big trees we kill an' leave standin'. . . . This hyar mesa is high an' dry, warm in winter an' cool in summer. It joins on to a big canyon where there's water an' grass for stock. An' it's the best place for bees in this country. I reckon Edd's pretty smart. He's shore goin' to do somethin' with his bee huntin'."

They entered the level forest, and Lucy was at once charmed and fascinated. This woodland differed from any she had visited. It was level, open in glades, aisles, and dense in thickets and patches. A dry hot fragrance of pine and cedar and juniper seemed to wave up from the brown-carpeted earth. How easy and delightful the walking here! As they penetrated deep into the forest the pines grew so huge that they actually thrilled her. Then the other trees were as large in proportion. Some of the junipers were truly magnificent, six feet thick at the base, symmetrical and spreading, remarkable for their checker-board bark and lilac-hued berries. Under every one of these junipers the ground was a soft gray-green mat of tiny needles, fragrant, inviting rest. Under the pines Lucy kicked up furrows in the dry depths of brown needles, and these places even more called her to tarry. A wonderful sweet silence pervaded this mesa forest. No birds, no squirrels, no deer or turkeys! Yet Denmeade pointed out tracks in every dusty trail. "Reckon game's all down by the water," he explained. "There's a gully runs right through this mesa, dividin' it in half. Shore is a wild place. I'll show you where an old she bear jumped on me. She had cubs, an' a mother bear is bad."

Lucy reveled in this exploration. The farther she followed Denmeade the more delighted she was with the wilderness and beauty, the color and fragrance of the forest.

"Oh, but it will be a shame to cut all these trees—and burn a hideous slash in this beautiful forest!"

"I reckon. Shore Edd says the same," replied Denmeade. "But we have to make homes. An' the forest, just like this, will surround the homesteads. We only cut an' clear land where there's water. A few acres slashed don't make much of a hole in this woods. . . . Look hyar. See between the pines, up there where the bluffs run down—it shows a break in the woods. That's the canyon I spoke of. It looks narrow an' short. Wal, it's wide an' long, an' it'll always be wild. It can't never be cut. An' there's many canyons like it, runnin' in under the Rim. . . . Miss Lucy, I come hyar twenty years ago. There's as many bear an' deer now as then. An' I reckon it'll be the same in twenty more years."

"I'm glad," breathed Lucy, as if in relief. How strange for her to feel that she did not want the wilderness despoiled! Indeed, she was responding fully to inherited instincts.

Denmeade led her on under the vast pines and through glades the beauty of which swelled Lucy's heart, and finally to the edge of a gully. She looked down into a green, white, brown, golden chaos of tree trunks, foliage, bowlders, and cliffs, trailing vines and patches of yellow flowers, matted thickets of fallen timber—in all an exceedingly wild hollow cut deeply into the mesa. Lucy heard the babble and tinkle of water she could not see.

"Edd aims to have his cabin hyar," explained Denmeade. "I heard him say once he'd clear an acre hyar, leaving these big trees, an' the forest all around. The crop field he wants a little ways off. He'd keep his bees down in the gully, clearin' out some. . . . Now you rest yourself while I climb down to the water. It's shore been a dry season, an' last winter the snows was light. I reckon I can get a good line on how much water there'll be in dry seasons."

Denmeade clambered down a steep trail, leaving Lucy above. Though she stood amid deep forest, yet she could see the Rim in two directions, and the magnificent looming tower stood right above her. It marked the bold entrance of the canyon. In the other direction Lucy looked down a slant of green, darkly divided by the depression made by the gully, to the rolling forest below, that led the eye on and on to the dim purple ranges. A cry seemed to ring out of the remote past, appealing to Lucy's heart. It stung her mind to flashing, vivid thought. Her immediate ancestors had lived a few hundred years in villages, towns, cities; the early progenitors from which

her people had sprung had lived thousands of years in
the forested wilderness, barbarians, nomads. She felt
it all so intensely. The giant seamy-barked pines, rough
and rugged, were more than trees. They had constituted
a roof for her race in ages past, and wood for fire. The
fragrance, the strength of them, were in her blood. Likewise of the cedars, the junipers, the gray and white
sycamores down in the gully, the maples and oaks, the
patches of sumach, all that spread colorful protection
around her. Deeper than sentiment, stronger than education, this passion claimed her for the moment.

"If I loved Edd Denmeade, how happy I could be in a
home here!"

It did not seem to be the Lucy Watson she knew
that whispered these involuntary words. They came from
beyond reason, intelligence, consideration. They just
flashed up out of instinct. She did not resent them,
though she stood aghast at intimations beyond her control. How impossible was fulfillment of them! Yet she
pondered why they had come. In vain! The loneliness,
the solitude, the grand imminence of the Rim, the silent
guarding pines, the eye-soothing softness of gray and
green—these physical things dominated her and would
not be denied.

"It is a *fact*," she whispered. "I *could* live here. . . .
I'd want Clara to be close. . . . I'd want to go back to
Felix now and then. . . . I'd want books, letters, papers
—to keep up with my idea of progress. . . . I'd want to
go on with my welfare work. But these are nothing. *They*
do not induce me to want to live in a log cabin. . . .
I am amazed at myself; I don't know myself. I am not
what I think I am!"

Lucy remained alone on the shady rim of the gorge for
half an hour—surely a critical and portentous time in
her realization of change. Yet, what seemed incredible
to her was the fact that she would not have changed
anything in the present. Perhaps she had given too much
thought to herself. Vanity! Mertie Denmeade was not
alone in this peculiar feminine trait. Lucy arraigned herself, and tried to persuade herself that she possessed

something of worldliness. All to little purpose! She was happier than she had ever been in her life and that was all there was to it.

Denmeade led back across the mesa by a shorter route, and down the slope by an old trail. Lucy trudged along in his tracks, vastly less curious than on the way up. It had been another full day. Her hands attested to the labor of it. And as to her mind, the shadows of the past seemed dim, fading away.

As they again approached level forest Lucy caught glimpses of the yellow clearing. She heard the discordant bray of a burro, then the shrill peal of childish laughter. She emerged on the edge of the timber in time to see the packed burros filing away through the corn, and on top of the last two sat Liz and Lize, triumphantly riding on sacks of beans. Edd strode beside them. Mrs. Denmeade and Allie were plodding on ahead. Far down the edge of the field Mertie and Bert appeared hand in hand, sauntering away toward the trail for home. Something about them, perhaps those linked hands, stirred Lucy to a divination of how little other people mattered to them. She had been right in her surmise. Propinquity was all that had been needed.

Denmeade cut across the corn-field, while Lucy wended her way back along the edge of the woods to the pine tree where she had left Clara. Perhaps Clara, too, had gone with the others.

The day was over. Sunset was gilding the Rim. Crickets had begun to chirp. The air had perceptibly cooled. Crows were sailing across the clearing. Faint and sweet came the shouts of the children.

Then Lucy espied her sister sitting with her back against the pine. Joe Denmeade stood near, gazing down upon her. If either was talking, Lucy could not hear what was said; but she inclined to the thought that on the instant there was no speech. They did not hear her footsteps on the soft earth.

Without apparent cause Lucy experienced a thrill that closely approached shock. How utterly she, too, was at the mercy of her imagination! Clara and Joe together,

in perfectly simple pose—what was there in that to
stop Lucy's heart? Verily she was growing like the Denmeades. On the other hand, there seemed profound
significance in Joe's gazing down upon Clara, as she
sat there, with the last touch of the sun making a golden
blaze of her hair. Joe had been hopelessly lost, from that
first sight of Clara. It had seemed of no great moment.
Lucy in her passionate devotion had thought only of her
sister. But Lucy had a flash of revelation. This wilderness
environment was marvelously strong. Lucy caught just
a vague hint of its elemental power—the earth, its
rugged beauty and vitality, its secret to unite and pro-
create, since the dawn of human life ages before. What
little people knew! They were but moving atoms dominated by nature.

"Oh, here you are!" called Lucy, to start the pensive
couple out of their trance. "I had the dandiest walk.
Climb, I should say. . . . And what have you two been
talking about all this time?"

"Joe came just this moment to tell me they were
going home," replied Clara, looking up at Lucy.

"Teacher, I was aboot to say she was goin' to get
well heah in the woods, an' that I'd heard her laugh
to-day," he replied, in his slow speech.

"How strange!" murmured Clara, as if mocking a be-
lief. She studied Joe with doubtful eyes, as if she refused
to believe the truth manifested in him.

Lucy wisely saw nothing, said nothing, though she
was stirred to speak.

"It has been a lovely day," she said as she turned
away. "Come, we must go."

"Wait, Lucy," complained Clara. "I may be getting
well, but I can't run."

"Make her hurry, Joe. It's late," replied Lucy, and she
crossed the devastated bean-field to enter the rustling
rows of corn. She did not look back. It was twilight
when she arrived at the tent, and wearied with exertion
and emotion, throbbing and burning, she threw herself
on the bed to rest a few moments.

Clara came just as darkness fell. "Are you there, Lucy?" she asked, stumbling into the tent.

"Shore I'm heah," drawled Lucy.

"Why did you leave me alone—to walk back with that boy?" queried Clara, plaintively. "He's falling in love with me—the fool!"

"Oh, Clara, he'd be a fool if he wasn't," retorted Lucy.

"But it'll only make him wretched. And you—you must stop believing I'm worthy of love."

"Maybe Joe is like me," said Lucy, and this reply silenced her sister.

CHAPTER X

September came, with the first touches of frost on the foliage, the smoky haze hovering over the hollow, the melancholy notes of robins and wild canaries, the smell of forest fire in the air.

Edd did not remind Lucy that he had promised to take her bee hunting. This, like so many things in the past, piqued her; and the more she upbraided herself for that the less could she forget it. Finally she said to him one night at supper:

"Edd, I thought you were going to take me bee hunting."

"Shore. Whenever you say," replied Edd.

"Then I say to-morrow," returned Lucy.

A clamor from the children and an excited little cry from Clara attested to the eagerness of others to share Lucy's good fortune. She was curious to see if Mrs. Denmeade would approve of some one else accompanying them. Lucy had in mind that among the people with whom she had associated in Felix it would hardly have been the proper thing for her to go with Edd into the woods alone.

Edd laughed down the importunities of the children.

"Nope, kids; you wait till I'm ready to cut down a bee tree not far away," he said to appease them. "I've got one located. . . . An' as for you, Miss Clara, I reckon you'd better not risk a long climb till you're stronger."

"Will you take me with the children?" asked Clara, wistfully.

"Shore. Reckon I'll be glad to have you-all packin' buckets of honey," drawled Edd.

"Edd, I seen the other day that Miss Lucy's boots wasn't hobnailed," spoke up Denmeade. "Reckon you mustn't forget to put some nails in them for her. Else she might slip an' hurt herself."

"Wal, now you tax me, I'll just naturally have to hobnail her boots," returned Edd, drily. "But fact was I wanted to see her slide around some."

"Very sweet of you, Edd," interposed Lucy, in the same tone. "Couldn't you wait till winter and find me some ice?"

"Say, slidin' down a slope of grass an' pine needles will take the tenderfoot out of you," he retorted.

"Oh, then you think I need that?" she queried.

"Wal, I reckon you don't need no more," he said, quaintly.

"Is Edd complimenting me?" asked Lucy, appealing to Mrs. Denmeade. She nodded smilingly.

"Thanks. Very well, Edd. I shall fetch my boots for you to hobnail. And to-morrow you may have the pleasure of watching me slide."

After supper she watched him at work. He had an iron last, upside down, over which he slipped one of her boots. Then with a hammer he pounded small-headed hobnails into the soles. He was so deft at it that Lucy inquired if he were a shoemaker.

"Reckon so. I used to tan leather an' make my own shoes. But I only do half-solin' now."

Presently he removed the boot from the last, and felt inside to find if any nails had come through.

"That one's jake," he said.

Lucy examined the sole to find two rows of hobnails

neatly and symmetrically driven round the edge. Inside these rows were the initials of her name.

"Well, you're also an artist," she said. "I suppose you want to make it easy for anyone to know my boot tracks."

"Wal, I can't say as I'd like anyone trailin' you," he replied, with a deep grave look at her.

Lucy changed the subject. When she returned to her tent dusk had fallen and Clara was sitting in the doorway. Lucy threw the boots inside and sat down on the lower step to lean back against her sister. Often they had spent the gloaming hour this way. The cool melancholy night was settling down like a mantle over the forest land. Bells on the burros tinkled musically; a cow lowed in the distance; a night hawk whistled his strange piercing note.

"Lucy, I like Edd Denmeade," said Clara, presently.

"Goodness! Don't let him see it—or, poor fellow, he——"

"Please take me seriously," interrupted Clara. "I believed I'd always hate men. But to be honest with myself and you I find I can't. I like Mr. Denmeade and Uncle Bill—and the boys. Edd is a wonderful fellow. He's deep. He's so cool, drawly, kind. At first his backwoodsness, so to call it, offended me. But I soon saw that is his great attraction for me. As you know, I've gone with a lot of city boys, without ever thinking about what they *were*. . . . I wonder. City clothes and manners, nice smooth white hands, ought not be much in the make-up of a man. Edd's old jeans, his crude talk and ways, his big rough hands—they don't repel me any more. I don't quite understand, but I feel it. He's good for me, Lucy dear. Do you know what I mean?"

"Yes. And I'm glad. You've had a bitter blow. No wonder you think now what boys are. . . . As for me, I don't really know whether Edd has been good—or bad for me"

"Lucy!"

"Listen. I'll tell you something," went on Lucy, and she related the story of Edd's taking her to the dance.

"How funny! How——" exclaimed Clara, laughing— "how I don't know what! . . . Lucy, I just believe it tickles me. If he had been rude—you know, fresh, I mean—I'd have despised him. But the way you told it. Oh, I think it's rich! I believe I would have liked him better."

Lucy might have confessed that deep in her heart she had done this very thing, herself, but the fact was not acceptable to her.

"Joe is the best of the Denmeades, and quite the nicest boy I ever knew," she said, earnestly. "What do you think of him, Clara?"

"It's dreadful of me, but I like to be with him," whispered Clara. "He's so—so sweet. That's the only word. But it does not fit him, either. He has the same strong qualities as Edd. . . . Lucy, that boy *rests* me. He soothes me. He makes me ashamed. . . . Tell me all about him."

"Well, Joe's ears will burn," laughed Lucy, and then she began her estimate of Joe Denmeade. She was generous. But in concluding with the facts about him that had come under her observation and been told by his people, Lucy held rigidly to truth.

"All that!" murmured Clara, thoughtfully. "And I'm the only girl he *ever* looked at? . . . Poor Joe!"

Next morning there was a white frost. Lucy felt it and smelled it before she got up to peep out behind the curtain of the tent door. The sun had just tipped the great promontory, a pale blaze that made the frost on grass and logs shine like an encrustment of diamonds.

"Ooooo but it's cold!" exclaimed Lucy as she threw on her dressing gown. "Now I know why Edd insisted on installing this stove. Any old morning now I'd wake up frozen!"

"Come back to bed," advised Clara, sleepily.

"I'll start the fire, then slip back for a little. Oh, I wonder—will we have to give up living out here when winter comes?"

The stove was a wood-burning one, oval in shape, and flat on top, with a sheet-iron pipe running up through the roof of the tent. Lucy had thought it sort of a toy affair, despite Edd's assertion as to its utility. He had laid the

pine needles and splinters and billets of wood, so that all
Lucy had to do was to strike a match. She was not an
adept at building fires, and expected this to go out. Instead it flared up, blazed, crackled, and roared. Fortunately Lucy recollected Edd's warning to have a care to
turn the damper in the stove-pipe.

"This stove is going to be a success. How good it feels!"

Then she noticed the neat pile of chips and billets of
redwood stacked behind the stove, and a small box full
of pine needles. Edd Denmeade was thoughtful. Lucy put
a pan of water on the stove to heat, and slipped back
into bed. Her hands and feet were like ice, matters that
Clara was not too sleepy to note. Soon the tent room
was cozy and warm. Lucy felt encouraged to think it
might be possible for her and Clara to occupy this lodging all winter. Edd had averred the little stove would
make them as snug as birds in a nest. To make sure,
however, that they could live outdoors, he had suggested
boarding the tent wall halfway up and shingling the roof.

"Sleepy-head!" called Lucy, shaking her sister.

"Ah-h! . . . I just never can wake up," replied Clara.
"It's so good to sleep here. . . . I didn't sleep much down
there in the desert."

"My dear, you've slept three-fourths of the time you've
been here, day as well as night. It's this mountain air. I
was almost as bad. Well, good sleep is better than wasted
waking hours. Now I'm going to be heroic."

By nine o'clock all trace of frost had vanished from
grass and logs. Edd presented himself at the tent. "Wal,
I'm a-rarin' to go."

"Yes, you are!" called Lucy, banteringly. "Here I've
been ready these last two hours."

"City girl! You can't line bees till the sun gets warm."

"Backwoods boy! Why not?"

"Bees don't work so early. You see, it's gettin' along
towards fall."

"I'll be right out. . . . Let's see—my gloves and knapsack. . . Well, sister mine, why do you stare at me?"

Clara was sitting at the little table, with speculative

gaze fastened upon Lucy. It made Lucy a little sensitive to her attire. This consisted of a slouch felt hat, a red scarf round the neck of her brown blouse, corduroy riding trousers, and high boots. On the moment Lucy was slipping on her gauntlets.

"Clara, it'll be a long hard tramp, up and down," declared Lucy, as if in self-defense.

"You look great," rejoined Clara, with one of her sweet, rare smiles. "I'm not so sure about your welfare work, in that get-up. I think it's plain murder."

Clara made an expressive gesture, to indicate Edd outside. Lucy was not quite equal to a laugh. Sometimes this realistic sister of hers forced home a significance that escaped her idealistic mind.

"If you only could go!" sighed Lucy. "I—I think I need you as much as you need me. . . . Don't forget *your* welfare work. Good-by."

Edd carried a gun, a small black tin bucket, and a package which he gave to Lucy to put in her knapsack.

"Ma reckoned you'd like somethin' to eat," he explained.

So they set off across the lane, through the strip of woods, and out into the sorghum-field. Lucy experienced an unaccountable embarrassment. She felt like a callow girl taking her first walk with a boy. She did not feel at all at her ease in this riding garb, though the freedom of it had never been so manifest. She was guilty of peering round to see if any of the Denmeades were in sight, watching them cross the field. She could not see anyone, which fact helped a little. Then she did not discover her usual fluency of speech. Finding herself alone with this stalwart bee hunter, facing a long day in the wilderness, had turned out to be something more than thrilling. Lucy essayed to throw off the handicap.

"What's in your little black bucket?" she inquired.

"Honey. I burn it to make a sweet strong scent in the woods. That shore fetches the bees."

"What's the gun for?"

"Wal, sometimes a bear smells the honey an' comes along. Bears love sweet stuff, most of all honey."

"Bears! In broad daylight?" ejaculated Lucy.

"Shore. One day not long ago I had four bears come for my honey. Didn't have no gun with me, so I slipped back an' hid. You should have seen the fun they had stickin' their noses an' paws in my bucket of honey. They stole it, too, an' took it off with them."

"You won't leave me alone?" queried Lucy, fearfully.

"Wal, if I have to I'll boost you up into a tree," drawled Edd.

"I wonder if this is going to be fun," pondered Lucy. Suddenly she remembered the proclivity for playing tricks natural to these backwoods boys. "Edd, promise me you will not try to scare me. No tricks! Promise me solemnly."

"Aw, I'm shore not mean, Lucy," he expostulated. "Fun is fun an' I ain't above little tricks. But honest, you can trust me."

"I beg your pardon. That about bears—and boosting me up into a tree—somehow flustered me a little."

Soon they crossed the clearing to the green wall of cedars and pines. Here Edd led into a narrow trail, with Lucy at his heels. His ordinary gait was something for her to contend with. At once the trail began to wind down over red earth and round the head of rocky gullies, choked with cedars, and downward under a deepening forest growth.

Lucy had never been on this trail, which she knew to be the one that led over the Rim. She thrilled at the thought of climbing to the lofty summit of that black-fringed mountain mesa, but she was sure Edd would not put her to that ascent without a horse. The low hum which filled her ears grew into the roar of brawling brook.

"Bear track," said her guide, halting to point at a rounded depression in the dust of the trail. Lucy saw the imprint of huge toes. Her flesh contracted to a cold creeping sensation. "That old Jasper went along here last night. Reckon he's the bear that's been killin' our little pigs. Pa shore will be rarin' to chase him with the hounds."

"Edd! Is there any danger of our meeting this old Jasper, as you called him?" inquired Lucy.

"Reckon not much. Shore we might, though. I often

run into bears. They're pretty tame. Hope we do meet him. I'd shore have some fun."

"Oh, would you? I don't believe it'd be very funny for *me*," declared Lucy.

"Wal, in case we do, you just mind what I say," concluded Edd.

Somehow his drawling confidence reassured her and she reverted again to the pleasurable sensations of the walk. The trail led down into a deep gorge, dense with trees large and small, and along a wildly bowlder-strewn stream bed, where the water roared unseen through its channel. Here towered the lofty silver spruces, so delicate of hue and graceful in outline. The sunlight filtered through the foliage. Everywhere Lucy gazed were evidences of the wildness of this forest, in timber and rocks and windfalls, in the huge masses of driftwood, in the precipitous banks of the stream, showing how the flood torrents tore and dug at their confines.

Lucy did not see a bird or squirrel, nor hear one. But as to the latter the roar of rushing water would have drowned any ordinary sound. Gradually the trail left the vicinity of the stream and began a slight ascent, winding among beds of giant bowlders covered with trailing vines. Lucy was particularly struck by the almost overpowering scent of the woodland. It appeared dominated by the fragrance of pine, but there was other beside that spicy tang. Through the woods ahead she caught glimpse of light and open sky. Then Edd halted her.

"I hear turkeys cluckin'," he whispered. "Hold my bucket, an' keep right close to me, so you can see. Walk Injun, now."

Lucy complied instinctively, and she was all eyes and ears. She could not, however, give undivided attention to the scene in front and at the same time proceed noiselessly. Edd walked slower and stooped lower as the trail led round a corner of thicket toward the open. Lucy saw a long narrow clearing, overgrown with small green cedars and patches of sumach shining red and gold in the sunlight. At the same instant she saw something move, a white-and-brown object flashing low down. Edd swiftly rose. The gun cracked so suddenly that Lucy was startled. Then followed a tremendous flapping of wings. Huge black-and-gray birds flew and sailed out of the clearing into the woods, crashing through the foliage. Next Lucy heard a loud threshing in the brush just in front, and a heavy thumping. Both sounds diminished in volume, then ceased.

"Wal, I reckon you'll have turkey for dinner to-morrow," said Edd, looking to his gun. "Did you see them before they flew?"

"I saw a flash. Oh, it went swiftly! Then you shot, and I saw them rise. What a roar! Did you kill one?" replied Lucy, excitedly.

"I shore did. It was a good shot. He was rarin' to get out of here," said Edd, as he walked forward through the patch of sumach.

Lucy followed him to the open place where lay a beautiful wild turkey, its shiny plumage all ruffled and disheveled, its wings wide, its gorgeous bronze-and-white tail spread like a huge fan. Lucy was astonished at the variety and harmony of the colors. This wild bird was as beautiful as a peacock.

"Gobbler, two years old," said Edd. "Just fine for eatin'. I'll hang him up in the shade an' get him on our way home. Shore it's risky, though, because there's cats and lions around."

He carried the turkey into the edge of the woods, where Lucy heard him tramping around and breaking branches. When he emerged again he led her to the upper end of this clearing, meanwhile telling her that his father had years before cut the timber and tried to cultivate the ground. It had not been a successful venture. A tiny stream of water ran through the upper end, making smooth deep holes in the red clay. Edd pointed out deer and turkey tracks, with muddy water in them. He followed the stream to its source in a spring at the head of the clearing. A small shallow basin full of water, weeds, and moss lay open to the sun.

"Wal, here's where we start," announced Edd, enthusiastically. "Listen to the hum of bees."

The air seemed murmurous and melodious with the hum of innumerable bees. What a sweet, drowsy summer sound! Lucy gazed all around.

"Oh, I hear them! But where are they?" she cried.

"Wal, they're flyin' around, workin' in the tops of these pine saplings," replied Edd.

"Do they get honey up there?" queried Lucy, in amaze.

"They shore get somethin'," replied Edd. "If you go climbin' round pine trees an' get your hands all stuck up with pitch an' sap you'll think so, too. I reckon bees get somethin' in these pines to help make their wax. . . . Now look down along the edge of the water. You'll see bees lightin' an' flyin' up. I've watched them hundreds of times, but I never made shore whether they drank, or diluted their honey, or mixed their wax with water."

"Well! Who'd have thought honeybees so interesting? . . . Yes, I see some. Will they sting me?"

"Tame as flies," returned Edd, easily.

Trustingly Lucy got down on hands and knees, and then lay prone, with her face just above the water. Here, at distance of a foot, she could see the bees distinctly. At once she noted several varieties, some yellow and black, which she knew to be yellow-jackets, some fuzzy and brown like the tame honeybee, and a few larger, darker. As she leaned there these wilder bees flew away.

Edd knelt to one side and pointed at the bees. "The yellow ones are jackets, an' she shore hates them."

"She! Who's she?" queried Lucy.

"Wal, I call the wild bees she. Reckon because I've caught an' tamed queen bees. Shore that's some job."

"I remember now. You told me in rainy season the yellow-jackets fought and killed the wild bees and stole their honey. These yellow bees are the ones. . . . They're pretty, but they're mean-looking."

"Hold still," said Edd, suddenly. "There's a wild bee, the kind I'm goin' to line to-day. He lit by that little stone."

"I see him," whispered Lucy.

"Wal, now look close. Is he drinkin' or movin' his legs

in the water? You see he's just at the edge. Look at his knees. See the little yellow balls? That's wax."

"How funny!" said Lucy, laughing. "Why, his legs look deformed, burdened with those balls! Where does he carry his honey?"

"I never was shore, but I reckon in his mouth. Some bee hunters think the yellow balls are honey. I never did. It tastes like wax."

"It's beeswax. I know what that is. But where does the bee use it?"

"Shore you'll see that when I cut down a bee tree."

Apart from Lucy's great sympathy with the singular passion this wild-bee hunter had for his calling she was quite fascinated on her own account. It needed very little to stimulate Lucy's interest, especially in a problem or mystery, or something that required reason, study, perseverance to solve. She was getting acquainted with bees. The yellow-jackets were lively, aggressive, busybody little insects that manifestly wanted the place to themselves. The wild bees had a very industrious and earnest look. At the approach of yellow-jackets they rose and flew, to settle a little farther away. Lucy espied bees all along the edge of the water. The big one Edd had called her attention to flew away, and presently another took its place. Lucy wished for a magnifying glass, and told Edd that if they had one they could tell exactly what the bee was doing there.

"By George!" ejaculated Edd, in most solemn rapture. "Shore we could. I never thought of that. Wal, I never even heard of a glass that'd magnify. Where can we get one?"

"I'll fetch you one from Felix."

"Lucy, I reckon I don't want you to go, but I'd shore love to have that kind of a glass."

"Why don't you want me to go?" asked Lucy, gayly.

"It's hard to say. I've heard the folks talkin'. Ma thinks it grand for Mertie. But I'm not so shore. Reckon Mertie will have a grand time. You're awful good to take her. But won't she get her head full of notions about clothes an' city boys?"

"Edd, you're worrying a lot, aren't you?"

"Yes," he said, simply.

"Haven't you faith in me? I'm going to satisfy Mertie's passion for pretty things. Once in her life! And I'm going to see that Bert Hall goes with us."

Lucy raised on her elbows to mark the effect of this statement upon her companion. For once his stoicism was disrupted. He seemed thunderstruck. Then his dark face beamed and his gray eyes shone with the piercing light Lucy found hard to face.

"Wal!—Who in the world's ever goin' to make up to you for your goodness?"

"Edd, it's not goodness, exactly," returned Lucy, somewhat affected by his emotion. "It's not my welfare work, either. I guess I'll get more out of it than Mertie and Bert. Real happiness, you know."

"Shore. But I know what I think."

Lucy dropped back to study the bees. A number of the wild species had settled down right under her eyes. They were of different sizes and hues, and the very smallest carried the largest balls of wax on his knees. She strained her eyes to see perfectly, and was rewarded by sight of an almost imperceptible motion of both their heads and legs.

"Edd, I believe they drink and wet their wax. Both. At the same time."

"Wal, shore I've reckoned that often. Now get up an' watch me line a bee."

This brought Lucy to her feet with alacrity. Edd's voice sounded a note entirely at variance with his usual easy, cool, drawling nonchalance. About most things he was apparently indifferent. But anything pertaining to his beloved bee hunting touched him to the quick.

"Now, you stand behind me an' a little to one side," he directed. "An' we'll face toward that far point on the Rim. Eagle Rock we call it. Most of the bees here take a line over there."

Suddenly he pointed. "See that one."

Though Lucy strained her eyes, she saw nothing. The wide air seemed vacant.

"Don't look up so high," he said. "These bees start low. You've shore got to catch her right close. . . . There goes another."

"I'm afraid my eyes aren't good," complained Lucy, as she failed again.

"No. Keep on lookin'. You'll line her in a minute."

Just then Lucy caught sight of a tiny black object shooting over her head and darting with singularly level swift flight straight away. It did not appear to fly. It swept.

"Oh, Edd, I see one! . . . He's gone."

"Shore. You've got to hang your eye on to her."

Lucy caught a glimpse of another speeding bee, lost it, and then sighted another. She held this one in view for what seemed an endless moment. Then having got the knack of following, she endeavored to concentrate all her powers of vision. Bee after bee she watched. They had a wonderful unvarying flight. Indeed, she likened them to bullets. But they were remarkably visible. No two bees left the waterhole together. There was a regularity about their appearance.

"Wal, you're doing fine. You'll shore make a bee hunter," said Edd, "Now let's face west awhile."

Lucy found this direction unobstructed by green slope and red wall. It was all open sky. A line of bees sped off and Lucy could follow them until they seemed to merge into the air.

"Why do some bees go this way and some that other way?" she queried.

"She belongs to different bee trees. She knows the way home better than any other livin' creature. Can't you see that? Straight as a string! Reckon you never heard the old sayin', 'makin' a bee line for home.'"

"Oh, is that where that comes from?" ejaculated Lucy, amused. "I certainly appreciate what it means now."

"Now shift back to this other bee line," instructed Edd. "When you ketch another, follow her till you lose her, an' then tell me where that is. Mark the place."

Lucy made several attempts before she succeeded in placing the disappearance of a bee close to the tip of a tall pine on the distant ridge.

"Wal, that's linin' as good as ever Mertie or Allie," asserted Edd, evidently pleased, and he picked up his gun and bucket. "We're off."

"What do we do now?" queried Lucy.

"Can't you reckon it out?"

"Oh, I see! We've got the bee line. We follow it to that pine tree where I lost the last bee."

"Right an' exactly," drawled Edd.

"Oh—what fun! It's like a game. Then where do we go?"

"Wal, I can't say till we get there."

"We'll watch again. We'll sight more bees. We'll get their line. We'll follow it as far as we can see—mark the spot—and then go on," declared Lucy, excitedly.

"Lucy, your granddad might have been a wild-bee hunter," said Edd, with an approving smile.

"He might, only he wasn't," laughed Lucy. "You can't make any wild-bee hunter of me, Edd Denmeade."

"Shore, but you might make one of yourself," drawled Edd.

Lucy had no reply for that. Falling in behind him as he headed across the clearing, she pondered over his words. Had they been subtle, a worthy response to her rather blunt double meaning, or just his simplicity, so apt to hit the truth? She could not be sure, but she decided hereafter to think before she spoke.

Edd crossed the clearing and plunged into the forest. As he entered the timber Lucy saw him halt to point out a tree some distance ahead. This, of course, was how he marked a straight line. Lucy began to guess the difficulty of that and the strenuous nature of traveling in a straight line through dense and rugged forest. She had to scramble over logs and climb over windfalls; she had to creep through brush and under fallen trees; she had to wade into ferns as high as her head and tear aside vines that were as strong as ropes.

They reached the bank above the roaring brook. As Edd paused to choose a place to get down the steep declivity, Lucy had a moment to gaze about her. What a wild, dark, deep glen! The forest monarchs appeared to

mat overhead and hide the sun. Boulders and trees, brook
and bank, all the wild jumble of rocks and drifts, and
the tangle of vines and creepers, seemed on a grand scale.
There was nothing small. The ruggedness of nature, of
storm and flood, of fight to survive, manifested itself all
around her.

"Wal, shore if you can't follow me you can squeal,"
shouted Edd, above the roar of the brook.

"Squeal! Me? Never in your life!" replied Lucy, with
more force than elegance. "If I can't follow you, I can't,
that's all. But I'll try."

"Reckon I didn't mean squeal as you took it," returned
Edd, and without more ado he plunged in giant strides
right down the bank.

Lucy plunged likewise, fully expecting to break her
neck. Instead, however, she seemed to be taking seven-
league-boot-steps in soft earth that slid with her. Once
her hands touched. Then, ridiculously easily, she arrived
at the bottom of the forty-foot embankment. Most amusing of all was the fact that Edd never even looked back.
Certainly it was not discourtesy, for Edd was always
thoughtful. He simply had no concern about her accom-
plishing this descent.

Crossing the brook had more qualms for Lucy, and
when she saw Edd leap from one slippery rock to another
she thought it was a good thing she had been put on her
mettle. Edd reached the other side without wetting a foot.
Lucy chose bowlders closer together, and by good judgment, added to luck, she got safely across, though not
without wet boots.

Then Lucy climbed after Edd up a bank of roots that
was as easy as a ladder, and thence on into the forest
again. A thicket of pine saplings afforded welcome change.
How subdued the light—how sweet the scent of pine! She
threaded an easy way over smooth level mats of needles,
brown as autumn leaves. Edd broke the dead branches
and twigs as he passed, so that she did not have to stoop.
On all sides the small saplings shut out the light and hid
the large trees. Soon the hum of the brook died away.
Footsteps on the soft needles gave forth no sound. Silent,

shaded, lonely, this pine swale appealed strongly to Lucy. Soon it ended in a rough open ridge of cedar, oak, and occasional pine, where Edd's zigzag climb seemed steep and long. It ended in an open spot close to a tree Lucy recognized.

"I thought—we'd never—get here," panted Lucy.

"That was easy. Can you pick out where we stood down in the clearin'?"

Lucy gazed down the slope, across the green thicket and then the heavy timber marking the channel of the brook, on to the open strip bright with its red sumach.

"Yes, I see the water," she replied.

"Wal, turn your back to that an' look straight the other way an' you'll soon get our—bee line."

She had not stood many moments as directed before she caught the arrowy streak of bees, straight over the ridge. But owing to the background of green, instead of the sky that had served as background, she could not follow the bees very far.

"Here's where we make easy stages," remarked Edd, and started on.

Open ridge and hollow occupied the next swift hour. Lucy had enough to do to keep up with her guide. The travel, however, was not nearly as rough as that below, so that she managed without undue exertion. She had been walking and climbing every day, and felt that she was equal to a grueling task. She had misgivings, however, as to that endurance being sufficient for all Edd might require. Still, she had resolved to go her very limit, as a matter of pride. Mertie had confided to Lucy that the ony time Sadie Purdue had ever gone bee hunting with Edd she had given out, and that, too, on a rather easy bee line. It would have to be a bad place and a long walk that would daunt Lucy this day.

Edd's easy stages proved to be short distances from mark to mark, at every one of which he took pleasure in having Lucy again catch the bee line.

"When are you going to burn the honey in your bucket?" asked Lucy, once, happening to remember what Edd had told her.

"I don't know. Maybe I won't have to," he replied. "If I lose the bee line, then I'll need to burn honey."

"It seems, if things keep on as they are, you'll lose only *me*," observed Lucy.

"Tired?"

"Not a bit. But if I had to keep this up all day I *might* get tired."

"We'll eat lunch under this bee tree."

"That's most welcome news. Not because I want the hunt to be short, at all! I'm having the time of my life. But I'm hungry."

"It's always good to be hungry when you're in the woods," he said.

"Why?" she asked.

"Because when you do get to camp or back home, near starved to death, everythin' tastes so good, an' you feel as if you never knew how good food is."

Lucy was beginning to appreciate what this philosophy might mean in more ways than applied to hunger. It was good to starve, to thirst, to resist, to endure.

The bee line led to the top of a slope, and a hollow deeper, rougher than any of the others, and much wider. Edd lined the bees across to the timber on the summit of the ridge beyond, but he was concerned because there appeared so little to mark the next stage. The pines on that side were uniform in size, shape, and color. There were no dead tops or branches.

"Now, this is easy if we go straight down an' up," said Edd. "But if we go round, head this hollow, I reckon I might lose our bee line."

"Why should we go round?" inquired Lucy.

"Because that'd be so much easier for you," he explained.

"Thanks. But did you hear me squeal?"

Edd let out a hearty laugh, something rare with him, and it was an acceptance that gratified Lucy. Thereupon he went straight down the slope. Lucy strode and trotted behind, finding it took little effort. All she had to do was to move fast to keep from falling. This mode of travel appeared to be exhilarating. At least something was exhilarating, perhaps the air. Lucy knew she was excited, buoyant. Her blood ran warm and quick. What an adventure! If only she could have felt sure of herself! Yet she did not admit to her consciousness where she felt uncertain. "I'll live this with all I have," she soliloquized, "for I might never go again."

The slope into this hollow was a delusion and a snare. From above it had appeared no denser than the others. It turned out to be a jungle of underbrush. Live oak, manzanita, buckbrush formed an almost impenetrable thicket on the southerly exposed side. Edd crashed through the oaks, walked on top of the stiff manzanita, and crawled under the buckbrush.

Water ran down the rocky gully at the bottom. How Lucy drank and bathed her hot face! Here Edd filled a canvas water bag he had carried in his pocket, and slung it over his shoulder.

"Shore was fun ridin' the manzanitas, wasn't it?" he queried.

"Edd, it's—all fun," she breathed. "Remember, if I fall by the wayside—I mean by the bee line—that my spirit was willing but my flesh was weak."

"Humph! Sometimes I don't know about you, Lucy Watson," he said dubiously.

When Lucy imagined she deserved a compliment it seemed rather disillusioning to hear an ambiguous speech like that. Meekly she followed him in and out of the clumps of brush toward the slope. Her meekness, however, did not last very long. Edd had the most astonishing faculty for bringing out all that was worst in her. Then by the time she had gotten halfway through a grove of large-leaved oaks she had forgotten what had inflamed her spirit. Every strenuous section of this journey had its reward in an easy stretch, where beauty and color and wilderness took possession of her.

Edd zigzagged up this slope, and the turns were so abrupt that Lucy began for the first time to feel a strain. Edd saw it and paused every few moments to give her time to regain breath and strength. He did not encourage her to waste either in speech. This slope stood on end.

The ridge proved to be a mountain. Lucy was compelled to dig heels and toes in the hard red earth, and often grasp a bush or branch, to keep from slipping back.

At last they surmounted the great timbered incline. Lucy fell on a pine mat, so out of breath that she gasped. She had an acute pain in her side. It afforded her some satisfaction to see Edd's heaving breast and his perspiring face.

"What're—you—panting about?" she asked, heroically sitting up.

"Reckon that pull is a good one to limber up on," he said.

"Oh-h-h! Are there—any worse pulls?"

"Shore I don't know. We might have to climb up over the Rim."

"Well," concluded Lucy, with resignation, "where's our bee line?"

"I got plumb off," confessed Edd, in humiliation, as if the error he had made was one of unforgivable proportions. "But, honest, sometimes it's impossible to go straight."

"I accept your apology, Edward," said Lucy, facetiously. "But it wasn't necessary. No human being—even a bee hunter—can pass through rocks, trees, hills, walls of brush, and piles of logs. . . . What'll we do now?"

"I'll walk along an' see if I can find her. If I don't we'll burn some honey. That'll take time, but it'll shore fetch her. You rest here."

Lucy could see the two clearings of the Denmeades nestling green and yellow in the rolling lap of the forest. How far she had traveled! She was proud of this achievement already. With her breath regained, and that pain gone from her side, she was not in the least the worse for her exertion. Indeed, she felt strong and eager to pursue the bee line to its end. Only by such effort as this could she see the wonderful country or learn something about the forest land. She was high up now, and yet the Rim still towered beyond and above, unscalable except for eagles. She was reveling in the joy of her sensations when Edd's step disrupted them.

"I found her. We wasn't so far off. Come now, if you're ready," he said.

"Edd, how far do bee lines usually run from where you find them?" asked Lucy.

"Sometimes miles. But I reckon most bee lines are short. Shore they seem long because you have to go up an' down, right over everythin'."

Rolling forest stretched away from the ridge-top, neither level nor hilly. Despite the heavy growth of pines the bee line seemed to penetrate the forest and still preserve its unwavering course. Lucy could see the bees flying down the aisles between the tree-tops, and she was unable to make certain that they curved in the least. Edd could line them only a short distance, owing to intervening trees. Progress here was necessarily slower, a fact that Lucy welcomed. Birds and squirrels and rabbits enlivened this open woodland; and presently when Edd pointed out a troop of sleek gray deer, wonderfully wild and graceful as they watched with long ears erect, Lucy experienced the keenest of thrills.

"Black-tails," said Edd, and he raised his gun.

"Oh—please don't kill one of them!" cried Lucy, appealingly.

"Shore I was only takin' aim at that buck. I could take him plumb center."

"Well, I'll take your word for it," rejoined Lucy. "How tame they are! . . . They're going. . . . Oh, there's a beautiful little fawn!"

She watched them bound out of sight, and then in her relief and pleasure to see them disappear safely she told Edd she was glad he was a bee hunter instead of a deer hunter.

"Wal, I'm not much on bees to-day," he acknowledged. "But that's natural, seein' I've a girl with me."

"You mean you do better alone?"

"I reckon."

"Are you sorry you brought me?"

"Sorry? Wal, I guess not. 'Course I love best to be alone in the woods. But havin' you is somethin' new. It's not *me*, but the woods an' the bees an' the work you're thinkin' about. You don't squeal an' you don't want to get mushy in every shady place."

Lucy, failing of an adequate response to this remarkable speech, called his attention to the bees; and Edd stalked on ahead, peering through the green aisles. The beautiful open forest was soon to end in a formidable rocky canyon, not more than half a mile wide, but very deep and rugged. Lucy stood on the verge and gazed, with her heart in her eyes. It was a stunning surprise. This deep gorge notched the Rim. Red and yellow crags, cliffs, ledges, and benches varied with green slopes, all steps down and down to the black depths. A murmur of running water soared upward. Beneath her sailed an eagle, brown of wing and back, white of head and tail, the first bald eagle Lucy had ever seen.

"Dog-gone!" ejaculated Edd. "Shore I was hopin' we'd find our bee tree on this side of Doubtful Canyon."

"Doubtful? Is that its name?"

"Yes, an' I reckon it's a Jasper."

"Edd, it may be doubtful, but it's grand," declared Lucy.

"You won't think it's grand if we undertake to cross."

"Then our bee tree is 'way over there some place," said Lucy, gazing at the blue depths, the black slopes, the yellow crags, the red cliffs. They would have looked close but for the dominating bulk of the Rim, rising above and beyond the canyon wall. All was green growth over there except the blank faces of the rocks. Ledges and benches, nooks and crannies, irresistibly beckoned for Lucy to explore.

"If! We're certainly going to cross, aren't we?" she queried, turning to Edd.

"Wal, if you say so, we'll try. But I reckon you can't make it."

"Suppose I *do* make it—can we go home an easier way?"

"Shore. I can find easy goin', downhill all the way," replied Edd.

"Well, then I propose we rest here and have our lunch.

Then cross! Before we start, though, you might let me see you burn some honey. Just for fun."

This plan met with Edd's approval. Just below they found a huge flat ledge of rock, projecting out over the abyss. Part of it was shaded by a bushy pine, and here Edd spread the lunch. Then while Lucy sat down to eat he built a tiny fire out on the edge of the rock. Next he placed a goodly bit of honey on a stone close enough to the fire to make it smoke.

"Pretty soon we'll have some fun," he said.

"Wrong! We're having fun now. At least I am," retorted Lucy.

"Wal, then, I mean some more fun," he corrected.

Whereupon they fell with hearty appetites upon the ample lunch Mrs. Denmeade had provided. Edd presently said he heard bees whizz by. But a quarter of an hour elapsed before any bees actually began to drop down over the smoking honey. Then Edd poured some of the honey out on the rock. The bees circled and alighted. More came and none left. Lucy asked why they did not fly away.

"Makin' pigs of themselves," he said. "But soon as they get all they can hold they'll fly."

By the time the lunch was finished a swarm of bees of different sizes and hues had been attracted to the honey, and many were departing. As they came from different directions, so they left. Edd explained this to be owing to the fact that these bees belonged to different trees.

"Do all these wild bees live in trees?" she asked.

"All but the yellow-jackets. They have holes in the ground. I've seen where many holes had been dug out by bears. . . . Wal, we played hob with the lunch. An' now I reckon it's high time we begin our slide down this canyon."

"Slide? Can't we walk?"

"I reckon you'll see. It'll be a slidin' walk," averred Edd. "Shore I'm goin' to have all the fun I can, 'cause you'll shore never go anywheres with me again."

"My! How terrible this sliding walk must be! . . . But I might fool you, Edd. I've decided to go to the dance with you, an' let Clara go with Joe."

"Aw! That's nice of you," he replied, with frank gladness. His face lighted at some anticipation. "Joe will shore be proud."

He walked out upon the ledge to get his bucket, driving the bees away with his sombrero, and when he had secured it he took a last long look across the canyon. Lucy noticed what a picture he made, standing there, tall, round-limbed, supple, his youthful leonine face sharp against the sky. He belonged there. He fitted the surroundings. He was a development of forest and canyon wilderness. The crudeness once so objectionable to her was no longer manifest. Was it because of change and growth in him—or in her? Lucy fancied it was the latter. Edd had vastly improved, but not in the elemental quality from which had sprung his crudeness.

"She'll be right across there," he said, pointing with long arm. "I can line her halfway across. Reckon I see the tree now. It's an oak, sort of gray in color, standin' on a ledge. An' it's got a dead top an' one big crooked branch."

"Very well, I'll remember every word," warned Lucy.

"I'll go ahead, so when you come slidin' I can grab you," he said.

"See that you don't miss me," replied Lucy, as she started to follow him down off the ledge. At first the descent, though steep, was easy enough. Had Edd zigzagged down she would have had no trouble at all. But he descended straight down over bare earth, rock slides, banks and benches, swerving only for trees and brush, and then taking care to get back again in alignment with whatever he had marked to guide him. Lucy could not go slowly, unless she sat down, which, despite an almost irresistible temptation, she scorned to do. Quite abruptly, without preparation, she found herself standing at the top of a wonderful green and brown slope dotted by pine trees and remarkable for its waved effect. It descended at an angle of forty-five degrees, an open forest standing almost on end! The green color was grass; the brown, pine needles. This place made Lucy's heart leap to her throat. An absolutely unaccountable and new species of fright assailed

her. Never in her life before had she seen a slope like that
or been attacked by such dread.

"Wal, here's where we slide," drawled Edd, gazing up
at her. "Whatever you do, do it quick, an' keep in line
with me."

Then he started down. His action here was very much
different from any before. He descended sidewise, stepping, or rather running, on the edge of his boots, holding
gun and bucket in his left hand, and reaching back with
his right. His position corresponded with the slant of the
slope. He slid more than he ran. His right hand often
touched the ground behind him. He left a furrow in grass
and needles. Forty or fifty feet below he lodged on a bench.
Then he straightened round to look up at Lucy.

"Wal, city girl?" he called, gayly. His voice was bantering, full of fun.

It lent Lucy recklessness. Through it she recovered
from the queer locked sensation.

"All right, country boy, I'm coming," she replied, with
bravado.

Then she launched herself, heedlessly attempting to
imitate Edd's method of procedure. A few swift steps
landed her upon the pine needles. Quick as lightning her
feet flew up and she fell. Frantically she caught the ground
with her hands and held on, stopping her momentum.
Both breath and bravado had been jarred out of her.

"Wal, you've started comin', so come on," called Edd,
never cracking a smile.

Lucy, holding on in most undignified manner, glared
down upon him, making one last desperate effort to keep
her equilibrium and her temper. If he had laughed or
smiled, she might have trusted him more.

"Did you get me here on purpose?" she demanded,
with magnificent disregard of reason.

"Shore. We're on our bee line. You couldn't be talked
out of it," he replied.

"I mean on this terrible hill," she added, weakening.

"How'd I know she'd make a bee line over this hill?"
he demanded.

Lucy, seeing that action, not talk, was imperative, got

up, and ran downhill right at him. She forgot his method of descending, but executed a very good one of her own. She ran, she flew, she fell, right upon Edd. He caught her outstretched hands and kept her from upsetting.

"Heavens!" gasped Lucy. "Suppose you hadn't been here?"

"Wal, you'd have slid some," he said. "But, honest, you did that fine."

"It was an accident," confessed Lucy as she fearfully gazed below. The next stage, to a bench below, seemed still steeper, and the one below that made Lucy's head reel.

"I'm sorry I called you city girl," he said, contritely. "For you're shore game, an' quick on your feet. You hunt bees like you dance."

Lucy's misery was not alleviated by the compliment, because she knew she was a sham; nevertheless, she felt a weak little thrill. Maybe she could go on without killing herself.

"Don't hang on to me," added Edd, as again he started. "That's not the way. We'll both slip, an' if we do we'll go clear to the bottom, same as if this hill was snow. . . . When I make it down there you come, same as you got here."

"Ha! Ha!" laughed Lucy, wildly. "Don't worry, I'll come."

Edd made a splendid achievement of the next descent, and halted in favorable position to wait for Lucy. It encouraged her. Stifling her vacillations, she launched herself with light steps, leaning back, and depending on her gloved hand. She kept her feet most of the distance, but landed before Edd in a sliding posture. On the next attempt a couple of pine trees made descent easy for her. Below that were successive stages calculated to give her undue confidence.

"Wal, this is plumb bad," ejaculated Edd, gazing below and to right and left. "But we can't climb back. An' it's worse on each side. Reckon there's nothin' to do but slide."

And he did slide and fall and roll, and finally lodge against a tree.

"Hey! you can't do worse than that!" he shouted. "Come on. Don't wait an' think. . . . Come a-rarin'."

Lucy was in a strange state of suspended exhilaration and acute panic. She was both inhibited and driven. Actually she closed her eyes on the instant she jumped. Then she ran. Her objective was Edd and she had to look. She expected to plunge head over heels, yet she reached Edd upright, and earned another compliment. They went on with varying luck, but at least they made remarkable progress. The farther down this slope they proceeded the thicker lay the mats of pine needles and the scanter grew the patches of grass. Naturally the needles slipped and slid downward. Also, trees and brush grew scarce. Then to make the situation worse the descent took a sharper angle and the benches cropped out farther apart. At last they reached a point where Edd seemed at a loss. The slope just below was not only more precipitous and longer than any yet, but it ended in a jump-off, the extent of which Edd could not determine.

"Lucy, I've played hob gettin' you into this," he said, in remorse.

"It was my fault," returned Lucy, frightened by his gravity. "Go on. Let's get down—before I lose my nerve."

All the nerve she had left oozed out as she watched Edd slide to the landing place selected below. He never took a step. He sat down and slid like a streak. Lucy thought he was going over the precipice. But he dug heels into needles and ground, and stopped his flight in the nick of time.

"Not so bad as it looked," he shouted. How far below he was now! "Come on. It's safe if you let yourself slide straight. So you won't miss me!"

But Lucy did not obey. She realized how silly she was, but she simply could not deliberately sit down and slide. She essayed to do as she had done above. And her feet flew higher than her head. She alighted upon her back and began to shoot down. She turned clear over on her face. Dust and flying needles blinded her. Frantically she dug in with hands and feet, and rolled and slid to a halt.

When she cleared her sight she found she had gotten out of line with Edd. He was crawling along the precipice to intercept her. Lying prone on the slippery slope, she had to hold with all her might to keep from sliding. Edd's yells, added to all that had happened, terrified her, and she clung there instinctively. It seemed a frightful drop to where Edd knelt. She would miss him and slide over the precipice. Inch by inch she felt herself slip. She screamed. Edd's voice pierced her drumming ears.

". . . darn fool, you! Let go! Slide!"

Lucy let go because she could no longer hold on. Then she seemed to rush through air and flying needles and clouds of dust. Swifter she slid. Her sight blurred. Sky and trees grew indistinct. She slid from her back over on her face, and plunged down. A mass of debris seemed to collect on her as she plunged. Suddenly she collided with something and stopped with terrific shock. She felt Edd's clutch on her. But she could not see. Again she was moving, sliding, held back, pulled and dragged, and at last seemed to reach a halt. Breathless, stunned, blinded, burning as with fire, and choked with dust, Lucy wrestled to sit up.

"You shore slid," Edd was saying. "You knocked us over the ledge. But we're all right now. I'll go back for my gun."

Lucy's mouth was full of dirt and pine needles; her eyes of dust. She sputtered and gasped, and could not see until welcome tears washed her sight clear. Then she found she was at the foot of the terrible slope. Edd was crawling up to the bench above. Her hair and blouse and trousers, even her boots and pockets, were full of dust, pine needles, twigs, and dirt. Standing up, shaking and spent, she essayed to rid herself of all she had collected in that slide. Incredible to believe, she had not sustained even a bruise that she was aware of. Then Edd came slipping down, gun and bucket in hand. As he reached her he seemed to be laboring under some kind of tremendous strain.

"No—use!" he choked. "Shore—I can't—hold it."

"What, for goodnesss' sake?" burst out Lucy.

"If I—don't laugh—I'll bust," he replied, suddenly falling down.

"Pray don't do anything so—so vulgar as that last," said Lucy, attempting hauteur.

But sight of this imperturbable backwoods boy giving way to uncontrollable mirth affected Lucy peculiarly. Her resentment melted away. Something about Edd was infectious.

"I must have been funny," she conceded.

Edd appeared incapacitated for any verbal explanation of how laughter-provoking she had been; and Lucy at last broke her restraint and shared his hilarity.

An hour later Lucy perched upon a ledge high above the canyon, exhausted and ragged, triumphant and gay, gazing aloft at a gray old oak tree that had breasted the winds and lightnings for centuries. Part of it was dead and bleached, but a mighty limb spread from the fork, with branches bearing myriads of broad green leaves and clusters of acorns. On the under side of this huge limb was a knot hole encrusted with a yellow substance. Beeswax. It surrounded the hole and extended some distance along the under side, changing the gray color of the bark to yellow. A stream of bees passed in and out of that knot hole. Edd had followed his bee line straight to the bee tree.

"She's a hummer," he was saying as he walked to and fro, gazing upward with shining eyes. "Shore, it's an old bee tree. Reckon that whole limb is hollow an' full of honey. . . . Easy to cut an' let down without smashin'! I'll save maybe fifty gallons."

"Aren't you afraid of those bees?" asked Lucy, seeing how they swooped down and circled round Edd.

"Bees never sting me," he said.

Lucy assumed that if there was no danger for him there would be none for her; and desiring to see the bees at close range as they streamed in and out of the aperture, she arose and approached to where Edd stood.

. Hardly had she raised her head to look up when a number of bees whizzed down round her face. In alarm Lucy struck at them with her gloves, which she carried in her hand.

"Don't hit at them!" shouted Edd, in concern. "You'll make them mad."

But it was too late. Lucy had indeed incurred their wrath and she could not resist beating at them.

"Oh, they're after me! . . . Chase them away! . . . Edd! . . ." She screamed the last as she backed away, threshing frantically at several viciously persistent bees. Then as she backed against a log and lost her balance, one of the bees darted down to sting her on the nose. Lucy fell back over the log. The bee stayed on her nose until she pulled it off, not by any means without voicing a piercing protest. Then she bounded up and beat a hasty retreat to a safer zone. For a moment she ached with the burning sting. Then the humiliation of it roused her ire. The glimpse she had of Edd through the saplings caused her to suspect that he had again succumbed to shameless glee. Else why did he hide behind the bee tree?

Lucy was inclined to nurse her wrath as well as her nose. At any rate, she sat down to tenderly hold the injured member. It was swelling. She would have a huge, red, ugly nose. When Edd came to her at length, looking rather sheepish, Lucy glared at him.

"That horrid old bee stung me right on my nose," she burst out. "Just for that I'll not go to the dance."

"I have some salve I made. It'll take out the sting an' swellin'," he replied, kindly.

"Does it look very bad yet?"

"No one'd ever see it," he comforted.

"Oh, but it hurts. But if it doesn't disfigure me for life I guess I can stand it."

He gazed thoughtfully down upon her.

"You stuck to me better than any girl I ever took on a bee hunt. I'm shore goin' to tell everybody. Pa an' ma will be tickled. Now I'm askin' you. Reckonin' it all, aren't you glad you had that awful spill an' then got stung?"

"Well," replied Lucy, gazing up at him just as thoughtfully, "I'm not glad just this minute—but perhaps I will be later."

Two hours of leisurely travel down a gradual descent, through a trailless forest, brought Lucy and her guide back to the brook. Edd had been careful to choose open woodland and the easiest going possible. Sunset found them crossing the clearing. Lucy could just wag along, yet she could still look up with delight in the golden cloud pageant, and at the sun-fired front of the Rim.

"Edd, you forgot the turkey," said Lucy as they entered the lane.

"Nope. It was only out of our way, comin' back. After supper I'll jump a hoss an' ride after it."

"Well, Edd, thank you for—our bee hunt."

As she passed the yard she waved and called gayly to the Denmeades, hiding to the last the fact that she was utterly spent. Clara heard her and flung open the door of the tent glad-eyed and excited. Lucy staggered up into the tent and, closing the door, she made a long fall to the bed.

"Oh—Clara," she whispered, huskily, "I'm killed! I'm dead! . . . Walked, climbed, slid, and stung to death! . . . Yes, *stung!* Look at my poor nose! . . . We found a bee line, and went a thousand miles—up and down. . . . I stuck to that wild-bee hunter. I *did,* Clara. . . . But, oh, it's done something to me! . . . What a glorious, glorious day!"

Clara leaned lovingly over her, and listened intently, and watched with sad, beautiful, wise eyes.

"Lucy dear," she said, gently, "you're in love with that wild-bee hunter."

CHAPTER XI

Late in October Lucy returned from Felix, where she had stayed four weeks instead of two, as she originally intended. Her work had so interested the welfare board that they considered the experiment a success, and they brought her in contact with other workers whom they wanted to have the benefit of Lucy's experience. Thus she had found herself rather an important personage in that little circle.

Though the stage arrived at Cedar Ridge late in the afternoon, Lucy did not want to tarry there till next day. She had a strange, eager longing to get back to her sister and to the place she called home, the lonely homestead under the Rim. That had been the cause, she thought, of her restlessness while in the city.

Bert and Mertie, vastly important about the change in their lives, hurried to his home to reveal their secret, assuring Lucy that they would come out to the ranch next day. Lucy hired one of the few automobiles in Cedar Ridge, and in charge of a competent driver she arrived at Johnson's just before sunset. Sam's younger brother offered to ride up to Denmeade's with her, and pack her baggage. As there was no school session during late fall and winter, Mr. Jenks had left with the understanding that he would return in the spring.

Once on horseback again, Lucy began to feel free. How long she had been gone! What changes had come! These were exemplified in the transformation fall had wrought in the verdure along the trails. Only the great pines had not changed, yet their needle foliage had a tinge of brown. The fern leaves that had waved so beautifully green and graceful were now crisp and shriveled; the grape vines were yellow; the brown-eyed daisies were all gone; the sycamore trees were turning and the cotton-woods had parted with their beauty. Likewise had the walnut trees.

In places where Lucy could see the Rim she was astounded and delighted. She had carried away a picture of the colored walls, but now there was a blaze of gold, purple, cerise, scarlet, all the hues of fire. Frost had touched maples, aspens, oaks, with a magic wand. It seemed another and more beautiful forest land that she was entering. Up and down, everywhere along the trail, her horse waded through autumn leaves. The level branches of spruce and pine, that reached close to her, were littered with fallen leaves, wrinkled and dried. How different the sound of hoofs! Now they padded, rustled, when before they had crunched and cracked.

The melancholy days had come. As the sunset hues failed Lucy saw purple haze as thick as smoke filling the hollows. The aisles were deserted of life, sear and brown, shading into twilight. She rode down into the deep forest glen and up out of it before overtaken by night. How comforting the dusky halls of the woodland! Assuredly she was going to find out something about herself when she could think it out. Sam's little brother talked whenever the trail was steep and his horse lagged close to Lucy's. Homely bits of news, pertaining to his simple life, yet Lucy found them sweet.

The hunter's moon lighted the last mile of the ride up to the Denmeade clearing. Weird, moon-blanched, the great wall seemed to welcome her. What had come to her under its looming shadow? Black and silent the forest waved away to the dim boundaries. Lucy forgot her weariness. The baying of the hounds loosened the thrills that had been in abeyance, waiting for this moment when she rode up the lane. She peered for the white gleam of her canvas tent. Gone! Had Clara moved into the cabin? Then she made out that the tent wall had been boarded halfway up and the roof shingled. A light shone through the canvas. Lucy could scarcely wait to get her baggage from the boy and to tell him what to do.

Her voice stirred scrape of chair and flying footsteps

inside the tent. The door swept open and Clara rushed out with a cry of welcome. Even in the poignant joy of the moment Lucy, as she folded Clara in a close embrace, missed the fragile slenderness that had characterized her sister's form. Then they were in the brightly lighted tent, where for a little the sweetness of reunion precluded all else.

"Let go of me, so I can see you," said Lucy, breaking away from her sister. "Oh, Clara!"

That was all she could say to this beautiful brown-faced radiant-eyed apparition.

"Yes, I'm well!" cried Clara. "Strong as a bear. Almost fat! I wondered what you'd think. . . . You see, your wilderness home and people have cured me. . . . More! Oh, sister, I'm afraid to say it—but I'm happy, too."

"Darling! Am I dreaming?" burst out Lucy, in a rapture. "What has happened? How have you done it? Who? . . . Why, I worried myself sick about you! Look at *me!* I'm thin, pale. And here you show yourself . . . Oh, Clara, you're just lovely! What have you been doing?"

"Simple as a b c, as Danny says," returned Clara. "When you left I just felt that I would get well and— and all right again—or I'd die trying. I took up your work, and I've done it. I worked every way they'd let me. I rode and climbed and walked every day with Joe. And eat? Oh, I've been a little pig!"

"Every day with Joe!" echoed Lucy, with eyes of love, hope, fear, doubt upon this strange sister. "Has *that* changed you so wonderfully?"

When had Lucy seen such a smile on Clara's face?

"Yes. But no more than taking up your work," she rejoined, with serious sweetness. "Joe cured my body. He got me out into the fields and the woods. I really wasn't so sick. I was weak, starved, spiritless. Then your work with the children, with all the Denmeades, showed me how life is worth living. I just woke up."

"I don't care who or what has done it," cried Lucy, embracing her again. "Bless Joe! . . . But, oh, Clara, if he was the way Edd said he was before I left—what is he now?"

"He loves me, yes," said Clara, with a dreaming smile.
Lucy's lips trembled shut on a query she feared to utter, and she endeavored to conceal her emotion by lifting her baggage to the bed.

"Well, that's no news," she said, lightly. "How's my wild-bee hunter?"

"I can't see any change," replied Clara, laughing. "You wrote me only twice, and him not at all."

"Him? Clara, did *he* expect to hear from me?" asked Lucy, facing about.

"I'm sure not, but he wanted to. Every night when he got home from his work—he's gathering honey now—he'd come to me and ask if I'd heard. I think he missed you and Mertie. He wondered how she'd get along in Felix."

"I ought to have written," said Lucy, as much to herself as to Clara. "But I found it hard. I *wanted* to. . . . I don't know where I stand. Perhaps now . . . Heigho! Well, as for Mertie, he needn't have worried about *her*."

"Lucy, I confess I'm curious myself," replied Clara.

"Mertie was just a crazy country girl who'd been badly influenced," went on Lucy. "She had good stuff in her, as I guessed, and she really cared for Bert. Mertie wanted something, she didn't know what. But I knew. And I gave it to her. I bought her everything she fancied and I took her everywhere. It did not seem possible to me that anyone could be so wildly happy as she was. And Bert? Goodness! It was good to see him. . . . They're married, and, I'm sure, settled for life."

"Married! Well, Lucy Watson, you *are* a worker. So that was why you took them to Felix?" replied Clara.

"Not at all. But it fell in with the natural order of things. Don't you breathe it. Mertie and Bert will be out here to-morrow to surprise the folks. They'll be glad. I wonder how Edd will take it."

"He'll be happy," mused Clara. "He loves that flipperty-gibbet. . . . So they're married. It seems about all young people can do."

"Are you speaking for yourself, or for me, sister?" queried Lucy, teasingly.

"Not for myself, surely. . . . Lucy, I think I hear Allie calling us to supper."

The welcome accorded Lucy in that simple household was something even more satisfying than the meed of praise she had received at Felix. Edd Denmeade was not present. His father said he was out, camping on a long bee hunt. Lucy tried to ward off conviction that his absence was a relief. Yet she wanted to see him. The feelings were contrary.

Lucy parried the queries about Mertie by saying that she would be home to-morrow to answer for herself. The clamor of the children was subdued by the delivery of sundry presents from town. For that matter, Lucy did not forget any of the Denmeades. She had remembered what joy a gift brought to them, one and all. For Edd she had purchased a magnifying glass and a field glass, for use in his study of bees.

"Sis, what'd you bring me?" queried Clara, jealously, when they were back in the tent.

"Myself. Is that enough?" teased Lucy.

"Of course. . . . Lucy, you must have spent a lot of money," said Clara, seriously.

"I shore did. All I had except what you wrote for. I have that."

"It's very—good of you," replied Clara.

"What'd you need so much money for?" asked Lucy, frankly. "It surprised me."

"It's—— I—— Well, there's a woman in Kingston," said Clara, averting her face. "I owed her money. I hated to tell you before, hoping she'd wait till I could earn some. But she wrote me."

"How did she know you were here?" queried Lucy, in surprise.

"I wrote to her first—about it," returned Clara.

"You mustn't owe money to anyone," said Lucy, decidedly. "Send her a money order from Cedar Ridge. . . . Don't look like that, dear. I'm glad to help you. What's mine is yours. . . . You'll be pleased when I tell you my salary was raised and my work highly recommended. I had to teach several new welfare workers."

And Lucy talked on and on, trying to chase away that strange look from Clara's face, and also to talk herself into a forgetfulness of questioning surprise and vague misgivings. Not in a month could Clara recover wholly from the past! Lucy was unutterably grateful for a change far beyond her hopes.

"It was warm in Felix. Here it's cold," said Lucy, shivering closer to the little stove. "But the frost, the air feel so good."

"We had six inches of snow," replied Clara, importantly. "I just loved it. Second snow I ever saw! But it melted off next day. . . . Edd and Joe fixed up our tent. Oh, when the wind howled and the snow seeped, it would have been great if you'd been here. I was a little afraid, all alone!"

"Snow already? Well, I missed it, didn't it? . . . Clara, let's stay out here all winter."

"Oh, I hope we can. I don't see what else we can do—not till spring. . . . Lucy, I've news for you. Mr. Denmeade told me that both the Claypools and Johnsons had complained to him because he was *keeping* you here so long. They say you're partial to the Denmeades, and that if you don't go to them soon they'll report you. I hope it's not possible for them to hurt you."

Lucy had expected to hear this very news. While in Felix she had anticipated it and prepared her employers for complaints of this nature.

"They can't hurt me, Clara," she rejoined, soberly. "I made this job and I can handle it to suit myself. But the Claypools and Johnsons are right. I *am* partial to the Denmeades, so far. I always meant to be fair and I shall try to be. Circumstances, however, make my duty harder than I thought it would be. Indeed, I was fortunate to come here first. I owe my success to that. Now I've got to face the music. We'll ride down to Claypool's and then to Johnson's, and arrange to go to them in the spring and summer. But we'll return here in the fall."

"We! Must *I* go with you?" exclaimed Clara.

"Must you? Why, Clara, of course you must go with me," declared Lucy, in amaze. "Whatever are you thinking of? How could I get along without you now?"

"I—I thought you might let me stay here," replied Clara, with confusion rare in her. "They have talked about it, and I'd hate to leave, to break into a strange family. Mr. Denmeade and Joe, the mother and children, all say they won't let you go. Edd says you'll *have* to go, and you will go because you're honest. . . . I'm selfish, Lucy. I hope you can do your welfare work from here. You could in all seasons but winter. We could ride horseback twice a day, even as far as Miller's. But if you can't see it that way, or let me stay here at least part of the time, of course I'll be glad to go, to work for you. I'm just a coward. These Denmeades have put something back in my heart. To live near that Sam Johnson would drive me wild. Mrs. Denmeade says the Spralls are bad, and Edd says you'll go there despite him or all of us. I met Bud Sprall one day when I was hunting squirrels with Joe. He was at the dance we went to in September. I caught him looking at me. And you should have seen him looking at me when I was with Joe. . . . Lucy, he couldn't have heard about me, could he?"

"I don't see how," declared Lucy, emphatically. " 'Way up here in this wilderness? Impossible! I did not hear about you even in Felix. I met all our old friends. But no one even hinted of what you fear."

Clara received this information with a stress of feeling disproportionate to its importance, Lucy thought, and she seemed singularly grateful for it.

"Lucy, there's bad blood between Edd and this Bud Sprall," went on Clara. "I've heard things not intended for my ears. You've got to hold in your wild-bee hunter or he'll kill Bud Sprall."

"Clara, I called Edd Denmeade my wild-bee hunter just for fun," protested Lucy. "I—I thought it would amuse you. But goodness! he's not mine! That's ridiculous! And I'm not responsible for his feuds. He hated Bud Sprall before I ever came here."

"That's perfectly true, Lucy, but the fact remains Edd

is yours whether you want him or not. And you *can* keep him from killing this fellow."

"What have I got to do?" demanded Lucy, flippantly. "I suppose you'll suggest that I—I throw myself into Edd's arms to keep him from becoming a murderer."

"It'd be noble welfare work, wouldn't it? And you like the boy!"

"I don't like him as much as that," muttered Lucy, doggedly.

"Well then, you're as fickle as I used to be. For when you came back from the bee hunt with Edd last month you were in love. Or else I don't know that little old disease."

"Nonsense, Clara!" exclaimed Lucy, greatly irritated and perplexed with her sister. "I was out of my head. Excited, full of the joy of the outdoors. I might have been in love with the forest, the canyon, the wildness and beauty of this country. I am so still. But that's——"

"Edd Denmeade and this wilderness are one and the same," interrupted Clara. "But pray don't mind my arguments, dearest Lucy. Sometimes you seem my little sister, instead of me being yours. We always disagreed. I suppose we always shall. I don't think you will ever care to live in Felix again. I know I never shall. And we can't help the effect we have on these boys. . . . Something will come of it, that's all. . . . You're tired, and I've worried you. Let's go to bed."

Next day Lucy was too devoted to getting settled and taking up the threads of her work to face at once the serious self-scrutiny that was inevitable. She welcomed any excuse to postpone it. Besides, she was weary of introspection. She felt like a fluttering leaf attached to a shaking twig and soon to be at the mercy of the storm. Always something was going to happen, but so far as she could tell it had not happened yet. Clara was an enigma. Despite the marvelous improvement in her, Lucy could not dispel a vague dread. It was intuitive, and resembled the shadow of a sword over her head.

She had a frank talk with Denmeade about the Claypools and the Johnsons. The old backwoodsman was honest and fair in his attitude toward them, in his statement of how much more they needed Lucy now than his own family. She could not delay her service in their behalf longer than early spring. He believed that Lucy could allay their jealous anxieties by going to see them and to plan with them for her coming. At the conclusion of this interview with Denmeade Lucy carried away the rather disturbing impression that the Denmeades had made her presence there a sort of personal triumph. She was living with them. What she had taught them, the improvements she had installed for cleaner and happier living, had only elevated them in their own regard above their neighbors. It made a bad situation.

Late that afternoon Mertie and Bert arrived in their best Felix clothes, mysteriously radiant.

"Clara, look," said Lucy, peeping out of the tent. "I knew nothing in the world would keep Mertie from arriving in that dress. She has ridden horseback—from Johnsons' anyway."

"She looks nice. It's a pretty dress," replied Clara. "Bert, though—isn't he perfectly killing? Acts like a young lord. . . . Well, I hope they'll be happy."

"Let's not miss this. They can't keep it longer. Why, it shines from them!"

"Excuse me, Lucy. You go. I'll see them later," returned Clara.

Though Lucy went out at once, she was too late to be present when the young couple confessed. As Lucy entered the yard an uproar began on the porch. Mertie and Bert had timed their arrival for an hour when the whole family was at home. The parental blessing had certainly been received. Lucy halted a moment to peep through the thin-foliaged peach trees. The children were screaming at the top of their lungs, yet that din could not quite drown the gay, happy, excited voices of the Denmeade women and the deep, hoarse tones of the men.

Lucy's eyes suddenly filled with tears and her heart throbbed with gladness. Only she knew just how re-

sponsible she had been for this happy event. Only she—
and perhaps Edd—had known the narrow verge Mertie
Denmeade had willfully trod. Therefore she tarried a
little longer at the fence, patting the noses of the smoking
horses.

When she did present herself to the family on the
porch the wild excitement had subsided.

"Reckon the boys an' girls will storm Mertie to-
morrow, shore," Denmeade was saying. "An' you want to
make ready for a high old time."

Lucy mounted the porch to gaze about her, smiling,
with pretended surprise.

"What's all the fun about?" she inquired.

"Wal now, Miss Lucy!" ejaculated Denmeade, rising
and actually taking off his hat. Then he seized her hand
in his big rough ones and beamed down on her, his
brown grizzled face as rugged as the bark of a pine, yet
expressive of the deepest feeling. "Wal now, you played
hob!"

That was all he had time to say before the children
enveloped Lucy, and Allie and Mrs. Denmeade for once
manifested their womanly appreciation of her goodness
to them. The boys were undemonstrative. Dick stood
like a tall sapling outlined against the open sky. Joe sat
in the background against the wall, quiet-eyed, intent.
Edd had evidently just come home, for his ragged leather
chaps and his jeans bore substance and odor of the
woods. He stood behind Mertie, who sat on the edge of
the table, pale with the passion of her importance and the
sensation she had created. She had her hands back of her,
holding to Edd's. The bright silk dress contrasted
strangely with the subdued colors around her. Bert stood,
foot on a bench, elbow on his knee, gazing adoringly
down upon his bride. His gaudy necktie matched her
gown.

"Howdy, city girl!" drawled Edd, to Lucy. He gave her
no other greeting. The deep gaze accompanying his
words was embarrassing and baffling to Lucy. She
laughed and retorted:

"Howdy, wild-bee hunter!"

Thereupon Mertie launched again into the wild and whirling recital that evidently Lucy's arrival had broken for the moment. When, presently, she paused for breath, Bert flicked the ashes off his cigarette and announced to Denmeade:

"Pa turned over the sawmill to me. Weddin' present!"

"Dog-gone me!" ejaculated Denmeade, vociferously. "If you ain't lucky—gettin' the mill an' Mert at one lick."

"Yep, my luck turned that day we had our bean pickin'," replied Bert, happily.

"Wal, to talk business, we've been runnin' up a log cabin for Joe's homestead, over on the mesa. 'Crost the gully from Edd's place. An' I'm wonderin' if you can saw an' deliver a lot of floor boards, door frames, an' such."

"I just can, you bet," declared the young man. "Give me your order. I'll deliver lumber at foot of the mesa trail in less than a week."

"Fine! You're a Jasper for rustlin'. Shore I expected to pack the lumber up on the burros. Long job, but Dick an' Joe can drive the pack while the rest of us work. Edd expects to be done cuttin' for honey soon. Then he can help. We'll have Joe's cabin done by the time snow flies."

"Get pencil an' paper so we can figure out just what lumber you want."

Father and son-in-law went into the kitchen, while Mertie broke into further elaboration of her romance. Lucy remained a few moments longer, fascinated by the rapt faces of the listening Denmeades, especially Edd. He seemed transfigured. Lucy suffered a twinge of remorse for having considered him a clod. How tremendously he had been affected by this happy settling of Mertie's affairs! More than once Lucy had heard it said that a Denmeade married was safe. Presently Lucy returned to her tent and unfinished tasks.

Supper was not ready until dusk, a fact which testified to the upsetting of the household. Then the lack of the usual bountiful meal was made up for by merriment. Lucy felt glad to free herself from an excitement that had begun to wear on her nerves. Moreover, she needed to be alone. As she passed Clara and Joe sitting on the porch steps she could just catch the gleam of their faces in the dim lamplight, Clara's pensive and sweet, and Joe's locked in its impassive youthful strength. Oh, boy and girl! thought Lucy with a pang. They could not help themselves. One called to the other. Clara's tragic childhood was fading into a past that was gone. She had to live, to breathe, to move; and this wilderness called to primitive emotions.

As Lucy halted a moment to pay her usual silent tribute to the black Rim above and the stars of white fire, she heard the gate creak, and then a quick step and jingle of spurs.

"Wait!" called Edd, with a ring in his voice. He could see her in the dark when she could not see him. The word, the tone halted her, and she seemed conscious of a sudden inward stilling. His tall form appeared, blacker than the darkness, loomed over her. Involuntarily Lucy took a backward step. Then Edd clasped her in his arms.

It was like the hug of a bear. Lucy's arms were pinned to her sides and she was drawn so close she could scarcely catch her breath. A terrible weakness assailed her. Not of anger, not of resentment! It was something else, strangely akin to a mingling of amaze and relief. Caught at last in her own toils!

"Oh—Edd!" she whispered, meaning to beg to be let go, but she never completed the appeal. Her arms moved instinctively upward, until stopped by the giant clasp that held her. What had she meant to do? How her mind whirled! He did not speak, and the moment seemed an age.

She felt the ripple of his muscles and the rough flannel of his shirt against her cheek. The scent of pine and honeybees and the woodland clung to his clothes. Lucy quivered on the brink of a tumultuous unknown.

Suddenly his arms uncoiled. Lucy swayed a little, not sure of her equilibrium.

"Shore I had to," he gasped, huskily. "Words don't come easy—for me. . . . God bless you for savin' Mertie!"

He plunged away into the blackness, his boots thumping, his spurs clinking. Lucy stood motionless, gazing into the gloom where he had vanished. Her heart seemed to take a great drop. Shivering, she went into the tent.

There she swiftly put a few knots of wood into the stove, set the damper, blew out the lamp, and hurriedly undressed for bed.

The darkness and the blankets were comforting. A faint crackle of burning wood broke the silence and tiny streaks of firelight played upon the tent walls.

"It was for Mertie he held me in his arms," whispered Lucy.

And she had taken it for herself. His gratitude had betrayed her. Lucy realized now that if her arms had been free she would have lifted them round his neck. She had not known what she was doing. But now she knew she loved him. Edd Denmeade, backwoodsman, wild-bee hunter! She suffered no shame in that. Indeed there was a hidden voice deep within her ready to ring the truth. She had sought to save and she had lost herself.

Lucy lay wide-eyed long after Clara slept, nestled with an arm around her, as in childish days. The night wind moaned through the forest, mournful, wild, lonely, as if voicing the inscrutable cry in Lucy's soul.

She had no regrets. She had burned her bridges behind her. The visit to Felix had clarified in mind all the perplexing doubts and dreads about the past. She and Clara had not had the training, the love, and the home life necessary to equip girls to deal with life happily. All her childhood she had suffered under the ban of position; all her girlhood had been poisoned by longings she could not attain, ignominies she could not avoid. She had grown to young womanhood terribly sensitive to the class distinctions so ruthlessly adhered to in all cultivated communities. She was old enough now to realize that true worth always was its own reward, and seldom failed of ultimate appreciation. But city life, multitudes of people, the social codes had all palled upon her. Never again could she live under their influence. Her victory over environment had come too late. The iron had entered Lucy's soul.

It was good to find herself at last. Every hour since her return to the Denmeades had been fraught with stirrings and promptings and misgivings now wholly clear to her. The wild-bee hunter, in his brotherly love, had hugged away her vanity and blindness. Poor groping Edd! It was what he was that had made her love him. Not what she wanted to make him! Yet the cold sensation of shock round her heart seemed to warm at the consciousness of his growth. Before her coming to the wilderness home of the Denmeades had he, or any of the children, ever thought of God? Lucy realized that the higher aspect of her work was missionary. Always she had been marked for sacrifice. In this hour of humility she delved out her acceptance.

Her sister slept on, with that little hand clinging close even in slumber. Lucy listened to her gentle breathing and felt the soft undulations of her breast. The mystery of life was slowly dawning upon Lucy. She had no wish to change what was, and the prayer she mutely voiced eliminated herself.

Outside the night wind rose, from mournful sough to weird roar. A hound bayed off in the forest. A mouse or ground squirrel rustled in the brush under the floor of the tent. The flicker of the fire died out. A frosty air blew in the window. These things were realities, strong in their importunity for peace and joy of living. It was only the ghosts of the past that haunted the black midnight hour.

CHAPTER XII

Denmeade's prediction was verified. Before noon of the next day the younger members of the neighboring families began to ride in, nonchalant, casual, as if no unusual event had added significance to their visit. Then when another string headed in from the Cedar Ridge trail Denmeade exploded.

"Wal, you're goin' to be stormed," he said, warningly, to the bride and groom. "Shore it'll be a Jasper, too."

"For the land's sake!" exclaimed his good wife. "They'll eat us out of house an' home. An' us not ready!"

"Now, ma, I gave you a hunch yestiddy," replied Denmeade. "Reckon you can have dinner late. Mrs. Claypool will help you an' Allie."

"But that young outfit will drive me wild," protested Mrs. Denmeade.

"Never mind, ma. I'll take care of them," put in Edd. "Fact is I've a bee tree only half a mile from home. I've been savin' it. I'll rustle the whole caboodle up there an' make them pack honey back."

"Mertie will want to stay home, dressed all up," averred his mother.

"Wal, she can't. We'll shore pack her along, dress or no dress."

Early in the afternoon Edd presented himself before Lucy's tent and announced:

"Girls, we're packin' that spoony couple away from home for a spell. The women folks got to have elbow room to fix up a big dinner. Whole country goin' to storm Mert!"

Clara appeared at the door, eager and smiling. "Edd, this storm means a crowd coming to celebrate?"

"Shore. But a storm is an uninvited crowd. They raise

202

hell. Between us, I'm tickled. I never thought Mertie would get a storm. She wasn't any too well liked. But Bert's the best boy in this country."

"*Maybe* he is," retorted Clara, archly. "I know a couple of boys left. . . . Edd, give us a hunch what to wear?"

"Old clothes," he grinned. "An' some kind of veil or net to keep from gettin' stung. Wild bees don't like a crowd. An' Sam Johnson thinks he's a bee tamer. This tree I'm goin' to cut is a hummer. Full of sassy bees. An' there's goin' to be some fun."

Lucy and Clara joined the formidable group of young people waiting in the yard, all armed with buckets. Lucy sensed an amiable happy spirit wholly devoid of the vexatious bantering common to most gatherings of these young people. Marriage was the consummation of their hopes, dreams, endeavors. Every backwoods youth looked forward to a homestead and a wife.

Mertie assuredly wore the bright silk dress, and ribbons on her hair, and white stockings, and low shoes not meant for the woods. Bert, however, had donned blue-jeans overalls.

The merry party set out, with Edd in the lead, and the gay children, some dozen or more, bringing up the rear. Edd carried an ax over his shoulder and a huge assortment of different-sized buckets on his arm. He led out of the clearing, back of the cabin, into the pine woods so long a favorite haunt of Lucy's, and up the gradual slope. The necessities of travel through the forest strung the party mostly into single file. Lucy warmed to the occasion. It *was* happy. How good to be alive! The golden autumn sunlight, the flame of color in the trees, the fragrant brown aisles of the forest, the flocks of birds congregating for their annual pilgrimage south— all these seemed new and sweet to Lucy. They roused emotion that the streets and houses of the city could not reach. Bert might have been aware of the company present, but he showed no sign of it. He saw nothing except Mertie. Half the time he carried her, lifting her over patches of dust, logs, and rough ground. Only where the mats of pine needles offered clean and easy travel did he let her down, and then he still kept his arm round her. Mertie was no burden for his sturdy strength. He swung her easily up and down, as occasion suited him. Lucy was struck by his naturalness.

Mertie, however, could not forget herself. She posed. She accepted. She bestowed. She was the beginning and the end of this great day. Yet despite exercise of the ineradicable trait of her nature, the romance of her marriage, the fact of her being possessed, had changed her. She had awakened. She saw Bert now as he actually was, and she seemed reaping the heritage of a true woman's feelings.

Aside from these impressions Lucy received one that caused her to sigh. Clara reacted strangely to sight of Mertie and Bert. Lucy caught a glimpse of the mocking half-smile that Clara's face used to wear. No doubt this bride and groom procession through the woods, the open love-making, oblivious at least on Bert's part, brought back stinging memories to Clara.

Edd led the gay party out of the woods into a beautiful canyon, wide and uneven, green and gold with growths, dotted by huge gray rocks, and trees. A dry stream bed wound by stony steps up the canyon. Edd followed this bowlder-strewn road for a few hundred yards, then climbed to a wide bench. Maples and sycamores spread scattered patches of shale over this canyon glade. A riot of autumn colors almost stunned the eyesight. The thick grass was green, the heavy carpet of ferns brown.

"Wal, there she is," said Edd, pointing to a gnarled white-barked tree perhaps a hundred paces distant. "First sycamore I ever found bees in. It's hollow at the trunk where she goes in. I reckon she's a hummer. Now you-all hang back a ways while I look her over."

Edd strode off toward the sycamore, and his followers approached, mindful of his admonition. They got close enough, however, to see a swarm of bees passing to and fro from the dark hollow of the tree trunk. Edd's perfect sang-froid probably deceived the less experienced boys.

He circled the sycamore, gazed up into the hollow, and made what appeared to be a thorough examination. Sam Johnson showed that he was holding back only through courtesy. The remarks of the boys behind him were not calculated to make him conservative. Sadie Purdue and Amy Claypool expressed diverse entreaties, the former asking him to cut down the bee tree and the latter begging him to keep away from it. Lucy had an idea that Amy knew something about bees.

Presently Edd returned from his survey and drew the "honey-bucket outfit," as he called them, back into the shade of a maple. Mertie draped herself and beautiful dress over a clean rock, as if she, instead of the bees, was the attraction. Lucy sensed one of the interesting undercurrents of backwoods life working in those young men. Edd's position was an enviable one, as far as bees were concerned. This was a bee day. Sam Johnson could not possibly have kept himself out of the foreground. There were several boys from Cedar Ridge, including Bert, who ran a close second to Sam. On the other hand, the boys who inhabited this high country, especially Gerd Claypool, appeared unusually prone to let the others have the stage. Joe Denmeade wore an inscrutable expression and had nothing to say. Edd was master of ceremonies, and as he stood before the boys, his ax over his shoulder, Lucy conceived a strong suspicion that he was too bland, too drawling, too kind to be absolutely honest. Edd was up to a trick. Lucy whispered her suspicions to Clara, and that worthy whispered back: "I'm wise. Why, a child could see through that *hombre!* But isn't he immense?"

"Sam, I reckon you ought to be the one to chop her down," Edd was saying, after a rather elaborate preamble. "Course it ought to fall to Bert, seein' he's the reason for this here storm party. But I reckon you know more about wild bees, an' you should be boss. Shore it'd be good if you an' Bert tackled the tree together."

"I'll allow myself about three minutes' choppin' to fetch that sycamore," replied Sam. "But Bert can help if he likes."

"Somebody gimme an ax," said Bert, prowling around.

Dick Denmeade had the second ax, which he gladly turned over to Bert.

"Bert, I don't want you gettin' all stung up," protested Mertie.

"No bees would sting me to-day," replied Bert, grandly.

"Don't you fool yourself," she retorted.

"Aw, she's tame as home bees," interposed Edd. "Besides, there's been some heavy frosts. Bees get loggy along late in the fall. Reckon nobody'll get stung. If she wakes up we can run."

"I'm a-rarin' for that honey," declared Sam, jerking the ax from Edd. "Come on, Bert. Start your honeymoon by bein' boss."

That remark made a lion out of the bridegroom, while eliciting howls and giggles from his admirers. Sam strode toward the sycamore and Bert followed.

"Reckon we-all better scatter a little," said the wily Edd, and he punched Gerd Claypool in the ribs. Gerd, it appeared, was doubled up in noiseless contortions.

"Serve Sam just right," declared Sadie, "for bein' so darn smart. He never chopped down a bee tree in his life."

"Well, if I know anythin' he'll never try another," added Amy. "Oh, Edd Denmeade, you're an awful liar. Sayin' wild bees won't sting!"

"Shore Sam wanted to cut her down. He asked me back home," declared Edd.

Some of the party stood their ground, notably Mertie, who rather liked the clean dry rock. Edd gravitated toward Lucy and Clara, presently leading them unobtrusively back toward some brush.

"Dog-gone!" he whispered, chokingly, when he was out of earshot of the others. "Chance of my life! . . . Sam's cut a few bee trees in winter, when the bees were froze. . . . But, gee! these wild bees are mad as hornets. I got stung on the ear, just walkin' round. She's been worried by yellow-jackets. . . . Now there's goin' to be some fun. She'll be a hummer. . . . Girls, put on whatever you fetched along an' be ready to duck into this brush."

"Edd, you're as bad as a cowboy," said Clara, producing a veil.

"Looks like great fun for us, but how about the bees?" rejoined Lucy.

"There you go, sister. Always thinking about the under dog! . . . Edd, do you know, I can't see how anyone could help loving Lucy," retorted Clara, mischievously.

"Shore. I reckon nobody does," drawled Edd. "Wal, Sam's begun to larrup it into my sycamore. *Now watch!*"

Sam had sturdily attacked the tree, while the more cautious Bert had cut several boughs, evidently to thresh off bees. Scarcely had he reached the objective spot when Sam jerked up spasmodically as if kicked from behind.

"Beat 'em off!" he yelled.

Then, as the valiant Bert dropped his ax, and began to thresh with the boughs, Sam redoubled his energies at the chopping. He might not have possessed much knowledge about wild bees, but he could certainly handle an ax. Quick and hard rang his blows. The sycamore was indeed rotten, for it sounded hollow and crackling, and long dusty strips fell aside.

Lucy stole a glance at Edd. He was manifestly in the grip of a frenzied glee. Never before had Lucy seen him so. He was shaking all over; his face presented a wonderful study of features in convulsions; his big hands opened and shut. All at once he burst out in stentorian yell: "Wow! There she comes!"

Lucy flashed her glance back toward the axman, just in time to see a small black cloud, like smoke, puff out of the hollow of the tree and disintegrate into thin air. Sam let out a frantic yell, and dropping the ax he plunged directly toward his admiring comrades.

"You darn fool!" roared Edd. "Run the other way!"

But Sam, as if pursued by the furies, sprang, leaped, wrestled, hopped, flew, flapping his hands like wings and yelling hoarsely. Bert suddenly became as if possessed of a thousand devils, and he raced like a streak, waving his two green boughs over his head, till he plunged over a bank into the brush.

Some of the Cedar Ridge boys had approached a point

within a hundred feet of the sycamore. Suddenly their
howls of mirth changed to excited shouts, and they broke
into a run. Unfortunately, they were not on the moment
chivalrously mindful of the girls.

"Run for your lives!" screamed Amy Claypool.

Lucy found herself being rushed into the bushes by
Edd, who had also dragged Clara. He was laughing so
hard he could not speak. He fell down and rolled over.
Clara had an attack of laughter that seemed half hysteri-
cal. "Look! Look!" she cried.

Lucy was more frightened than amused, but from the
shelter of the bushes she peered forth, drawing aside her
veil so she could see better. She was in time to see the
bright silk dress that incased Mertie soaring across the
ground like a spread-winged bird. Mertie was noted for
her fleetness of foot. Sadie Purdue, owing to a rather
short stout figure, could not run very well. Sam, by
accident or design, had fled in her direction. It did not
take a keen eye to see the whirling dotted circle of bees
he brought with him. Some of them sped like bullets
ahead of him to attack Sadie. Shrieking, she ran away
from Sam as though he were a pestilence. She was the
last to flee out of sight.

Presently Edd sat up, wet-faced and spent from the
energy of his emotions.

"Reckon I've played hob—but dog-gone!—it was fun,"
he said. "Shore Sam's a bee hunter! I'll bet he'll look like
he had measles. . . . Did you see Sadie gettin' stung? She
was that smart. Haw! Haw! Haw!"

Joe came crawling to them through the bushes. For
once his face was not quiet, intent. He showed his
relationship to Edd.

"Say, Sam will be hoppin' mad," he said.

"He shore was hoppin' when last I seen him," replied
Edd. "Wal, I reckon I'll have to finish the job. You
girls stay right here, for a while, anyhow."

Whereupon Edd pulled a rude hood from his pocket
and drew it over his head and tight under his chin. It
was made of burlap and had two rounded pieces of
window screen sewed in to serve as eyeholes. Then

putting his gloves on he got up and tramped out toward the sycamore. Lucy left Clara with Bert, and slipped along under the bushes until she reached the end nearest the tree. Here she crouched to watch. She could see the bees swarm round Edd, apparently without disturbing him in the least. He picked up the ax, and with swift powerful strokes he soon chopped through on one side of the hollow place, so that the other side broke, letting the tree down with a splitting crash. After the dust cleared away Lucy saw him knocking the trunk apart. The swarm of bees spread higher and wider over his head. Lucy could hear the angry buzz. She felt sorry for them. How ruthless men were! The hive had been destroyed; the winter's food of the bees would be stolen.

"Hey, Joe!" called Edd. "Round up that outfit to pack honey back home. There's more here than we got buckets to hold. Tell them I'll fetch it part way, so they won't get stung no more."

Lucy caught glimpses of the members of the party collecting a goodly safe distance away, along the edge of the timber. Judging by gestures and the sound of excited voices coming faintly, Lucy concluded that the storm party was divided in its attitude toward Edd. Sadie Purdue evidently was in a tantrum, the brunt of which fell upon Sam. Amy's high sweet laugh pealed out. Presently the girls were seen entering the forest, no doubt on their way back to the cabin; the boys showed indications of standing by Edd, at least to the extent of waiting for him to collect the honey.

Lucy saw him filling the buckets. He used a small wooden spoon or spade with which he reamed the honey out of the hollow log. She was intensely eager to see this bee hive and Edd's work at close hand, but felt it wise to remain under cover. The screams of the girls who had been stung were a rather potent inhibition to curiosity.

The honey had a grayish-yellow cast and a deep amber color, from which Lucy deducted that one was the comb, the other the honey. When Edd had filled four buckets he took them up and proceeded to carry them toward the waiting boys. A number of bees kept him company. How grotesque he looked with that homemade hood over his head!

"Hey! you better lay low," he called to Lucy, seeing her peeping out of her brushy covert, "unless you want your pretty little pink nose stung!"

"Edd Denmeade, my nose isn't little—or pink!" protested Lucy.

"Wal, no matter; it shore will be pink if you don't watch out. Didn't you get stung on it once?"

Halfway between the bee tree and the boys Edd set the buckets down on a rock, and cutting some brush he covered them with it. Then he shouted:

"Pack these home, you storm-party honey suckers!"

Upon his return to the fallen sycamore he scraped up a bundle of dead grass and sticks, and kindled a fire, then added green boughs to make a heavy smoke. Lucy saw him vigorously slap his back and his legs, from which action she surmised that he too was getting stung. Next with two leafy boughs he made an onslaught on the whirling shining mill-wheel of bees. He broke that wheel, and either killed or scattered most of the swarm. Then he proceeded to fill more buckets, which he carried away as before. Meanwhile Joe and Gerd Claypool had come for the first buckets.

Lucy crawled back through the bushes to where she had left Clara. She found her prone on the grass, her chin propped on her hands, musingly watching the proceedings.

"Funny how we are," she said. "It's a long time since I felt so good over anything. Sam and Sadie were immense. . . . Pride—and conceit, too—go before a fall!"

"You remember I was stung on the nose by one of these wild bees," replied Lucy. "It hurts terribly."

They remained in the shade and security of this covert until Edd had filled all his buckets.

"Hello, girls! Go back through the bushes to the bank, an' get down," he called. "Wait for us below."

Lucy and Clara scrambled away into the thicket and down into the stream bed, which they followed to the woods. Joe and Gerd and Dick came along laden with heavy buckets, and rather harassed by a few persistent bees.

"Keep away from us," cried Lucy. "I've been initiated into the wild-bee fraternity."

"But Clara hasn't," replied Joe.

"Young man, if you know when you're well off, you'll not lead any wild bees to me," warned Clara, gathering up her skirts ready to flee into the woods. She was smiling, yet earnest. How pretty she looked, her eyes flashing, her brown cheeks flushed, her blue veil flying round her golden hair! Lucy saw what Joe saw.

Next Edd came striding out of the willows, down into the gully. He carried four buckets, all manifestly laden. He had removed his hood, and his face was wet with sweat and wreathed in smiles.

"Run along ahead till she gets tired followin' me," he called to the girls.

They were not slow to act upon his advice, yet did not get so far ahead that they could not see the boys coming. The forest seemed so shady and cool after the hot sunny open.

"Why does Edd speak of bees as she?" queried Clara, curiously.

"He told me once he had captured and tamed queen bees, and after that always called bees she, whether collectively or individually. It is funny."

"He'll be making you queen bee of his hive some day," said Clara, tantalizingly.

"Oh, will he? It requires the consent of the queen, I imagine. . . . As to queen-bee hives, Joe's is being built, I hear."

Clara squeezed Lucy's arm and cringed close to her, as if to hide a shamed or happy face. "Oh, what will become of us? . . . When I don't *think,* I'm full of some new kind of joy. When I *remember,* I'm wretched."

"Clara, we are two babes lost in the woods," declared Lucy, half sadly. "But if you must think, do it intelligently. We could be worse off."

"I love it here," answered Clara, swiftly, with a flash of passion.

Then Edd's halloo halted them. Presently Lucy had opportunity to see wild honey fresh from the hive. The buckets were full of the yellow combs and amber honey, all massed together, in which numbers of bees had been drowned.

"Shore it's got to be strained," explained Edd.

"What'll become of the bees—those you didn't kill?" she inquired.

"Wal, now, I wish you hadn't asked that," complained Edd. "Shore you always hit at the sufferers. . . . Lucy, I hate to treat a bee tree like we did this one. But I can't capture an' tame the old swarms. They're too wild. I have to destroy them. Sometimes I burn them out. . . . She'll hang round that sycamore, an' starve to death or freeze. It's too bad. I reckon I'm no better than the yellow-jackets."

That bee-tree episode had taken the younger element of the storm party away from the Denmeade home for the greater part of the afternoon, a fact for which Mrs. Denmeade was devoutly thankful. She and Allie, with the kind assistance of the Claypool women, prepared on short notice an adequate feast for this formidable array of uninvited guests.

Lucy learned this, and much more, upon her arrival at the cabin. Mertie had torn the bright silk dress and was inconsolable. She did not seem to mind so much the sundry stings she had sustained. But Sadie Purdue almost disrupted the hilarious and joyful tone of the occasion. She had been severely stung on hands and arms and face. Sam Johnson, however, was the one who had suffered most. All the members of that expedition, except Lucy and Clara, had reason to vow vengeance upon Edd.

"Oh, wait, you wild hunter of bees! Wait till you're married!" was the reiterated threat.

"Shore I'm safe," drawled Edd. "No girl would ever throw herself away on me."

Sam took his punishment like a man, and made up

for the ravings of his *fiancée*. She had the grace, presently,
to get over her fury. And by supper-time, when Mertie
was won back to a happy appreciation of the honor of
having the largest storm party ever known in that country,
the jarring notes were as if they had never been.

All the chair, bench, and porch space was necessary
to seat this merry company. It was quite impossible for
Lucy to keep track of what followed. But she had never
seen the like of that dinner. Uproarious, even violent, it
yet gave expression to the joy and significance of marriage in that wilderness.

White mule flowed freely, but in marked contrast with
its effect at the dances, it added only to the mirth and
the noise. After dinner the young people nearly tore the
cabin down with their onslaughts upon the bride and
groom, the former of whom they hugged and kissed, and
the latter mauled. Dancing was not on this program.
Then, evidently, for the young backwoodsmen present, it
was a natural climax to fly from their felicitations of the
bride to salutations to the possible brides-to-be in that
gathering. They were like young bears.

Lucy and Clara fled to the security of their tent, and
refused to come out. Certain it was that both of them
were more than amused and frightened. Manifestly a
storm party on a bride was regarded as an unexampled
opportunity.

"Whew!" gasped Clara, with wide eyes on Lucy. "I
thought cowboys were wild. But alongside these fellows
they're tame."

"Deliver—me!" panted Lucy. "Almost it'd be—safer
to be—in Mertie's boots!"

The celebration, however, turned out to be as short as
it had been intense. Before dark the older people were
riding down the lane, calling back their merry good-nights,
and not long after the boys and girls followed. Soon the
homestead of the Denmeades was as quiet as ever; and
a little later, when Lucy peeped out, yard and cabin were
shrouded in the blackness of the melancholy autumn
night.

CHAPTER XIII

It was midwinter. Lucy's tent was cozy and warm, softly colored with its shaded lamplight, falling on bear rugs and bright blankets, on the many paper pictures. The Clara that sat there beside the little stove, occupied with needlework, was not the Clara who had arrived at Cedar Ridge one memorable day last summer. Lucy was having leisure for books.

The tent seemed to be full of the faint fragrance of juniper, and that came from the wood which the little stove burned so avidly. Lucy was wont to say that of all Clara's homestead accomplishments that of feeding wood to a fire was what she did best and liked most. "Maybe I'll have to *chop* wood myself some day. I could do worse," was Clara's enigmatic reply.

Outside, the snow seeped down, rustling like the fall of leaves on dry grass, floating softly against the window. No mournful wail of wind broke the dead silence. The homestead of the Denmeades was locked in winter. Lucy and Clara had long since grown used to it. For a while they had suffered from cold, but that was owing to their susceptibility rather than severe weather. Denmeade's heavy bear rugs on the floor had added much to the comfort of the tent. The girls wore woolen sweaters and no longer noticed the cold. At ten o'clock they went to bed, enjoying to the utmost this most important factor of outdoor life. Night after night, for weeks, they had spent like this, reading, sewing, studying, writing, talking, and then sleeping.

The zero mornings had put them to the test. With the fire long dead, the cold was practically the same inside as outside. They had taken turn about kindling a fire, and the one whose morning it was to lie snug and warm in

214

bed while the other slipped out into the icy air seldom failed to tease and crow.

When the tent was warm they got up and dressed, and made coffee or tea, and cooked some breakfast. No matter how deep the new-fallen snow, there was always a path shoveled from their tent to the cabin, Edd and Joe vying with each other to see who could beat the other at this task. Lucy's work now was confined to instructing the children, and Clara was studying hard to enable her to take Mr. Jenks's place as teacher of the school. The afternoons were usually sunny and clear. After a snowstorm the warm sun melted the snow away in a few days. But there were unexampled opportunities to tramp and romp and play in the snow, things in which the girls found much pleasure. They had been born and brought up in a snowless country, where the summers were torrid and the winters pleasant.

The Denmeades, however, might as well have been snowed in. Lucy marveled at this, and came to understand it as a feature of backwoods life. The men kept the fires burning and fed the stock, outside of which they had nothing, or thought they had nothing, to do. The women cooked, sewed, and washed, almost as actively as in summer. No visitors called any more on Sundays. They saw no outsiders. Once a week Dick or Joe would ride down to Johnson's for the mail, or for supplies that had been sent for. It seemed a lonely, peaceful, unproductive existence.

Edd, being the eldest of the Denmeade boys, had received the least schooling, a fact he keenly deplored, and through these winter days he laboriously pored over the books Lucy gave him. Joe was the keenest of the children, as well as the quietest, and he seconded Edd in this pursuit of knowledge.

Lucy and Clara had supper with the Denmeades, which they endeavored to serve before dark. Sometimes, when the meal was late, the light in the kitchen was so dim they could hardly see to eat. After supper the children and young people would make a rush into the other cabin where Denmeade kept a huge log or stump burning in the open fireplace. Mertie was gone, and her absence seemed a benefit. Allie and Joe were the thoughtful ones who helped Mrs. Denmeade. Seldom was a lamp lighted until Edd stamped in to resort to his books.

Every time the door was opened the dogs would try to slip in, and always one or more of them succeeded, and occupied a warm place in front of the fire. The children played until put to bed. Uncle Bill was not long in climbing to his bed in the attic. Denmeade smoked his pipe and sat gazing at the blazing log. How many hours of his life must have been spent so! Lucy and Clara always passed part of the early evening hours in this living room. Seldom or never did they have a moment alone with the boys. It was a family gathering, this after-supper vigil in front of the big fire.

Denmeade typified the homesteader of that high altitude. Winter was a time of waiting. Almost he was like a bear. Spring, summer, fall were his active seasons. The snow, the sleet, the icy winds of winter shut him in.

Lucy counteracted this growing habit in the boys. She convinced them that winter was the time to improve the mind and to learn something of what was going on in the outside world. Her success in this she considered equal to any of her achievements here. The old folks, of course, could not be changed; and Lucy confined herself to the children. Many times she thought of how all over the wild parts of the west, in high districts, children and young people were wasting golden hours, with nothing to do but what their parents had done before them. What a splendid work she would accomplish if she could make known the benefits of home instruction! But it really did not seem like work. Thus the winter days and nights passed.

The coming of spring was marked by Allie Denmeade's marriage to Gerd Claypool. These young people, wise in their generation, invited everybody to their wedding, which took place in Cedar Ridge. Lucy and Clara remained at home with the children.

March brought surprisingly fine weather, the mornings and evenings cold, but the middle of the day sunny and warm. Soon the wet red soil dried out. The men, liberated from the confines of winter, were busy taking up the tasks that had been interrupted by the first fall of snow. One of these was the completion of Joe's cabin. Lucy, using a walk with the children as excuse, climbed the mesa trail to see the men at work. Clara did not want to go. She was more studious and complex than ever, yet seemed strangely, dreamily happy.

The mesa, with its open glades, its thickets of red manzanita, its clumps of live oak, and giant junipers and lofty pines, manifested a difference hard to define. Lucy thought it had to do with spring. The birds and squirrels and turkeys voiced the joyfulness of the season.

Joe's homestead edifice was a two-cabin affair, similar to that of the Denmeades. Lucy particularly liked the clean, freshly cut pine and its fragrant odor. She urged Joe to build in several closets and to insist on windows, and kitchen shelves, and a number of improvements new to the cabin of the backwoodsman.

"Joe, are you going to live here alone?" queried Lucy.

"On an' off, while I prove up on my homesteadin' patent," he replied. "You see, I have to put in so many days here for three years before the government will give me the land."

His frank answer relieved Lucy, who had of late been subtly influenced by a strangeness, an aloofness, in Clara, which mood somehow she had attributed to Joe's infatuation for her. The boy had no pretense. His soul was as clear as his gray eyes. Lucy was compelled to believe that the erecting of this cabin was solely to forestall a threatened invasion of the mesa by other homesteaders.

On the way home Lucy stopped awhile at the beautiful site Edd had selected for his cabin. She found that thought of the place, during the fall and winter months, had somehow endeared it to her. Long communion with the secret affection of her heart had brought happiness with resignation. She knew where she stood; and daily she gathered strength to bear, to serve, to go on, to find a wonderful good in her ordeal.

The forest had wrought incalculable change in her. It was something she felt rush over her thrillingly when she approached the green wall of pine and entered it, as if going into her home. She thought more actively, she worked better, she developed more under its influence than in the city. This she knew to be because the old bitter social feud under which her youth had been oppressed was not present here. Lucy was ashamed of that relief, but she could never change it.

As she was soon to go to the Claypools to take up her work there, Lucy knew it might be long before she had the strange, inexplicable joy of dreaming here in this spot of perfect solitude and wild beauty. So while the children played at keeping house among the bears and turkeys, she gazed around her and listened and felt. She was quite at the mercy of unknown forces and she had ceased to beat and bruise her heart against them, as might have a bird against the bars of its cage. Above all, there came to her the great simple fact of a harmony with this environment. She could not resist it and she ceased to try.

Mr. Jenks arrived at the Johnsons' in the latter part of March and attended the meeting of the school board. He wanted to turn over the teaching to Clara, but in case she did not accept the position he would be glad to remain another summer. Denmeade returned from that board meeting to place a proposition squarely before Clara. And in his own words it was this: "Reckon we don't want to change teachers so often. Every schoolmarm we've had just up an' married one of the boys. Wal, if you will agree to teach two years, whether you get married or not, we'll shore be glad to let you have the job."

"I give my word," replied Clara, with a firmness Lucy knew was a guerdon that the promise would be kept.

What struck Lucy markedly on the moment was the fact that Clara did not disavow any possibility of marriage.

The deal was settled then and there, and later, when the girls had gone to the seclusion of their tent, Clara evinced a deep emotion.

"Lucy, I'll be independent now," she said. "I can pay my debt . . . I—I need money——"

"My dear, you don't owe *me* any money," interposed Lucy, "if that's what you mean."

Clara's reply was more evasive than frank, again rousing in Lucy the recurrence of a surprise and a vague dread. But she dismissed them from her consciousness.

"We'll have to settle another thing, too," said Lucy. "Once before you hinted you didn't want to go to Claypool's with me."

"I don't, but I'll go if you insist," rejoined Clara.

"If you will be happier here than with me, by all means stay," replied Lucy, in a hurt tone.

"Don't misunderstand, Lucy, darling," cried Clara, embracing her. "I'm used to this place—these Denmeades. It's like a sanctuary after——" She broke off falteringly. "It will be hard enough for me to teach school, let alone live among strangers. . . . And aren't you coming back here in the fall?"

"I don't know. It depends," answered Lucy, dubiously. "Well, it's settled then. You will live here. I suppose you'll ride horseback to and fro from the schoolhouse. That would be fine."

"Yes. Joe or Dick will ride with me every day, so I'll never be alone."

Lucy turned away her face and busied herself with papers on her table.

"Clara, have you anything particular you want to tell me?"

"Why—no," came the constrained and low reply.

Lucy divined then that there was something Clara could not tell her, and it revived the old worry.

Edd Denmeade, alone of all the family, did not take kindly to Lucy's going to the Claypools. The others, knowing that Clara was to continue to live with them and that Lucy would probably come back in the fall, were glad to propitiate their neighbors at so little a loss.

"But, Edd, why do you disapprove?" Lucy demanded, when she waylaid him among his beehives. She did not want to lose her good influence over him. She wanted very much more from him than she dared to confess.

"I reckon I've a good many reasons," returned Edd.

"Oh, you have? Well, tell me just one," said Lucy.

"Wal, the Claypools live right on the trail from Sprall's to Cedar Ridge."

"Sprall's! . . . What of it?" demanded Lucy, nonplussed.

"Bud Sprall rides that trail."

"Suppose he does. How can it concern me?" rejoined Lucy, growing irritated.

"Wal, it concerns you more'n you think. Bud told in Cedar Ridge how he was layin' for you."

"I don't understand. What did he mean?"

"Lucy, that *hombre* isn't above ropin' you an' packin' you off up over the Rim, where he holds out with his red-faced cowboy pard."

"Nonsense! The day of the outlaw is past, Edd. I haven't the least fear of Bud Sprall. Indeed, so little that I intend some day to take up my work with the Spralls."

Wheeling from his work, he loomed over her, and fastening a brawny hand in her blouse he drew her close. His eyes flashed a steely fire.

"You're not goin' to do anythin' of the kind," he said, darkly.

"Who'll prevent me?" queried Lucy.

"If you go to Sprall's I'll pack you back if I have to tie you on a hoss."

"You—will?" Lucy's voice broke in her fury.

"Shore you bet I will. Reckon you haven't forgot that dance I made you go to. I wasn't mad then. Wal, I'm as mad as hell now."

"Why do you presume to interfere with my work?"

"Can you crawl in a hog-pen without gettin' dirty?" he demanded. "I reckon your work is somethin' fine an' good. I don't begrudge that to Sprall's. But you can't go there, unless just in daytime, an' then with somebody. . . . You think I'm jealous. Wal, I'm not. Ask pa an' ma about this Sprall idea of yours."

"But, Edd, weren't you somewhat like Bud Sprall once? Didn't you tell me I helped you? Might I not do the same for——"

Edd shoved her away with violence.

"Ahuh! So you want to work the same on Bud? . . .

Wal, the day you make up to him as you did to me I'll go back to white mule. . . . An' I'll kill him!"

As he stalked away, grim and dark, Lucy shook off a cold clutch of fear and remorse, and ran after him.

"Edd! You must not talk so—so terribly!" she cried, appealingly. "You seem to accuse me of—of something. . . . Oh! that I haven't been fair to you!"

"Wal, have you, now?" he queried, glaring down at her.

"Indeed—I—I think so."

"Aw, you're lyin'. Maybe you're as deep as your sister. Shore I'd never deny you'd been an angel to my family. But you worked different on me. I was only a wild-bee hunter. You made me see what I was—made me hate my ignorance an' habits. You let me be with you, many an' many a time. You talked for hours an' read to me, an' worked with me, all the time with your sweet, sly girl ways. An' I changed. I don't know how I changed, but it's so. You're like the queen of the bees. . . . All you told me love meant I've come to know. I'd do any an' all of those things you once said love meant. . . . But if you work the same on Bud Sprall you'll be worse than Sadie Purdue. She had sweet, purry cat ways, an' she liked to be smoothed. That was shore where Sadie didn't cheat."

"Cheat! . . . Edd Denmeade, do you mean—you think I made you love me—just to save you from your drinking, fighting habits?" queried Lucy, very low.

"No. I reckon I don't mean that. You just used your—yourself. Your smiles an' sweet laugh—your talk—your pretty white dresses—your hands—lettin' me see you—lettin' me be with you—keepin' me from other girls—workin' on me with yourself. . . . Now didn't you? Be honest."

"Yes. You make me see it. I did," confessed Lucy, bravely. "I'm not sorry—for I—I—"

"Wal, you needn't figure me wrong," he interrupted. "I'm not sorry, either. Reckon for my family's sake I'm glad. Shore I have no hopes of ever bein' anythin' but a lonely wild-bee hunter. . . . But I couldn't stand your workin' that on Bud Sprall."

"You misunderstood me, Edd," returned Lucy. "I couldn't have done what you imagined. Now I fear I can never do anything. . . . You have made me ashamed. Made me doubt myself."

"Wal, I reckon that won't be so awful bad for you," he drawled, almost caustically, and left her.

This interview with Edd befell just before Lucy's time of departure to the Claypools, most inopportunely and distressingly for her. Edd had declared a great, and what he held a hopeless, love for her. Lucy suffered an exaltation embittered by doubt, distress, even terror. The sheer fact that he loved her was a tremendous shock. Not that she had not known of his affection, but that he had arisen out of his crudeness to her ideal of love! She could not overcome her pride in her power to uplift him. It was sweet, strange, sustaining, yet fraught with terrors for her. It forced her into a position where she must find out the truth and bigness of love herself. She could not trust this new elemental self, this transformation of Lucy Watson in the wilderness. She must have long lonely hours—days —nights to fight the problem. What terrified her was the memory of that beautiful mesa homestead and the thought of Edd Denmeade's love. Together they threatened to storm her heart.

Next morning Lucy was ready early for her departure. She had entirely overlooked what kind of an occasion it might be, but she soon discovered that it was not to be joyous. The children were pitiful in their grief. Lucy felt as if she had died. They were inconsolable. Mary was the only one of them who bade her good-by. Mrs. Denmeade said she was glad for the sake of the Claypools.

"Wal, Miss Lucy," said Denmeade, with his rugged grin, "reckon by the time you get through with the Claypools an' Johnsons you'll find us all gone to seed an' needin' you powerful bad."

"Then I'll be happy to come back," replied Lucy.

Clara, however, gave Lucy the most thought-provoking surprise of this leave-taking. Evidently she had cried before getting up, and afterward she was pale and silent.

When Edd and Joe arrived with saddle horses and the burros, Lucy, after taking out her baggage to be packed, returned to find Clara had broken down. Lucy could not understand this sudden weakness. It was not like Clara. They had a most affecting scene, which left Lucy shaken and uncertain. But she had the sweet assurance of Clara's love and reliance upon her. For the rest her sister's emotion seemed a betrayal. Lucy felt that in Clara's clinging hands, her streaming hidden eyes, her incoherent words. But in the few moments of stress left her before departure she could neither comfort Clara nor find out any adequate reason for this collapse.

"Hey!" called Edd, for the third time. "Reckon the burros are rarin' to go, if you ain't."

Lucy left Clara face down on the bed. Before she closed the door she called back, softly: "Don't be afraid to trust me with your troubles. I'll share them. . . . Good-by."

Lucy had seen the Claypool clearing, but she had never been inside the cabins. There were two families and many children, all assembled to greet her. Allie and Gerd still lived there, pending the clearing of a new tract of forest near by. They took charge of Lucy and led her to the little hut that had been constructed for her use. It had been built of slabs fresh from the sawmill, and these boards, being the outside cut from logs, still retained the bark. The structure was crude, yet picturesque, and it pleased Lucy. The inside was the yellow hue of newly cut pine, and it smelled strongly of the woods. Lucy had to laugh. What a wonderful little playhouse that would have been—if she were still a little girl! It had one window, small, with a wooden shutter, a table, and a closet, a shelf, and a built-in box couch, full of fragrant spruce. A deer skin with the fur uppermost lay on the floor. In the corner nearest the door was a triangular-shaped shelf, three feet above the floor, and under it sat a bucket full of water and on it a basin and dipper and lamp.

Allie and Gerd were plainly proud of this lodging house for Lucy.

"It's pretty far from the cabins," concluded Gerd, "but there's a big bar for your door. Nothin' can get in."

"I am delighted with it," declared Lucy.

Edd and Joe drove the pack burros over to Lucy's new abode and carried her bags in. She noted that Edd was so tall he could not stand upright in her little room.

"Wal, I reckon Gerd shore didn't figure on your entertainin' me," drawled Edd, with a grin.

"It's pretty nice," said Joe, practically. "With your rugs an' pictures, an' the way you fix things up, it'll be Jake."

Edd lingered a moment longer than the others at the door, his big black sombrero turning round in his hands.

"Wal, Lucy, do I go get me some white mule an' hunt up Bud Sprall?" he queried, with all his cool, easy complexity.

Lucy felt the sting of blood in her cheeks. When she stepped toward him, as he stood outside and below, one foot on the threshold, his face was about on a level with hers. Lucy looked straight into his eyes.

"No, you don't, unless you want me to call you again what hurt you so once."

"An' what's that? I disremember."

"You know!" she retorted, not quite sure of herself.

"Wal, I reckon you won't need do that," he said, simply. "I was only foolin' you about the white mule. I wouldn't drink again, no matter what you did. An' I reckon I wouldn't pick a fight, like I used to."

Lucy had been subjected to a wide range of emotions through the last twenty-four hours, and she was not prepared for a statement like this. It wrought havoc in her breast. In swift impulse she bent forward and kissed Edd on the cheek. Then as swiftly she drew back, slammed the door, and stood there trembling. She heard him gasp, and the jingle of his spurs, as slowly he walked away.

"There! I've played hob at last!" whispered Lucy. "But I don't care. . . . Now, my wild-bee hunter, I wonder if you'll take that for a Sadie Purdue trick?"

CHAPTER XIV

Congenial work with happy, eager, simple people made the days speed by so swiftly that Lucy could not keep track of them.

She let six weeks and more pass before she gave heed to the message Clara sent from the schoolhouse by the Claypool children. From other sources Lucy learned that Clara was the best teacher ever employed by the school board. She was making a success of it, from a standpoint of both good for the pupils and occupation for herself.

Joe Denmeade happened to ride by Claypool's one day, and he stopped to see Lucy. Even in the few weeks since she left the Denmeades there seemed to be marked improvement in Joe, yet in a way she could hardly define. Something about him rang so true and manly.

During Joe's short visit it chanced that all the Claypools gathered on the porch, and Gerd, lately come from Cedar Ridge, narrated with great gusto the gossip. It was received with the interest of lonely people who seldom had opportunities to hear about what was going on. Gerd's report of the latest escapade of one of the village belles well known to them all was received with unrestrained mirth. Such incident would have passed unmarked by Lucy had she not caught the expression that fleeted across Joe Denmeade's face. That was all the more marked because of the fact of Joe's usually serene, intent impassibility. Lucy conceived the certainty that this boy would suffer intensely if he ever learned of Clara's misfortune. It might not change his love, but it would surely kill something in him—the very something that appealed so irresistibly to Clara.

The moment was fraught with a regurgitation of

Lucy's dread—the strange premonition that had haunted her—that out of the past must come reckoning. It remained with her more persistently than ever before, and was not readily shaken off.

Some days later, one Friday toward the end of May, Lucy rode down the schoolhouse trail to meet Clara and fetch her back to Claypool's to stay over Sunday. It had been planned for some time, and Lucy had looked forward to the meeting with both joy and apprehension.

This schoolhouse trail was new to her, and therefore one of manifold pleasure. It led through forest and glade, along a tiny brook, and on downhill toward the lower country.

Lucy was keen to catch all the woodland features that had become part of her existence, without which life in this wilderness would have lost most of its charm. Only a year had passed since first it had claimed her! The time measured in work, trial, change, seemed immeasurably longer. Yet Lucy could not say that she would have had it otherwise. Always she was putting off a fateful hour or day until she was ready to meet it. Her work had engrossed her. In a few weeks she had accomplished as much with the Claypools as she had been able to do for the Denmeades in months. She had learned her work. Soon she could go to the Johnsons. Then back to the Denmeades! To the higher and wilder forest land under the Rim! But she was honest enough to confess that there were other reasons for the joy. Lucy lingered along the trail until a meeting with the Claypool and Miller children told her that school was out. They were riding burros and ponies, in some cases two astride one beast, and they were having fun. Lucy was hailed with the familiarity of long-established regard, a shrill glad clamor that swelled her heart with its message.

"Hurry home, you rascals," admonished Lucy, as she rode back into the trail behind them. Then she urged her horse into a lope, and enjoyed the sweet forest scents fanning her face, and the moving by of bright-colored glades and shady green dells. In a short time she reached the clearing and the schoolhouse. She had not been there for a long time. Yet how well she remembered it!

At first glance she could not see any horses hitched about, but she heard one neigh. It turned out to be Baldy, and he was poking his nose over the bars of a small corral that had recently been erected in the shade of pines at the edge of the clearing. Lucy tied her horse near and then ran for the schoolhouse.

The door was open. Lucy rushed in, to espy Clara at the desk, evidently busy with her work.

"Howdy, little schoolmarm!" shouted Lucy.

Clara leaped up, suddenly radiant.

"Howdy yourself, you old backwoods Samaritan!" returned Clara, and ran to embrace her.

Then, after the first flush of this meeting, they both talked at once, without any particular attention to what the other was saying. But that wore off presently and they became rational.

"Where's Joe?" queried Lucy, desirous of coming at once to matters about which she had a dearth of news.

"He and Mr. Denmeade have gone to Winbrook to buy things for Joe's cabin."

"Are you riding the trails alone?" asked Lucy, quickly.

"I haven't yet," replied Clara, with a laugh. "Joe has taken/good care of that. Edd rode down with me this morning. He went to Cedar Ridge to get the mail. Said he'd get back to ride up with us."

"You told him I was coming after you?"

"Shore did, an' reckon he looked silly," drawled Clara.

"Oh! Indeed? . . ." Lucy then made haste to change the subject. She had not set eyes upon Edd since the day she had shut her door in his face, after the audacious and irreparable kiss she had bestowed upon his cheek. She did not want to see him, either, and yet she did want to tremendously.

"Let's not wait for him," she said, hurriedly.

"What's wrong with *you?*" demanded Clara. "Edd seems quite out of his head these days. When I mention you he blushes. . . . Yes!"

"How funny—for that big bee hunter!" replied Lucy, essaying a casual laugh.

"Well, I've a hunch you're the one who should blush," said Clara, dryly.

"Clara, sometimes I don't know about you," observed Lucy, musingly, as she gazed thoughtfully at her sister.

"How many times have I heard you say that!" returned Clara, with a mingling of pathos and mirth. "Lucy, the fact is you *never* knew about me. You never had me figured. You were always so big yourself that you couldn't see the littleness of me."

"Ahuh!" drawled Lucy. Then more seriously she went on: "Clara, I'm not big. I've a big love for you, but that's about all."

"Have it your own way. All the same, I'm going to tell you about myself. That's why I sent word by the children. You didn't seem very curious or anxious to see me."

"Clara, I was only in fun. I don't want to—to know any more about you—unless it is you're happy—and have forgotten—your—your trouble," rejoined Lucy, soberly.

"That's just why I *must* tell you," said her sister, with swift resolution. "I *did* forget because I *was* happy. But my conscience won't let me be happy any longer until I tell you."

Lucy's heart contracted. She felt a sensation of inward chill. Why had Clara's brown tan changed to pearly white? Her eyes had darkened unusually and were strained in unflinching courage. Yet full of fear!

"All right. Get it over, then," replied Lucy.

Notwithstanding Clara's resolve, it was evidently hard for her to speak. "Lucy, since—March the second—I've been—Joe Denmeade's wife," she whispered, huskily.

Lucy, braced for something utterly different and connected with Clara's past, suddenly succumbed to amaze. She sat down on one of the school benches.

"Good Heavens!" she gasped, and then could only stare.

"Darling, don't be angry," implored Clara, and came to her and knelt beside her. Again Lucy felt those clinging, loving hands always so potent in their power.

"I'm not angry—yet," replied Lucy. "I'm just flabbergasted. I—I can't think. It's a terrible surprise. . . . Your second elopement!"

"Yes. And this made up for the—the other," murmured Clara.

"March the second? That was the day you took the long ride with Joe? Got back late. On a Saturday. You were exhausted, pale, excited. . . . I remember now. And you never told me!"

"Lucy, don't reproach me," protested Clara. "I meant to. Joe wanted to let you into our secret. But I couldn't. It's *hard* to tell you things."

"Why? Can't I be trusted?"

"It's because you do trust so—so beautifully. It's because you are so—so good, so strong yourself. Before I did it I felt it would be easy. Afterwards I found out differently."

"Well, too late now," said Lucy, sadly. "But how'd you do it? Where? Why?"

"We rode down to Gordon," replied Clara, hurriedly. "That's a little village below Cedar Ridge. We hired a man to drive us to Menlo. More than fifty miles. There we were married. . . . Came home the same way. It was a terrible trip. But for the excitement it'd have killed me."

"March the second! You've kept it secret all this time?"

"Yes. And want still to keep it, except from you."

"Clara—I don't know what to say," rejoined Lucy, helplessly. "What on earth made you do it?"

"Joe! Joe!" cried Clara, wildly. "Oh, let me tell you. Don't condemn me till you hear. . . . From the very first Joe Denmeade made love to me. You could never dream what's in that boy. He loved me. My refusals only made him worse. He waylaid me at every turn. He wrote me notes. He never let me forget for an hour that he worshiped me. . . . And it grew to be sweet.

Sweet to my bitter heart! I was hungry for love. I wanted, needed the very thing he felt. I fought—oh, how I fought! The idea of being loved was beautiful, wonderful, saving. But to fall in love—myself—that seemed impossible, wicked. It mocked me. But I *did* fall in love. I woke up one morning to another world. . . . Then I was as weak as water."

Lucy took the palpitating Clara in her arms and held her close. After all, she could not blame her sister. If no dark shadow loomed up out of the past, then it would be well. Then as the first flush of excitement began to fade Lucy's logical mind turned from cause to effect.

"Clara, you didn't tell Joe about your past," asserted Lucy, very low. She did not question. She affirmed. She knew. And when Clara's head drooped to her bosom, to hide her face there, Lucy had double assurance.

"I couldn't. I couldn't," said Clara, brokenly. "Between my fears and Joe's ridiculous faith in me, I couldn't. Time and time again—when he was making love to me—before I cared—I told him I was no good— selfish, callous little flirt! He would only laugh and make harder love to me. I tried to tell him about the cowboy beaus I'd had. He'd say the more I'd had, the luckier he was to win me. To him I was good, innocent, noble. An angel! He wouldn't listen to me. . . . Then when I fell in love with him it wasn't easy—the idea of telling. I quit trying until the night before the day we ran off to get married. Honestly I meant seriously to tell him. But I'd hardly gotten a word out when he grabbed me— and—and kissed me till I couldn't talk. . . . Then— I was sort—of carried away—the—the second time."

She ended in a sobbing whisper. All was revealed in those last few words. Lucy could only pity and cherish.

"You poor child! I understand. I don't blame you. I'm glad. If you love him so well and he loves you so well— it must—it *shall* come out all right. . . . Don't cry, Clara. I'm not angry. I'm just stunned and—and frightened."

Clara responded to kindness as to nothing else, and her passion of gratitude further strengthened Lucy's resolve to serve.

"Frightened! Yes, that's what I've become lately," she said. "Suppose Joe should find out—all about me. It's not probable, but it *might* happen. He would never forgive me. He's queer that way. He doesn't understand women. Edd Denmeade, now—he could. He'd stick to a girl—if—if—— But Joe wouldn't, I know. At that I can tell him *now,* if you say I must. But it's my last chance for happiness—for a home. I *hate* the thought that I'm not the angel he believes me. I know I could become anything in time—I love him so well. Always I remember that I wasn't wicked. I was only a fool."

"Dear, regrets are useless," replied Lucy, gravely. "Let's face the future. It seems to me you should tell Joe. After all, he hasn't so much to forgive. He's queer, I know——"

"But, Lucy," interrupted Clara, and she looked up with a strange, sad frankness, "there was a baby."

"My God!" cried Lucy, in horrified distress.

"Yes . . . a girl—my own. She was born in Kingston at the home of the woman with whom I lived—a Mrs. Gerald. She had no family. She ran a little restaurant for miners. No one else knew, except the doctor, who came from the next town, and he was a good old soul. In my weakness I told Mrs. Gerald my story—whom I'd run off with—all about it. She offered to adopt the baby if I'd help support it. So we arranged to do that."

"That was the debt you spoke of," replied Lucy, huskily. "Why you needed money often."

"Yes. And that's why I was in such a hurry to find work—to take up this teaching. . . . She had written me she would return the child or write to its—its father unless I kept my part of the bargain. I was so scared I couldn't sleep. . . . I was late in sending money, but I'm sure it's all right."

"You married Joe—with this—hanging over you?" queried Lucy, incredulously.

"I *told* you how that came about. I know what I felt. I suffered. But it all came about. It happened," answered Clara, as if driven to desperation.

"Only a miracle can keep Joe from learning it some day."

"Miracles sometimes happen. For instance, your giving me a home. And my love for this boy! . . . You can never understand how close I was to death or hell. . . . Kingston is a long way off. This is a wilderness. It might happen that God won't quite forget me."

"Oh, the pity of it!" wailed Lucy, wringing her hands. "Clara, how can you repudiate your own flesh and blood?"

"I had to," replied Clara, sadly. "But I've lived with the memory, and I've changed. . . . I'll meet Mrs. Gerald's demands, and some day I'll make other and happier arrangements."

"If you only hadn't married Joe! Why, oh, why didn't you come to me?" cried Lucy.

Clara offered no reply to that protest. She straightened up and turned away.

"I hear a horse," she said, rising to look at Lucy.

"Must be Edd," returned Lucy, nervously.

"Riding pretty fast for Edd. You know he never runs a horse unless there's a reason."

The sisters stood a moment facing each other. Perhaps their emotions presaged catastrophe. Outside the sound of rapid hoofbeats thudded to a sliding halt. Lucy was occupied with anticipation of being compelled to face Edd Denmeade. Less prepared than at any time since her sentimental impulse at Claypool's, she could not on such short notice master her feelings.

Nevertheless, under the strain of the moment she hurried toward the door, to make her hope that the arrival was not Edd a certainty.

Clara went to the window and looked out.

Lucy reached the threshold just as her keen ear caught the musical jingle of spurs. Then a step too quick and short for Edd! In another second a tall slim young man confronted her. He wore the flashy garb of a rider. Lucy wondered where she had seen that striking figure, the young, handsome, heated red face with its wicked blue eyes. He doffed a wide sombrero. When Lucy saw the blaze of his golden hair she recognized him as the individual once pointed out to her at Cedar Ridge. Comrade of Bud Sprall!

"Howdy, Luce! Reckon your kid sister is heah," he said, coolly.

Lucy's heart seemed to sink within her. Dread and anger leaped to take the place of softer emotions now vanishing.

"How dare you?" she demanded.

"Wal, I'm a darin' *hombre*," he drawled, taking a step closer. "An' I'm goin' in there to even up a little score with Clara."

"Who are you?" queried Lucy, wildly.

"None of your business. Get out of my way," he said, roughly.

Lucy blocked the door. Open opposition did much to stabilize the whirl of her head.

"You're not coming in," cried Lucy. "I warn you. Edd Denmeade's expected here any moment. It'll be bad for you if he finds you."

"Wal, I reckon Edd won't get heah pronto," rejoined this cowboy, impertinently. "I left my pard, Bud Sprall, down the trail. An' he's a-rarin' to stop Edd one way or another. Bud an' I have been layin' for this chance. Savvy, Luce?"

She gave him a stinging slap in the face—so hard a blow that even her open hand staggered him.

"Don't you believe it, Mr. Red-face," retorted Lucy, furiously. "It'd take more than you or Bud Sprall to stop Edd Denmeade."

"Wild cat, huh? All same Clara!" he ejaculated, with his hand going to his face. The wicked eyes flashed like blue fire. Then he lunged at her, and grasping her arm, in a single pull he swung her out of the doorway. Lucy nearly lost her balance. Recovering, she rushed back into the schoolhouse in time to see this stranger confront Clara. For Lucy it was a terrible thing to see her sister's face.

"Howdy, kid! Reckon you was lookin' for me," he said.

"*Jim Middleton!*" burst out Clara in queer, strangled voice. Then she slipped limply to the floor in a faint.

For Lucy uncertainty passed. She realized her sister's reckoning had come, like a lightning flash out of a clear sky, and it roused all the tigress in her. Running to Clara, she knelt at her side, to find her white and cold and unconscious. Then she rose to confront the intruder with a determination to get rid of him before Clara recovered consciousness.

"So you're Jim Middleton?" she queried, in a passionate scorn. "If I had a gun I'd shoot you. If I had a whip I'd beat you as I would a dog. Get out of here. You shall not talk to my sister. She hates you. Nothing you can have to say will interest her."

"Wal, I'm not so shore," returned Middleton, without the coolness or nonchalance that before had characterized his speech. He looked considerably shaken. What contrasting gleams of passion—hate—wonder—love—changed the blue gaze he bent upon Clara's white face! "I've a letter she'll want to read."

"A letter! From Mrs. Gerald?" flashed Lucy, quivering all over as his hand went to his breast.

"Yes, if it's anythin' to you," retorted the cowboy, shaking a letter at her.

"Mrs. Gerald wants money?" Lucy went one.

"She shore does," he answered, resentfully.

"I suppose you're going to send it to her?"

"I am like hell!"

"Also I suppose you'll want to right the wrong you did Clara? You'll want to marry her truly?" demanded Lucy, with infinite sarcasm.

"You've got the wrong hunch, Luce," he replied, laughing coarsely. "I jes want to read her this letter. Shore I've been keepin' it secret these days for her to see first. Then I'll tell Joe Denmeade an' every other man in this woods."

"Haven't you made Clara suffer enough?" queried

Lucy, trying to keep her voice steady and her wits working.

"She ran off from me. I reckon with another man."

"You're a liar! Oh, I'll make you pay for this!" cried Lucy, in desperation.

Suddenly she saw him turn his head. Listening. He had not heard her outburst. Then Lucy's strained hearing caught the welcome clatter of hoofs. Quick as a flash she snatched the letter out of Middleton's hands.

"Heah, give that back!" he shouted, fiercely.

Like a cat Lucy leaped over desks into another aisle, and then facing about, she thrust the letter into the bosom of her blouse. Middleton leaned forward, glaring in amaze and fury.

"I'll tear your clothes off," he shouted, low and hard.

"Jim Middleton, if you know when you're well off you'll get out of here and out of the country before these Denmeades learn what you've done," returned Lucy.

"An' I'll beat you good while I'm tearin' your clothes off," he declared as he crouched.

"Edd Denmeade will kill you!" whispered Lucy, beginning to weaken.

"Once more," he hissed, venomously, "give me that letter. . . . It's my proof about the baby!"

And on the instant a quick jangling step outside drew the blood from Lucy's heart. Middleton heard it and wheeled with muttered curse.

Edd Denmeade leaped over the threshold and seemed to fill the schoolroom with his presence. Blood flowed from his bare head, down his cheek. His eyes, like pale flames, swept from Lucy to Middleton, to the limp figure of the girl on the floor, and then back to Lucy. The thrill that flooded over her then seemed wave on wave of shock. He had been fighting. His clothes were in rags and wringing wet. He advanced slowly, with long strides, his piercing gaze shifting to Middleton.

"Howdy, cowboy! I met your pard, Bud Sprall, down the trail. Reckon you'd better go rake up what's left of him an' pack it out of here."

"The hell you say!" ejaculated Middleton, stepping to

meet Edd halfway. He was slow, cautious, menacing, and somehow sure of himself. "Wal, I'd as lief meet one Denmeade as another. An' I've shore got somethin' to say."

"You can't talk to me," returned Edd, with measured coldness. "I don't know nothin' about you—'cept you're a pard of Sprall's. That's enough. . . . Now go along with you pronto."

The red of Middleton's face had faded to a pale white except for the livid mark across his cheek. But to Lucy it seemed his emotion was a passionate excitement rather than fear. He swaggered closer to Edd.

"Say, you wild-bee hunter, you're goin' to heah somethin' aboot this Watson girl."

Edd took a slow easy step, then launched body and arm into pantherish agility. Lucy did not see the blow, but she heard it. Sharp and sudden, it felled Middleton to the floor half a dozen paces toward the stove. He fell so heavily that he shook the schoolhouse. For a moment he lay gasping while Edd stepped closer. Then he raised himself on his elbow and turned a distorted face, the nose of which appeared smashed flat. He looked a fiend inflamed with lust to murder. But cunningly as he turned away and began to labor to get to his feet, he did not deceive Lucy.

"Watch out, Edd! He has a gun!" she screamed.

Even then Middleton wheeled, wrenching the gun from his hip. Lucy saw its sweep as she saw Edd leap, and suddenly bereft of strength she slipped to the floor, back against a desk, eyes tight shut, senses paralyzed, waiting for the report she expected. But it did not come. Scrape of boots, clash of spurs, hard expulsions of breath, attested to another kind of fight.

She opened wide her eyes. Edd and Middleton each had two hands on the weapon, and were leaning back at arm's-length, pulling with all their might.

"I'm agonna bore you—you damn wild-bee hunter!" panted the cowboy, and then he bent to bite at Edd's hands. Edd gave him a tremendous kick that brought a bawl of pain and rage from Middleton.

Then began a terrific struggle for possession of the gun. Lucy crouched there, fascinated with horror. Yet how the hot nerves of her body tingled! She awoke to an awful attention, to a dim recollection of a fierce glory in man's prowess, in blood, in justice. Edd was the heavier and stronger. He kept the cowboy at arm's-length and swung him off his feet. But Middleton always came down like a cat. He was swung against the desks, demolishing them; then his spurred boots crashed over the teacher's table. They wrestled from there to the stove, knocking that down. A cloud of soot puffed down from the stovepipe. The cowboy ceased to waste breath in curses. His sinister expression changed to a panic-stricken fear for his own life. He was swung with violence against the wall. Yet he held on to the gun in a wild tenacity. They fought all around the room, smashing desk after desk. The time came when Middleton ceased to jerk at the gun, but put all a waning strength in efforts to hold it.

When they were on the other side of the room Lucy could not see them. What she heard was sufficient to keep her in convulsive suspense.

Suddenly out of the corner of her eye she saw Clara sit up and reel from side to side, and turn her white face toward the furiously struggling men.

"Clara—don't look!" cried Lucy, huskily, almost unable to speak. She moved to go to her sister, but she was spent with fright, and when Clara's purple eyes fixed in an appalling stare, she quite gave out. Then crash and thud and scrape, harder, swifter, and the whistle of men's breath moved back across the room into the field of her vision. Edd was dragging Middleton, flinging him. The fight was going to the implacable bee hunter.

"Let go, cowboy. I won't kill you!" thundered Edd.

Middleton's husky reply was incoherent. For a moment renewed strength seemed to come desperately, and closing in with Edd he wrestled with the frenzy of a madman.

Suddenly there burst out a muffled bellow of the gun.

Edd seemed released from a tremendous strain. He staggered back toward Lucy. For a single soul-riving instant she watched, all faculties but sight shocked into suspension. Then Middleton swayed aside from Edd, both his hands pressed to his breast. He sank to his knees. Lucy's distended eyes saw blood gush out over his hands. Dragging her gaze up to his face, she recoiled in a fearful awe.

"She—she was—" he gasped, thickly, his changed eyes wavering, fixing down the room. Then he lurched over on his side and lay doubled up in a heap.

Edd's long arm spread out and his hand went low, to release the smoking gun, while he bent rigidly over the fallen man.

"It went—off," he panted. "I was only—tryin' to get it—away from him. . . . Lucy, you saw."

"Oh yes, I saw," cried Lucy. "It wasn't—your fault. He'd have killed you. . . . Is he—is he?——"

Edd straightened up and drew a deep breath.

"Reckon he's about gone."

Then he came to help Lucy to her feet and to support her. "Wal, you need a little fresh air, an' I reckon some won't hurt me."

"But Clara! . . . Oh, she has fainted again!"

"No wonder. Shore she was lucky not to see the—the fight. That fellow was a devil compared to Bud Sprall."

"Oh! . . . Edd, you didn't kill him, too?" implored Lucy.

"Not quite. But he's bad used up," declared Edd as he half carried her across the threshold and lowered her to a seat on the steps. "Brace up now, city girl. Reckon this is your first real backwoods experience. . . . Wal, it might have been worse. . . . Now wouldn't you have had a fine time makin' Bud an' his pard better men? . . . There, you're comin' around. We need to do some tall figurin'. . . . But I reckon, far as I'm concerned, there's nothing to worry over."

After a moment he let go of Lucy and rose from the step. "Lucy, what was it all about?" he queried, quietly.

She covered her face with her hands and a strong shudder shook her frame.

"Wal," he went on, very gently, "I heard that fellow ravin' as I come in. But all I understood was 'proof about the baby.' "

"That was enough to hear, don't you think?" replied Lucy, all at once recovering her composure. Out of the chaos of her conflicting emotions had arisen an inspiration.

"Reckon it was a good deal," he said, simply, and smiled down on her. "But you needn't tell me nothin' unless you want to. I always knew you'd had some trouble."

"Trouble!" sighed Lucy. Then averting her gaze she continued: "Edd, I ask you to keep my secret. . . . The baby he spoke of—was—is mine."

He did not reply at once, nor in any way she could see or hear express whatever feeling he might have had. Lucy, once the damnable falsehood had crossed her lips, was stricken as by a plague. When she had thrown that off there was a horrible remorse pounding at the gates of her heart. Her body seemed first to receive the brunt of the blow she had dealt herself.

"Wal, wal—so that's it," said Edd, in queer, broken voice. He paused a long moment, then went on, in more usual tone: "Shore I'll never tell. . . . I'm dog-gone sorry, Lucy. An' I'm not askin' questions. I reckon it doesn't make no difference to me. . . . Now let's think what's best to do. I'll have to send word from Johnson's about this fight. But I'm goin' to see you home first, unless you think you can get there all right."

"That depends on Clara. Come with me."

They went back into the schoolhouse to find Clara showing signs of returning consciousness.

"Please carry her outside," said Lucy.

As he lifted the girl in his arms Lucy's fearful gaze roved round the room. Amid the ruins of the crude furniture lay the inert form of Jim Middleton, face down, hands outstretched in a pool of blood. Though the sight sickened her, Lucy gazed until she had convinced herself that there was no life in the prostrate form. Then she hurried after Edd and reeled out into the sunlight and the sweet fresh air. Edd carried Clara to the shade of pines at the edge of the clearing.

"I'll go down to the brook," he said. "Reckon we don't want her seein' me all over blood."

Presently Clara's pale eyelids fluttered and unclosed, to reveal eyes with purple abysses, hard for Lucy to gaze into. She raised Clara's head in her arms.

"There, dear, you're all right again, aren't you?"

"Where is he?" whispered Clara.

"Edd's gone down to the brook to fetch some water. He's all right."

"I mean—*him!* . . . Ah, I saw!" went on Clara. "Edd killed him!"

"I fear so," said Lucy, hurriedly. "But it was an accident. Edd fought to get the gun. It went off. . . . Don't think of that. God has delivered you. I have the letter Mrs. Gerald wrote Middleton. He did not betray you. And now he's dead. . . . Edd knows nothing about your relation to this cowboy. See that you keep silent."

Edd returned at this juncture with a shining face, except for a wound over his temple; and he handed his wet scarf to Lucy.

"Wal, shore she's come to," he drawled, with all his old coolness. "That's good. . . . Now I'll saddle up her horse an' pretty soon she'll be able to ride home."

"I think she will," returned Lucy. "But what shall I say about—about this?"

"Say nothin'," he replied, tersely. "I'll do the talkin' when I get home. . . . An', Lucy, on my way to Johnson's I'll take a look at my old friend Bud Sprall. If he's alive, which I reckon he is, I'll tell him damn good an' short what happened to his pard, an' that he'll get the same unless he moves out of the country. These woods ain't big enough for us two."

"He might waylay you again as he did this time— and shoot you," said Lucy, fearfully.

"Wal, waylayin' me once will be enough, I reckon.

Bud has a bad name, an' this sneaky trick on you girls will fix him. They'll run him out of the country."

While Edd saddled Clara's horse Lucy walked her to and fro a little.

"Let's go. I can ride," averred Clara. "I'd rather fall off than stay here."

Edd helped her mount and walked beside her to where the trail entered the clearing. Lucy caught up with them, full of misgiving, yet keen to get out of sight of the schoolhouse.

"Go right home," said Edd. "I'll stop at Claypool's on my way up an' tell them somethin'. Shore I won't be long. An' if you're not home I'll come a-rarin' down the trail to meet you."

"Oh, Edd—be careful!" whispered Lucy. She hardly knew what she meant and she could not look at him. Clara rode on into the leaf-bordered trail. Lucy made haste to follow. Soon the golden light of the clearing no longer sent gleams into the forest. They entered the green, silent sanctuary of the pines. Lucy felt unutterable relief. How shaded, how protecting, how helpful the great trees! They had the primitive influence of nature. They strengthened her under the burden she had assumed. Whatever had been the wild prompting of her sacrifice, she had no regret for herself, nor could she alter it.

Clara reeled in her saddle, clinging to the pommel; but as she rode on it appeared she gathered strength, until Lucy came to believe she would finish out the ride. And what a tragic ride that was! Clara never once looked back, never spoke. The pearly pallor still showed under her tan. Lucy felt what was going on in her sister's soul, and pitied her. Scorn for Clara's weakness, anger at her duplicity, had no power against love. The reckoning had come and the worst had befallen. Lucy experienced relief in the knowledge of this. Clara's future must be her care. It was not right, but she would make it right; it was not safe, yet she must insure its safety. And all at once she realized how she loved Edd

Denmeade, and that eventually she would have gone to him as naturally as a bird to its mate. Then the green forest seemed to pierce her agony with a thousand eyes.

CHAPTER XV

At the conclusion of that ride Clara collapsed and had to be carried into her tent, where she fell victim to hysteria and exhaustion. Lucy had her hands full attending to her sister and keeping the kindly Denmeades from hearing some of Clara's ravings.

Next day Clara was better, and on Sunday apparently herself again. To Lucy's amaze she announced she could and would go back to school next day.

"But, Clara—how *can* you, considering——" faltered Lucy.

"I know what you mean," replied her sister. "It'll be rather sickening, to say the least. Yet I'd prefer to be sick than have the awful feeling of dread I had before."

Nevertheless, Lucy would not hear of Clara's going to teach for a least a week. Amy Claypool would be glad to act as substitute teacher for a few days, or failing that, the pupils could be given a vacation. Clara did not readily yield this point, though at last she was prevailed upon. During these days Lucy avoided much contact with the Denmeades. It was not possible, however, not to hear something about what had happened.

Upon his return Edd had conducted himself precisely as before the tragedy, a circumstance that had subtle effect upon Lucy. By degrees this bee hunter had grown big in her sight, strong and natural in those qualities which to her mind constituted a man. From Joe she learned certain developments of the case. Bud Sprall, late on the day of the fight, had been carried to Johnson's,

the nearest ranch, and there he lay severely injured.
Middleton had not been removed until after the sheriff
had viewed his remains on Saturday. Gossip from all
quarters was rife, all of it decidedly favorable to Edd.
The dead cowboy had not been well known at Cedar
Ridge, and not at all by the name of Middleton.

On Monday Lucy returned to her work at Claypool's,
leaving the situation unchanged so far as she was concerned. She and Edd had not mentioned the thing that
naturally concerned them both so vitally; nor had Lucy
confessed to Clara what she had taken upon herself.
There would be need of that, perhaps, after the sheriff's
investigation.

Lucy's work did not in this instance alleviate a heavy
heart. Once more alone, away from the worry about
Clara's health and the excitement of the Denmeades,
she was assailed by grief. Clara's act, viewed in any
light possible, seemed a sin, no less terrible because
of unfortunate and mitigating circumstances. It was something that had been fostered long ago in the family.
Lucy had expected it. She blamed the past, the lack of
proper home training and ideals, the influence inevitable
from her father's business.

After her work hours each day she would walk off
into the deep forest, and there, hidden from any eyes,
she would yield to the moods of the moment. They
seemed as various as the aspects of her trouble. But
whatever the mood happened to be, grief was its dominant note. Clara had gotten beyond her now. She was
married, and settled, providing Joe Denmeade was as
fine a boy as he seemed. But if Clara's true story became
public property and Joe repudiated her, cast her off—
then her future was hopeless. Lucy could not face this
possibility. It quite baffled her.

Then there was something else quite as insupportable
to face. Sooner or later she must take up the burden she
had claimed as her own. It would be hard. It meant
she must abandon her welfare work there among the
people she had come to love. They needed her. She
would have to go farther afield or take up some other

kind of work. It was not conceivable that her sister's child could be left to the bringing up of strangers. That would only be shifting the responsibility of the weak Watson blood upon some one else. It did not make in the least for the ideal for which Lucy was ready to lay down her life.

Perhaps hardest of all was the blow to what now she recognized as her unconscious hopes of love, dreams of happy toil as a pioneer's wife. She knew now, when it was too late, what she could have been capable of for Edd Denmeade. She had found a fine big love for a man she had helped develop. She would rather have had such consciousness than to have met and loved a man superior in all ways to Edd. Somehow the struggle was the great thing. And yet she had loved Edd also because he was self-sufficient without her help. How she cared for him now, since the killing of one enemy and crippling of another, was hard for her to define. So that this phase of her grief was acute, poignant, ever-present, growing with the days.

She found out, presently, that going into the forest was a source of comfort. When there seemed no comfort she went to the lonely solitude of trees and brush, of green coverts and fragrant wild dells, and always she was soothed, sustained. She could not understand why, but it was so. She began to prolong the hours spent in the woods, under a looming canyon wall, or beside a densely foliaged gorge from which floated up the drowsy murmur of stream. All that the wild forest land consisted of passed into her innermost being. She sensed that the very ground she trod was full of graves of races of human beings who had lived and fought there, suffered in their blindness and ignorance, loved and reared their young, and had grown old and died. No trace left! No more than autumn leaves! It seemed to be this lesson of nature that gradually came to her. Thereafter she went to the woods early in the mornings as well as the afternoons, and finally she had courage to go at night.

And it was at night she came to feel deepest. Darkness emphasized the mystery of the forest. Night birds and crickets, prowling coyotes with their haunting barks, the wind sad and low in the pines, the weird canopy of foliage overhead studded with stars of white fire—these taught her the littleness of her life and the tremendousness of the spirit from which she had sprung. She was part of the universe. The very fear she had of the blackness, the beasts, and the unknown told of her inheritance. She came at length to realize that this spell engendered by nature, if it could be grasped in its entirety and held, would make bearable all aches of heart and miseries of mind. Her contact with actual life covered twenty little years in a town, among many people; her instincts, the blood that beat at her temples, the longings of her bones, had been bred of a million years in the solitude and wild environment of the dim past. That was why the forest helped her.

A Saturday in June was the day set for an investigation of the fight that had resulted in the death of Jim Middleton. It would be an ordeal for which Lucy had endeavored to prepare herself.

But from what she heard and saw of the people interested she judged the day was to be rather a gala one. Certainly the Denmeades were not worried. Lucy did not see Edd, but Joe seemed more than usually cheerful, and evidently he had prevailed somewhat upon Clara. If she had any misgivings as to what might develop, she certainly did not show them. She rode by with Joe and the other Denmeades before Lucy was ready. Allie and Gerd dressed up for the occasion as if they were going to a a dance. Lucy rode with them as far as Johnson's where she was invited to go the rest of the way in a car with Sam and other of the Johnsons. During this part of the ride Lucy had little chance to think or brood. The party was a merry one, and their attitude toward the occasion was manifested by a remark Sam finally made to Lucy:

"Say, cheer up. You're worryin' about this investigation. It won't amount to shucks. Everybody in the country is glad of what Edd did. Shore there won't be any court proceedings. This whole case would have been over long ago an' forgotten if Bud Sprall hadn't been too bad crippled to talk. Just you wait."

Lucy found some little grain of assurance in Sam's words, and bore up under her dread. Perhaps she worried too much, and felt too deeply, she thought. Sam drove as if he were going to a party, and the twenty miles or more seemed as nothing. Cedar Ridge was full of people, to judge from the horses, cars, and vehicles along each side of the main street. When Sam halted with a grand flourish before the hotel Lucy was thrilled to see Edd Denmeade step out from a motley crowd. He was looking for her, and he smiled as he met her glance. He read her mind.

"Howdy, Lucy! Reckon you needn't be scared. Shore it's all right," he said, pressing her hand as he helped her out. "Howdy there, you Sam! Just saw Sadie an' she shore looks pert. Howdy, you-all!"

Lucy was conducted into the hotel parlor by the sheriff, who seemed very gallant and apologetic and most desirous of impressing her with the fact that this meeting was a pleasure to him.

The magistrate she met there appeared equally affable. He was a little man, with sharp blue eyes and ruddy shaven face, and he had only one arm.

"Wal, now, it was too bad to drag you away from thet good work we're all a-hearin' aboot," he said.

"Judge," spoke up the sheriff, "we got Edd's story an' now all we want is this girl's. She see the fight over the gun."

"Set down, miss, an' pray don't look so white," said the magistrate, with a kindly smile. "We see no call to take this case to court. Jest answer a few questions an' we'll let you off. . . . You was the only one who see the fight between Edd an' thet cowboy?"

"Yes. My sister had fainted and lay on the floor," replied Lucy. "But just at the last of it I saw her sit up. And after, when I looked back, she had fainted again."

"Now we know thet Harv Sprall threw a gun on Edd——"

"Sprall!" interrupted Lucy. "You're mistaken. The other fellow was Bud Sprall and he wasn't in the school-room. Edd had the fight for the gun with——"

"Excuse me, miss," interrupted the judge in turn. "The dead cowboy was Harv Sprall, a cousin of Bud's. He wasn't well known in these parts, but we got a line on him from men over Winbrook way. . . . Now jest tell us what you saw."

Whereupon Lucy began with the blow Edd had delivered to the so-called Harv Sprall, and related hurriedly and fluently the details of the fight.

"Wal, thet'll be aboot all," said the judge, with his genial smile, as he bent over to begin writing. "I'm much obliged."

"All! May—I go—now?" faltered Lucy.

"Go. I should smile. I'm escortin' you out. Not thet we're not sorry to have you go," replied the sheriff, and forthwith he led her out to where the others were waiting on the porch.

Lucy came in for considerable attention from the surrounding crowd; and by reason of this and the solicitude of her friends she quickly regained her composure. Presently she was carried away to the house of friends of the Johnsons. She wondered where Clara was, and Joe and Edd, but being swift to grasp the fact that the investigation had been trivial, she was happy to keep her curiosity to herself.

During the several hours she remained in town, however, she was destined to learn a good deal, and that by merely listening. The name Jim Middleton was mentioned as one of several names under which Harv Sprall had long carried on dealings not exactly within the law. He had been known to absent himself for long periods from the several places where he was supposed to work. If Bud Sprall had known anything about his cousin's affairs with Clara, he had kept his mouth shut. The investigation had turned a light on his own unsavory reputation, and what with one thing and another he was liable to be sent to state prison. The judge had made it known that he would give Sprall a chance to leave the country.

It seemed to be the universally accepted idea that the two Spralls had planned to waylay Edd or Joe Denmeade, and then surprise the young school-teacher or overtake her on the trail. Their plans had miscarried and they had gotten their just deserts; and that evidently closed the incident.

Lucy did not see Edd again on this occasion, and some one said he had ridden off alone toward home. Clara and Joe did not show inclination for company; and they too soon departed.

Before dark that night Lucy got back with the Claypools, too tired from riding, and weary with excitement and the necessity for keeping up appearances, to care about eating, or her usual walk after supper. She went to bed, and in the darkness and silence of her little hut she felt as alone as if she were lost in the forest. To-morrow would be Sunday. She would spend the whole day thinking over her problem and deciding how to meet it. If only the hours could be lengthened—time made to stand still!

That Sunday passed by and then another, leaving Lucy more at sea than ever. But she finished her work with the Claypools. July was to have been the time set for her to go to the Johnsons or the Millers. When the date arrived Lucy knew that she had no intention of going. Her own day of reckoning had come. Somehow she was glad in a sad kind of way.

The Denmeades welcomed her as one of the family, and their unstinted delight did not make her task any easier. They all had some characteristic remark to thrill and yet hurt her. Denmeade grinned and said: "Wal, I reckon you're back for good. It shore looks like a go between Joe an' your sister."

Meeting Clara was torturing. "Well, old mysterious, get it off your chest," said her sister, with a shrewd bright look. "Something's killing you. Is it me or Edd?"

"Goodness! Do I show my troubles as plainly as that?" replied Lucy, pathetically.

"You're white and almost thin," returned Clara, solic-

itously. "You ought to stay here and rest—ride around
—go to school with me."

"Perhaps I do need a change. . . . And you, Clara—
how are you? Have you found it hard to go down there
—to be in that schoolroom every day?"

"Me? Oh, I'm fine. It bothered me some at first—especially that—that big stain on the floor. I couldn't scrub
it out. So I took down a rug. I'm not so squeamish as
I was. But I go late, and you bet I don't keep any of my
scholars in after school hours."

"Don't you ever think of—of——" faltered Lucy,
hardly knowing what she meant.

"Of course, you ninny," retorted Clara. "Am I a clod?
I think too much. I have my fight. . . . But, Lucy, I'm
happy. Every day I find more in Joe to love. I'm going
to pull out and make a success of life. First I thought it
was for Joe's sake—then yours. But I guess I've begun
to think of myself a little."

"Have you heard from Mrs. Gerald?" queried Lucy,
finally.

"Yes. As soon as she got my letter, evidently it was
all right again. But she never mentioned writing to Jim."

"She would be glad to get rid of her charge—I imagine?" went on Lucy, casually.

"I've guessed that, myself," rejoined Clara, soberly.
"It worries me some, yet I——"

She did not conclude her remark, and Lucy did not
press the subject any further at the moment, though she
knew this was the time to do it. But Lucy rather feared
a scene with Clara and did not want it to occur during
the waking hours of the Denmeades.

"Have you and Joe told your secret?" queried Lucy.

"Not yet," replied Clara, briefly.

"Where is Joe now?"

"He's working at his homestead. Has twenty acres
planted, and more cleared. They're all helping him. Edd
has taken a great interest in Joe's place since he lost interest in his own."

"Then Edd has given up work on his own farm. Since
when?"

"I don't know. But it was lately. I heard his father talking about it. Edd's not the same since he—since that accident. Joe comes home here every night and he tells me how Edd's changed. Hasn't he been to see you, Lucy?"

"No."

"Of course Edd's down in the mouth about you. I don't think killing that cowboy worries him. I heard him say he was sorry he hadn't done for Bud Sprall, too, and that if he'd known the job those two put up on him there'd have been a different story to tell. . . . No. It's just that Edd's horribly in love with you."

"Poor—Edd, if it s so!" murmured Lucy. "But maybe you take too much for granted, just because Joe feels that way about you."

"Maybe," replied her sister, mockingly. "Edd will probably come home to-day with Joe, as he hasn't been here lately. Take the trouble to look at him and see what you think."

"Are you trying to awaken my sympathies?" queried Lucy, satirically.

"I wish to goodness I could," returned Clara, under her breath.

Lucy realized that she was not her old self, and this had affected Clara vexatiously, perhaps distressingly. Lucy strove against the bitterness and sorrow which in spite of her will influenced her thought and speech. She would not let another day go by without telling Clara what she had taken upon herself. That would be destroying her last bridge behind her; she could go forth free to meet new life somewhere else, knowing she had done the last faithful service to her family.

The Denmeade boys came home early, but Lucy did not see Edd until at supper, which, as usual, was eaten on the porch between the cabins. He did seem changed, and the difference was not physical. He was as big and brawny and brown as ever. Sight of him reopened a wound she thought had healed.

"Come down an' see my bees," he invited her after supper.

The time was near sunset and the green gully seemed

full of murmuring of bees and stream and wind. Edd had added several new hives to his collection, all of which were sections of trees that he had sawed out and packed home.

"How'd you ever keep the bees in?" she asked, wonderingly.

"I stuffed the hole up an' then cut out the piece," he replied. "It can't be done with every bee tree, by a long shot."

For once he seemed not to be keen to talk about his beloved bees, nor, for that matter, about anything. He sat down ponderingly, as a man weighted by cares beyond his comprehension. But the stubborn strength of him was manifest. Lucy had at first to revert to the thought that the flying bees were harmless. With them humming round her, alighting on her, this association of safety did not come at once. She walked to and fro over the green grass and by the sturdy pines, trying to bring back a self that had gone forever. The sun sank behind purple silver-edged clouds, and the golden rim stood up to catch the last bright flare of dying day.

"Wal, you're leavin' us soon?" queried Edd, presently.

"Yes. How did you know?" replied Lucy, halting before him.

"Reckon I guessed it. . . . I'm awful sorry. We're shore goin' to miss you."

That was all. He did not put queries Lucy feared she could not answer. He showed no sign of thoughts that pried into her secret affairs. Somehow he gave Lucy the impression of a faithful animal which had been beaten. He was dumb. Yet she imagined his apparent stolidity came from her aloofness. Lucy, in her misery, essayed to talk commonplaces. But this failed, and she was forced to choose between falling on her knees before him and flying back to the tent. So she left him sitting there, and then from the bench above she spied down through the foliage upon him until dusk hid him from view.

Was she a traitor to the best in herself? Had she not betrayed this backwoods boy who had responded so nobly to every good impulse she had fostered in him? But blood ties were stronger than love. How terribly remorse flayed her! And doubts flew thick as leaves in a storm. Nevertheless, she could not weaken, could never depart in any degree from the course she had prescribed for herself. That was a dark hour. Her deepest emotions were augmented to passion. She was reaching a crisis, the effect of which she could not see.

Later the moon arose and blanched the lofty Rim and the surrounding forest. Black shadows of trees fell across the trail and lane. The air had a delicious mountain coolness, and the silence was impressive. Lucy drank it all in, passionately loath to make the move that must of its very momentum end these wilderness joys for her. But at last she dragged herself away from the moonlit, black-barred trail.

She found Clara and Joe sitting in lover-like proximity on the rustic bench near the tent. As she approached them she did not espy any sign of their embarrassment.

"Joe, I want to have a serious talk with Clara. Would you oblige me by letting me have her alone for a while?" said Lucy.

"If it's serious, why can't I hear it?" queried Joe.

"I can't discuss a purely family matter before you," returned Lucy. "I'm going away soon. And this matter concerns us—me—and things back home."

"Lucy, I belong to your family now," said Joe, as slowly he disengaged himself from Clara and stood up.

"So you do," replied Lucy, laboring to keep composed. "What of it?"

"I've a hunch you haven't figured us Denmeades," he rejoined, rather curtly, and strode away.

"What'd he mean?" asked Lucy, as she stared down at Clara, whose big eyes looked black in the moonlight.

"I'm pretty sure he meant the Denmeades are not fairweather friends," said Clara, thoughtfully. "He's been trying to pump me. Wants to know why you're here and going away—why you look so troubled. . . . I told him, and Edd, too, that I wasn't in your confidence. It's no lie. And here I've been scared stiff at the look of you."

"If you're not more than scared you're lucky. Come in the tent," said Lucy.

Inside, the light was a pale radiance, filtering through the canvas. Lucy shut the door and locked it, poignantly aware of Clara's lingering close to her. Her eyes seemed like great staring gulfs.

Lucy drew a deep breath and cast off the fetters that bound her.

"Clara, do you remember the day of the fight in the schoolhouse—that you were unconscious when Edd arrived?" queried Lucy, in low, forceful voice.

"Yes," whispered Clara.

"Then of course you could not have heard what Jim Middleton said. He was about to leap upon me to get the letter I had snatched. He threatened to tear my clothes off. Then he said it was his proof about the baby. . . . Edd ran into the schoolroom just in time to hear the last few words. . . . Later he said he'd heard—and he asked me—whose it was. I told him—mine!"

"Good—God!" cried Clara, faintly, and sat down upon the bed as if strength to stand had left her.

"I spoke impulsively, yet it was the same as if I had thought for hours," went on Lucy, hurriedly. "I never could have given you away . . . and I couldn't lie—by saying it—it was somebody's else."

"Lie! It's a—terrible lie!" burst out Clara, hoarsely. "It's horrible. . . . You've ruined your good name. . . . You've broken Edd's heart. *Now* I know what ails him. . . . But I won't stand for your taking my shame—my burden on your shoulders."

"The thing is done," declared Lucy, with finality.

"I won't—I won't!" flashed her sister, passionately. "What do you take me for? I've done enough."

"Yes, you have. And since you've shirked your responsibilities—cast off your own flesh and blood to be brought up by a greedy, callous woman—I intend to do what is right by that poor unfortunate child."

Her cutting words wrought Clara into a frenzy of grief, shame, rage, and despair. For a while she was beside herself, and Lucy let her rave, sometimes holding her forcibly from wrecking the tent and from crying out too loud. She even found a grain of consolation in Clara's breakdown. What manner of woman would her sister have been if she had not shown terrible agitation?

At length Clara became coherent and less violent, and she begged Lucy to abandon this idea. Lucy answered as gently and kindly as was possible for her under the circumstances, but she could not be changed. Clara was wildly importunate. Her conscience had stricken her as never before. She loved Lucy and could not bear this added catastrophe. Thus it was that Clara's weak though impassioned pleas and Lucy's efforts to be kind yet firm, to control her own temper, now at white heat, finally led to a terrible quarrel. Once before, as girls, they had quarreled bitterly over an escapade of Clara's. Now, as women, they clinched again in such passion as could only be born of blood ties, of years of sacrifice on the part of one, of realization of ignominy on the part of the other. And the battle went to Lucy, gradually, because of the might of her will and right of her cause.

"You can't see what you've done," concluded Lucy, in spent passion. "You're like our father. Poor weak thing that you are, I can't blame you. It's in the family. . . . If only you'd had the sense and the honor to tell me the truth!—Before you married this clean simple-minded boy! Somehow we might have escaped the worst of it. But you *married* him, you selfish, callous little egotist! And now it's too late. Go on. Find what happiness you can. Be a good wife to this boy and let that make what little amends is possible for you. . . . I'll shoulder your disgrace. I'll be a mother to your child. I'll fight the taint in the Watson blood—the thing that made you what you are. To my mind your failure to make such fight yourself is the crime. I don't hold your love, your weakness against you. But you abandoned part of *yourself* to go abroad in the world to grow up as you did. To do the same thing over! . . . You are little, miserable, wicked. But you are my sister—all I have left to love. And I'll do what you cannot!"

Clara fell back upon the pillow, disheveled, white as death under the pale moonlit tent. Her nerveless hands loosened their clutch on her breast. She shrank as if burned, and her tragic eyes closed to hide her accuser.

"Oh, Lucy—Lucy!" she moaned. "God help me!"

CHAPTER XVI

Lucy walked alone in the dark lane, and two hours were but as moments. Upon her return to the tent she found Clara asleep. Lucy did not light the lamp or fully undress, so loath was she to awaken her sister. And exhausted herself, in a few moments she sank into slumber. Morning found her refreshed in strength and spirit.

She expected an ordeal almost as trying as the conflict of wills the night before—that she would have to face a cringing, miserable girl, wrung by remorse and shame. But Clara awoke in strange mood, proud, tragic-eyed, and aloof, reminding Lucy of their youthful days when her sister had been reproved for some misdemeanor. Lucy accepted this as a welcome surprise, and, deep in her own perturbation, she did not dwell seriously upon it. The great fact of her crisis crowded out aught else—she must leave the Denmeade ranch that day, and the wilderness home which was really the only home she had ever loved. Delay would be only a cruelty to herself. Still, the ordeal was past and she had consolation in her victory. At least she would not fail. This was her supreme and last debt to her family.

Never before had the forest been so enchanting as on that summer morning. She punished herself ruthlessly by going to the fragrant glade where she had learned her first lessons from the wilderness. Weeks had passed, yet every pine needle seemed in its place. Woodpeckers hammered on the dead trunks; sap suckers glided head down ward round the brown-barked trees; woodland butterflies fluttered across the sunlit spaces; blue jays swooped screechingly from bough to bough; red squirrels tore scratchingly in chattering pursuit of one another. Crows and hawks and eagles sailed the sunny world between the forest tips and the lofty Rim. It was hot in the sun; cool in the shade. The scent of pine was overpoweringly sweet. A hot, drowsy summer breeze stirred through the foliage. And the golden aisle near Lucy's retreat seemed a stream for myriads of Edd's homing bees, humming by to the hives.

Lucy tried to convince herself that all forests possessed the same qualities as this one—that the beauty and charm and strength of it came from her eye and heart—that wherever she went to work she now could take this precious knowledge with her. Trees and creatures of the wild were ministers to a harmony with nature.

A forest was a thing of infinite mystery, a multiple detail, of immeasurable design. Trees, rocks, brush, brooks could not explain the home instinct engendered in the wild coverts, the shaded dells, the dark caverns, the lonely aisles, the magnificent archways. The green leaves of the trees brought the rain from the sea and created what they lived upon. The crystal springs under the mossy cliffs were born of thirsty foliage, of the pulse in the roots of the trees. These springs were the sources of rivers. They were the fountains of all life. If the forests perished, there would be left only desert, desolate and dead.

Lucy sat under her favorite pine, her back against the rough bark, and she could reach her hand out of the shade into the sun. She thought for what seemed a long time. Then she forgot herself in a moment of abandon. She kissed and smelled the fragrant bark; she crushed handfuls of the brown pine needles, pricking her fingers till they bled; she gathered the pine cones to her, soiling her hands with the hot pitch. And suddenly overcome by these physical sensations, she lifted face and arms to the green ——— py above and uttered an inarticulate cry, poi- wild.

ustling in the brush startled her; and as if in

answer to her cry Edd Denmeade strode out of the green wall of thicket, right upon her.

"Reckon you was callin' me," he said, in his cool, easy drawl.

"Oh-h! . . . You frightened me!" she exclaimed, staring up at him. He wore his bee-hunting garb, ragged from service and redolent of the woods. His brown brawny shoulder bulged through a rent. In one hand he carried a short-handled ax. His clean-shaven tanned face shone almost golden, and his clear gray eyes held a singular piercing softness. How tall and lithe and strong he looked! A wild-bee hunter! But that was only a name. Lucy would not have had him any different.

"Where'd you come from?" she asked, suddenly realizing the imminence of some question that dwarfed all other problems.

"Wal, I trailed you," he replied.

"You saw me come here? . . . You've been watching me?"

"Shore. I was standin' in that thicket of pines, peepin' through at you."

"Was that—nice of you—Edd?" she faltered.

"Reckon I don't know. All I wanted to find out was how you really felt about leavin' us all—an' my woods."

"Well, did you learn?" she asked, very low.

"I shore did."

"And what is it?"

"Wal, I reckon you feel pretty bad," he answered, simply. "First off I thought it was only your old trouble. But after a while I could see you hated to leave our woods. An' shore we're all part of the woods. If I hadn't seen that I'd never have let you know I was there watchin' you."

"Edd, I do hate to leave your woods—and all your folks—and you—more than I can tell," she said, sadly.

"Wal, then, what're you leavin' for?" he asked, bluntly.

"I must."

"Reckon that don't mean much to me. Why must you?"

"It won't do any good to talk about it. You wouldn't understand—and I'll be upset. Please don't ask me."

"But, Lucy, is it fair not to tell me anythin'?" he queried, ponderingly. "You know I love you like you told me a man does when he thinks of a girl before himself."

"Oh no—it isn't!" burst out Lucy, poignantly, suddenly, strangely overcome by his unexpected declaration.

"Wal, then, tell me all about it," he entreated.

Lucy stared hard at the clusters of fragrant pine needles she had gathered in her lap. Alarming symptoms in her breast gave her pause. She was not mistress of her emotions. She could be taken unawares. This boy had supreme power over her, if he knew how to employ it. Lucy struggled with a new and untried situation.

"Edd, I owe a duty to—to myself—and to my family," she said, and tried bravely to look at him.

"An' to somebody else?" he demanded with sudden passion. He dropped on his knees and reached for Lucy. His hands were like iron. They lifted her to her knees and drew her close. He was rough. His clasp hurt. But these things were nothing to the expression she caught in his eyes—a terrible flash that could mean only jealousy.

"Let me go!" she cried, wildly, trying to get away. Her gaze drooped. It seemed she had no anger. Her heart swelled as if bursting. Weakness of will and muscle attacked her.

"Be still an' listen," he ordered, shaking her. He need not have employed violence. "Reckon you've had your own way too much. . . . I lied to you about how I killed that cowboy."

"Oh, Edd—then it wasn't an accident?" cried Lucy, sinking limp against him. All force within her seemed to coalesce.

"It shore wasn't," he replied, grimly. "But I let you an' everybody think so. That damned shunk! He was tryin' his best to murder me. I had no gun. . . . I told him I wouldn't hurt him. . . . Then what'd he do? He was cunnin' as hell. He whispered things—hissed them at me like a snake—vile words about you—what you were. It was a trick. Shore he meant to surprise me—make me lose my nerve . . . so he could get the gun. An'

all the time he pulled only the harder. He could feel I
loved you. An' his trick near worked. But I seen through
it—an' I turned the gun against him."

"Oh, my God! you killed him—intentionally!" exclaimed Lucy.

"Yes. An' it wasn't self-defense. I killed him because
of what he called you."

"Me! . . . Oh, of course," cried Lucy, hysterically. A
deadly sweetness of emotion was fast taking the remnant
of her sense and strength. In another moment she would
betray herself—her love, bursting at its dam—and what
was infinitely worse, her sister.

"Lucy, it don't make no difference what that cowboy
said—even if it was true," he went on, now huskily.
"But—were you his wife or anybody's?"

"*No!*" flashed Lucy, passionately, and she spoke the
truth in a fierce pride that had nothing to do with her
situation, or the duty she had assumed.

"Aw—now!" he panted, and let go of her. Rising, he
seemed to be throwing off an evil spell.

Lucy fell back against the pine tree, unable even to
attempt to fly from him. Staring at Edd, she yet saw the
green and blue canopy overhead, and the golden gleam
of the great wall. Was that the summer wind thundering
in her ears? How strangely Edd's grimness had fled!
Then—there he was looming over her again—eager now,
rapt with some overwhelming thought. He fell beside her,
close, and took her hand in an action that was a caress.

"Lucy—will you let me talk—an' listen close?" he
asked, in a tone she had never heard.

She could not see his face now and dared not move.

"Yes," she whispered, her head sinking a little, drooping away from his eyes.

"Wal, it all come to me like lightnin'," he began, in a
swift, full voice, singularly rich. And he smoothed her
hand as if to soothe a child. "I've saved up near a thousand dollars. Reckon it's not much, but it'll help us start.
An' I can work at anythin'. Shore you must have a little
money, too. . . . Wal, we'll get your baby an' then go far

off some place where nobody knows you, same as when you come here. We'll work an' make a home for it. Ever since you told me I've been findin' out I was goin' to love your baby. . . . It'll be the same as if it was mine. We can come back here to live, after a few years. I'd hate never to come back. I've set my heart on that mesa homestead. . . . Wal, no one will ever know. I'll forget your—your trouble, an' so will you. I don't want to know any more than you've told me. I don't hold that against you. It might have happened to me. But for you it would have happened to my sister Mertie. . . . Life is a good deal like bee huntin'. You get stung a lot. But the honey is only the sweeter. . . . All this seems to have come round for the best, an' I'm not sorry, if only I can make you happy."

Lucy sat as if in a vise, shocked through and through with some tremendous current.

"Edd Denmeade," she whispered, "are you asking me—to—to marry you?"

"I'm more than askin', Lucy darlin'."

"After what I confessed?" she added, unbelievingly.

"Shore. But for that I'd never had the courage to ask again. . . . I've come to hope maybe you'll love me some day."

This moment seemed the climax of the strain under which Lucy had long kept up. It had the shocking power of complete surprise and unhoped-for rapture. It quite broke down her weakened reserve.

"I—love you *now*—you big—big——" she burst out, choking at the last, and blinded by tears she turned her face to Edd's and, kissing his cheek, she sank on his shoulder. But she was not so close to fainting that she failed to feel the effect of her declaration upon him. He gave a wild start, and for a second Lucy felt as if she were in the arms of a giant. Then he let go of her, and sat rigidly against the tree, supporting her head on his shoulder. She could hear the thump of his heart. Backwoodsman though he was, he divined that this was not the time to forget her surrender and her weakness. In the quiet of the succeeding moments Lucy came wholly into a realization of the splendor of her love.

It was late in the day when they returned to the clearing. Hours had flown on the wings of happiness and the thrill of plans. Lucy forgot the dark shadow. And not until they emerged from the forest to see Clara standing in the tent door, with intent gaze upon them, did Lucy remember the bitter drops in her cup.

Clara beckoned imperiously, with something in her look or action that struck Lucy singularly. She let go of Edd's hand, which she had been holding almost unconsciously.

"Wal, I reckon your sharp-eyed sister is on to us," drawled Edd.

"It seems so. But, Edd—she'll be glad, I know."

"Shore. An' so will Joe an' all the Denmeades. It's a mighty good day for us."

"The good fortune is all on my side," whispered Lucy, as they approached the tent.

Clara stood on the threshold, holding the door wide. Her face had the pearly pallor and her eyes the purple blackness usual to them in moments of agitation. She did not seem a girl any longer. Her beauty was something to strike the heart.

"Lucy—come in—you and your gentleman friend," she said, her voice trembling with emotion. Yet there was a faint note of pride or mockery of self or of them in it.

"Wal, Clara, you may as well kiss me an' be done with it," drawled Edd, as he entered behind Lucy. "For you're goin' to be my sister two ways."

Clara's response was electrifying. Her face seemed to blaze with rapture and the swift kiss she gave Edd admitted of no doubt as to her acceptance of Edd's blunt speech. But she made no move to approach Lucy.

Joe Denmeade sat on the edge of the bed, white and spent. Sight of him caused Lucy's heart to leap to her throat.

"Howdy, Lucy!" he said, with a smile that was beautiful. "Is my brother Edd talkin' straight?"

"Yes, Joe, I'm going to be doubly your sister," she replied.

"I couldn't ask no more," he rejoined, with deep feeling.

There followed a moment of constraint. Lucy could not grasp the situation, but she felt its tensity. Then, trembling, she turned to face Clara.

"I have told Joe," said Clara as Lucy met her eyes.

Lucy received this blow fully, without preparation, and following hard on stress of feeling that had left her spent. Her intelligence was swift to accept the wondrous and almost incredible fact of Clara's regeneration, but her emotions seemed dead or locked in her breast. Mutely she stared at this beloved sister. She saw an incalculable change, if she saw clearly at all. She might have been dazed. In that endless moment there was a slow action of her own mind, but something she expressed wrought havoc in Clara. The glow, the rapture, the exaltation that so enhanced Clara's beauty, suddenly faded and died. Even her moment of supreme victory had been full of thought of self. But Lucy's agony transformed it.

"I—told him," burst out Clara, sobbing. "I couldn't *stand* it—any longer. I *wanted* him to know. . . . I could have gone on—living a lie—if you had not taken my— my shame. But that was too much. It killed something in me. . . . So I told him I couldn't let you do it. I must do it myself. And I gave Joe up. . . . But, Lucy, he forgave me! . . . He will stand by me!"

"Oh, Joe—how splendid—of you!" gasped Lucy, and with the hard utterance her bound faculties seemed to loosen. She ran to Joe's side. "But how can you meet this—this terrible situation?"

Joe took her trembling hands in his.

"Why, Lucy, don't be upset!" he said. "It's not so bad. If Clara had told me long ago I reckon you'd both been saved a lot of heart-breakin'. . . . There's only one way. The preacher who married Clara an' me will keep our secret. An' he'll marry us again. We'll just leave out tellin' anybody that this—this cowboy forgot to marry Clara himself."

"Yes—yes!" cried Lucy, wildly.

"Reckon thet's aboot all," continued Joe, with his rare smile. "Clara an' I will tell the folks, an' leave at once. . . . An' we'll come back with the baby!"

Here Edd Denmede strode to a position before them, and though he seemed to be about to address Joe, he certainly looked at Lucy.

"Reckon you'd do well to have the parson meet you in Cedar Ridge an' marry you there," he said.

Lucy could have laughed had she not been fighting tears. "Edd, are you talking to Joe—or me?"

"Lucy, would you marry me at the same time?" he queried, hoarsely.

"I—I fear the crowd at Cedar Ridge. They'll storm us," faltered Clara.

"Shore we can fool them," returned Edd.

"All right. We've settled it all," said Joe, in a grave kind of happiness. "I'll go in an' tell the folks."

"Wal, I'm goin' with you," rejoined Edd as Joe rose. They strode out together, and Edd's brawny arm went round his brother's shoulder. "Joe, I reckon it's as good one way as another. It's all in the family. The three of them'll be Denmeades."

Lucy closed the tent door after them and turned to her sister. Clara's eyes were shining through tears.

"Aren't they good?" she murmured. " 'It's all in the family,' Edd said. Either he or Joe would have been happy to be father to my baby. . . . Oh, I did not appreciate them. I did not understand Joe—or you—or myself. . . . I did not know what love was. . . . Now I can atone for the past."

At sunset Lucy escaped the hilarious Denmeades and slipped into the forest, to hide in an unfrequented glade. She had to be alone.

The profound transformations of the day were less baffling and incredible once she found herself in the loneliness and solitude of the forest. Life was real and earnest, beautiful and terrible, inexplicable as the blaze of the setting sun, so fiery golden on the rugged towering

Rim. In the depths of the quiet woods she could understand something of simplicity. For her and Clara life had been throbbing and poignant. For the Denmeades life seemed like that of the trees and denizens of the forest.

The sun sank, the birds ceased their plaintive notes, and a dreaming silence pervaded the green world of foliage. Late bees hummed by. The drowsy summer heat began to cool.

Lucy's heart was full of reverent gratitude to whatever had wrought the change in Clara. Love, suffering, the influence of nature, all had combined to burn out the baneful selfish weakness that had made Clara a victim to circumstances. And these were only other names for God.

How inscrutably had things worked to this happy end! She tried to look backward and understand. But that seemed impossible. Yet she realized how stubbornly, miserably, she had clung to her ideal. If she had only known the reward!

The great solemn forest land was after all to be her home. She would go on with her work among these simple people, grateful that she would be received by them, happy that she could bring good to their lonely homes. The thing she had prayed most for had become a reality. If doubt ever assailed her again, it would be of short duration. She thought of the bee hunter. She would be his wife on the morrow!

Dusk mantled the forest. A faint night wind arose, mournful and sweet. Lucy threaded her way back toward the clearing. And the peace of the wilderness seemed to have permeated her soul. She was just one little atom in a vast world of struggling humans, like a little pine sapling lifting itself among millions of its kind toward the light. But that lifting was the great and the beautiful secret.